WITH A DEEP LAUGHTER that was totally an expression of malign hatred and ineffable wickedness, Tharizdun took the cambion Iuz into his monstrous right hand and lifted him high.

"Observe the view as your Master sees it," Tharizdun bellowed, still with a voice brimming with evil mirth. Then the terrible god tossed the cambion up, caught him again, and squeezed. A piercing shriek came from Iuz as his bones were splintered, organs ruptured.

Tharizdun's talonlike nails sank deeper into his victim's flesh as he looked down with satisfaction at his handiwork. Then the glowing eyes of pure purple looked up from the corpse of Iuz clutched in his hand and out across the chitinous plane. "Now for you, little champion!"

Gord's knees sagged, his spirit quailed. Gord had found some measure of revenge against the ones who had made his childhood a nightmare of fear, hunger, and self-disgust. But his reason told him that no additional evening of the score would ever occur hereafter. He steeled himself.

"If I must go," he said, "then why not go as a wolf rather than a rabbit?"

COME ENDLESS DARKNESS

by Gary Gygax

Burning for revenge and carrying the hopes of the world with him, Gord takes the battle against Evil into its own dark domain

Cover art by Ray Rubin

Edited by Kim Mohan

GORD THE ROGUE™ Books
COME ENDLESS DARKNESS

First Printing, March 1988
Printed in the United States of America

Distributed to the book trade by the Berkley Publishing
Group, 200 Madison Avenue, New York NY 10016

9 8 7 6 5 4 3 2 1

I S B N : 0-441-11446-6

New Infinities Productions, Inc.
P.O. Box 657
Delavan WI 53115

Dedication

This book is especially for Alexander Hugh Hamilton Gygax. Even though he's far too young to read it now, I hope one day he will pick it up and experience the excitement and adventure in its pages the same way I did with such heroes as Conan and John Carter when I was a boy.

Other books by Gary Gygax

Saga of Old City

Artifact of Evil

Sea of Death

Night Arrant

City of Hawks

Preface

AT ONLY A FEW WEEKS OF AGE, Gord suddenly became an orphan. He was quite unaware of the fact, of course, but it impacted his life in a bizarre and cruel fashion. His parents, knowing what threatened them, had left him in the company of an old friend, a kindly sorcerer. But instead of being watched and kept in safety for a brief time while his parents were eluding the murderous evil that pursued them, the infant became the target of the same deadly force that was visited upon his father and mother.

Fortunately, many magical protections surrounded the little Gord. He and the woman who was to be his nursemaid were thus hidden from the malign ones who hunted them — she magically transformed and disguised as the crazed and ugly crone known as Leena, and Gord as an ignorant urchin unaware of his birth and heritage. Together they dwelled in the crumbling filth and stark poverty of the slums of Greyhawk's Old City.

But then deprivation, sorrow, and cold — perhaps with some assistance from the evil magics seeking them both — slew the unfortunate and unsightly woman, Gord's only companion, before the lad was twelve. Alone thereafter, Gord managed to escape a

series of harrowing challenges, learn the craft of beggary, and even receive some training as a thief.

That period was in some ways more enjoyable
than what he had previously been through; for one
thing, at least he didn't have to worry any longer
about starving. In other ways, it was worse for him
than his earlier life had been. In any event, this time
came to an end when warfare erupted between crimi-
nal elements of Greyhawk. Taking this opportunity
for revenge, Gord escaped from his indenture to the
cruel and sadistic murderer Theobald, master of all
beggars in the city. After having seen to Theobald's
much-deserved demise, young Gord and his friend,
San, another little beggar lad, ventured forth uncertain if they would be hunted down and slain by the
Thieves Guild as other beggars had been. Both found
refuge among the young students dwelling in the uni-
versity area of the city. There too they found a tutor.
In time both boys actually managed to become official
students during the day, paying their own way from
the proceeds of what they practiced in the night . . .
thievery!

Older, more learned, and an apt swordsman, Gord
eventually left the grim City of Hawks behind in order
to sail the great lakes and waterways of Oerth with
the Rhennee, the so-called gypsy bargefolk of his
world. During his time with them and their land-
loving cousins the Attloi, Gord learned still more
about thieving, acrobatics and gymnastics, life, and
love. Still not much wiser, however, the young adventurer began to rove here and there throughout the
eastern lands. In the bandit city of Stoink he met a
one-eyed troubador named Gellor, with whom he
would later become fast friends. In fact, Gellor was
responsible for getting Gord out of prison after he had

immersed himself in an ill-fated love affair with a beautiful woman named Evaleigh. During this period of his life Gord also met a number of other brave stalwarts, among them Chert the iron-thewed hillman and Curley Greenleaf, a half-elven ranger and druid. The three of them had some desperate adventures indeed. A full-scale battle, life-and-death duels, and combats with demons were suddenly the stuff of daily routine for Gord.

After deciding he had taken in quite a sufficiency of that sort of thing for a time, Gord convinced the barbarian Chert to return to Greyhawk with him. The pair of them lived a fast and easy life on the easy pickings of the city. They did have many rich hauls by practicing their "night arrantry," but eventually Chert could stand the confines of urban life no longer. He departed, and Gord carried on alone — undaunted, it seemed. Then another unfortunate experience with another beautiful woman brought about a change in his life. Gord became wiser and more cynical. Yet he still sought three things: who he really was, what had become of his parents, and exactly what meaning his life had.

Both Gellor and Curley Greenleaf had given Gord some inkling of his purpose in the past, which is what got the young man thinking about such serious matters in the first place. Possibly unrealized by Gord, both had also influenced him for the better in other ways. Thus, when Gord discovered he had an enchanted ring that not only enabled him to change from man to panther and back as he willed, but also saved him from death and carried him safely to the domain of the Catlord, he reached a plateau of maturity. In early adulthood but already with a lifetime of dangers and experiences behind him, Gord the

Rogue was ready to do something other than thieving his way to vast sums of loot and then spending it on drinking and carousing.

Rexfelis the Catlord and Basiliv, the mighty worker of spells known as the Demiurge, combined to convince Gord that he was instrumental in a quest that was taking place — a quest to recover a terrible relic from a bygone era. They explained to him that a millennium and more had passed since Tharizdun, the Darkest of Evil, King of Wickedness, Emperor of all the Netherplanes, was brought to ruin. The forces of Weal and Nature had combined to defeat the malign Tharizdun, but slay him they could not. Instead, they drugged him with a magical sleep from which there was virtually no awakening, chained him with enchanted powers, and then walled him in a prison that was in an otherworldly no-space. In this way Tharizdun was to be exiled until the end of time, a captured and slumbering incarnation of everything bad in the multiverse.

Unfortunately, even this imprisonment had a price for the jailers. His foes could not accomplish the binding without unavoidably leaving a means by which all could be undone. Just as a key can be used to both lock and unlock, the great artifact that made possible Tharizdun's incarceration could also be used to free him. The makers of it knew that even the strongest of magics could not destroy the key, so the relic was divided into thirds and each part carefully hidden far from the others. Each so-called Theorpart was a mighty artifact of powerful evil force in itself. If conjoined, the three portions were the key to the awakening and return of the dreaded king of evil.

Eventually, one of the forces of evil did locate one of the Theorparts. The vile society that worshiped devildom and called itself the Scarlet Brotherhood managed to find the Initial Key, known as the Awakener. When this occurred, Tharizdun stirred in his lightless cell in no-when and sent forth thoughts of sleeping evil. This effect empowered the possessors of the first of the keys to locate the whereabouts of the second one. In fact, Gord himself had taken part in the force that fought against the minions of evil to prevent their capture of this second portion of the ancient relic.

In the course of events, the demons who also sought the thing were triumphant. Iuz, a part-demon, part-human fiend, managed to gain the second portion and thus become a terrible force for evil. Yet, this outcome was not entirely to the detriment of those who opposed wickedness. Demonkind did not seek to reawaken Tharizdun, for if that occurred the mighty evil of that being would force them into submission. If Good sought to conceal the second portion of the terrible relic, at least the demoniacal possessors who gained it also sought to keep it from the minions of the hells, who would favor reawakening the slumbering lord of all darkness. A near stalemate had thus occurred — but now the Final Key held the balance of power, and it could not be allowed to fall to either the Brotherhood or the servants of Iuz. Rexfelis and the Demiurge enlisted Gord to seek out and try to take the last portion of the relic, thus preserving the balance that would keep Tharizdun entombed.

Such an undertaking seemed worthwhile to Gord. He despised the evil ones and understood the threat that Tharizdun posed to all not of their ilk. Agreeing to serve, the young thief set off into the hinterland in search of the last Theorpart. The trail of clues took him deep into the Ashen Desert, a veritable sea of

11

dusty death in whose center lay a lost and buried city. Deep beneath the powdery ash of the desert, created by a terrible magical war fought at the time of the forging of the relic, Gord discovered the last portion of the thing, just as he had been told.

But finding it was one thing and keeping it quite another. At the moment of potential triumph, Gord was deserted by his dark-elf companion Leda and confronted by the evil-serving dwarf Obmi, the champion of Iuz. The dwarf left Gord for dead and fled the buried ruins with the Final Key, thinking that he would soon place it in the hands of his master. Leda, however, and Gord, too, followed on Obmi's heels. Even as Leda overcame her counterpart Eclavdra, a truly evil dark elf, so too did Gord battle Obmi in a fearsome combat to the death.

Finally the young adventurer overcame the wicked dwarf despite the black powers Obmi commanded. In part Gord's victory was due to his ability to assume the form of a panther. Then, a demon stood before him and offered Gord the very artifact he had sought, the prize for which he and Obmi had fought. Vuron, the alabaster-white lord of the Abyss, henchman of the demon king Graz'zt, spoke with Gord and explained much. Eventually Gord came to the only conclusion he could: Graz'zt must have the Theorpart, for only an evil power could maintain a hold on an object of such vileness. There was a terrible price to be paid for that decision, even though it seemed the correct thing to do. Vuron, for reasons of his own, would not take the key unless Leda also willingly accompanied him — so all three had to descend into the abyssal netherplanes. Leda understood this and agreed. Despairing, Gord also consented. For the third time in his life, he had loved and lost.

Feeling but half-alive, Gord traveled on with his new band of comrades. Soon they took ship and sailed into the southern seas of Oerik — the name of the great continent on which is found the City of Greyhawk. As traders in the wild jungles there, as island explorers, and as buccaneers too, the young thief and his friends went. They earned fabulous treasures and gained untold wealth, only to lose it just as readily in games of chance or mishaps in some exotic city of the many lands of the southwestern seas. Eventually the pain of Gord's loss became only a dull ache that upset his quiet moments and disturbed his sleep.

Gord had finally become a full-fledged man, and one with wisdom beyond his years. Still a daring thief and a willing roisterer, he was no longer altogether uncertain of himself or what he stood for. Despite that, he remained ignorant of his background. Who had his parents been? Why had he been abandoned in the slums? Those questions and others remained unanswered, and when he thought about them — which was often — they troubled him.

The saga now continues with Gord aboard a ship in the southern waters off Oerik. Much is in store, not only for Gord but for those who share this episode of his life with him. . . .

Chapter 1

THE LEADEN SKY lowering above seemed to press flat the dull waters of the sea. The lean ship sat upon those waveless waters as does a little fowl in the center of a great pewter salver, alone, awaiting a certain fate. The air was as motionless as the water. Heat and oppressive silence were the vessel's only companions in the middle of that forsaken ocean desert. No creak of plank, no rattle of rigging, not a splash of wave or whisper of motion in canvas.

A dark-winged sea bird gently gliding high above the cog saw scattered bodies littering the ship's weathered decking, their forms as still as the sails and cords. The bird croaked raucously, flapped its great wings, and soared away. Again the vessel was alone, bearing its cargo of dead upon the dead-gray, becalmed sea. All was quiet, until . . .

"It is gone."

"Are you sure?"

"Yes. It is gone."

A group of corpses suddenly became animated. The five arose and peered carefully around them. One gave a low whistle, and the remaining litter of dead forms likewise stirred and began to move about.

"The trick worked, Cap'n, but how long can this

game go on?" The man who rumbled the question was a stockily built old salt, sailing master of the ship, known to one and all simply as Barrel. He looked expectantly at the man he had addressed — his boon companion, the vessel's captain, and in fact leader of all aboard.

Gord was a seasoned traveler, experienced on land and sea, but he felt more at home swindling some dishonest noble or fighting a fell monster than trying to outwit whatever unseen powers worked against the ship now. Without revealing his own uncertainty, the young adventurer leveled his gray eyes calmly so as to look Barrel squarely in the face as he replied.

"Sea hags and sirens have failed to waylay us. We weathered the storm sent next. Now, we've managed to fool that ill-omened bird of evil into believing all of us have died from thirst. I'd say we have the enemy on the run, old friend!" Gord turned and looked at the old priest who had taken ship with them on Keoland's coast. "What say you, good cleric?"

Abbot Pauncefot was forthright and direct. "Oh, we have managed to fox them well enough," he barked, "but the workings of demons are not so quickly done. Even if they suppose us all dead, they'll not be through with us until bones of men and ship lie rotting on the floor of the deep!"

A buzzing of fearful exchanges sprang up among the crewmen at that. Barrel set his mouth tightly, almost as if in imitation of the thin-lipped priest. Gord frowned and thought furiously. Could he repair the damage the cleric's words had done? "Grist for our mill," Gord said with a jauntiness that he hoped would hearten the men. "They've tossed their best at us and failed. Whatever else might happen along can be something to batten on. What with our good abbot's powers, master Dohojar's magics, and the stout steel of our weapons, no fiend of the netherworld can harm us now."

"Never tempt demons!" This new admonition from the cleric countered whatever bolstering of flagging spirits Gord had just managed to accomplish. Abbot Pauncefot cared not a whit for anything but the truth . . . as he saw it. "The benisons bestowed by mine own Great Lord are but petty powers when compared to those of the evil ones who seek to destroy this vessel and all aboard. It is no fault of Rao that I am too small to channel more than a trickle of the benefit he could bestow."

"You have seen to our drink and sustenance, good abbot," the homely Barrel said. "Your prayers and divinations have brought us all through 'til now. . . ."

The elderly priest squared his thin shoulders and looked grimly at the men who had gathered close to hear the exchange. Forsaking the compliment Barrel had just paid him, Pauncefot saw instead an opportunity to address a higher issue. The abbot spread wide his arms and spoke loudly for all to hear. "Salvation of the sort I have provided is temporary. To be truly saved, you must give yourselves unto Him who is All." Before the priest could say more, growls and mutterings arose from the crowd.

"We are of the sea," one crewman called. "We trust and believe, abbot, but there are times and places for—"

"Silence!" Gord shouted. "I am your captain. All of you, quiet!" Then the small, dark-haired thief turned to the cleric, saying, "It is your good counsel and great spells we need, Abbot Pauncefot, not preaching. Even now the evil might be again massing to attack us."

It was as if the cleric had been awaiting just this sort of opportunity. His face was stern and his voice thundered. "It is not these men whom the demons and dark forces seek to destroy — no! It is you, Gord — you, the disbeliever. I cannot fathom you, but I think you are not far removed from those who threaten to carry us all into some watery hell!"

First the *Sovereign Sea Lion*, next *Stormeater*, then *Seablade*, and now *Silver Seeker* — many of those present had been on each of those ships with Gord. What the priest had just uttered was worse than blasphemy to them, a blasphemous lot anyway. Dirks suddenly appeared in clenched fists, and threats flew thick and fast. Perhaps this self-righteous priest would make an acceptable sacrifice to Brocam the Sealord! Even the young thief, though he did not give the cleric's words any credence, felt a surge of hatred and a desire to see the abbot's blood stain the dun waters around the ship as it lay becalmed.

"This is the next attack of the enemy, Gord Zehaab! Listen, friends, bold sailors and shipmates all!"

This voice of reason came from Dohojar, the only man among them all who seemed unaffected by rage. The dark man native to far-off Changar was a spellworker, an aspiring mage, but despite his uniqueness one of the group nonetheless. His magic was of the West, his inner powers thus slightly different from what the others were used to, and he sensed the black force that lay unseen upon *Silver Seeker* as a dark octopus surrounds a mollusk it is about to devour. "Think now," Dohojar continued when all ears were turned to him. "Would you harm the one who has given us our lives this past fortnight? And you, holy man — do you really dare to condemn this one who champions the fight against all evil?"

18

Dohojar's admonition contained sufficient accuracy to give everyone pause. The old abbot started a chant to counteract malign sendings, while the Changa used his own spell-working art to ward off dark magical forces being visited upon them. Gord, Barrel, and the two dozen crewmen stood sheepishly by. It was humiliating to realize that the enemy had almost managed to bring another of its attacks to fruition so insidiously that none but the perceptive little Changa had noticed. "Use whatever rituals and talismans you have to assist our comrades," Gord told the officers of *Silver Seeker*. "And tell your men the same," he added in a hushed voice as the priest and the mage continued their work.

"I cannot make the magic leave," Dohojar finally said with a gasp.

"Nor can I do more than force the evil of it but a little way from us," Abbot Pauncefot said slowly. "Yet that may be enough for the time if we are carefully on guard. To know the presence of the enemy is to be armed against attacks."

"Well and good, stout friends," the burly Barrel said. "I still have the problem of being dead in the water, and the Azure Sea is no place to be becalmed in for long!"

The old cleric prayed and gave the crew his blessings against the black anger sent upon them by the forces of the netherworld. Then Pauncefot retired to his tiny cabin to meditate. "What now, cap'n?" Barrel asked. He was grim-faced, for the sun was near the horizon. Soon it would vanish to the west, and then they would be pinned to the flat sea with the darkness surrounding them. "In the dark, our powers will wane, and those of evil grow — and not even a sliver of a moon to lend us strength."

19

Gord motioned for Barrel and Dohojar to come to his side, and then he addressed the full assemblage of crewmen. "We must hold moot now. I need your counsel. Unless a strong course of action can be determined, I will have to accept the abbot's advice."

"What do you mean, Zehaab?" Dohojar looked at his comrade with true puzzlement, for he had heard nothing from the priest that he could interpret as advice to Gord. "The man said nothing but the ugly things put into his head by demonshine!"

"Not quite, Dohojar, not quite. The enemy doesn't care a jot for the life of anyone aboard *Silver Seeker* but for me. That much of what the abbot said was pure truth. Somehow, those vile ones who seek me have managed to succeed. If I get away from the ship, then it . . . and all of you . . . will be safe."

"You have no proof of that, lad," Barrel said, neglecting for once to address Gord by his official title — an office conferred by Barrel, Dohojar, and the rest by vote during the time when they sailed aboard the *Sovereign Sea Lion* more than a year ago. Since then most of their original band had left for home or some personal quest, but the new members who had joined were of like mind. Gord, once beggar-boy, then thief and swordsman, now buccaneer, was their leader. "I say we lower our boats and row us the hells out of this demon-made calm!"

The other crewmen had muttered among themselves while these exchanges were taking place. They were all anxious to strike back at their unseen tormentors in any fashion they could.

"We're all with you, captain," one of the newest of the lot called. He was an ordinary sailor but felt emboldened to speak because of the easy relationship on this ship between officers and men.

"I jined up when the old *Lion* lef' fer southern waters, matey-boy," a leathery-visaged salt said to the first speaker. "You've jes' said what all o' us think!"

Gord took in that and more of the same kind of commentary from the rest of the men. "Thanks, all of you," he said, "but I think I have to say a bit against myself. You just listen up a tad. Many of you have been a part of our band for as long as we've been one. We've sailed to the savage coasts together, been to exotic ports, fought pirates and sea monsters, and done a bit of privateering ourselves in the process." There were nods and murmurs at that, and several of the men grinned as they patted a girdle or fingered a gem-set earring or golden bracelet taken as their share of booty. The young adventurer allowed them their moment to recall that, then went on. "And during that time you'll recall I managed to call most of the decisions right, aye?"

"Aye, that you did, cap'n," Barrel said, speaking for all of the men.

"Well, we're in a pickle now, my lads; it's a devilish tight place, too. If the priest isn't actually one of us, Abbot Pauncefot is a good man and true nonetheless. He said that I was the target of the attacks, and I vow by the green beard of Brocam he was dead accurate!"

"There is no way we can sacrifice you, Gord Zehaab, to save ourselves," the Changa said loudly.

Gord looked absolutely astounded at that. "Sacrifice? Who the hells mentioned that? I'm not ready for Brocam's Briny Bier or any other grave quite yet, mate!"

There was nervous laughter at that, and Dohojar was embarrassed. "But you said . . ."

"I said that I'd get you and *Seeker* off the demons' hook if I could. That doesn't mean I'm consigning

21

myself to drowning or anything like it. Most of you know that I have fought against lesser sorts of demons and others who serve evil, just as you know that once I was a city-bred thief. Somehow I seem to be singled out, not to say cursed, to forever get in the way of the great forces that contend for mastery of our world. Like you, I would be content to fight a little, frolic more, and seek excitement where I may."

Because there were comments of ribald sort at that, Gord allowed a momentary pause before he spoke further, but time was short, and he had to press ahead rapidly. "Listen well now, lads! In my dreams of late I keep hearing a call. It has come to me more and more frequently these past few weeks. I have ignored the omen so far, thinking it imaginary and meaningless, but now I rue that choice, for it has put you all at peril."

The young man allowed that to sink in a moment. "I am indeed being called elsewhere," he continued. "The foes of the evil ones who hunt for my soul are in need of me. Had I heeded their summons sooner, then you would all be in Safeton's snug harbor now, drinking and wenching. The priest spoke naught but fact when he said I was the target of the demonkin who plague *Silver Seeker* now. Somehow they have found me and now use their fell sendings to try to destroy me."

"If that be the case, Gord, then I'll join ye in the fight," Barrel said firmly.

Dohojar nodded agreement. "I too am by your side, Zehaab!"

Before there was a general rush of that sort of thing, Gord raised his hand. "Hold! Avast! Then we'd be back where we are now. I am here to tell you that I will have to leave you — all of you. *Seeker* needs you

22

all to survive the side effects of whatever dark things have been sent for me. My departure will draw off some of the ill, but much might still find its way to you!"

"Will you stride across the waters of the sea? Or have you wings?" That sarcastic query came from one named Reppon, first mate of the ship and a doughty sea-warrior who had seen much of the world in his travels.

"Neither," Gord replied with a laugh. "But I have certain friends, shall we say — beasts of the ocean. I think it likely that I can call upon them to carry me safely hence to wherever it is I must go — and that destination will be known to them."

The rim of the sun was just touching the watery horizon when the moot finally ended. What decided it all so quickly was not entirely Gord's decision. An immense wall of black clouds was suddenly visible to the north — great, anvil-headed clouds that shot upward in contorted forms, nightmare shapes with writhing bodies and leering, fearsome faces. Dark layers overtopped even these mighty clouds, and bright lightnings made the looming wall flicker and flash eerily. It was Barrel who concluded the assembly then and there. "That there's a hellstorm, boys!" he announced. "If the cap'n can leave and take it from us, we just might live to tell of it!"

Dohojar dithered and fretted as Gord began a ritual to summon the "friends" he had referred to. "I am willing to help you with this calling, Zehaab," the dark-skinned man pleaded. "How can you refuse?"

But the young adventurer would not relent. He was confident that he could manage. "My friend," he finally said to the Changa, "even though you are a mage, you aren't acceptable to the ones who might agree to bear me from this place. Now go away so I can finish!" Dohojar slunk off, and Gord completed his ritual. The words he uttered and the gestures he made were the parts of a cat-summoning dweomer that had been taught to him by Rexfelis the Catlord. His dreams, he thought, were messages sent by Rexfelis, so perhaps the Catlord would supply the means of transportation. After all, he reasoned, weren't the great sea lions faithful subjects of Rexfelis? That remained to be seen. He waited a few minutes but got no results, so he began the ritual again, performing it more carefully this time.

A gurgling and a growl made Gord start. He had been so wrapped up in repeating the charm properly that he hadn't seen the darker shape rise in the darkening gray of the sea's depths. The lionlike head that suddenly broke the surface was huge — thrice the size of a true lion's — and of a greenish tinge.

"Who braves the calling of Leoceanius?" The challenge came in a roar, sounding like the rush and retreat of a huge breaker.

"Gord, associate of Rexfelis and friend of all cats, summons one who is vassal to the Lord of Felines."

Before the young man could say or do anything more, the monstrous sea cat rose up and grabbed him with its gigantic forepaws. "About bloody time, too," the creature growled, as it bore Gord from the ship's deck off into the leaden-hued waters. "Get on my back and hold fast to my mane, or I'll not be held accountable for your fate," said Leoceanius gruffly. There was no chance to protest. Floundering, Gord managed to do as the sea lion demanded, grasping and holding fast for dear life, for even as he spoke the creature was swimming off at a speed unimaginable to a man.

"What of my belongings, O Master Lion of the Seas?"

The sea lion gave a coughing roar, its version of a laugh. "You have much of power with you, man. I read clearly in your own mind that what is behind on that wooden float is naught of importance to you. Even were it otherwise, there would be no help for it. Ere you could get your possessions, the black sending would strike."

They were slicing through the calm waters at an angle that took them eastward and slightly away from the oncoming mountains of cloud. The *Silver Seeker* was already little bigger than a dot behind them. What the creature said was true. All of his possessions that Gord considered truly valuable were with him. He wore his short sword and his dagger, his cat's-eye ring and his amulet of protection, plus a few other cherished things safely contained in a dweomered coffer no bigger than a thimble.

"Go to it, Leoceanius! Let's see a real turn of speed!" Gord cried with a laugh to match that of the sea lion. Let his companions aboard the ship keep the gold and gems he had left there. So too the good shirt of elfin chain mail that was in his sea chest, and the extra blade he had hidden beneath a false floorboard in his quarters — a longsword of dark metal that he had brought back from the city deep beneath the Ashen Desert. Those things he truly regretted leaving, but perhaps they would save another one's life one day. The mail shirt would fit Dohojar, although the Changa would have to forsake his spellworking while he had it on. And both Dohojar and Barrel knew of the sword and where it was concealed, so Gord was sure it would eventually be brought out and put to good use by someone. At any rate, there was no point in worrying about those things any more. "And where do we go?" Gord asked the lion.

"Well away from that," the great water-creature roared, giving its mighty head a shake to indicate the advancing tempest. "Only I do not think I can go fast enough."

That gave Gord pause. He turned slightly to eye the wall of ebon clouds and saw that indeed the storm was coming down upon them at tremendous speed. The dark, lightning-shot center of the tempest had altered its course too. The whole front was now bearing toward them, going eastward just as they did. The fading sunlight was now so dim that he could see nothing more, but Gord imagined that *Silver Seeker* was now well away from the worst of the storm, for the leading gusts of wind would be more than enough for the ship to begin beating westward.

"What makes the roiling?" the young adventurer managed to shout above the rising wind. He had seen the splashing of something off to their right and slightly ahead.

"My fellows," Leoceanius roared so as to be heard. "They converge to escort us to safety. A bad sign, for it means some worse foe than the storm draws near!"

In minutes the now-dark waters were made lighter by the foam and froth of a score of great sea lions cleaving the rising waves. They offered greetings to Leoceanius as their liege, the master of all their kind. It surprised Gord, however, to be saluted as well by these creatures — and especially because they hailed him as prince. Leoceanius surged to his right, bearing the young adventurer directly away from the evil cloud-wall that was rolling down upon them at terrible speed. "What news?" the sea lion roared to his followers.

"It is the sea hag, Udyll, who has raised the tempest," came the faint reply. Although the wind tore away at even the great bass voice of the sea cat, Gord could discern the speech well enough to hear the fear in the creature's voice. "The hag hunts for the man you bear even now — she and her pack of sharks!"

Leoceanius shook his great mane. "Even as fast as I can go, the hag's tempest closes upon us. It will strike soon, and at its edge will be her death-fish. Burdened as I am, Gord, we are no match for sharks and hag."

"I have my sword!" Gord grabbed the hilt of the short blade buckled around his waist as he shrieked into the howling gale that now battered them and broke the tops of the ever-heightening waves of the Azure Sea into horizontal sheets of spray that stung like blizzard-whipped sleet.

"Save your breath!" came the sea cat's roar. "I go deep for safety!"

"What?" Gord couldn't believe his ears. The monstrous sea cat roared something about an undine's grotto, and then dived. There was no choice now. Gord held onto the deep green mane and concentrated on breath control. How deep they plunged into the salty waters of the Azure Sea, how fast they were descending, he had no idea. But the time seemed an eternity, since he did not have a chance to take a deep breath before they went under.

As part of his normal regimen of exercise, Gord practiced various breathing techniques, including the talent of holding his breath. In dangerous circumstances, even so slight a thing as a whispered exhalation could give a thief away. If he had a chance to prepare for it, Gord could maintain activity and not intake a breath of air for more than two minutes. But now his lungs felt as if they were bursting. Gord expelled some of the air from them in tiny spurts. That helped the burning in his chest only a little, and it made him conscious of the pain of pressure in his ears.

A blackness more impenetrable than the dark of the storm-ridden sea was closing over the young adventurer when he felt a change of motion. Leoceanius was no longer sounding but swimming laterally. Gord could feel the touch of thick strands of kelp striking him as the sea lion whipped through what must have been a veritable forest of the growth. Then he had to let out the last of his air, and seconds later the overwhelming dark conquered Gord and he remembered no more.

* * *

"Those drowned ones who I have seen before were not so handsome as he."

Hearing that startled Gord into full wakefulness. His eyes saw a watery cave softly illuminated by a radiance that seemed to play between rose pink and the rich vert of a prize tourmaline. The walls were of stone, but coral branches of a reddish hue shot from them, and the sea plants that grew in profusion seemed to have been artfully arranged within the grotto so as to divide its space into private little nooks. Then he saw the undine.

Her skin was quicksilver and her waist-length tresses the color of rich emeralds. The coral that graced the undersea cave was shamed by the brightness of the undine's full lips. As green as her hair were her long nails, but the sea nymph's perfect breasts were tipped with the hot color of coral to match her mouth. Gord stared in wonderment at the creature, and finally his gray eyes met the green and gold orbs of the undine. At that she smiled, and Gord saw her mouth was filled with pearly little teeth as sharp as those of a barracuda. This anomaly shocked him, and he tore his eyes from her.

The undine laughed, a sound most strange in this watery place; yet Gord heard it plainly, as well as her voice saying, "Welcome to my home, hero. Will you linger here with me a spell?"

"No!" The reply came not from Gord, for the young adventurer was ready to agree. Leoceanius suddenly appeared beside him, and Gord became aware that the whole pride of sea cats was there in the grotto. The place was deceptively large, or else enchanted in some fashion. "We all, this man included, request sanctuary, Kharistylla. We will have no need to linger beyond the prescribed period for such."

"Request? Prescribed? My, my, Leoceanius, how formal your demand," the undine replied with a hint of mockery in her sweet contralto. "Yet I have no quarrel with Udyll. Why should I heed you?"

"Your power weaves a net of concealment about us now, undine," the huge sea cat rumbled. "You have already helped us, as I suspected you would graciously do, and thus cast your lot. But if she discovers what you have done, you know the hag would deal with the likes of you no more gently than with me . . . or this human who is her current prey."

The undine smiled, again showing her sharp teeth. Gord didn't find them quite so disturbing this time. "Agreed, great sea cat. I grant you sanctuary. Still," she said with a lingering appraisal of Gord, "I see no reason not to . . . detain . . . this man you carried here beyond the time the rest of you decide to leave."

"He is a champion of Balance," the monstrous sea lion rumbled. "Not even you would dare to disturb that!"

Kharistylla undulated closer, rested her hands on Gord's hips, and lightly caressed the thimble-sized container she found fastened to the right side of his belt. She smiled to herself, took Gord's hand, and spread it so as to reveal his palm. He noticed that her fingers were webbed, connected by a nearly transparent membrane. After the undine had studied it for a bit, she released his hand and stared into the young adventurer's eyes. That made his head reel, and Gord uttered an involuntary gasp, slamming the door on his thoughts at the invasion he sensed.

"Quick — quick and strongly barred, Gord. But not so fast that I didn't see," the undine said with a small smile. "You are indeed what the sea cat claims, yet you are not entirely informed or willing. Come, then. Balance has others to spend their lives on behalf of its cause. You and I are much alike, and we both give due homage to the middle way. Be my champion and dwell here in Kharistylla's domain for a time."

Her voice was sweet and laden with promise. Gord's own voice was filled with regret as he replied. "If that were my rede, gracious lady, I would gladly tarry here with you for as long as it pleased you. It has ever been my fate, though, to be driven by storm and tempest to some strand that is not of my own choosing. Soon I must leave this element, somehow, to return to the world of air and earth. The ones who call me cannot be denied, but when I am done perhaps we can . . ."

The undine flashed him her strange smile and pressed a pearl of pale green into his hand, the same hand whose palm she had studied so carefully. "I think not, Gord-Dark-Destiny. Although I cannot discern your past nor see your future, my feelings tell me that this will be our only meeting. But who can say? I am not the arbiter of things. I am one who, as you, meets what comes."

"The danger passes," growled Leoceanius. "Sooner than I would have thought, but good for us. While the hag is distracted, we must make haste."

"All well and good," said Kharistylla. "Swim away if you feel you must, but leave the human safe with me and protect yourselves by doing so. The hag will certainly ignore you if you go alone."

"Yes," countered the sea lion. "But we cannot preserve the Balance by abandoning our charge."

"Trust me," the undine said sweetly but firmly. "When the peril is entirely past, the one we both cherish will be free to go. And he does have a means of leaving without your aid — this I know."

That statement puzzled Gord, but he was in no position to argue. Better, he thought, to take his chances with the undine's claim than to endure another underwater ride on the back of Leoceanius.

The sea lion seemed to take Kharistylla's words for granted. Instead of contending with her further, the creature swam to his fellows and softly growled some instructions. Then he came back to Gord. "Fare thee well, prince," the sea lion grumbled warmly.

"Nay, my friend," Gord responded. "I am no prince. It was you who made the royal gesture, else I and my comrades should have been in the deep darkness by now. Fortune be with you and yours, Leoceanius."

The sea lion let out a rumble in reply, dipped his head in salute to Kharistylla, and then was gone.

"Do not concern yourself, Gord-My-Guest," the

31

undine said reassuringly. "They will miss the hag. And now we have a brief time of safekeeping, so let us make what we can of it!"

Gord could not pass beyond the confines of the undine's grotto. Her enchantments kept them secure within it and enabled him to breathe its salty waters as easily as the sea lions had done. Now, thanks to the pearl given to him by Kharistylla, he was able to move, see, and feel just as the undine did within the grotto. It was a far more magnificent place than Gord had perceived. Its enchanted spaces went on for great distances in all directions, with chambers and secret gardens that even natives of the sea could not discern. Water sprites and saltwyrds were there in numbers to serve their mistress, and all forms of poisonous sea creatures — snakes, fish, and worse — were always hovering at the fringes of the place to guard against intrusion; possibly to prevent unwanted egress as well. Gord didn't care; he wouldn't go where he was not allowed and had no intention of forcing his way out of the place, either.

"It is your inner force which draws me," the beautiful sea spirit said. "You have such strength within you, such a raw energy and purpose. I do not have that, you know. Otherwise, I too would be opposing the hag and all of her ilk."

"I will share my energy with you, Kharistylla," the young adventurer volunteered with sincerity. His ingenuousness made the undine laugh in her rich, sensuous voice.

"Don't look hurt, dear lad. I meant no injury but am touched by so fine an offer. If only it were that easy. You are one of many forces, I a being of but one elemental power. My own energy is very great — far greater than yours, Gord, in certain, limited ways. Yet beyond this small place which is mine I weaken and become far less. No infusion can change that, else no undine would I be. Enough of this! Come, now, and let us enjoy all of the wonder of this grotto."

A while later Gord asked Kharistylla of events above the waters of the sea that covered them. "The storm has passed," she told him, "and ancient and ugly old Udyll gnashes her broken fangs and drives her packs of sharks hither and thither seeking aught. The little ship which bears your friends lies leagues and leagues away, never fear. A southerly breeze has come to counter the foul blast from the north, and that good zephyr drives the vessel beyond the hag's reach and into the waters of that place near to where you call home."

"Woolly Bay?"

"Ah, yes. I see from the pictures in your mind that is what you call the waters I spoke of. Without your force aboard the ship, Udyll cannot see it. She is in a terrible fury because you are nowhere. Soon I think she will give up her hunt and go to her masters to tell them you have passed beyond the ken of material and elemental spheres."

"How do you know all this?"

"Hags are the greatest of the evil elemental powers, Gord-My-Sweet, but undines are the greatest of the rest — those of Balance, as it were. My powers and dweomers are much stronger than any sea hag's, in most ways, and always so within my own domain. I can sense all that happens here in this sea and a good bit of the events in adjoining waters as well. Poor, stupid Udyll could not even pierce the net of my concealment of you when she was within a league of that which she sought!"

"She was that close to us?"

"Closer, even . . . but no matter. The time you may stay grows short now. I have gifted you, and we have exchanged forces to that extent which is permissible. Now, Gord, will you leave me some token of yourself?"

"I . . . I . . ." he stammered, trying to think of something suitable. All of the fine jewels and pretty things he had accumulated as a sea rover were aboard the *Silver Seeker*. What little he had with him seemed inappropriate for gifting. Then he recalled the secret magical coffer. Inside it was, among other things, a talisman that he had kept as a souvenir. He reached into his belt, slipped the tiny coffer out, and touched it so that it would open. He had no fear of the water, for despite its everpresence, no drop of it wetted his garments or actually touched his skin.

As the container unlocked itself, it grew. The undine laughed and clapped her hands as it expanded before her eyes into a lovely vessel of inlaid wood and ivory fully large enough to hold a small fortune in treasure. "I only wish I had placed my good mail shirt herein," Gord said ruefully as he viewed the interior. There were only a few small items inside, a battered old box being the largest. This was a relic from his childhood. He had never been able to fathom its secrets, but he was sure it was somehow something important to him. For the moment, he passed it over in favor of one of the smaller items.

"Here, Kharistylla," he said with feeling, "I give this to you." He picked up a little pouch of some exotic skin and withdrew from it an amber piece of cabochon form. Inside the golden oval was a spider.

"That is lovely!" the undine exclaimed. "And it is a potent talisman too. How came you by such a piece?"

"That is a long tale, dear lady of the sea, and one which by your own words we have no time for. Suffice to say that I gained it and kept it at great personal peril. For a time my liege lord, Rexfelis, made use of it — I paid it over to him by his demand for a favor. Then one day he simply restored it to me without a word of explanation. No matter, for now it is yours."

Kharistylla kissed him with her perfect, coral-red lips, then laughed. "I shall keep it and treasure it. Perhaps you do not realize it, but such a thing as this extends my power no small amount. With it, I can move upon the sphere of earth, metal, or wood. Better still, I can walk unhindered on the material plane for as long as I choose — even to dwell in a city among men such as you will pose no problem to me with this!"

Gord was happy that he had pleased the undine with the gift. "Perhaps we will then meet in Greyhawk," he suggested.

Kharistylla gave him a sorrowful smile. "Nay, that I see not. Yet, perhaps somewhere . . . but there is more, dear Gord! Your Rexfelis is a deep one, he is. This he gave to you for a reason beyond mere generosity, I think. A single touch of your belt, earlier, told me that."

"What do you mean, Kharistylla?"

"The amulet will serve to open a portal for you to your liege lord's place. He bestowed such dweomer to it in most puissant form before returning it to you, that is clear."

"I will remember to thank him when I see him," Gord said dryly. "Now let us enjoy the last of the time remaining between us here." That the undine was most happy to agree to.

Chapter 2

THE FLANAESS SHOOK to the tread of marching armies. The land writhed under the lash of fire and sword, spell and conjured monster, as its creatures fled the bellow of iron horns and the boom of thundering drums. The hordes of the cambion Iuz were on the move, and their advance was as inexorable as the march of time.

The attack had begun abruptly, without warning. The masses of humanoids from the land of Iuz had swarmed forth to bring death and destruction to all who opposed the cambion. Their massing had been veiled by the great powers of Iggwilv, the mother of all black witches, and the demon queen Zuggtmoy. The two of them and Iuz controlled the evil magic of the Initiator, the middle portion of the Theorpart, one of the keys to the loosing of all wickedness, and they used it well.

The Vesve Forest was taken; then the lands beyond its western verge, all the way south to the Velverdyva River, fell to the invaders. From forest and mountains came swarms of evil creatures to join the victorious forces of the cambion. The great walls and men of the city of Chendl barred the advance into Furyondy's heartland, but the northern part of that kingdom was gone, and grinning orcs and slobbering gnolls roamed freely north of the Crystal River.

Legions of troops swept through the Horned Society, the lands that had formerly bowed to the Hierarchs, and into the Shield Lands. Not even the vaunted Knights of the Shield could prevail against the forces of Iuz, and the survivors among that number huddled on their fortress island in the Nyr Dyv, praying that the waters of that lake would protect them.

Far to the east the story was much the same. The haughty men of Tenh died bravely in defense of their country, but they died in vain, for bandits, mercenaries, and the newly allied warbands from the Barrens rode across the sovereign ducal state in mere weeks. Trolls from the fens and ogres and giants from the high mountains joined in their destruction of that land.

Thereafter all of the north bowed fully to the cambion. Fierce horse nomads rode beneath the wolfhead standard to threaten their southern neighbor, while those who followed the great tiger banner made war in Iuz's vile name farther to the west. Fierce men of the Hold of Stonefist marched south to join the humanoids and the army of bandits threatening the Theocracy of the Pale. The demon armies held bridgeheads that were like swords poised above Urnst, stabbing Furyondy's flank, and the elven state of Highfolk.

The Flanaess reeled, and councils met. How could such a thing have occurred? What defense or counterattack could be made? Then the armies of the Great Kingdom in the south, and the Scarlet Brotherhood's disciplined regiments too, attacked northward. All thought of a counteroffensive was hurled to the winds. Nyrond, its friends and allies, and the few other unconquered free states of the Flanaess knew that their survival now stood in question. The evil that served devils advanced northward in counterpoint to the demon-serving hordes that rolled south. All good was caught between these two, and there was growing despair in the land.

The evil of the south was weak. Its greatest force, the Theorpart known as the Awakener, was no longer in their hands. Its might had been requisitioned by the Dukes of Hell, and there is no recourse to their demands. The evil of the north, that of witch, demon and cambion demigod, was great, for the malign strength of the Initiator was theirs to use. The Final Key, the Unbinder, was held by the lords of the Abyss, and so while the denizens of the hells used one portion of the evil relic to fight against the demon hosts that threatened them on otherworldly planes, Iuz was free to use his own Theorpart to crush all who dared oppose his will.

While men and demihumans and humanoids made war in and on the Flanaess, all of the netherworld likewise fought in that domain. The albino demon lord Vuron led the demons' attack upon those who would wrest the Theorpart from his liege, Graz'zt. His genius was great, and the swarming demon creatures who obeyed Vuron's commands overran their foes time after time. Up from the unspeakable depths of the Abyss swarmed more and more demons eager to serve. More and more of the lords of the Abyss named Graz'zt as monarch of their foul plane. Only the mightiest of the princes — Zortolagon, Orcus, Mandrillagon, and Ushablator the Chaos Horror — remained opposed to the new king. Of course they fought each other as well as Graz'zt, so although those who refused fealty commanded fully half of all demoniacal power, their own factiousness made them impotent.

Vuron strode across the pitchy plane of Tarterus and hammered on the gates of Hades itself. Cacodaemons from Pandemonium marched with daemon and demon under Vuron's command. There they were met by the legions of the hells, now likewise armed with a mighty instrument of evil, and Nerull's glooms shook under the impact of the crash of devil and demon ranks colliding.

The gods of Weal then fell upon the marches of the Nine Hells, harried Pandemonium, and brought destruction to any sort of evil found campaigning outside its own black realm. Some assistance too they gave to the men and demihumans of Oerth, but none of it was enough. The lords of light themselves were at odds, and Iuz's strength was too great for anything but a completely unified opposition.

The very stuff of creation groaned under the weight of the magic and power unleashed in the manifold battles across space, time, and probability. On the gameboard of the multiverse, the pawns and pieces of black swept outward to slay those of dull purple, rust red, and other colors. Those of gold captured pieces of tawny and red, while the forces of white fell upon gray, and the blue position remained aloof. Huddled in the center, the little array of emerald warriors formed itself into a ring and waited.

The One of Greatest Evil still lay comatose, fettered, and locked in unbreachable imprisonment. Perhaps the incarceration would not last forever, yet at the moment there seemed to be no need for his release. Fear and terror, strife and slaughter, reigned everywhere, and the malign was surely coming into ascendance. All portions of the Theorpart were in play now; conjoined or not, their evil influence was growing ever stronger, more pervasive. Perhaps this darkness was what kept the forces of Good from uniting. At any rate, that was not a topic for debate. The only fact that mattered was that demoniacal hordes were marching triumphantly, both on Oerth and throughout the planes of the netherworld.

* * *

"An emissary from Hades is here, dread master."

Vuron gave his full attention to the ahazu-demon who addressed him. The lank, long-armed monster was known as Talonclasp. The demon's ability was great, and Vuron had recently promoted the ahazu to command of the Cacodaemon Horde. The force was still posted as his own guard, so the ahazu-demon was remaining as Vuron's chief of staff until the cacodaemons were moved into combat.

"Emissary?" Vuron asked with a sneer. "What minion of Nerull dares venture into my hand so?"

Talonclasp managed to meet the pink eyes of the albino demon lord without submissiveness or challenge evident in his own gaze. "The netherhag Sekculintig is the visitor, Lord Vuron. She is coven-mistress of all—"

"Yes, yes. I know who the hag is, and I am aware of her power as well," the albino interrupted. "Now why would Nerull send her . . . or has she come of her own volition?" The question was obviously Vuron's way of thinking aloud, so the ahazu stood rigidly silent. Vuron noted this and approved. "Did she volunteer anything, Talonclasp?"

"No, dread master. The hag simply commanded that I announce her to you personally."

"As I had presumed," Vuron said with a trace of satisfaction. "You performed with precise duty, ahazu, which is rare in any sort of demon, let alone your ilk. You have confirmed your merit. Fetch the hag to me, then make certain none other disturbs us."

"Yes, my lord," said Talonclasp as he exited. In a second he and the emissary were back in the brazen pavilion that housed the Master of the Hordes in the field. Immediately upon announcing the arrival of the hag, the ahazu-demon was away again, and Sekculintig and Vuron stood confronting one another. The hag knew she was expected to speak first, and so she did.

"Greetings, you pale and sexless lump of shit," she said.

"And to you, ugly heap of putrescence which not even a disease-crazed goat would copulate with," Vuron countered.

That made Sekculintig cackle with mirth. "You are so good at clever comebacks, whitey!"

"You inspire that in all, I think," the albino demon lord said dryly. "But let us put pleasantries aside and get down to pressing matters — such as why you have placed your worthless being into my grasp!"

The hag cackled maniacally again, the sound reverberating horribly inside the vast metal space of the pavilion. "Are you so sure of your powers?" she said snidely. "Perhaps the Empress of Hags has something up her sleeve, eh?"

The great demon's hand reached for an ebon ziggurat on the stand next to him. "Say something meaningful, hag, or I shall terminate this interview."

"You are unlike others the Abyss, Vuron," Sekculintig fairly purred in response. "You are greater . . . and could be more so!"

"Is that so?" the albino said without emotion.

"Oh, yes, Vuron. That you know. I would not dare to try to lie to you in the very nexus of your strength. I am here on behalf of Infestix and all those who support the Ultimate One of Nullity. The dukes of the hells vie, each seeking the honor of serving as Tharizdun's left hand. Infestix sends me to offer the honor to you!"

"Tharizdun is still bound," spat Vuron. "And is Nerull so sure he is the right hand that he can offer the left?" The demon lord purposely would not use Infestix's true name, preferring to refer to the lord of Hades by the name he used for his avatar on the plane of Oerth. Some used the names interchangeably, but Vuron considered "Nerull" to be of lesser status than "Infestix" and so made the distinction.

The hag fought to control her rage, suppress her anxiety. If she could somehow convince the albino demon lord to turn his coat and support Hades, then she would certainly become the right hand of Infestix. But Sekculintig herself would be in jeopardy if she failed in persuading Vuron to take up the cause of Tharizdun. "The slumber is broken, pale lord. The confines weaken and the shackles corrode, for the artifact is active."

She let that sink in for a moment, then Sekculintig crooned on. "None can deny that Infestix leads the array who will free the Darkest, so is there any question as to which of Evil's princes will be placed on the right?"

"Perhaps. What merit places me on the left?"

"Without you the demons will splinter and offer no resistance. You, and the Theorpart you wield, would bring the matter into swift resolution!"

"I am one weak lord amongst a myriad of great

demons," Vuron offered, slyly watching the coven-mistress of hags.

"Don't try to beguile me, you colorless maggot! Has not Graz'zt granted you fully a tithe of his power? And the six and sixty greater and lesser who bow to that inky shoat have likewise allowed trickles of their puissance to flow to you. How can you portray yourself as weak? Turds fall from your silly mouth!"

The albino demon lord was taken aback — not by the words themselves, but by how much they revealed about what the netherhag knew. In truth, Vuron realized full well that at this moment he was possibly the most powerful of all demons. Powers had been bestowed upon him, others gained in conflict, others drained from the lesser demonlings who virtually worshiped him. Demogorgon in all his might would quail before him if Vuron chose to reveal his strength. How foolish he had been to assume he alone understood that. "Possibly, Sekculintig, I am almost as powerful as you seem to imagine," he conceded. "Still, you mentioned the six and sixty who bow to Graz'zt. I will reveal a secret and tell you that there are now more. My Lord Graz'zt commands fully one-half of the Abyss. Of what use is Vuron before that demonic assemblage?"

"Fagh! That collection is nothing more than violent bullies, moronic giants, and gibbering destroyers who will be at each other's throats in no time without you and the Theorpart to weld them into servitude. Graz'zt is no better than the other princes. Without you he would be another little kinglet in the howling maelstrom of contention."

"Have a care how you speak, hag!"

"Don't try that tone on me, Vuron. I see the gleam in your pink eyes. You are as lustful for power as any

— even more so, I would guess, for you have no other lusts, do you?" Sekculintig's screeching cackle of laughter at her own wit was such that she didn't notice the low sound from the albino demon's throat or see his face harden.

"If I attempted to desert Graz'zt's horde, even I would be overwhelmed by those lesser lords and greater demons who are loyal to him. To attempt that by using the ancient tool of Evil I have charge of would merely compound the numbers who would try to prevent it."

"I thought so," the netherhag gloated. "You are as corruptible as any devil, daemon, or hag! Well, albino, know that you will have help when you show the demon fartbag the price of making war on Hades. Does that satisfy you?"

"What, that empty assurance? You take me for one of the dolts of the Abyss? You will learn otherwise, hag. The blandishments you offer are meaningless. This audience is ended."

"Wait! I offer no empty promises, Lord Vuron. Pazuzeus will assist you in making transference to The Pit. Your own Talonclasp sides with us, and his cacodaemons will attack and spread disorder to mask your coming over to Tharizdun's cause!"

"Then all is certainly finished."

"What?" Sekculintig was uncertain of the demon lord's meaning.

"Thank you," Vuron replied as he opened his alabaster lips and allowed a withering blast of pure energy to shoot forth. The vomited force struck the netherhag with a soundless roar that devoured her being totally. In Hades, Infestix screamed in pain, for he had sent his essence with Sekculintig to spy out the demon lord's reaction, to measure Vuron. When his minions rushed to him, Infestix merely told them to send for Laudilewis immediately. That hag was the next in line for coven-mistress. Infestix would need the powers wielded by the hags more than ever now.

The ahazu was another matter. Vuron took his time, maiming and killing Talonclasp over a period of many days. As rampaging demons under Vuron's control decimated the ranks of the cacodaemons, devouring the leaders of the planned rebellion and destroying others for example and pleasure, the albino demon lord tortured and questioned his former officer. The ahazu-demon had been imbued with devilshine and with the dweomers of Hades as well. That one had long been a traitor. Carefully peeling his consciousness as if the ahazu were an onion, Vuron found the truth beneath skins of deception and subterfuge. Then he caged what mewling little portion of Talonclasp remained and prepared to hasten back to the Abyss.

Vuron's departure for the Abyss came slightly after Iuz's thrusts southward in the Flanaess had virtually ceased. Much fighting, pitched battles, and sieges aplenty were still occurring. But the advancing companies of demoniac evil were no longer driven from within. The enemy of Good no longer rolled onward as if it were an invincible juggernaut. Now its commanders were mere men or monsters — vile sorcerers, ruthless killers, unfeeling creatures of undeath. Gone were Iuz, the cambion's demon ally Zuggtmoy, and the great witch Iggwilv.

The pale lord of the Abyss cursed himself when he cast forth his witch-sight from his pavilion on Tarterus and discovered what had occurred, fully a week after the withdrawals had taken place. Vuron knew at that moment that he had indeed pulled the truth from the ahazu-demon; what he saw happening on Oerth confirmed Talonclasp's reluctant admission that Iuz and his Theorpart were being brought into play against Graz'zt. Had he not been so filled with his own pride, his belief in his own accomplishments, Vuron thought, then he would have seen the matter coming to light sooner. Now it might be too late.

The crux of the problem was Iuz, of course. The half-demon, offspring of Iggwilv and Graz'zt, hated his father more than he hated most things. Iggwilv was probably behind the ploy, since she also despised Graz'zt and was perhaps even more devious than her cambion son. But what part did Zuggtmoy and her clan play? Cursing the prospect of a two-front war, forcing him to divide his forces between Tarterus and the Abyss, Vuron appointed one of his lieutenants to serve as liaison between his headquarters and those of the demon lords who commanded the various hordes in the field. Then he disappeared in a silent, purple-black shimmering, gating from the frontiers of Tarterus back to the home realm of demonkind. Perhaps he would be in time to save Graz'zt and prevent the defeat of the Abyss by its foes.

* * *

"Where have you been?" The question was an accusation, the voice a snarling scream.

"Serving you as I then thought best, my king," Vuron said evenly.

Graz'zt, his giant ebony frame tense on his massive chair of state, was obviously not about to accept so reasonable a reply. "There has been a shift of power here! Why didn't you warn me, Vuron?" As he spoke, crackling motes of dark energy came from his body, forming an aura of negativity that sucked in little bolts of electricity from the dim atmosphere of the huge chamber. These crackles played in sudden bursts around the demon king and made his aspect even more terrible.

The tall, straight body of the albino demon lord bent in subjection. "It was the power of Initiator, my king. That force, and the emissions of your own Theorpart too, masked the turn of events."

"Give it to me!" Graz'zt screamed. "You were trusted with the most important assignment, and you failed! Where is Unbinder? I want it now!"

"As you wish, King Graz'zt." The albino held forth both of his long, powerful hands, palms upward. His pink eyes glazed, then burned a ruby hue. The black, conical shape of the third portion of the mighty relic appeared in his pale hands. As if it were upon a cushion, Vuron presented it, dropping down to one knee as he did so. "Your Theorpart, my king," he intoned ceremoniously.

The black demon snatched the dark object from Vuron, the Theorpart becoming nearly invisible as Graz'zt clutched it to his massively muscled chest. Then its strange dweomer came into play. The crackling energies around the demon king were drawn to it and absorbed in a lightless flash that was still somehow perceptible. The effect was instantaneous on Graz'zt. He seemed to grow larger and more awesome. "Get out!" he shouted at Vuron. "I will hold council soon. Be prepared! Your failure will be judged then."

"I hear and stand always ready to serve, my king," the albino said quietly as he bowed his head and withdrew. Graz'zt was paying no attention, clutching Unbinder and drawing in great waves of energy with it. Vuron made no sound as he left the hall. The tall, stick-thin, and leathery-skinned albino stood out among the weird nightmare of demons in the palace, not only because of his alabaster skin but because of the power he held. As steward to Graz'zt, he commanded instant homage from all there save a few princes and one or two demon lords holding high office.

As Master of the Roving Hordes, Vuron was the third most powerful general in his king's growing domain. Only Prince Yeenoghu and Lord Kostchtchie were superior in rank — and that only theoretically, for the albino demon lord controlled fully two-thirds of all the troops inhabiting Greater Mezzafgraduun, the name given to the layers of the Abyss that were under Graz'zt's purview. Vuron flinched inwardly at that thought. He *had* been in such a position of power. Now . . . who could say? From the sly glances and covert whisperings he evoked, Vuron knew that word, as usual, was sweeping through the grand palace: "Vuron is in disfavor," went the mutterings. "Beware when you speak to him, or you too might suffer the wrath."

With bearing, gaze, and controlled gesture the near-skeletal albino commanded and got every bit of respect and obedience due him, but not one jot more. None came fawning to ask favors. No groveling and begging supplicants lurked outside his personal suite. Vuron shrugged and ignored that. Excellence and commitment would tell in the end. A pair of hulking skurda guarded the portal. The flat, lifeless eyes of the scorpion-demons seemed to grow even more dead as he passed, but both were otherwise perfect in appearance and demeanor. The albino carefully closed the door to his chambers and locked it fast with a spell. Then, using his secret word of passage, Vuron went into the inner cyst where all of his vital information was kept. He floated above the concave floor in the center of the space, looking down upon a holographic map of the Abyss.

Mezzafgraduun, three hundred thirty-third layer of the Abyssal Plane, glowed with a deep, opaline luster. There were twenty-nine levels above it and thirteen below that had a paler though similar hue. Those were the layers now conquered and made part of the greater kingdom of Graz'zt. The realms of Kostchtchie, Yeenoghu, and the newly joined Baphomet shimmered in tones of color that indicated their past status. In all, six dozen strata of the plane were now bound to Graz'zt — counting only the useful, productive ones. Adding in the various shunned layers and forsaken backwaters, virtually a quarter of the whole plane was under the control of the obsidian king of demons. Little markers and strange, floating sigils showed demon gatherings, hordes, powers, and magics in play. Fully half of all of these indicators were of the silvery black sheen of Graz'zt and his minions.

At a mental command, the sphere of the demoniac realm altered and the whole of the netherworld replaced it. More of the dark opalescence appeared, demonstrating the extent of Graz'zt's power, the sweep of what was in actuality the first demon empire. If each plane of the dark realm was likened to a continent, then Graz'zt had spread his power out to engulf two and was threatening a third, from a base that was but a portion of the demon-land. Masses of red and purple glyphs writhed along a line described by similar markings of glowing black and smoky color, the place where the front of the advancing horde of demons was met by devil legions and daemon divisions. At a thought, Vuron could cause any such marking to expand and reveal details of its representation, whether it was an auxiliary legion of second-rate dreggals, elite maniples of evil-horned devils, or the battalions of Nerull himself. The demon lord impassively noted that every advance he had planned seemed stalled, and there were possible reverses taking shape. But that was secondary and must wait until later. He concentrated once again, and the view shifted again, so that the sphere of the Abyss now filled the chamber.

Vuron floated gently through the phantom replications of the demon strata. These layers wavered and changed as the demon lord sought here and there. Nothing! "This is not actual," the stick-thin demon said aloud. He closed his red-pink eyes and concentrated. He still maintained a link to the Theorpart. Carefully, so as not to alert Graz'zt, he drew power from the matrix that was Unbinder, letting the great evil force of the artifact flow through him. Its energy filled Vuron, spilled out, and surrounded him with a field of terrible strength.

"Now let us see," the demon lord cried, and intoning mind-shattering syllables in his sing-song incantation, Vuron knitted, shaped, and focused the power that he had leeched into a palpable cluster of tentacles. These he sent into the phantom projection, and as they entered the projection they too became ethereal and vanished, small things lost in the greatness. But the force within them dwarfed all else, and suddenly the maplike depiction shimmered, flickered, and changed.

"Now I see you!" It was a cry of triumph, for the seemingly quiet layers that surrounded the domain of Graz'zt became hot with the glow of enemy forces at work. Triumph turned quickly to disbelief, disbelief to

agony, as Vuron comprehended the extent of the debacle. Graz'zt's fury had been spewed forth upon the
albino because the stratum of the cataboligne demons had been wrested from the king's grasp by an
unexpected assault. Vuron was certain that Graz'zt
envisioned it as nothing more than a minor revolt in
the provinces, so to speak. The albino demon lord
now grasped the fullness of the enemies' strength.

Up from the depths swept the forces of the slime-
demon queen Zuggtmoy and her cohort Szhublox.
With them were the standards of Demogorgon, Var-
Az-Hloo, and a score of other demon lords. Even as
Vuron's gaze took in the advance, the mass of hostile
sigils was brightened. It now gleamed with the glyphs
of the hordes of Mandrillagon and Abraxas with their
lesser vassals as well. The combined host was awesome in its strength and numbers, and Graz'zt had
no intelligence of its approach.

The revealed energies above were no better. There
was the unmistakable rune of the cambion Iuz and
beside it that of the witch Iggwilv. Both were incandescent with the power of the Initiator. "They cluster
like dung beetles around a massive pile of turds!"
Vuron grated aloud as he saw the sigils of the demon
princes and lords that hovered nearby. Orcus to the
right, Azazel and Bulumuz there too. Eblis was to the
left, with Lugush and Marduk. Close by was Socoth-
benoth, positioned as if to prop up the cambion. Behind all of them trailed a cluster of lords and greater
demonlings, their trains, and their demon soldiers.

Between these two jaws lay the newly won kingdom of his lord Graz'zt. The bands and hordes guarding its frontiers were few, scattered, weak. The advancing adversaries would crack them like a nut in a
vise. Vuron shouted an awful word of power. The

scene vanished, and the whole secret chamber shook as it was drained by the magical utterance. The albino cared not. The place had served its purpose.

Vuron strode into the antechamber of Graz'zt's own suite in the royal wing of the sprawling palace. The massive guristhoi who served as the dark demon king's bodyguards tried to prevent the albino demon lord from entering. Steel-hard scales, colossal muscles, and fearsome attack powers were of no avail, of course. The tall, thin demon lord brushed the sentinels aside with a small gesture. His personal efficacy would have been sufficient alone, and Vuron still bore the massive infusion of the black force from the Theorpart as well. The guristhoi were frozen immobile instantly. The huge valves of hematite swung open at his approach, and the albino strode into the sanctum sanctorum of Graz'zt without heralding of other sort.

The six-fingered demon king sprang up from his couch. He had evidently been deep in discussion with certain of his advisors. The dark elf Eclavdra, his great high priestess, was there, as were Ogrijek, lord of the winged zubassu; the flame-demon Palvlag; and Nergal, the Justicier. Maps and papers littered the table around which their seats were clustered. "How dare you?" Graz'zt boomed. "This time, pale dog, you have gone too far!"

Vuron prostrated his thin body full length upon the mirror-polished jet slabs of the chamber floor; but almost as he so supplicated himself the albino was on his feet again. Unnaturally long arms waving, Vuron plunged ahead with what he had to do. Graz'zt actually turned pale at this, his ebon color fading to a dark ashen hue, for he saw what could only be the passes needed to summon power and use it. Vuron is here, thought Graz'zt, to assassinate me!

Graz'zt took a step back, and his hand grasped the icy metal of Unbinder desperately. "No, my liege!" Vuron shouted. "Look!"

The strange movements Vuron had completed caused a high-pitched twanging to fill the room, and at the same moment three-dimensional images appeared on either hand. "Behold the faces of your enemies, King Graz'zt!"

"Are you mad? Play you the gnomish buffoon, Vuron?!" Graz'zt barely glanced at the shadowy figures that moved and seemed to pantomime speech. The great demon had the Theorpart firmly in hand now and drew himself up to his full height, looming over even the tall albino.

"Send him to nothingness, great king!" The voice that urged Graz'zt to use the power of the evil artifact was that of Ogrijek.

"Please withhold your ire, my lord Graz'zt," came Eclavdra's clear voice sweetly. "Isn't that Iuz there, with Orcus?"

Lowering the conical device slowly, Graz'zt turned his gaze from the pink eyes of his albino warlord and steward to look where the dark-elf priestess was pointing. Sure enough, there was the cambion in his demoniacal form speaking with grand gestures to none other than the ram-headed king of vampires and their ilk. "What's this?" the demon king roared, again assailing Vuron with words. "You affront me with such scum in my own inner chambers?"

The nerve-jangling whine accompanying the ghostly images suddenly ceased and was replaced by a voice: ". . . to fall upon my gross and stupid sire and utterly crush him and all his vomit-sucking little—"

The bland face of the corpulent Orcus split, the woolly muzzle showing teeth appropriate to a shark's maw rather than that of so innocuous a creature as a sheep. "Silence!" the great demon bleated. "There — see there! Phantom forms in the mist." Iuz's skin tone deepened from its light red to a fuchsia color, but nevertheless the cambion kept quiet and gazed in the direction Orcus indicated. Both appeared to be staring straight into Graz'zt's own eyes.

"An omen, and a potent one," hissed Iggwilv as she too stared. "That the vapors rising from the Cyanic Fens should take the form of 'dear' Graz'zt even as we march for his stronghold is a great portent. We shall thus immerse him in such stuff when he falls into our hands!"

As this occurred, Vuron made further passes, and the perspective suddenly altered to one that was above the figures. This Graz'zt noted, even as his main attention stayed upon the trio. "Omen? My scepter tells me it was something more dire than a foretelling, witch," the gross Orcus said in his blaring baah. "Yet there is no sense of it now, and the apparition too has vanished. . . ."

"Attend me, King of Unlife," Iuz said in his demanding tone. "I wield the uncheckable might of Initiator. With it, I . . . we all . . . will overthrow the usurper. If the Font of Witchdom says it is a portent, then so it is!"

Orcus made some sort of reply, but his voice died away as Graz'zt turned away from that tableau in order to observe the other phantasms elsewhere. His eyes fixed on Zuggtmoy in her repulsive fungoid form, with the equally disgusting slime lord Szhublox, chimerical Demogorgon, and the other vile demons who attended them. "We will divide all of the Abyss between us," Demogorgon's rasping hiss said clearly throughout the chamber, "and all who do not fight with us now will be subjected to final termination upon our victory!"

"Just so, Abyssal Prince," Zuggtmoy's booming, rotten voice sounded in agreement. "All that was the claim of Graz'zt, and the fiefs of his curs too, will be ours to divide."

"What of the high priestess Eclavdra?" Var-Az-Hloo asked. "I have heard of the drow's beauty and skills. . . ."

"I think that none will say thee nay should you choose to claim her as booty, handsome one," the fungoid demon queen fairly chortled, "if she somehow survives the coming devastation of her lord and master's false kingdom!"

"Enough!" Graz'zt was a lightless blur, his form barely recognizable. Great energies were being drawn to him, and the effect was startling even to Vuron, who had done a similar feat not so long ago. "I see now that I was in error, my steward. When did you discover this?"

"But a short time ago, my king. I came without regard to protocol or heed for my own well-being."

Graz'zt snarled, but the ferocity was directed at the images of the demon enemies. "They make alliance against me because of Iggwilv's urging and the Theorpart's power. If the witch and her sprat had brought Initiator's might to me, the whole of the Abyss united could not oppose my will. They conjoin from fear and greed. Yet they *are* allied. . . ."

"Dogs who snap and snarl at each other, mighty king," said Ogrijek, lord of the zubassu-demons, in his most ingratiating tone. "They will devour each other, great Graz'zt, if you will but assign me more hordes to oppose them. My winged killers alone are not enough!"

Palvlag, not to be outdone, urged that he and his flame-demons be assigned to a major position immediately so as to smash the coming attack, even as the Justicier, Nergal, being the most powerful of the trio, demanded that he be awarded command of both of them and their followers. The three-way debate was stopped short by Graz'zt.

"You three will all have important commands . . . under me! Get ready, for I go to crush Demogorgon and his pack of scum myself. Now get out! Be ready whenever I call. You, high priestess, stay here with Vuron. I will assign you duties now." Not daring to complain, let alone offer protest, the three demon lords skulked out, casting sidelong glares at Vuron and the drow Eclavdra.

Vuron spoke first after the trio had left. "I trust not the zubassu thegn—"

"Trust!? I trust none . . . except my handmaiden, here, and you, Vuron. Now be silent, for I rule here. With Kostchtchie and that lot will I go. You, Vuron, will speed south even as I march north. Because you have employed the Theorpart so well, I again entrust its power to you. I have drawn strength aplenty from it, and I also have my sword and the Eye of Deception. Remember, though, steward, that I will always keep contact with Unbinder."

"And what is my assignment, my king?" Eclavdra asked.

"To stand beside Vuron. To assist him, and to watch him too. Yeenoghu and a dozen others of power will also be there, but Vuron is to have overall command. You, Eclavdra, are his lieutenant and my watchdog."

The drow bowed her beautiful head in silent acceptance, showing nothing except that by so doing.

The albino demon likewise bowed in homage. "I hear and obey, king," Vuron muttered deferentially. Graz'zt actually smiled at the pale demon lord, his fiery green eyes showing something as akin to true respect and friendship as is possible for such beings. Vuron saw that, bowed lower, and continued, "And if Iuz should come forth with his Theorpart? . . ."

The smile turned to a savage, wolfish snarl. "Ah, my steward, if I could only be there for such an event! Yet I am confident you will know how to deal with that gross idiot should that happen. It is the witch you must beware of most. Have care should she come forth!"

Both Vuron and Eclavdra nodded and started to depart. Graz'zt stopped them short with what seemed like an afterthought. "The full council will meet in one hour. I had thought to discuss other matters. . . . Come with the rest, but both of you are to say nothing. Listen only. At the conclusion, you two will remain behind, for I will need your assessment of the lords present. As I told you, I trust none fully; most of that lot must be watched." Then Graz'zt left them, and his two closest servants quickly made their way to their own places to prepare.

Chapter 3

"THIS IS MOST UNEXPECTED. . . ."

Gord spoke those words softly, and it was an understatement. A moment or two before, he had been in an undersea grotto with the undine Kharistylla. She had told him it was time. "Time for what?" he had asked. Then, following her instructions, he had simply touched the amulet while thinking of Rexfelis the Catlord.

The beautiful undersea grotto and the even lovelier undine had suddenly wavered, become insubstantial, and for an instant Kharistylla's smiling eyes had seemed to become as large as saucers just before she vanished from his sight. Gord spoke, blinked, and shook his head, because he now stood before the assembled lords of Balance.

"He is changed," Basiliv the Demiurge said to no one in particular. Then, to Gord: "Welcome, prince. Leoceanius said we should expect you about now, and so here we stand gathered."

A murmur rose up from several of those in Rexfelis's private chamber. Of the score of powerful personages there, perhaps seven or eight had met and spoken with the young adventurer in the past. Among them were the Master Cat, of course; the Demiurge

Basiliv; the archwizards Mordenkainen and Tenser; and the King of Shadow.

"I present Gord," Rexfelis said formally, coming to the young man's aid. "Some of you have been intro- duced to the Prince of Panthers before this." Then he made introductions of some of those present whom the young adventurer had not met. "My Lords of the Cabal," he began, nodding to indicate four strange no-longer-humans near the back of the chamber. Then, sweeping his gaze and his arm slowly around the room, he named others. "Gord, this is the Master of Swords — perhaps a foster sire of yours, I think. Here is Lord Hewd, Lord Donal, Murlon, Lord Keogh, Venerable Yocasta, Venerable Nastan. And here is the Active Hand of Dweomer, the Archimage, of course, for the highest of magic never himself interferes. . . ."

Demi-gods, quasi-deities, the most powerful of hu- mans. Somehow, Kharistylla had found out exactly when he was supposed to make his appearance, and Leoceanius had played a role he was unaware of. The whole experience was simply too much for Gord to comprehend. "I . . . I . . . What is the problem? Am I being judged?" he blurted out.

"Droll fellow," the quasi-deity known as Lord Keogh drawled with barely suppressed mirth. "If that were the case, the whole lot of us would have to stand beside you."

"Yet, not a bad idea that," suggested the Mad One of Magic. "Let's round up those demi-humans — the elves, dwarves, gnomes, that whole lot — and stand trial together!"

"There's no point trying to find that bunch," Lord Hewd said, tugging absently at his little beard. "They're all off fighting against demons and devils, you know."

Shadowking raised a dark eyebrow at that exchange, and Rexfelis seemed about to interject something, but the four Hierophants of the Cabal spoke in unison. "Enough, sirs!" they said. Then one of them continued. "This young prince is true and truly puzzled. Let us deal with matters at hand in a fashion likely to produce results, ere we find ourselves grappling with fiends from the nether regions ourselves!"

"Thank you, my lords," Gord said to the Hierophants after an audible swallow of relief. "I have had to face demons and devils before, and I think even this assemblage is preferable to that."

"Too bad, too bad," caroled the Mad Archimage. "We're here to see that you do just that!"

At that the Catlord took a hand. "I apologize, Prince Gord," he said formally. Then he took the young man by his arm and steered him to a nearby chair. Rexfelis pushed Gord down, seated himself in the next tall chair, and waved casually to the others to take their positions. "Let us all take our places, and I shall explain to our champion what is to take place. Agreed?"

There were various spoken and unspoken assents, and in a moment or two the whole strange assembly, the gathering that included the majority of the powers who represented Balance, was seated in a semicircle in the large, low-ceilinged chamber. "Thank you all, lords and ladies," Rexfelis intoned. "Hear what I have to tell to Gord of Greyhawk, acknowledged by me and you all as a peer, titled the Prince of Panthers by birthright and by virtue of accomplishment such that none may question."

"Hear, hear!"

"Get on with it!"

Gord was now more confused than before, and at

the same time a bit excited. What was this about "birthright"? Perhaps, for some reason he could not fathom, he was finally about to learn of his heritage. But he and Rexfelis had spent long hours together before this, and surely the Catlord had already told him all there was to tell. Gord held his tongue, but his mind reeled. He dared not hope, but could not keep from doing so. . . .

The Catlord gave cold looks to both who had spoken, first Basiliv and second the crotchety old Mordenkainen. He cleared his throat with a sound that was a cross between a purr and a growl, then continued. "As you know, Gord has served the cause of Balance for longer than he has realized, but actively and most willingly of late. In recognition and explanation of his services, I have acknowledged his heritage to some of you. I now tell this to the rest of you, and Gord himself, for the first time: His father, my own great-grandson, was the sole heir of my kind's Seventh House. By birthright and his own deeds he has fully earned that heirship . . . and more. That is another story, however. I will stick with the business our council has before it."

At that point Gord could no longer contain himself. "You've known all along?" he asked, anger overriding the excitement he felt.

Rexfelis showed little emotion, but his huge, dark eyes had a tinge of sadness as he replied. "Yes, Gord, I have known all along. I do not ask your forgiveness, for there is nothing to forgive. Perhaps you'll understand when you know more, perhaps not. Too many sought you — too many of such deadly power and fell purpose that not even all of us here, let alone simply me, could keep them from you had they fully understood just who and what you were . . . or are, rather."

"Just what is that?" Gord's voice was calm, but an inner glow coming from his gaze bespoke his rage and sadness at being kept uninformed for so long.

"The one foretold . . . the one foreordained to fight the final battle."

The Catlord's last words curtailed Gord's rising fury, stopped it cold. "I am fated to fight . . . the *final* battle?" he asked.

"No, no, Rexfelis," the ancient priest, Nastan, said loudly in his cracked voice. "Not any of us can so order. We are mere predictors — searchers for clues is a better term, perhaps."

"Well, I don't care who ordered it, actually," Gord said harshly. "I have some say. And why this damned secrecy? If this has been foreordained, then who or what could prevent it? Why not tell all?"

Rexfelis spoke again. "Not so fast. What is foretold is this: Should you attain your maturity, manage to survive and not be polluted by evil, or made narrow by some rigid conceit, then you would be the one to bear the banner for us."

Gord started to open his mouth, but the Catlord silenced him with a stern look. "Mind you, prince, that I speak of no guarantees. Attend my words; let your ears hear. You alone can fight for us. None of those who espouse Law or Chaos must be allowed to prevail. Balance is the force that has a champion, one to carry the contest to Unrelenting Darkness.

"That much alone is foretold — the outcome of the battle is not prescribed. No hint is even given. Yet, your even being able to contest with the great enemy was sufficient to make the vile ones quail. You had to be protected — and kept ignorant so as not to reveal some clue unwittingly — until we could reveal this knowledge to you."

"The years in miserable suffering, the horrors of that bastard Theobald and beggary, the whole course of my life . . ."

"Necessary — and generally secretly assisted for the better by our agents, or simply directed by your own mind, Gord. In fact, what you did, what you accomplished, what you are — all of that is your own doing."

"And just what does all of this mean?"

"Who can say? Not even the best of us is so great as to venture into such suppositions. Yet, prince, I think you yourself know the answer well enough. You see all sides of the question, judge, and act. Each year you grow, your perspective heightens, and the change is evident. You perceive the great conflict which now embroils all. It is a deadly game which will decide the fate of your world and ours too, whether of material sort or not."

Gord shook his head in denial. "That is no game, and I am no pawn in it."

"To some it is a game," Basiliv the Demiurge said gently. "It is a helpful analogy to use, though. The ones we contest with, even those we seek to aid, see it as such, you know."

"How can this be called a game? Lives being played with, lost. . . . It is monstrous!"

"There is a prize at stake, Gord," Basiliv said in reply to the heated denial. "It is a contest. You have played the game of life and death often enough yourself, I think."

"It was for survival, and against those who knew full well the consequences of loss. Each was an able and skilled opponent, and I took only the lives of those who needed to die," Gord countered with less anger but iron determination filling his voice.

"Most arrogant and judgmental!" This came in unison from the four who were the head of the Cabal, the strange Hierophants. "We object to your attitude, Gord. If you do not dismiss such thinking from yourself immediately, you will be an unfit champion." Though the four spoke at one time, they were of one mind and one voice so utterly that the words came from each of them simultaneously. The effect was eerie and rather unsettling, but Gord would not be dissuaded.

"I am not champion. I have no wish to play this game! Let the hells, the demons, all of you find some other pawn to push around!" Gord was ready to rise and leave, although he didn't know where he would go or what the reactions of these mighty ones of Balance would be when he tried to evacuate. At this juncture he no longer cared. It was just too much for a mortal spirit to bear.

Rexfelis stopped him, smiling gently. "You are right. You need not be a pawn. Do not 'play.' Those who seek evil, death, misery, enslavement for all who do not serve them willingly will gloat and be filled with glee at your decision, Gord. They have long sought to eliminate you from the contest. Your quitting will serve almost as well as your death, I think."

That made Gord sink back down and stare at the Catlord. "Better, better," Rexfelis said softly. "Long have you played unwittingly, without our direction, although our other active forces in the game supported you when they could. Then you took part at the direction of Balance, but without full knowledge of what was involved. Even should you choose to leave now, Gord, I think that too would simply be part of the play. You, like us, cannot escape by simply wishing to."

Gord could do little but shrug. "Then I am no champion at all. I am a piece which wanders aimlessly about, doing nothing of significance and unable to direct my course. Let one of you powerful beings serve as the banner-bearer. Who amongst you all is not more puissant than I?"

"Fairly put, young Gord," a slow and heavy voice said. All in the chamber were completely still at the sound, and Gord looked over to the place where the words had come from. "Yet there is a bit of each of us to go with you, and then you will be both less and more than any of us," the being continued.

That meant nothing to him, but Gord was unsettled by what he saw. Nothingness and yet something occupied a place in the hall, and none of the other occupants of the place were near the space. "I am at a disadvantage . . . Lord of . . . Nothingness? I cannot see you, nor do I know your title or realm."

"I am All and Nothing, prince. You were not far from the mark. It is sufficient to say that in my own limited way I am part of Balance in that I contest with life and death, chaos and order. Normally I would not take part in any struggle, for in the end I will triumph over all that way.

"However," the measured, plodding voice spoke on, "the advent of Tharizdun has forced me to assist the Lords of Neutrality. Thus a portion of my essence will be yours to call upon, should you step forward and serve willingly."

Advent? So the terrible force of total evil *was* advancing. That knowledge had a great effect upon the young thief, and Gord forgot to ask just what the so-called 'All and Nothing' was. Instead he turned to the Master of All Cats. "Explain more of this to me, please," he asked simply, settling back in his chair for the first time since he had been thrust into this assemblage.

Rexfelis proceeded to tell him about the emerging struggle that put Balance into so exposed a position in the very center of all. With occasional interjections from the great personages and virtual deities in the chamber, the Catlord related how he and the others had sought to confound the machinations of devils and demons without recourse to a particular champion. Although they, as the sovereigns of Neutrality, knew that there was a prophecy regarding such a singular figure, even they could not be certain, so they had played on while keeping careful guard over the one who might one day be needed — by all the multiverse, not just by Balance. Gord's parents had been, together, a minor force in the game, and they had been betrayed into vulnerability by pieces of their own color. Sadly, they had been eliminated and yet thus fulfilled a part of the foretelling, for behind them remained a tiny spark of potential.

"Amidst the webs of magic and energy, Gord, even that mote could have been discerned by our foes — your foes, of course, as well as ours," said Rexfelis. "Alone we could not have hidden your spark of possibility, but still the evil ones could not seem to locate you. Another hand was involved."

After a few questions, the narration continued as before. Rexfelis and Lord Donal spoke of how they had seen Gord become an able young beggar and thief, occasionally protected, always observed, but never interfered with. "When you left the city, prince, and set off with the Rhennee, you suddenly entered the field as a pawn," Lord Donal noted. "You were not played — you placed yourself upon the board!"

After noting that Gord's successes, as well as his

failures, not only moved him around the area of the contest but also made his relative strength change, just as an advancing pawn becomes more threatening to the opposing force, Rexfelis explained that Gord himself promoted his worth to above that of a mere foot soldier. "By continually winning over evil adversaries, and by not just staying well away from their influence but becoming more and more firmly convinced to uphold your ever-strengthening beliefs in freedom and choice, you grew from an inconsequential if well-placed pawn into a multi-powered piece."

Shadowking and the Demiurge added their own comments then, and Gord was amazed still more. He turned to the person introduced to him earlier as the Master of Swords. "Blademaster, you assisted me?"

"Even so skilled a thief as you, one whose gymnastic feats are of the highest sort, does not acquire weapons skill — or such weapons as you have possessed, Gord, without a bit of help, shall we say," the Master of Swords confirmed in his quick manner. His thin lips smiling, the Lord of All Blades added, "And I shall do so again if you will."

Each of those present assured the young man that he had done some small thing to assist him. Then Rexfelis spoke again. "Now, Gord, you are Prince of Panthers. That acknowledged status bestows but little additional power upon you, for you are already a knight in service to Balance. As a willing champion, however, you will command those spaces adjacent to you as well; thus will you be equipped to the best of our ability to face the Ultimate Foe."

"What choice have I?" Gord said finally. "Whether willing or willy-nilly, it would seem I am fated. I have no love for our foes, no commonality with those who oppose them. Balance is my only understanding. To accept conviction of its purpose, then, is but to admit what I am."

"There are shades and tints, intensity and pallor, even in the whole of Neutrality, Gord," Lord Hewd told him. "Whatever the exact ethos may be, all of us recognize that in order to have our liberty to remain as we are, and for all others to do likewise, the Ultimate Darkness must not be allowed to prevail."

"Am I not proof of the different shades and tints?" Gord asked rhetorically.

"No," said the slow voice of the nothingness that seemed to fill a whole corner of the hall, "but my presence with Balance is."

Before more could be said, the four Hierophants arose and in unison placed their mark upon Gord. The sensation for him was like a burning wave washing over his body, and the young thief nearly fainted. Then each of the others there likewise gave some touch or sign as their gift. Energy shot through Gord's body, made his nerves tingle, his brain float. So much power, so many diverse agencies! He was glad indeed to be sitting when it occurred.

"Basiliv and I will escort you from here, prince," the Catlord said when the last of the Lords of Balance had finished placing their tokens of power with him. "I have more to say, for above all my own aegis is over you. The Demiurge too has instructions."

* * *

"Now I will begin at the beginning," the Master of Cats said when the three of them were alone in a small library that served as Rexfelis's personal study. "You are the offspring of my seventh son, the ninth of my great-grandchildren to attain status above that which was theirs by birthright. With the acceptance just given by the Lords of Balance, none of my own, not any of the scions of the other houses, dare to contest you."

"What do you mean?" Gord asked. This was all too confusing still.

"Each of the Nine Houses vies for supremacy with the others. Each would have its own become king. I cannot interfere . . . much, anyway, else I would be no Lord of Catkind. But your own father had no such aspirations. He knew of the prophecy and above all sought to see it come true. He and your mother were the deadliest foes of Tharizdun and his servitors."

"What was my mother's name? My father's?"

"Of course. Forgive me, Gord. The pressures of this time made me remiss. Your mother was called Ataleena. She had second sight and could have been a great wizardess. She had violet eyes, you know — perhaps from her distant elvish blood. Your father was named Karal, and he loved your mother more than just about anything in the planes. It was she who convinced him to desert the confines of this place, Gord, and to fight the enemy elsewhere. I don't think I forgave her for that until I first met you. . . ." Rexfelis said half to himself. Then, recapturing his train of thought, he went on.

"Ataleena knew of the prophecy regarding Tharizdun's return from her mother, who had learned it from her own mother, and so on. All of those women were seeresses. Good folk. Karal named you after his wife's house. Your mother was Ataleena Carona, and your given name is Carl — was, I must say. Despite its humble origin, Gord is now your name, and one which has power. You must keep it. Does Prince Gord Carl Quapardus suit you?"

70

After a minute came the reply. "The name Gord is what I am accustomed to. It seems sufficient."

"So it shall be for the time. I'll be brief about the rest," Rexfelis said softly. "Others of your kin betrayed both your father and mother. Too late the traitors repented. Your parents were slain by agents of evil, directed by one of its most terrible minions." When Gord's face started to darken with anger, the Catlord waved him to settle him down and hurried on. "I brought much sorrow upon those responsible, and they paid dearly, as much from their own guilt as from any punishment of mine. Not one of the perpetrators survives now," he added with sorrow for the act of betrayal, not for loss or mourning. "The malign ones rejoiced at first, but then discovered that they had not fully completed their mission. Despite their best, or worst, efforts, not the greatest of devils or vilest of netherlords could quite discover whom they sought. Even now I think they do not know, but that will soon change!"

Basiliv the Demiurge spoke then. "You have been destined to become the sole one able to contest with the greatest of evil beings, Gord. While your kin squabbled over who was to become the chief heir to Rexfelis's domain, and the powers of evil hatched their plots to find and gather the Theorparts, you went about your own business. Unknown and unknowing, you were tried and tested, heated, hammered, forged, and tempered to become the weapon of all who deny evil."

"There are many of Balance far stronger than I — even with what you have given to me." Gord stated this as a fact, not meaning to be argumentative.

"True. Even had all of us nobles of Balance been present at the conclave, and all bestowed all the force

71

they could upon you, still there would be others stronger than you. I do not know how to explain the state of affairs, save to say that the foretelling is what it is."

Gord gave up on that line of thought and turned back to Rexfelis. "Tell me more about my father and mother," he said.

"First," said the Catlord, "the box." Gord knew immediately what Rexfelis was referring to — not his magical carry-all, but the battered wooden coffer he carried within it. Gord had been keeping it safe, either in his possession or carefully hidden somewhere in the city of Greyhawk, ever since claiming it as a child. Old Leena, the brutal, cantankerous woman who served as his guardian during his early youth, had kept the box away from him and even taunted him with her possession of it — because she had somehow known that it and its contents were meant for him instead of her. She had learned, quite accidentally, how to open it, but she had never imparted that information to Gord, and he was only able to get it away from her after she died in her bed one day.

"It is carefully dweomered," Rexfelis continued. "Speak either your mother's or your father's name while holding it, and it will open to reveal its contents." Unbeknownst to Gord, this was why old Leena had been able to open it, at least partially. Her name was quite similar to the name of Gord's real mother — and, as it turned out, there was a minor flaw in the first stage of the magical protection surrounding the box. Thus, she could get the main compartment open by saying "Leena," but because she never voiced the full word "Ataleena," she never knew of the real treasure hidden beneath the container's false bottom.

"Inside you will find portraits of your parents and

a history of what they had done, written in the language of catfolk. Your father even said therein that he hoped you would not fail the coming tests."

"He knew what I was to become?"

"Perhaps. The document is not exactly clear, but it gives hints. Read it when we are done here, and then judge for yourself." Rexfelis held up a hand to keep Gord from responding to that and added one more vital fact. "Beneath a secret panel, which is opened by saying the same name a second time, you will find a necklace containing nine black sapphires." The Cat-lord allowed himself a thin smile as he said that.

"Are they . . . ?" Gord asked, barely able to contain his anticipation. They must be the same ones, he thought in answer to his own unvoiced question — the same ones he had risked his life to regain during his time in the Land of Shadow and then been forced to relinquish in order to leave that eerie place.

Not even Rexfelis knew the full history of these gems. They had been in the coffer when old Leena had held it, but had been magically removed from the container a few years after her death as the box lay buried in a secret place in Greyhawk. When Gord came back from one of his adventures and reclaimed the box, he had no way of knowing that its contents had been tampered with in the meantime by sorcerous forces aligned with those that had been trying to discover and destroy Gord. Fortunately for him, the box was not under magical surveillance when he returned to Greyhawk and dug it up; by that time, the search for him had gone in another direction, and the box was forgotten about, thought to be unimportant.

The sapphires were eventually set into a glorious necklace, and the piece of jewelry was so highly treasured that it ended up as the property of a high priest of Nerull. Then it was subsequently acquired by one of the major denizens of Shadowland, a terrible lich-creature called Imprimus. It was this evil being whom Gord vanquished in order to gain the sapphires for himself. He had thought of them only occasionally since using them to gain egress from Shadowland, and had not really expected to see them again.

"Yes, the sapphires are back inside the coffer, Gord, as you will see when you examine the box. The necklace which they are again formed into is your badge of royalty, bequeathed to you by your father. It proclaims its wearer as the Prince of the Ninth House, the Prince of Panthers. The sapphires have traveled far and wide over the years, but they have really always been your property — yours to keep, yours to use some day."

Rexfelis paused, but Gord was at a loss for what to say. He had taken in so much information so rapidly that he simply did not know how to comment or what to ask. He did not understand how the gems could have been placed inside the box without his knowledge, but he had long known that the workings of magic were beyond his ability or his desire to comprehend. Then the Catlord continued, seemingly anxious to disclose the rest of what he cared to reveal.

"The ring I gave you was also left to you by your father. Karal himself would have kept it, I think, had he been sure of surviving long enough to see you wear it. There is a little more I can tell, but this is not the time. Suffice to say that regardless of other events, the Ninth House will attain the rule of all the feline kingdom if you survive, Gord. In fact, I would abdicate to you at this moment, save that it would avail neither of us anything. Destiny has removed much from our hands."

The Demiurge took over at this point, for it seemed difficult for the Catlord to continue. "We lords of Neutrality are in a poor position, you see, and in comparison to those who surround us we are quite weak. The rulers of the hells alone outnumber us ten to one, and few of us are stronger than the greatest of those dukes. What you saw at the gathering represents barely half of those with enough power to have a hand in charting the course of Balance. Some others are bound to their own elements and see naught but the eternity of that. A few contest with the upper planes, some others fend off total order or wild randomness as needs be. Some are fully engaged in the physical struggle against the forces of the Abyss or Hades or the hells' legions. And some are . . . gone." Basiliv looked at Gord briefly, then continued. "If all of the Lords of Balance took the field, that would free a far greater number of our opponents to contest against our presence. That would spell our doom. If your grandfather— "

"That is properly great-grandfather," Rexfelis harrumphed in interjection.

"If your great-grandfather, or I, or some other should try alone, then the evil ones would know immediately and send two or more of their own mightiest ones to stop us. There is no other way save what we have told you. You are unknown now, your sudden increase in power unsuspected by the enemy. And you play chess well, I hear."

"I play several sorts of chess fairly well," Gord acknowledged, "and *at* many forms of the game too." Those last words were delivered with a sidelong glance toward Rexfelis, as Gord recalled the times the Catlord had bested him in one or another obscure forms of the game.

75

"Yes, just so," the Demiurge said with a smile. "You understand that the value of a piece is in its power of movement and area of command. In this so-called game, though, we must also deal with the fact that not every piece can exert pressure upon any opposing contestant. A pawn is powerless against a minor piece, a minor piece of no use against a greater piece.

"In this play there are many grades of pawns, levels of minor pieces, and ranks of major ones. Unless near-parity exists, the lesser cannot prevail against the greater, and the more powerful will usually succeed in slaying the weaker. Time and again you have done for one or other of the evil pieces — humans, monsters, demons. Still, the enemy cannot reckon properly what you are. When you move into the main field again as the champion sent by Balance, none will recognize your true powers until too late — we hope! If that is so, then you will become the second most powerful figure in the multiverse."

"The second?"

"Tharizdun is the first," Basiliv said heavily.

"And I must then seek out that one?"

"If you attain to the second station, Prince Gord," the Demiurge assured him, "you will have no need to seek out the Absolute Darkness. He will find you."

"How can I hope to succeed?" The young man looked from Catlord to the Demiurge questioningly.

"The Master of Nothingness and All has sided with us," Basiliv stated after hesitating. "That one is perhaps now the second-greatest force in the multiverse, but you must always beware such a being, just as one watches the scorpion."

"Why be so enigmatic about him or it? I must have information!"

"No more can be said," Basiliv replied. "You will know in time, if that is given to any of us. If I speak too much, I might distort the foretelling."

"Nonsense!" It was evident from his expression that Rexfelis disagreed with Basiliv's last statements, but it had not been the Catlord who had spoken just now. The voice had come from a shadowy corner.

"Shadowking?" Gord asked uncertainly.

"No," the slow and icy voice answered from yet another location in the chamber. "Master Entropy — at your service, prince and champion."

That made Gord start. "You are of ultimate chaos!"

"Never. I will consume the wild motion, eliminate randomness as I do order, wipe out death by removing life, burn out life and slay darkness into nothing. I am truly neutral, the actual balance of all. I am nothingness and everything — in their proper states."

"Beware!" Rexfelis and Basiliv spoke in unison, but Gord ignored both of them.

"How will you help?" he asked the unseen figure.

"My aid comes now in the form of information. One of your most important tools is a sword. Many of your fine associates will appreciate the weapon and its forms. You have it now, the dark blade you brought from the buried capital of the forgotten realm of the Suloise."

"I own it indeed," Gord admitted, "but it is of no special value."

"More than you suppose," the nothingness countered. "Still, the sword is not all it can be, on that point I agree." Was there mockery in the voice? Gord wasn't certain.

"You will assist me in making it truly potent?"

"I have already, by giving you this knowledge. This has been most painful, prince and champion, for it defies all I stand for and drains my particular force cruelly," Master Entropy intoned monotonously, as if speaking to a slow and measured beat. "There is no more I shall say, no more I can do. Now, Gord, all is in your hands."

With that, the presence of the strange being faded away. Basiliv and Rexfelis, seeming to take their cues from that occurrence, silently rose from their seats. Gord did the same, and moments later was alone in his chamber.

* * *

Elsewhere, elsewhen, the tides of evil weakened in their surge, and the men of the kingdoms and nations of Oerth who opposed the dark and wicked pushed their enemies back a little, slaughtering many in so doing. Stalemate positions occurred in the netherworld, and the great war being fought in the Abyss raged, but neither side advanced.

Master Entropy was at work. Creation and life — vitality even of demoniacal or negative sort — slipped away into nothingness. Nothingness grew and was strengthened, and was content.

"We are lost," the Demiurge said lamentably when he, Rexfelis, and Gord reconvened a few hours later — hours during which weeks of time had passed on Oerth. "Now truly are we placed between the void and the bottomless pit!" Rexfelis nodded and looked grim. What Basiliv said was too true, and there seemed to be no escape. Entropy was perhaps better, if nonexistence of anything but nothingness could be accepted by those who were sentient. "Never should we have accepted Master Entropy, not in an eternity of days!"

"Lost or not, I have much to do," Gord said energetically. "Time will decide if that one is to triumph or not, but if I am to believe what I have been told, it is up to me to face and defeat Tharizdun." He spat as he said that name. "What can you tell me of the power of the sword Master Entropy spoke of?"

"I am as unaware of that as you, Gord," Rexfelis replied. "Basiliv?"

"Would I could be of assistance," the Demiurge said. "Perhaps if I could see the weapon and spend a little time examining its aura. . . ."

"There will be a bit of time for that, my old friend," Rexfelis said. "Gord will soon be presented to all of my subjects, including the peers who are his kins-folk. There will be a short ceremony, longer speeches, and much growling of useless sort. I will name him first of all our sort after me before he sets forth on the mission we have for him."

"I will certainly stay for two reasons, then," Basiliv said, mustering up a weak smile. "Let us see the dark blade now, for soon we will be too busy for anything except such work as we need accomplished." Basiliv and the Catlord turned expectantly to Gord, both casting their gazes toward the scabbard at his waist. Gord's face was blank.

"Well? Bring forth the blade!" the Demiurge said.

"This is not it," Gord said, touching the sheath. "The sword that Master Entropy spoke of is hidden aboard *Silver Seeker*, and where that ship is I can't tell you," he said sadly.

Chapter 4

"WE ARE NOW MOORED in Safeton's deep harbor, pious brother."

The bent old cleric looked up with weak, rheumy eyes from the prayerbook he was reading. "Thank you, shipmaster, but please call me simply Brother Donnur. 'Pious' is too worthy an honorific for a mendicant pilgrim," the ancient fellow added gravely.

"Of course," the captain of the little trading vessel said quickly. Then he turned and hurried above. Despite the priest's gentle demeanor and kindly ways, there was something about him that Shipmaster Rench found disquieting. "Ah, balls," the sailor muttered to himself. "Likely nothin' more than the fact I'm a lost and wicked heathen, it is." Nonetheless, Rench would be glad to see the back of the old cleric's dirty brown robe as the man went down the gangplank of his ship.

Safeton, northernmost of the ports that dotted the long Wild Coast, was a thriving town of some five thousand souls that Shipmaster Rench and his vessel, the *Sea Turtle*, called upon regularly. When the ship was tied fast to the long mole in Safeton Harbor, the town officials only barely checked papers, manifest, and passengers. Instead they greeted the captain as a long-lost comrade, took the usual bribe, and were soon off to the nearest tavern to share a few bumpers of ale with Rench and his officers.

Nobody even noticed Brother Donnur's departure from the ship, Rench included. The bent priest hobbled away and was lost in the throng that teemed around the cargoes and market stalls of the waterfront district. When he was safely away, where none of the crew of the *Sea Turtle* could see him, the man exchanged his brown robes for a dark overcoat hanging outside someone's door, straightened his spine, and strode on, looking nothing at all like the withered cleric that had been on the ship.

The very day that *Sea Turtle* raised anchor and headed south for other ports of call, a patched-up ship passed her, heading for its own place along the long quay. That vessel was none other than *Silver Seeker*, stopping at Safeton to take on water and provisions before sailing northward. She was bound for passage up the Selintan River to Greyhawk, and Barrel, her new captain, wanted to find and hire a pilot to make certain that the journey didn't bring craft and crew to grief. Deep-water sailing was something the burly man knew well, but he was veteran enough to realize also that navigating upriver was another matter altogether.

"Ahoy, mates! I expect we're goin' to be here no more than three days — two, if I find the man I'm lookin' for sooner," Barrel announced after the ship was moored. "Debauch yerselves to your black hearts' content, boys, but be back aboard before sunup Starday — else I'll sail without ye!"

With Dohojar at his side, the burly captain began a careful canvassing of the dives along the town's waterfront horseshoe, seeking the services of a freshwater pilot. A drink here, a copper coin there, and soon enough Barrel had the names of a half-dozen navigators who did their sailing up and down the Selintan. That was no surprise, for the City of Greyhawk was a thriving center of commerce. By then, however, both the Changa and Barrel were sufficiently drunk to know it was time to retire back aboard their ship.

"C'mon, my fine brown friend," Barrel said with a happy smile as he clapped his arm around the little Changa's narrow shoulders and steered him toward the door of the saloon. "We'll sleep now, an' tomorrow find our navigator."

"Oh, yes, Barrel, yes," Dohojar agreed, likewise grinning in happy inebriation. "Gord Zehaab himself would understand the correctness of such wisdom." The two lurched out the exit and were soon snoring in their cabins in *Silver Seeker*.

After Gord's sudden departure, the storm had veered enough to enable them to survive the tempest. After repairs and more jury-rigging, they had headed for Telmstrand on the east portion of Ulek's coast for proper refitting. Before sailing on, the two had held a moot with the rest of the crew to decide what course they should chart. When Dohojar had suggested that the best place to find Gord was the city of Greyhawk, the issue was settled. Now, after sailing around the Pomarj peninsula and along the Wild Coast up Woolly Bay, they were almost there.

Next evening, Barrel discovered that having the names of navigators was one thing and finding the men attached to them was quite another. He had all but run out of possibilities when he found someone who said he could help. "This here's the busy time, matey," a squint-eyed barkeep explained. "Most o' the men ye're lookin' fer've hauled anchor already, but fer the right fee I can find ye a likely pilot." With that, he held out his hand and waited.

Barrel made a ferocious face — an easy enough thing to do with a visage as homely and scarred as his — but the barkeep did not flinch. So the captain reached into his purse and began counting out the thick copper discs that the fellow was waiting for. At ten the squint-eyed man leered and closed his hand. "That'll do — I ain't no greedy-gut!" he said. "I'll have one o' me boys fetch 'im, an' he'll be here inside an hour. Have a drink on th' house whilst yer awaitin'." Dohojar looked uncertain, but his comrade shrugged and ordered each of them small beer.

Just about an hour later, though, true to his word, the squint-eyed proprietor nodded toward the door. "There, sirs! Didn't I tell ye? There's yer navigatin' man now!"

The man he indicated was a very tall, skinny one standing straight as a mast just inside the door. Barrel's first impression was not a good one — the man simply didn't look like a sailor. "You better have steered me true, gleed-eye, else I'll be fixin' it so's you sing soprano hereafter," the captain growled as he eyed the supposed pilot.

"Arrr," the barkeep rumbled with a smirking grin. "Yer mos' welcome ta try anything ye like, cap'n. I be no easy mark. Yet that 'un is what I tol' ye he was, by Skunar! If'n he ain't, I'll do the cuttin' o' me barnacles m'self!"

Mollified, Barrel motioned to Dohojar, and the two elbowed their way over to where the tall man stood waiting. The burly seaman stood back as Dohojar stepped up and asked, "Are you the pilot-man I have asked for?"

The fellow looked down at the little Changa without moving his head. Then he looked up and straight at Barrel. "I don't know your game," he said, addressing the burly sailor, "but I don't think I like it."

As the thin man started to leave, Barrel caught him politely by his coat sleeve. "Avast, navigator! A man can't be too careful now, can he? Especially in these waters!"

"That's right," the tall fellow said in clipped fashion. "Take me, for instance. I'm having nothing to do with you."

"Would a golden orb change your mind?"

The tall, thin body suddenly froze in its progress out of the tavern. Then the man turned, expressionless, looking hard at Barrel. "No," he said finally, his face immobile and his lips barely moving. "My life is worth more than that."

Dohojar nudged his comrade, and the burly sailor grudgingly said, "All right then, mate, make it a pair of orbs . . . if you can navigate my ship up the Selintan safely to Greyhawk."

The tall pilot didn't reply. Instead he went over to an empty table nearby, sat down, and looked at Dohojar and Barrel. The two joined him, Dohojar signaling to the barkeep for service. "I may take that offer, captain," he said as a bumper of wine was placed on the stained board before him.

"Barrel. Cap'n Barrel."

"But I'll see the color of your coins first."

The Changa held the purse, and at his friend's nod slipped two gold coins out and displayed them so that only the three of them sitting at the table could see their gleaming yellow. "A fortune for such work, I think," Dohojar commented.

"Shows how little you know about navigation upriver," the tall, hard-faced pilot said as he reached over casually and took the coins. He hefted them, tested one with his teeth, and then smiled a smile as thin as himself. "Call me Graves. Pilot Graves. Your ship is the *Silver Seeker*?"

"Aye," Barrel admitted with surprise. He didn't remember saying his ship's name to the barkeep, so how could this man have known? Well, he supposed, word about such things does have a way of getting around the docks. . . . "And I'll take back those orbs 'til you be coming aboard her!" he added.

Stone-faced, the thin man placed the pair of gold coins back into the Changa's hand. "Naturally. One I'll take upon boarding, one when I've seen you safely docked along Greyhawk's quay. We sail with the morning tide, Captain Barrel. The Selintan is low this time of year, and likely to get lower before the autumn rains start. Your ship has a deep keel, and I don't guarantee anything if you want to tarry here."

"That you needn't fear, pilot," the burly seaman growled. "Be aboard afore sunup, and we'll set sail with the morning wind." Graves stood up and stalked off, still stiff and straight as a spar, not saying another word. "He's an odd sodder," Barrel remarked to the Changa as the lanky form disappeared into the darkness outside.

"Very much so, I am thinking," Dohojar concurred without his usual toothy smile. "Perhaps we should be seeking another one to navigate, Barrel Captain."

"Bloody small chance of that," Barrel said, although he more or less agreed with Dohojar. The man made him uneasy, too, but there was nothing to be done for it. "A month earlier and we'd have had our pick o' pilots for such work," he explained, "and if we could stay in port here for another month until rainy season, we'd have a shot at another school of the blasters looking for a berth. But right now, mate, we've no choice. It's the tall beggar or no pilot at all."

* * *

There was little wind, so the journey to the mouth of the Selintan took a full two days and nights to accomplish. The sea's color changed where the rush of fresh water spilled from the broad mouth of the river. When the sun rose on the third day, the tall pilot called Graves took command of *Silver Seeker*, for the next two hundred fifty miles of the journey would be along the turns and twists of the river. Sweeps more than sails would be required to get the vessel upstream. The crewmen grumbled about this but were ready enough for the work, because they were anxious to drop anchor at Greyhawk and regain their leader, Gord. Their enthusiasm was dampened by the pilot's presence; none of the men liked the stiff navigator. At the same time, this lent a measure of additional effort to their task; these seamen also wanted to finish the long, cramped trek up the Selintan in order to get the pilot off their ship.

If Graves was aware of the dislike he engendered in the ship's master, officers, and crew, he ignored it. The tall, narrow form was seemingly fixed to the poopdeck of *Silver Seeker* as permanently as her mizzenmast. The helmsman at the tiller had to look smart and obey instantly whenever the pilot spoke. Graves was an unrelenting taskmaster and would brook not the slightest infraction, while slowness or sloth was punished by a sharp word and his unwavering stare. Oddly, the sailors feared his gaze, so Graves got his obedience.

Sand bars and snags were thus avoided, for the navigator seemed to know the Selintan as if it had been personally dug by him. Both moons were near full, so after the first night the ship sailed on after sunset instead of anchoring. The seamen manning the sweeps were allowed to sleep in shifts, but the pilot seemed to need only a few hours rest. When Luna set, Graves retired to his tiny cabin for the short time left before dawn. Even as the sky turned red heralding the approaching sun, the gaunt navigator would appear again on deck, ready for another stint.

"He's a weather-witch," one of the mates mumbled to Barrel.

The shipmaster grinned. "If that be the case, he is a fine one indeed, lad! Not a hint of foul weather since we left Safeton, and a south wind's air to gently blow us along against the current of this narrow stream. We should always have such a one as he aboard." Unconvinced, the mate made a sign to ward off ill fortune and stumped away.

"Perhaps the man is right, Barrel Captain," Dohojar said softly, still apprehensive. "Not even you can bear to be near that fellow for long."

The burly captain turned and stared at Graves for a moment as the man stood pillarlike, his eyes fixed on the river ahead. There was a mixture of admiration and near-loathing in the captain's gaze. "He's a fine sailor, Dohojar. Even if he only navigates waters such as these, that one could be a wonder at sea, I'm thinking — only no crew would serve under him!"

"Perhaps," the Changa said softly in reply, "that is why he is a pilot instead of a captain."

"Must be," Barrel growled, and with a shrug he turned and went forward to attend to something there. With Graves piloting the ship, there was little left for Barrel to do, and he felt disinherited. He would be happy enough to have Gord as the captain of the vessel once again. The sooner the better, in fact. But he had been and would remain sailing master, with the work attendant in maintaining *Silver Seeker* resting squarely upon his broad shoulders. For now, whether the man was a good pilot or not, he would be comfortable again only when Graves left his ship.

"Here, you bun-blasting lubber! Just because we've left the clean salt water to sail into this muddy ditch is no reason to be slovenly!" Barrel shouted to one of the crew. The sailor blenched, for he had been caught loafing and knew what was coming. "Coil that rope and then go below for tar. You'll be handling a lot of rope soon, and when I come back I'd better see you doing so smart and lively!" At that the hand hurried below, as Barrel shouted for the bosun to bring to the deck all the cordage in need of tarring.

Three days later, as they came near the city, luck turned against them, Graves' supposed powers notwithstanding. The morning was dull and dark. Layers of clouds obscured the sunrise, and visibility was restricted to a bowshot. "Sweeps only, captain, and put a man in the bow chains with a lead line. I'll have to know the depth of the channel if we're to move at all," the tall man commanded with, as usual, no expression in his voice.

Barrel tried to respond just as emotionlessly, but his scarred visage and his voice both showed a hint of strain, perhaps from the weather conditions, possibly from the attitude of the navigator. "You keep the ship moving," he said, "and don't worry about my role. I'll see the crew is standing by to jump to as needed."

Graves looked over his shoulder at the burly sea-man, and his thin lips shifted into a faint smile. "Yes, of that I'm sure, captain," he called back over the distance between them. His voice was hollow-sound-ing in the still air.

Late in the forenoon the sky grew darker still, the wind rose suddenly, and scattered rain began to pat-ter down. "Haul away on those sweeps!" Graves actu-ally shouted from his station near the tiller. "Greyhawk's just there," the tall man cried, his long, scrawny arm sticking out ahead like a scarecrow's. "Bend your backs, and we'll make a safe anchorage before the worst of this storm comes!"

Barrel likewise shouted the order from where he stood amidships, for the wind and rain were gaining intensity by the second, and he thought the pilot's command might have been lost to the men toward the bow. But the effort was unnecessary; the navi-gator's voice seemed to cut through the weather as a knife, and all the sailors assigned to the long oars were already redoubling their efforts. None wanted to be caught where they were if a heavy storm broke.

Between the sheets of rain Dohojar caught glances of a dark shape ahead and to starboard. He pointed, and Barrel nodded.

"Right he was, Changa," the captain shouted to be heard over the howl of the ever-strengthening rain-storm. "That must be the walls o' the city! Not more 'n a mile to go!"

Lightning flashed to the west. It was evident that they would be lucky to make half the distance needed before they were in the thick of it. "Set the jibsails! And raise the mainsail abaft!" Barrel bellowed. "We either make anchorage or get driven aground soon," he cried to his friend before hurrying aft to see to the raising of the lateen sail there. It was going to be a tricky business.

Dohojar watched as the crew hurried to raise the sails, the oarsmen strained to haul the ship ahead with their long and heavy sweeps, and another pair of sailors struggled with the tiller in obedience to the pilot's commands. "By the gods," the Changa muttered as the vessel seemed to come alive and leap ahead. "I thought storms at sea were the only danger, but this river seems a nasty place to be now!"

The occasion for that observation was the rushing passage of a massive tree being carried downriver by the rising current. Had it struck *Silver Seeker*, the trunk would have stove in her planking. As it was, the tree nearly struck one of the larboard sweeps. The impact would probably have injured or killed one or more of the men working it. Nothing untoward happened, though.

The near-gale made the sails as hard as iron, driving the ship up against the rush of the Selintan's waters like a spawning salmon cleaving the current. They moved a half-mile past the first portion of the walls of the city before Dohojar saw the helmsmen shove the tiller hard and the sails suddenly drop, thundering as they flapped before being caught up. He barely heard the orders being shouted, but there was no doubt about it. They had made the harbor and would soon be in Greyhawk.

"Let go the anchors!" Graves shouted. Barrel sped to see that the pilot was heard and obeyed. In a minute they were secured bow and stern. "No chance to moor at the quay," Graves said in a shout as the captain of the ship came back. "We must remain in Hook Harbor until the storm passes." He nodded then and stalked off to go below. Despite the fierce blasts of wind, the tall man moved with an unbent spine and unbowed head, as if he was immune to the fury of mere natural phenomena.

"When will this filthy weather pass?" Dohojar asked as he watched the tall form of the pilot disappear belowdecks, his gaze momentarily distracted by a brilliant flash of lightning.

Thunder boomed and rolled overhead, forcing Barrel to pause before he could answer. "This ain't like a hurricane, lad," he said with his head bent down to bring his words close to the shorter Changa's ear. "I'll wager she'll blow herself out in less than an hour."

The thunder and lightning did soon move on toward the southeast, and the rain slackened shortly thereafter.

"You are right, friend," Dohojar said, giving Barrel his best grin. "It passes. Let us get our navigator back on deck so we can dock."

"Not so fast, Dohojar," the captain told him. "I don't like the feel of the air."

Barrel peered intently westward and let his gaze sweep on around to the north. He saw blackness and flickering light. "There's another one headin' toward us now, and it looks worse than the last. Go forward and see that the lads there are alert. *Seeker* might drag her anchor, and I don't want to see her busted up after coming all this way!"

The foul weather continued through the afternoon, and around twilight it was obvious that they would have to await the morrow to leave ship. "Slumgrub!" Barrel called to the cook. "Try to give the crew something good to eat for a change, so's they'll be satisfied to stay aboard one more night afore headin' for a brothel." The ship's cook grinned and promised his best. That made Barrel guffaw, for none of the man's dishes ever tasted good. "Issue an extra tot o' brandy too," he cried to Slumgrub, "and that'll help to kill the taste o' your swill!"

* * *

The wind died down before midnight. The heavens were now dark and quiet, with nary a flicker of lightning nor a rumble of thunder. Heavy clouds blanketed the sky, though, and spattering showers fell irregularly and without warning. Standing watch was an uncomfortable job in weather like this. Thrommel, a junior lieutenant, had charge of that duty, with Hornfoot and Blinky currently on guard forward and aft. Every few minutes Thrommel would walk up one rail and check the bow, then head back along the other to see if Blinky, who was at the stern, was alert. Those two would have a four-hour stint, and then they'd be relieved.

"Damn their sleepy eyes," Thrommel muttered softly. "They'll be able to turn in a couple of hours from now, and I'll still be marching around topside in this shitty stuff," he complained, dashing rain from his brow with an irritated sweep of his hand. Just then he heard a sound from Hornfoot's duty station.

The lieutenant considered calling out, then decided to move up quietly to see for himself. River pirates were common enough, and perhaps even this close to a major city some of those scum might think *Silver Seeker* an easy morsel.

Thrommel had his cutlass in hand even as that thought ran through his mind. He'd split many a skull with its heavy blade, and he had no fear of any attackers. One shout from him, and a dozen doughty salts would be on deck and ready to fight. Dohojar too, with his spell-binding, would be there to handle things of that nature. This was no vessel to be boarded by river rats, no indeed.

Creeping carefully in the darkness, Thrommel arrived at a place where he could see Hornfoot's sentry station. The sailor was on his feet, leaning against the foremast, his back to the lieutenant. No one else was around, and there was no sound to indicate any trouble.

Thrommel stepped up beside the seaman, his bare feet making only a whisper of sound in the night. "Everything okay, matey?" he hissed to Hornfoot. When the sailor didn't reply, Thrommel grabbed him by the shoulder and tried to turn him around. He was angry, for the fellow could only be snoozing as he stood.

Hornfoot barely budged, so the lieutenant stepped around and confronted the sailor. Then he saw that Hornfoot was held fast to the mast by a thick-hafted javelin driven through his chest. Both of the man's eyes were gouged out too, and Thrommel's surprise and shock at the sight prevented the lieutenant from shouting an alarm for a couple of seconds as he caught his breath. It was the last breath he would ever take.

Something very dark and huge seemed to emerge from the shadows alongside the lieutenant as if it had been a part of the murkiness. The thing came upright suddenly, towering above him by more than a head. Thrommel didn't have a chance to be shocked by the appearance of this fiend, because the only glimpse he got of it was just the barest of ones, out of the corner of his eye. Before he could do more than turn his head slightly in the direction of the movement, massive arms shot out and horny hands clamped themselves upon the seaman. One covered his face, while the long fingers of the other tightened around Thrommel's throat. The arms moved, the hands twisted, and a dry, snapping sound came from his neck. The man's body jerked and twitched, but that was mere nervous reaction, for it was already dead.

The netherfiend that had killed Thrommel stopped for a moment to enjoy the work it had just done, quickly devoured the man's eyes, and then turned toward the stern of the ship. "Blinky!" it shouted in a voice that was identical to the lieutenant's. "Get forward here and help me with Hornfoot. The stupid fool's managed to drink himself dead drunk!"

The sailor heard that and came forward on the run. There might be some of the liquor left, and he didn't want to miss out. In his haste, he mistook Hornfoot's body for the waiting lieutenant and stumbled over Thrommel's corpse, but the fiend was already lunging and caught him before Blinky could hit the deck. "Hello, my fine little human," the monstrous thing piped in an obscenely high-pitched voice. Then it proceeded to kill him slowly, not caring that Blinky's screams were rousing the rest of the men. The netherfiend had already grown bored of doing in humans one at a time. It had been fun surprising these three, but the killings had only whetted its appetite.

As most of the crewmen rushed onto the deck from below to confront whatever attacker had come, an altogether different scene was unfolding in the stern cabins of *Silver Seeker*. There, Graves stood in the main room, in the quarters that had been Gord's but were temporarily being used by Barrel. The pilot's arrival had roused Barrel from sleep just a few seconds before Blinky's death screams had sounded.

"Give me the sword, dungball, and I might let you live," the towering stick of a man said softly. The navigator was now garbed in robes of sorcerous fashion, instead of the plain garments of a seafarer, and his eyes burned with an inhuman, malign fire.

Without replying, Barrel sprang to his feet, his own sword drawn and ready, for he kept it always beside him on the cot. "Stuff this in your skinny bilge, Graves!" the seaman snarled under his breath, taking a vicious swing at his enemy as he spoke.

The image did not move as he cut through it, and Barrel knew right away that his blade had whistled through empty air. The tall man was not really standing where he seemed to be. He chuckled evilly at the miss. "Know me now by my full name of Gravestone — which also foretells your future, you stupid turd!" the man cackled. "Just drop your silly weapon now and show me where the sword is. Then I'll kill you swiftly and painlessly."

Again Barrel cut at the man, only this time he scythed his cutlass so that it swept in a much wider arc. Barrel was an old campaigner and knew not a little about dweomers and the like. The so-called pilot, who had now revealed himself to be some sort of spell-binder, was certainly protected by a magical displacement, a trick that bent the light and made the eyes see something in a place other than where it was. He shouted as he swung, putting all his might into the blow. Again it sliced only empty air.

At that instant Blinky began screaming from abovedecks; either that noise or Barrel's shout, or perhaps both, roused Dohojar from his slumber in the next cabin. "Devils take you!" Barrel panted as he saw that his second attack was as useless as the first had been.

"More likely *I* to take *them*," the phantom figure said mockingly. "For that last stroke I will see you die more slowly, fool; but yield what I ask, and I might have some mercy when you beg." Actually, Gravestone had no desire for an easy surrender now. His bloodlust was rising, and he relished the coming sport. He bided his time, for he could hear Dohojar rustling about, and he knew that the captain's comrade would soon join him in the aft cabin.

As if on cue Barrel called out, "Dohojar, to me! We are attacked!" The shout went unheard by most of the men on board, for they were already rushing forward to help Blinky. But the Changa heard it well enough and immediately came to his friend's aid on the run.

For Dohojar, one look at the scene before him was sufficient. "Very bad!" he cried aloud, even as he began to conjure the most potent spell he had at his command.

"That's not the half of it, lad!" Barrel answered as he desperately sought some way to bring harm to the insubstantial figure. "The blaster just isn't there!" he added by way of advising his shipmate what they were up against.

Just then Habber, first lieutenant to the sailing master, burst into the cabin with a sword in one hand and an axe in the other. In his rush he bumped into Dohojar and caromed off the Changa's back, nearly knocking both of them down in the process. "Uff! Shit!" he cried, catching himself and trying to stand on guard against whatever attacker was at hand.

The spell he had been trying to work was spoiled in the collision, so Dohojar changed tactics instantaneously, forgetting the loss because there was no help for it. "Quick, Habber-Lieutenant," he said as he pointed toward the far corner of the ill-lighted cabin. "Throw your axe where the shadows are thick there!" The confused sailor complied even though it was an order that seemed to make no sense. Habber cocked his arm and sent the weapon spinning across the short space in one quick motion.

A sharp gasp of pain came from the place, and then a shout of rage. The figure of the false pilot disappeared from the center of the cabin, and the man was suddenly visible crouching in the corner of the place. One of Gravestone's long arms could be seen through a tear in his baggy-sleeved robe, the place where Habber's axe had sliced cloth and cut flesh in its flight. The gaunt face of Gravestone was awful to behold as he stood hunched and shaking with rage in the low-ceilinged space. "I'll play with you no longer!" he screeched.

Barrel tried to get an attack in then, moving toward Gravestone with his cutlass held before him. Again Habber brought trouble by being too precipitous. He rushed the enemy at the same time, a movement that caused him and the burly sailing master to collide briefly. That was all the advantage Gravestone needed. He brought a sound from down deep in his narrow chest and allowed its abomination to clamber up his throat and gush from his mouth. The terrible sound was wrapped in the vilest of evil and had fell power. As the word was spewed forth, the air thickened, and dark streaks of energy leaped and coalesced. Habber toppled soundlessly, stone dead, while both Barrel and Dohojar were thrown back as if struck by a great hand.

"Now, maggots, you are mine!" Gravestone stepped deliberately toward the two stunned men with gleeful

triumph plainly evident on his ancient face. The visage he showed now was his actual one — very old
and totally evil. It was filled with demoniacal emotion,
the joy of anticipating what was to come. Suddenly
his expression changed to surprise.

"Not so easy, old pole of wickedness!" Dohojar exclaimed as he saw the darts of energy he had summoned up strike home, burning the leathery skin of
the evil mage's face where they touched. With greater
fury than before, Gravestone spun and reached for
the Changa, his fingers like talons. Extremities that
looked like tentacles shot from those clawed hands
and wrapped in a deadly embrace around Dohojar's
neck. His agonized writhing was proof enough of their
effect, even without the hissing of his flesh where the
tentacles' acidic secretion ate away the skin and
seared deeper still.

"Godsdamn you!" screamed his friend as he witnessed the horror of whatever magic Gravestone was
employing to slay the Changa. "This will stop you!"
Barrel struck a blow with his cutlass that did not
miss, catching Gravestone full across one of his upper arms. Yet something prevented it from having real
effect. While the tall man seemed to be shaken by the
attack, and he loosed his terrible tentacles from
Dohojar, the weapon's sharp edge had somehow
failed to sever the man's arm from his body as it
should have.

Gravestone moved back quickly, still crouching,
and now shaking his right arm as he glared balefully
at his foes, but he bore no apparent wound from the
cutlass. "You can't be unhurt. . . ." the burly seaman
said in consternation.

"Oh, but I can be," Gravestone said as he locked
his feral eyes full upon those of Barrel. The thick,

ropy growth that had sprung from his fingers had disappeared when the cutlass struck his arm, but now Gravestone's long digits were themselves writhing like adders. "Drop that sword," Gravestone commanded icily.

Barrel's face relaxed, and as that happened, his grip on the heavy cutlass began to loosen. Then, with an ear-splitting war cry, the burly seaman had the weapon firmly again and held straight forth as he lunged to bury its point in the tall man's heart. "I'll drop *you!*"

The move failed to catch Gravestone by surprise, however. Instead, his narrow body seemed to twist aside as would a serpent's, and as Barrel extended himself in completion of the useless thrust, the man's fingers thrust out and into Barrel's body. No longer snaky in the least, Gravestone's digits were now as stiff as steel bars and tipped with razor-sharp nails that had sprouted long, tearing barbs.

The finger-knives sunk home, the hands following, until they clasped what they sought. Then Gravestone reversed his motion and heaved backward. Barrel, his side torn and gushing blood, fell to the gory deck, lifeless. The useless cutlass clattered down beside him, and the tall man laughed a rolling paean of evil triumph.

"That was too quick, too easy," Gravestone said then, turning to where Dohojar lay semi-conscious, one hand feebly trying to wipe away the fiery pain where tentacles and acid had made a ruin of his neck and lower jaw. "Does it hurt?" he asked solicitously as he bent closer to the Changa in order to watch the effects of the pain from a better vantage point. Dohojar tried to say something, but Gravestone reached forth and with a single finger welded the dark lips together, leaving what looked like a frightful red scar where Dohojar's mouth had been.

"No, no, little maggot," Gravestone crooned softly. "I'll have no more puny spells from you to pain me. Instead, we will play a game, you and I. If you hold up well, then you win! And as your reward, I'll finish you myself rather than giving you to Krung. Come now, let's begin!"

* * *

Later, when he came upon the deck, he found the netherfiend, the beast he had called Krung, happily crouched in the center of a pile of corpses, plucking delicacies from first one, then another of the bodies. When the thing saw Gravestone, it clutched one of the corpses and then stood, holding the form as if it were a doll. "I have eaten well, master. Thank you for such sport."

"That's nice, Krung. I too have had amusement and am quite satisfied." As he spoke, the evil man held a long, thin bundle in his left arm, almost as if he were mimicking the fiend with the dead body it held as a prize.

Gravestone gestured, and the netherfiend hurried toward the tall spell-binder. "Shall I make fire to burn the ship?" it asked.

Gravestone shook his head. "No, let's leave a mystery for them, Krung. Dispose of the corpses here however you like. Just don't leave them to be found. I am going now. You may return to your own plane when you've done your work." With that, Gravestone the priest-wizard turned and went to a place where he could lower one of the ship's little boats, then make his way to shore.

It amused him to depart this way. Although he could magically transport himself away if he desired, he had decided to row downstream, dock at the quay, and enter Greyhawk like any other honest traveler. Such mundane acts helped to make life more interesting, he thought to himself. The use of great magicks was best reserved for moments like the ones he had just experienced . . . savored! He would miss performing these occasional acts of drudgery when he became a lord of the lower spheres, but that was the way of things.

Musing thus, Gravestone tossed his parcel into the dinghy, picked up the oars, and began to row away from the now-quiet *Silver Seeker*. The rapid current of the Selintan carried the boat quickly once he brought it out of the shelter of the harbor, and in minutes it was lost from the sight of the eyes that glared after it. The netherfiend was angry at having its feast interrupted and cut short, and now it vented its wrath in Gravestone's direction.

"Big-headed shit!" Krung spat as it began to grab up the bodies sprawled on the deck and heave them into the air. At the apogee of its trajectory, each one suddenly vanished. When the netherfiend had mangled and tossed the last one, it got down on the deck and used its broad and leathery tongue to lap up all traces of blood. The tongue made a rasping sound as it passed over the planks, and when it was finished the thing spat out splinters and cursed again. "One day, you skinny human, one day you too may fall into my clutches. . . ."

Krung snarled and looked around. The area was clean. There might be other bodies below, but that was not its concern. Gravestone had specified that the bodies "here" be disposed of, so the fiend was satisfied that it had fulfilled the letter of the command. It was not about to clean up after any mess that Gravestone might have made below.

"I have done enough," the thing growled. "Let the human worry about the rest, if he cares so much about his mystery."

Making a shrill humming noise through its broad, flat nose, the netherfiend started to perform the ritual that would return it to its home in the pits. When the first pale rays of the dawn's light began to wash the eastern horizon a few minutes later, Krung was no longer to be seen.

Chapter 5

IT IS PRACTICALLY IMPOSSIBLE to discover just where the mansion begins or ends. Positioned as it is among little swales, surrounded by trees and flowering shrubs, no eye can follow its lines. The place is large, and probably covered with some magic as well. For all the time Gord had spent in and around Rexfelis's own palace, the young adventurer was now quite unsure as to exactly where he and the Catlord's steward were going.

"I feel rather silly, Lord Lowen, marching around out here in all this finery," Gord finally said, gesturing as he spoke to indicate his velvet garments and the glittering jewels that adorned the costume.

"Tush! Our king has directed this promenade to occur," the steward said without irritation. "Therefore, Prince Gord, this is what you and I shall do."

Gord simply didn't understand. At a time like this, when the fate of the entire multiverse was at stake, such a waste of time seemed bizarre if not lunatic. "We have been at this ambling for over an hour now, lord steward. Perhaps it pleases everyone — although from the strange glances we've gotten I think otherwise — but I for one am no longer amused. There is that of import at hand which cannot—"

"We will do as commanded," the old fellow said firmly, taking Gord firmly by his arm and quickening their pace. "Besides, we are almost finished now. See those tall yews ahead? That is where we began this walk."

At the moment, Gord was quite unable to distinguish ash from elm, let alone recognize a particular clump of yew trees. Agitated or not, the young man maintained sufficient poise to recognize the merit of complying with Lowen's guidance. It was better to spend a few more minutes completing the business, whatever it was, than to fly off impatiently. "Very well," Gord allowed in a grudging tone, "we shall go on to those trees, but not one step thereafter. I must hurry inside and prepare myself."

At that the old steward smiled and patted his charge on the shoulder. "By all means, prince, by all means. We shall go immediately inside once past these yews, through that broad portal over there. And you shall indeed prepare yourself."

"That means shedding this finery and readying for more deadly work."

"No, what you said and what I meant are quite different," Lord Lowen said with a tinge of amusement in his deep voice. Gord was confused but elected not to press the matter. They walked in silence for a couple of minutes, and then the steward added, "Now we come to the place of entry, prince. Are you ready to enter?"

"Yes. . . ." Gord let that trail off, for Lowen had sounded most formal and had spoken those last words loudly. Even as he had said "yes," Gord's eyes had fallen upon two lines of guards, stiffly arrayed so as to form a double line leading into the mansion that was the Catlord's palace. "But I think we must find another door, steward," the young adventurer said under his breath. "Some ceremony is in progress here, and it would not be meet to interrupt."

"Have no concern, prince," Lord Lowen said as softly in reply. "We will not be intruding — quite the contrary." As the two strode on, the nine armored warriors on either hand saluted. Lowen's grip would not allow anything but for Gord to proceed on into the hall before them.

Great thumps suddenly sounded. "Prince Gord Carl Quapardus now enters this hall! Who will display flattened ears?" The bellowing came from Raaph, major domo of the palace.

Lowen had tugged him to a halt, so Gord had a moment to scan the scene. During the time they had been out walking, a transformation had been effected in the place. A semicircular dais had been erected in the leftmost portion of the big room. It supported nine groups of tall chairs. Each group had two on the higher level of the stand and four below on the lower tier. All six seats of each group were occupied by grandly arrayed men and gorgeously dressed women. To either side of the uppermost chairs stood pages, while below the lower four seats of each group stood a fully armored knight.

Gord's gaze settled upon each of the uppermost figures in turn. They were the noble heads of the Nine Houses, with their chief henchmen occupying the lower chairs. Here was the Scion of Smilodons in cloth of gold, bedecked with a necklace of nine huge golden beryls. Closest to his vantage point was House Lynx, its prince adorned in gray spidersilk vestments, a glitter of diamonds serving as his badge of nobility.

To Gord's right hand was another large dais. Thereupon he noticed the emblems and ensigns of those creatures who were associated with catkind — sea lions, true sphinxes, dragonnes, tiger sharks. Those beneath these blazons appeared to be men and women, but the young adventurer knew that such appearance was but one of the forms possible for them. The chief one of the leopard seals nodded almost imperceptibly as Gord's eyes briefly met hers. Then another voice brought his eyes elsewhere.

"None questions the coming." Rexfelis said those words in a normal tone, but they seemed to fill the whole of the huge hall.

"There is no challenge!" agreed the major domo.

The Lord of Cats arose from the throne he had been stiffly sitting upon. As he did so, the other creatures in the chamber followed suit, rising to their feet as their sovereign had done. Then the realization struck Gord: Rexfelis had stood to greet . . . him!

"Go forward to our lord, prince," Lowen hissed. "I will follow just behind." Gord began to walk slowly ahead. He felt very uncomfortable, as though the hundreds of eyes in the chamber were burning holes in him. Yet proceed he did, and none hindered the forty-nine paces he took as he advanced to stand before the Catlord.

"You have walked around the Place of All Cats?"

Gord looked at Rexfelis, consciously noting for the first time that he wore a gold diadem set with a variety of gems. Never before had the young man seen him wear a crown of any sort. Without delay and with no need of prompting, Gord answered truthfully and simply. "I have, lord."

"I then announce to all the Peers of this Realm that I have considered and found you most worthy of all. I name you Heir to the Domain of Catkind. Kneel, Prince Quapardus."

Gord did as he was told. Then Rexfelis took the diadem from his own head and placed it upon Gord's brow. "Arise, Crown Prince Gord, and sit beside me."

After the Lord of Cats said those words, another great thumping arose. "All hail Crown Prince Gord!" commanded the stentorian voice of the major domo. The assembled folk complied immediately and gave nine great shouts. In such a din, who could say if the cheers were full of happiness and respect, or discontent and envy? It made no difference, for the deed was accomplished.

"I am at a loss, Lord Rexfelis," Gord said quietly as the Master Cat took him to a newly brought second throne. They both sat, and the others in attendance took their seats again too. "It is an honor and station I don't think I deserve — in fact, am most uncomfortable with. Besides, at a time such as this, what use is this position and the ceremony associated with it?"

"Blunt, too blunt," Rexfelis muttered back. "Think you that being a monarch is an insignificant task? In time you will get used to it . . . if we have such time granted. As to that, and your last comment, prince, the one who champions Balance must be of both proper station and have the support of all. You being of catkind, it is required that all the nobles of the dominion recognize you as such. . . . Enough of this now! We are being rude to our peers. Speak to them!"

Apparently he had no choice. Lately Gord had found that circumstance to be more and more frequent. Wondering if he was simply growing more perceptive of what had always existed, or if fate was intervening, Gord stood to do as Rexfelis had commanded. Naturally, all the assemblage then rose once again, even the Catlord. Disconcerted yet more, the young man managed to utter a few words, gracefully accept the accolades then given him by the princes of the other eight of the Nine Houses, those from the allied ones, and so forth. After an interminable time, Rexfelis gestured for all others to be seated and spoke a lengthy speech that ended in an invitation to the royal feast.

More thoughts were racing through his mind than he could cope with, more emotions were bathing his psyche than Gord had ever experienced. The sudden rush of information, of knowledge, and of purpose was too much. Where should he be? What should be done? How to accomplish what had to be done? Cold fear was deep within him: What if this all was an enormous lie? A dream? Or, worst of all, what if everything was true — but he proved unequal to the task? Also, he had to wonder why all this ritual and pomp was necessary now. There was so much more to learn, so many more important things to be done: What use was this revel?

The rest of the day was a blur for him. Lady Tirrip was there, but she was distant and formal instead of the warm, loving woman-cat she had once been with him. Equally stiff and reserved were all the others of catkind he had known before, whether as friend and companion or as rival. They were respectful, but distant and . . . afraid?

It occurred to Gord then that he was no longer like any of them at all, even Rexfelis. The infusion of power by the Lords of Balance, the words of that which called itself All and Nothing, his own commitment — all had combined to make him singular. There was no way he could relate to any of the others here. He was indeed a champion, and that set him apart. There was nothing to be done about it. Those who had identified, if not selected, him as the one to contest against the Ultimate Evil had set in motion a series of events that neither they nor he could reverse. The facts of his parentage and infancy, Gord's past life, the honors of the day: Each and every aspect of what had gone before and was now transpiring had no meaning to him except as they bore upon the thing to come.

At the stroke of midnight, Gord turned to the Catlord. "Your will in this matter has been accomplished, Lord Rexfelis. I thank you. I sense a new energy emanating from those folk here and flowing to me. For that too am I thankful. But I can bear this charade no longer. Now it is time for me to leave and seek the path which will bring me to the foe I am meant to confront. May I have your leave?"

"I . . ." Rexfelis looked with his own strange eyes into the deep, gray pools of his heir. There was such pain and purposeful resolve there that the Lord of Cats was unable to say more for a moment. Then he looked away. In his heart he felt deep sorrow for this one, one of his own, to whom had passed such a terrible burden. Rexfelis was sad that he himself had labored long and with exacting care to bestow that weight. That Rexfelis had not apportioned the fate, only recognized it, made little difference in the Catlord's feelings. "I grant it, of course, prince. You and I must meet again before you begin, though, for there is news of importance just arrived today."

"Why haven't you told me before now?"

"The naming of you as my heir had to be accomplished, and done in the manner I myself set forth centuries ago."

Of course, the young man thought. Rexfelis had been master of all felines since there had been such a deity. Idly, Gord wondered why the Catlord would now find it desirable to abdicate. It was but a fleeting thought, one of little consequence under the circumstances. If Tharizdun triumphed, then there would be no Catlord, no heir. If Gord prevailed, it seemed quite likely to him that he would become something other than the new Lord of Cats. Odd. . . . "Very well. Let us go someplace where there is privacy."

By this time the celebration had become quite festive. It was not difficult for both of them to leave the hall unnoticed. Sovereign and crown prince notwithstanding, the noble folk of this realm meant to enjoy the proclaimed celebration to the full. Considering the heritage of all concerned, independence and general lack of interest in something so relatively insignificant as those two when compared to the food, drink, and company was indeed natural.

Shadowy galleries at either end of the hall provided space for many nonfeline attendees. Among them, incognito, were Basiliv and a host of others concerned with the coming duel. Several of these personages joined them as Gord and Rexfelis headed along the corridor leading from the great room to one of the Catlord's quiet chambers.

"Have you news for us, Demiurge?"

Basiliv nodded, but somberly. "My agents discovered that *Silver Seeker* put into port at Telmstrand and then sailed for the Wild Coast. As that place is beyond my sphere, so to speak, I passed the information along to the Lesser Hierophants."

"That is where I was called in." The voice was familiar, and Gord turned quickly to see if his ears were deceiving him. "Congratulations, *Prince* Gord," Gellor said with a slight bow and a big smile quickly hidden by the inclination of his head.

"You one-eyed devil!" Gord cried. Then he stepped

over and hugged the sinewy body of the grizzled troubador, forgetting decorum entirely. "Where have you
been? Are you well?"

"Time for that later, please," Rexfelis said curtly.
"You urged this matter on, Gord. You must now accept the consequences."

"Urged? I *am* the matter, as far as everyone is concerned. If I opt to tarry with an old comrade, then all
of you will have to wait until I've decided otherwise!"

Gellor shook his head slightly. "You are right, my
friend, but so is your grandsire. There will be time for
personal talk later — and with other old friends besides myself — but now we should stick to the affair
of the *Silver Seeker* and your sword." He looked at the
young face, noting that the gray eyes had darkened
somehow and aged. They were older now, as old as
the world, and there was no youthfulness or thoughtless joy there, none of the recklessness that had
made him a gallant thief and carefree adventurer.
Gord returned the study, then nodded for Gellor to
continue.

"The druids of the Suss, and certain priests too,
were sent word. They in turn passed information
along to other agents of ours. We knew within hours
of her dropping anchor that *Silver Seeker* and your
shipmates were in Safeton." Gellor paused a moment
to shrug helplessly. "Information is one thing, decision is another. By the time word had reached us and
we could hold council to decide how best to approach
the captain — Barrel, I believe, was his name— "

"What do you mean, *was*?!" Gord's face was set in
hard lines as he shot that interruption at Gellor.

"Oh . . . I am getting ahead of myself, and most
stupidly so," the troubador said with a sigh. He
reached across the little distance between himself

and his friend and clasped Gord's forearm. "Your comrades came to grief, my friend. Now, please allow me to tell this in chronological fashion. I'll come all too soon to the part you want to hear. . . . What indeed you *must* hear."

"Go on, then." His voice was toneless, but Gord managed a small smile to show Gellor that he understood the difficulty of his comrade's position.

Gellor released his hold on Gord's arm and continued without haste, for precise detail was needed. "We were in council, and therein it was decided to have several of us go to the town and speak with the captain of the vessel and your associate Dohojar, the Changa."

Before Gellor could say more, Gord allowed himself to interrupt again. There was something he had to know, and it was an essential part of the whole. "How were you aware of Dohojar? Barrel? Even the ship?"

"All of our energies are not spent on watching the foe, Gord," Basiliv said. "You have been informed of our constant vigilance in the distant past, from the time you were but a babe. Can you doubt that we do not continue to observe at all times? After all—"

"I have protection against such intrusion," Gord said flatly.

"Of course, we cannot watch you directly, but events around you are sufficient indicators of your whereabouts and actions. Then a spy here, an informant there, and agents sent to a locale discover all the details. We have known who to watch exactly. Fortunately, the evil ones have only been able to suspect. What is known to Balance is barely guessed at by those of the netherrealms."

"Where was I?" Gellor said with a hint of irritation.

"Sending a delegation to see Barrel and Dohojar in Safeton," Gord supplied.

"Thank you. That is what was decided by the Lesser Hierophants. It took a while to round us all up — Chert, Greenleaf, and me. By the time we arrived in Safeton, the *Silver Seeker* had raised anchor and sailed away five days earlier. Fortunately, we quickly discovered that she had left with a man calling himself Graves, who claimed to be a river pilot able to navigate up the Selintan." The troubador raised a finger to make sure that Gord didn't interrupt him further. "Unfortunately, we also found out that the so-called pilot had paid a third party to get aboard the ship as its navigator; it seems the man wanted this particular job very much.

"It was easy to guess that your mates were making for Greyhawk, Gord. Obviously, they were heading north up the river for that destination. Presumably you had arranged to meet them in the city if you became separated, or you had arranged to join up there at some given time. No matter. . . . We immediately sought out the chief one of Balance in Safeton, and she arranged for us to arrive in Greyhawk's vicinity within hours. The three of us were already inside the city's high walls when tragedy happened aboard your ship."

"Barrel is dead, then," Gord said heavily. It was a statement, not a question.

"Dead and worse. So too your Changa comrade, Dohojar. Both of them were slain ruthlessly by the pilot, the man calling himself Graves."

"How can you know for certain? If neither could be raised and both are still dead, then—"

"The murderer was careless. No, I should say that he was careless with one of his agents. There was a

115

series of violent thunderstorms on the day that *Silver Seeker* came upriver to Greyhawk. The weather was so foul as to preclude docking at a quay or jetty. The ship was taken on up into Hook Harbor, and when the sun rose in a clear sky next morning was seen riding peacefully at anchor there.

"One of our men told us that the customs officials of the city were going out to investigate her, so we immediately hired a wherryman to scull us out to the ship. We brought along someone of sufficient authority in the government to be sure there would be no problems for your shipmates. However, when we got alongside the vessel, there was no sign of life. The deck was empty and nobody answered our hail. We knew the customs cutter would be there soon, so all of us clambered aboard and sought someone to tell what was going on."

"There was no sign of foul play?" Gord asked.

"Not on deck," Gellor replied. "It was as clean as if just holystoned. Forward belowdecks it was the same — everything left as if the crewmen had stowed their gear and were standing by for inspection. But the aft cabins were a different tale, let me assure you. Violence and magic and pain. Each was etched there, and the remains of both of your comrades were left as they had fallen . . . or been slowly killed."

"Say on, and spare me no detail," the young champion said sternly. "Of this business I will know all."

Following came an exacting description of what Gellor and the others had observed and deduced. "Our personage from government was a cleric, one of both high standing and accomplishment. That priest used his powers to attempt a bringing back of both dead men. It was to no avail. Barrel and Dohojar had been sent past the veil from where they could be recalled. So too it was with normal questioning of that vibratory force that lingers after the spirit has gone.

"The venerable priest was not one to yield to evil so easily, though. He worked long and painstakingly to divine what had occurred, to gain a clue about what had transpired aboard *Silver Seeker*. He gained enough for us to follow a thread. As there was nothing else to do, no trace of your sword or other things you had left aboard, Gord, we removed both bodies quietly and buried them with proper rites there in the harbor's deep waters.

"Then, yesterday, we met with two other great spell-binders come to assist the priest in the tracing of the single thread he had gained. Mordenkainen, despite the pressures of the cambion's hordes attacking his lands, arrived by the use of certain objects and words given to him by the Demiurge. Tenser was present thanks to assistance directly from the Archimage himself.

"Carefully, so as not to arouse attention from watchers of the evil ones, the work was done. The clue was sufficient to reveal that a netherfiend was involved in the slaughter, and only a few of such monsters can be so employed. By careful selection and questioning of those beings who attend to the matter of transference through the portals that wend their way from the foul pits to the material worlds, it was discovered which fiend was involved."

"That one's name?" Gord demanded harshly.

"Krung. One of the most disgusting and potent of the thirty-three able to move out of the nether pits."

"Let us go to where you have it prisoned and force all from its vile throat!" Gord sprang to his feet and started for the door.

"Easy, my friend, easy there," Rexfelis said sooth-

GORD THE ROGUE

ingly. "Please return to your place a moment, for the
troubador has more to tell you, I am certain."

"That is true, Lord of Cats," Gellor said. "Do listen,
please, Gord. We dared not force the netherfiend into
returning to this plane for fear of alerting its master
and all the lords of evil. Instead, we attempted to
discover which sorcerous servant of the pits commanded service from Krung."

"With what result?"

At that the one-eyed troubador smiled a wolfish
smile. "A most enlightening result, my dear comrade,
a most enlightening one indeed! There are some of
the elements which defy Neutrality and serve Evil.
There was the matter of the long series of violent
storms which came too conveniently for coincidence.
Although we dared not delve into the lower realms in
our quest for truth, those of elemental air were more
than open to us. Greenleaf alone was able to trace
down and summon the one which had served to call
forth the storms which enabled the murderous work
to be done in secret. We forced the truth from the
thing, a creature called Vashmilkusom. Then we imprisoned it safely to await a time when it will be
convenient for us to return it to its own place and
execute it."

Gord allowed himself a moment to feel satisfaction, then inquired, "The elemental revealed who had
summoned it to bring the storms?"

"Oh yes, eagerly too . . . after a time. The sum-
moner, the one who commands the service of the
netherfiend Krung, is one you might actually have
heard of. He is from Greyhawk and uses many different appellations. It took us only a few hours to discover that, but we do not have his true name."

"Enough beating around the bush, Gellor," Gord

118

said in the hard, impatient tone he had used so frequently of late. "What aliases does the scum use?"

"Undron Nalvistor is the one you may have heard, Gord. That is the name that the Assassins Guild of Greyhawk knows him by. Beanpole is the appellation that the urchins of the Low Quarter use, while his older neighbors there refer to him as Norund, a dotty gemner. Certain of the city's oligarchs utilize his talents, thinking the man to be named Rundon Tallman, a mystic and seer of no small power."

After pondering a minute, Gord shook his head slowly. "Odd. I have not heard those names at all. This one is a spider!"

"Spider and adder as well," Gellor concurred with a look of disgust and loathing on his lined countenance. "Yet not so clever as he thinks himself to be — not by half! He used the air elemental to travel swiftly and safely from Greyhawk to Hardby. Then he masqueraded as a cleric, calling himself Brother Donnur, and insinuated himself onto a vessel bound for Safeton. How he knew that *Silver Seeker* was making for that same port speaks volumes in testimony of his connections with the nether realms.

"When he arrived in Safeton slightly in advance of *Seeker*, which was coming from the opposite direction, he assumed the guise of Graves, a navigator and river pilot. He fabricated a suitable tale, applied bribery freely, and got aboard *Seeker* as the one who would guide it safely up the Selintan to Greyhawk. That he did, but in the end only so that he could torture and murder the ship's captain and crew outside the city's high ramparts.

"His vile servants know his name as Gravestone. So too his masters use that name, in all likelihood. He is a rarity — perhaps a nonesuch, considering just who this Gravestone must bow down to. The creature is a demonurgist of great power. We have not discovered which of the abyssal spheres are in his thrall, but we will, we will. Powerful and clever — invisible until now — but no supra-genius. Gravestone left a clear trail from his meddling with elementals and others of that ilk. He can no longer hide from us, Gord!"

"And he has the sword?"

"Aye. Donnur the mendicant cleric entered Greyhawk the very morning of the frightful killings aboard *Silver Seeker*. By close querying we discovered that the supposed priest carried with him a sword-sized parcel. Man, weapon, and whereabouts — we have them all!"

Basiliv and Rexfelis exchanged glances. "That is fine work, Gellor," the Demiurge said then. "No wonder so many of our associates in the alliance speak so highly of your talents. One small matter, though. It seems that this . . . Gravestone knows far too much. How, for instance, did he know that the sword was there aboard that ship? What intelligence does this demon-binder have?"

"More than mere demons, even lords of their vile kind," the troubador said with conviction. "Tenser posed the same question. How can it come to pass that this one knew to find the right vessel at the right time and take from it the sword?"

Gord stood and raised his right hand, slowly turning it into a fist. "Because there is a traitor amongst us," he spat through clenched teeth.

"Just so," the Demiurge agreed. "Not one highly placed, however. It would be worse otherwise. Someone who professes to serve Balance is actually a carefully masked double agent. It can only be one of those

placed so as to pass information, a relay." Basiliv
turned to the Catlord. "When Gord told us that he
had left the sword on board the ship, who was it that
took the information out to pass along to the rest of
the network?"

"Prince Lurajal and Prince Raug," Rexfelis replied
slowly, obviously weighing each in his mind as he
spoke, trying to fathom which of the two might be
leagued with Evil.

"Let us summon them to us, then." Gord said the
words before the Demiurge could. "One or the other,
we will have the truth quickly enough!"

"Have a care, Lord of Cats," Basiliv said instantly.
"Either of them could undo us now. Both have at
worst an inkling — at best, certain knowledge — that
Gord is the foreordained champion. Whichever one of
those two is the spy and traitor, he must be itching to
convey that information to the masters of evil. Do not
alert either Raug or Lurajal of the true reason for
their summoning. The guilty one will certainly have
some means of escaping, some portal to carry him
away instantly to the nether realms!"

"They shall both believe that they are to accompany their cousin, Gord, on his imminent visit to the
material world," Rexfelis said with a tigerish snarl.
"Have no fear. Both will come quickly enough upon
hearing that . . . only one of them will hasten to us
for the wrong reason!"

It was open and shut as far as Gord was concerned. In his mind the young champion dismissed
Lurajal from consideration. There could be no real
suspicion about that one. Not only had he become
Gord's fast friend, but he was too open, too uncom-
plicated a person to manage such duplicity as what
had occurred. In short, Lurajal was just not bright or

clever enough to manage such black treachery. Raug, on the other hand . . . .

Rexfelis called one of his servitors into the room. After giving a carefully worded set of instructions, the Catlord told them all to compose themselves and to wait. It was only a few minutes before both of the suspects came eagerly into their presence.

Raug bowed stiffly, showing not a little cold jealousy on his face when it came to paying his respects to the new crown prince, Gord. On the other hand, when Lurajal entered he did not bother with protocol and went straight to the young man and hugged him. "Gord!" Lurajal purred. "High time they recognized you as prince and heir!"

"Does that suffice?" Gord said aloud, looking from Rexfelis to Basiliv and then finally glaring at Gellor and Raug.

The latter scowled. "I have no idea what you mean . . . prince," Raug said.

Lurajal didn't bother to inquire at all. "When do we seek out the enemy?" he asked Gord.

"Enough, all of you," the Lord of Cats said, looking meaningfully at the young champion. His glance told Gord to shut his mouth and keep it that way. "Now then — you, Raug, and you, Lurajal, of House Panonca. Do you both stand ready and willing to serve me in a matter of life and death?"

"Yes, Lord of Us All," the two replied in chorus.

"Good. It is all settled, then. Gord will need two such stalwarts as you in what lies ahead. Before you equip yourselves for the mission, however, there is one thing further I require of you. Go to the crown prince and pledge your fealty and life to him!"

There was no hesitation from Lurajal, but Raug rumbled ominously, deep in his chest, a scowl plainly written on his face, and made no move to comply with Rexfelis's command. "I am your right arm!" Lurajal exclaimed, dropping to one knee before Gord as he spoke and holding both hands before him.

"And you?" Rexfelis asked ominously, staring at Raug.

The big fellow tried to remove the look of enmity from his face. "I . . . I . . . have some difficulty, lord, accepting him . . . the Prince of Panthers . . . as my liege," Raug finally blurted in a growl.

"Here to me, then, and let it be as it may. You shall not go," said the Master of Cats.

Raug stared at him only a moment, then shrugged and stepped to stand beside Rexfelis. "I will be obedient, lord . . . but Gord and I have been at odds often, and it will take time. I wish to serve you in this cause, but another in my stead is better, I suppose."

Rexfelis smiled in an agreeable, knowing way when Raug said that. "Yes, it is only honest to admit your weakness thus," he replied. Turning to the others, the Catlord then spoke sharply. "Have a care when you take Lurajal! He will resist to the death!"

Basiliv had anticipated the matter fully. His hand shot forth and touched the dark young scion of jaguars on the forehead, and Lurajal dropped as if he had been poleaxed.

"There, my friends," said Rexfelis sadly. "The Demiurge has taken care of the traitor in our midst."

Lurajal wasn't dead — only unconscious, Basiliv explained. He would be questioned immediately when he awakened in an hour or so. Raug was completely taken aback and bewildered, but the Catlord took him aside and patiently went over the whole affair for his benefit. While this was occurring, Gord looked from Gellor to the Demiurge. "I would have wagered my life against Raug and on him," he said, pointing to the prone Lurajal.

"And lost, too," the one-eyed troubador observed. "Then again, I would probably have made the same misjudgment as you . . . until it came time to pledge an oath of fealty."

Basiliv nodded. "That was the undoing of Lurajal. He was too ready, and Raug too honest. Lucky for us that both did not agree readily, for then we would have had to use some potent spells to discern the truth — and that might have allowed Lurajal an opportunity to make good an escape. But no trick or enchanted object will save that one now," the Demiurge noted. "Even now there are spell-workers and priests hastening here with armed warriors. Soon Lurajal will be stripped, chained, and put to the question in a place where none of his magic will work. Soon we will know his master's name and perhaps more; the evil ones he serves will not guess the fate of their agent until it is too late, I think. For once, we are ahead in this deadly game!"

Chapter 6

REVELRY AND LAUGHTER filled the Blue Lantern Tavern's long, narrow confines — not overly loud and boisterous, but enough so that the musicians hesitated to resume their playing.

The four veteran players didn't mind. Why should they? All the more time for them to drink and laugh themselves. Soon enough the crowd in this place would begin to demand more of their art — and that of the girl who danced to their melodies.

For now, though, the musicians would allow the crowd's amusement to run its course while they enjoyed the relative calm of the eddy. In fact, several others near their back table seemed to be doing much the same, deep in drink and close conversation during the break before sensuous music and writhing dancer would again drive the patrons of the Blue Lantern into a frenzy of noise over which no voice in conversation could prevail.

"Typical crowd," the drummer offered rather idly.

"Not so! This is the third round of potables those kind gentlemen at the nearby table have furnished us in appreciation for my playing." This came from the viellist, who was remarkably haughty for one of his occupation.

The fat musician who played the sackbut eyed the patrons to whom the viellist had referred. Garbed in nondescript clothing, these four were as unlikely a group as any he had ever known to send musicians drinks in appreciation of their musical talents. The fellow was quite intelligent enough, and a realist as well, so he accepted the harsh fact that if they were virtuosos they would be performing for nobles, not seedy denizens of a Foreign Quarter tavern. "The dancers are graceless or lumpy or both," the sackbut player supplied in answer to the viellist's boast. "They feed us drink to *keep* us from playing."

At that the virginal player laughed, nearly choking on his ale and splattering the viellist with a shower of the brown liquid in the process. Sniffing disdainfully, the latter man arose, brushed at the droplets and announced, "It is past time for us to play again. Let us by all means put our respective theories to the test. I say it is my artistic renditions of these common folk melodies which generate such enthusiasm!"

Still sniggering, the virginal player followed him, so the other two decided to get on with it as well. Just as they were mounting the low platform whereon they performed, the sackbutist happened to glance toward the door. A pair of hooded men there were motioning toward the table where the four who had bought the musicians their drinks were seated. A bald half-elf positioned so as to be able to watch the entrance noticed the two strange figures, said something to his friends, and all four arose and left the tavern in the wake of the hooded pair.

The viellist refused to speak to anyone the rest of the night.

Outside the Blue Lantern Tavern the four plainly dressed men joined the pair of heavily cloaked way-

farers who had gestured to them. All six walked rapidly along Hardcobbles Way, entered Lost Lane, and
disappeared into the deep darkness there. A drunken
fellow weaving along across the street from them
burst out in a ribald song, took a few more steps,
then fell into the gutter in a drunken stupor. The
sound of his singing disturbed a cat or rat elsewhere,
for there was a clatter just after the last off-key notes
died away. Then the street was quiet.

"We are being followed."

"Very perceptive, Chert," Gellor whispered dryly.
"There seems to be some sort of relay setup, I believe,
designed so that we wouldn't notice that which you
immediately spotted," the one-eyed bard added softly.
The big hillman's sixth sense was keen, and Gellor
did not want to discourage Chert from using it to the
fullest.

"There are at least two men on the rooftops
above," Gord hissed. "Watch that we aren't caught
unawares if they try to rain death upon us in this
narrow place."

Curley Greenleaf, uncomfortable in this urban wilderness, started to walk faster. Gellor unobtrusively
caught hold of the druid-ranger's cape and tugged on
it to slow his pace. "Let's not alert the enemy and let
them know we're aware of them," he said in his soft
whisper. The sound didn't carry more than a few feet.
Then, loudly enough for any nearby to hear, he
asked, "How far is this place you're taking us to?"

One of the hooded figures turned and replied
casually, "Just a little way ahead. We'll arrive soon
enough, I assure you."

Lost Lane had several narrower alleyways leading
from it, but it terminated in a close called Heart's
Desire. Not only did the street there make a vaguely

127

heart-shaped bow among the buildings of the close, but the establishments there were of the sort sought out by those abroad at night. There were dens where exotic substances could be consumed, houses of pleasure, and gambling establishments of unusual sort. There were many such places in the Foreign Quarter, but no others quite so varied or expensive as these. In fact, outside of certain places in the Garden and High Quarters, the whole of Greyhawk offered no establishments of higher quality than were to be found in Heart's Desire. It was therefore quite plausible that the half-dozen men would be where they were.

"Thieves, or . . . ?" Gord muttered, allowing the question he had whispered to the troubador to trail off meaningfully.

"Killers, I think — meaning to make their work look like that of street bandits if need be," the one-eyed man replied. "Being where we are, they'll hold off, awaiting our exit from whichever of these houses of iniquity we should choose."

Being very much familiar with the operations of both assassins and thieves, and knowing such places as Heart's Desire as well, Gord shook his head, even though the negatory gesture could not be seen in the all-but-lightless lane. "No, Gellor. They'll certainly strike when we're inside and diverted from wariness by the pleasures of the place we're in. Tell the others — I am certain of it."

One of the hooded men pointed to a flight of stone stairs leading to a cellar door. Narrow windows of deep amber glass, dirty and coated with grime, allowed a faint glow from within to illuminate the steps slightly. "Mind now. We're going down here to Hegmon's Underground . . . a place you're sure to like!" the man said. With laughter and rude jesting of the sort that a group out for such sport would make, the six clumped down the stairway and entered through the old door at the bottom.

It was a little brighter inside, but not much. They found themselves in a longish, narrow foyer that ran the whole length of the building's front. There were three curtained doorways on the far wall, and through the center one came a huge man, his muscles running to fat from dissipation and age, but not one to provoke nonetheless.

"Welcome, strangers! I am Hegmon, and my establishment is yours. Name your pleasure and pay the coin. No customer is ever allowed to leave unsatisfied!" The beefy fellow was not speaking idly. He was assessing the six, mentally weighing their status and purses as well, as he allowed a bland smile to lift his face slightly. However, the expression softened his eyes not a jot.

"A quiet room in the rear, first," the taller of the two hooded men murmured in reply to the invitation. "We will indulge in Flowers of Thratus Kaloid to heighten our senses — agreed?"

Nods and words of assent came from the other five, so the massive proprietor stepped to his right, waving the group to follow. "This way then, if you please, worthy gentlefolk," he said, and proceeded to take them to a smallish room toward the back of the basement. As he opened its door, Hegmon held out his hand. "The salon is yours at a mere copper the hour, and the essences you require are one silver noble each. That comes to one hundred twenty-five bronze zees."

"My pleasure," Gord said with a wink to the beefy fellow as he counted out six nobles and a common

129

into the man's fat hand. "Here's another noble for you, sir," he added as a seventh silver coin appeared in Hegmon's palm, "to see that the heady vapors arrive soon and no one disturbs us until after they are done!"

"Of course. It is always thus in Hegmon's Underground," the fellow said with his insincere smile. "I will order that none disturb you until you ring the bell there," and the beefy proprietor closed the door as he gestured to the pull cord adjacent to it. In a few minutes an ugly old Flan opened the door and wheeled in a little cart with six earthenware flasks of odd design upon it. Saying nothing, she placed the containers before them, so that each of the six was supplied with the sense-altering drug. Without looking up or speaking, the woman then departed, shutting the door firmly behind her.

Gord, Gellor, Chert, and Greenleaf were ranged around one side of the round table in the room, while the two cloaked men were opposite the four. Both of them now threw their hoods back just a little. Anyone viewing the room through a spy hole would still not be able to distinguish them, but the four others could see their eyes and lips. One was the wizard Allton, from the Circle of Eight. The second man was a high priest named Timmil, who was associated with Tenser the Archmage. The latter gave a small wink as he drew forth a bottle from his heavy cloak. "Let us have a sip of this old Adri, a redoubtable brandy, before we sample those Flowers of Kaloid, eh?"

With laughter and much ado, the bottle was passed from hand to hand, each of them seeming to swill heartily from its contents and sigh or cough appropriately after swallowing. Gord's turn came, and he went through the act. It was bad-tasting stuff, thick and bitter. He knew it was an antidote to the narcotic effects of the vapors they would soon have to inhale. "Whoosh! Powerful stuff, comrade," he said, passing the flask along to Allton, who in turn gave it back to Timmil after taking his drink from it. "Now for the really invigorating stuff," Gord said to the company. "Come, let's enjoy!"

All six moved as close to the table as their chairs would permit, drew their container of vapors near, and hunched over so as to be able to unstopper, inhale, and restopper without losing the fumes that shot from the ceramic pot as it was warmed by each person's grasp around its smaller, bottom bulge. While seeming to be lost in enjoyment of the stuff, the six were actually busy exchanging conversation by sign. It flashed around the table like this:

"Are we watched?"

"Every move . . . typical of this kind of dive."

"What can be overheard?"

"Every word spoken."

"What should we do then?"

"Eliminate the one spying on us!" That sign came from Gellor.

Gord then signaled, "I see the place and the hidden door which is by it."

"Do the work," came a general series of signs.

The young thief stood, slowly inhaling deeply as he did so. "The last of the essence is gone," he finally said ruefully, "but what euphoria! I am full of every sense and feeling!" In truth, he did feel somewhat giddy and sensual, but each deep breath he took seemed to mix with the counter-agent he had drunk to nullify the narcotic vapors. Otherwise, there was no question he would have been thoroughly intoxicated by the heady stuff he'd just inhaled.

"I need to move, to experience," Gord announced to the other five, who were still in the process of sniffing up the last of the Flowers of Thratus Kaloid from their flasks. So saying, the young man stepped here and there around the room, moving quickly and as if filled with agitated energy. Seeing his nod, the others stood and began to act oddly, reaching into robes, drawing forth daggers, and so on. Whoever watched would certainly have his gaze riveted upon these strange activities.

The secret entrance to the room was hidden about three feet above the floor, its edges masked by supporting posts set into the wall and by strips of wood bracing them. It took the eye of a master thief to discover the not-quite-proper fit and note faint smudges from careless hands — where no hand should have been placed unless its owner was eight feet tall. Next to this panel was a long, irregular crevice in a ceiling timber, as if the ancient beam had dried and cracked from age. That too wasn't quite right, and Gord could discern that the "crack" was really only about an inch deep. That was obviously the spy hole.

As his associates commenced their strange behavior, the young thief began tracing the outline of the hidden portal with sensitive fingers — searching, pressing, seeking the hidden means of opening it. Come on, I know it's here somewhere, he said to himself, all the while hoping that the watcher had no means of locking the panel to prevent just such unwanted entry as Gord had in mind.

He found a strip of wood that moved sideways. Gord gave a gesture at this discovery, and his comrades began to talk loudly and laugh. Their noise filled the chamber, and the click the panel made as Gord shoved the strip of old oak to the side was in-

audible in the din. With an effortless heave, the
young thief was up and into the space revealed as the
portal swung inward to the left. Trusting his in-
stincts, Gord sprang up and to the right with his dagger ready. He could just make out a figure there,
peering intently through the crack at the antics in the
room below. A swift blow with the pommel of his
weapon, and the surprised spy was unconscious.

"Move this cockroach," Gord called softly into the
bedlam. Chert took one long stride and grabbed the
limp form from where Gord had thrust it partially out
of the secret opening in the wall. With the body out of
the way, the young adventurer was able to move
along the narrow passage and see if there was a nearby means of exit. A couple of minutes later he thrust
his head into the room again. "This way, everybody.
There's a back door!"

With one of the chairs jammed firmly against the
regular door, and the unconscious spy now firmly
bound and gagged, the others clambered up and into
the little inter-wall passage as quietly as they could.
The last in was Gellor, and he carefully shut the panel behind him. Gord was creeping along to the right,
with Allton, Greenleaf, Timmil, Chert, and Gellor following in that order. Gord and Gellor both had the
ability to see in the dark, so they needed no illumination. The vision of the other four was aided by the
soft glow of a magical brooch that Allton wore at his
throat. The wizard simply touched the piece of jewelry
when he entered the dark tunnel, and it began to give
off light immediately.

After ascending four steps, the file of silent men
came to a plain wooden door. "The other side appears
to be the back of a cabinet," Gord hissed over his
shoulder. "Mind your heads as you go through."

They exited in a dirty, disused room, formerly a large pantry or something like that. "Where now?" Allton inquired, looking at the young champion in the faint light from his brooch. "I am lost."

"We passed through the rear wall of Hegmon's, into another structure which abuts it," Gord explained. "From the looks of this room, the place is deserted. All we need to do is find a way to the front and depart. No one will look for us back there," he added, thumbing to indicate the underground lair, "for at least a half-hour. That's more than enough time to lose ourselves in Greyhawk."

"This all seems to be a lot of shit," Chert said. "Why not just take out whoever it is that's laying for us and be done with it?"

"That, my dear fellow," Timmil replied in a patient manner, "would give our enemy too precise a measure of our strength."

"It might just tell us who in the hells is after us!" the barbarian warrior muttered in exasperation. He did not like running away from any fight.

Gord opened the door that led on into the rest of the place. "If you must chat, do it as you go, please. We need to move quickly," he said, and then suited his actions to his words by slipping out.

After passing through several abandoned rooms they came to the front of the building, marked by shuttered windows and a barred door. "This is tricky," the young thief said in admiration. "Opens from outside and in as well," he said, demonstrating the latter by pivoting the brace that held the bar and giving the outer door a shove. It opened noiselessly on greased hinges. "Just duck under the bar — it's affixed permanently." Soon all six were outside and away without anyone around to see their escape.

Gord took them through a subterranean route so that they passed out of Old City and into Clerksburg unmolested. After entering a small inn there, Gord exchanged a few words with its owner, handed over a small stack of coins, and that was that. They were now safe and unobserved — for a time, at least — and could get down to the business at hand. Once the group was closed off in a private room on the third story of the place, Gord began the meeting.

"You are here to assist us, gentle priest and worthy mage, I know. But how is it that we were picked up by agents of our foes so quickly? I noticed none until you two joined us. . . ." He let that statement trail off as he stared at both of the men.

Timmil answered without hesitation. "I fear I am the cause of it all. You see, the agents of Evil here know full well my efforts against them and on behalf of Balance. I did my utmost to avoid any who might follow when I went to meet the good wizard here and then seek you four out at the tavern," he explained. "That is why we motioned you out when we arrived there."

"True," Allton confirmed. "Both of us sensed something was amiss on our way to the Blue Lantern, and then I noticed we were being followed by hostile folk. But we are now secure, so let us pass on to more pressing matters."

All of them looked at Gord. He nodded a curt agreement. "Very well, I suppose that will do. You have our man under surveillance?"

"Yes. Various of our operatives keep watch on his quarters night and day, and he is followed most discreetly wherever he goes. I don't believe that this . . . Gravestone? Undron Nalvistor? . . . has noticed any of it, either."

The substance of that last claim seemed quite unlikely to Gord, but he made no comment. "You can tell me then, at any given time, just where our object of interest is?"

"Yes, but the appropriate observer will have to be contacted first, of course."

"And you, wizard Allton — is there anything you can add?"

The man shook his head, looking squarely at Gord with his large, intelligent eyes of deep brown. "I came to this city only a few days ago at the behest of my lord, Tenser. Until this very night, I have avoided contact with anyone connected to the organization, so as to remain invisible to the foes of Balance. I know who — and what — we seek, and I am happy to be a part of the group who will accomplish the thing," he stated with pride in his tone. Then he paused for a second and added, "Glad too that I have strong allies, for this man is not one I would face alone!"

"Yes," said Gord. "To counter the malign power of this Gravestone, we have swords, stealth, and spells — I hope in sufficient quantity and of such quality that he and his vile servants will fall as grain before a scythe. If he gets an inkling of what we plan, though, that one will have such a force to greet us that we will be meat in his pot." Gord looked around at all their faces after saying that. None of them showed fear.

"I will get Brool," Chert boomed, referring to his great battle axe, "and we can take the scum before sunrise!"

"That's fine, my old comrade," Gord said with a smile that showed he meant to take the fight to their foes soon indeed. "Gellor and I will wait here while you and Curley go to our cache and bring everything there to this inn. You'll draw no attention if you hur-

ry, for it isn't too late for honest folk to be abroad yet
in this part of Greyhawk." They had left the hillman's
axe and certain other bulky items in safekeeping with
a friend, one who knew both Chert and Gord from the
old days when the two had practiced their larcenous
trade and roistered in the city. His quarters were but
a few blocks distant, and the pair could be there and
back inside an hour, even with the precaution of a
circuitous route and careful observation for possible
followers.

"Now, what about you two?" Gord continued, addressing the wizard and the cleric after Chert and
Greenleaf had departed. "Do you need to go forth to
gather up any materials for the expedition?"

"I am already prepared," Allton said. "What I do
not have will probably be useless anyway."

The cleric looked resigned. "I am as ready as I
shall ever be for work such as we must face," he ventured. "I have a foreboding feeling about this assault,
but I am ready to do my utmost to see to its success.
I have said my prayers and meditated, equipping myself thus. And I do have my stout mace," the man
concluded, patting the object beneath his robes.

"Do we venture against the demonurgist when the
others return?" asked Allton.

"I'll decide that when they come back," Gord responded. "Let's wait to find out what Chert and Curley might have run into before we make a plan of
action." Both dweomercraefter and priest agreed that
such was sound reasoning, so the four remaining
members of the team settled back with their own
thoughts to await the return of the big hillman and
the half-elven druid and forester.

Not very much later the two came back, Chert
lugging a large case and Greenleaf only slightly less

137

burdened. They might well have been travelers laden with the baggage of their sojourning.

"Well?" Gord asked abruptly in greeting.

"The thoroughfares are alive with evil ones," the half-elf said as he let his heavy satchel drop.

"Curley's right, Gord," the brawny hillman confirmed. "Every hard-hearted whore and gimlet-eyed cutpurse in Greyhawk is abroad tonight — and not on routine business, either. They're all about cruising to spot something for the thugs lurking in the background. Couldn't be any other reason than us."

"The word got out fast, then," Gellor said with a soft whistle. "Did any of them make you?"

"Pretty unlikely," Greenleaf said with assurance. "I had a cap on, so nobody would spot me as part elven, and Chert does a pretty good job of making himself smaller. My guess is that they have been told to look for a group of six, whether moving as a gang or broken into threes or twos and traveling loosely together. I'm sure they noticed us, but when nobody else was near us, they switched their attention elsewhere."

"Good enough," said Gord. "Judging by the looks of it, I'd say you returned with everything you went for."

"Yes — and then some," Chert replied with a bit of a scowl, hefting the case he had carried back. "Good thing I have such a strong back, or that little straw of yours might have broken it."

"Straw?" Gord was perplexed.

Chert unfastened the straps holding the case shut and pulled forth a weapon the big barbarian had not seen before this evening. "Are you trying to tell me this *isn't* yours?" he asked. "If I had known that—"

"Gods!" Gord gasped in amazement. "It *is* my blade! But how . . . ?"

"It was in our gear, that's all I know," said Chert. "You must have had it well hidden until now."

"Better than you could imagine, Chert," said Gellor with a thin smile.

Gord reached out, took the scabbard, and withdrew the sword it held. The blade was keen, long, and the blackest of black in color. It was the very weapon that had been presumed lost into the hands of Gravestone — the object that had indirectly cost Barrel and Dohojar and the rest of the crew of the *Silver Seeker* their lives.

"How . . . ?" Gord asked again, this time directing his gaze to Gellor.

"I could surmise," replied the one-eyed troubador, "but the *how* of the matter is of no real import right now. The important thing is that the blade has been wrested from the hands of Gravestone and returned to its rightful purveyor. A good sign for the coming contest, I'd venture."

"Possibly," said Gord, reflecting on the near-miracle that had just occurred. Despite Gellor's advice, he wondered just how the sword had been taken from Gravestone — and how many of their allies might have been killed in the effort.

"So let's go after the blaster!" Chert boomed. "I can give Brool some exercise, and you can show the rest of us what that ebony sword can do."

Gord raised a hand as though trying to calm down his companion. "It is also possible, Chert, that our adversary will be even more angered and doubly dangerous now, because he has lost the item that he went to such great trouble to gain. We must be especially cautious."

Chert sighed heavily. "I know what that means," he said. "We all might as well get comfortable." He flopped down on the floor, put his head on the hard leather of the case he'd brought, and closed his eyes.

"What is he saying?" Timmil asked the group at large.

Gord replied. "We can't move as a group tonight without being spotted and Gravestone likely being alerted. We'll wait until sunup to move. He'll not be expecting us to come in broad daylight." With that, he sat down, put his feet up on a low table nearby, and likewise closed his eyes. "Get some rest, everyone. You'll need to be at your best come morning."

In a few minutes all conversation died away. Each man did his best to relax and conserve energy for the coming confrontation. Soon only the sputtering of the lamp's wick as it burned could be heard; then that was drowned out by the barbarian's rumbling snores.

One of the six watched the others through slitted eyes, but not one of the five stirred in unnatural fashion. They were, it seemed, strong in mind and firm in their purpose. That pleased the watcher, for although the principal burden of this mission was squarely on his shoulders, he knew he would need the help of all of them to succeed. Thinking that, Gord turned his head a little so that when the sun came up its rays would strike his face through the slats of the shuttered little window. Then, grasping the hilt of the black sword, he let his thoughts drift, and soon he too was asleep.

Chapter 7

AT FIRST GLANCE IT SEEMED a featureless, endless plane — not that anyone would wish to even glance at it in the first place. Its putrid hue was sufficient to make all but the most hardened guts writhe with nausea, the eyes to water, the mind to seek sanity in delusions so as to escape the thought of such an abomination actually existing.

The rotten dun of the plane was far from featureless. It was shot through with veins of stuff that looked like coagulated blood, and craterlike openings dotted here and there resembled massive, open sores in which pools of pus festered. Other portions of the landscape manifested themselves suddenly. Here a wormy thing suddenly rose up, splattering the noisome stuff of the place in reeking gobbets that splattered and rained down for seconds after its upheaval. Then the maggoty monstrosity was sucked back into the corruption, the putrescence absorbing the foul lumps greedily. There first one and then another strange growths shot up. Soon a forest of the ulcerous things had been extruded, so that their angry red and slowly dripping green stood out in stark contrast to the less colorful but no less disgusting flatness from which these excrescencies had been thrust.

In addition to the assault upon the visual and the olfactory senses, so too the very sounds of this place ravaged the ears. Disgusting slobberings, vile smackings and slurpings, terrible rendings competed with a cacophony of shrieks and teeth-paining screeches, accompanied by litanies of hollow groanings and gibberings along with sounds that could only be the slow splintering of bones.

Was this the floor of the lowest hell? No, not that pleasant a place by any means. This was the three hundred sixty-sixth layer of the Abyss, a place called Ojukalazogadit by those who cared to identify it.

As the expanse pulsed and twitched and parts of it grew or shrank, were silent, or gave out their horrid sounds, it geysered forth streams of thick, steaming liquid at unexpected places and of varying colors of revolting sort and appropriate odor. Parts of it took on lives of their own, dashed madly off as if trying to escape the place on stubby, misshapen appendages, only to be swallowed by some suddenly appearing maw or be caught and torn to stinking gobbets of gore by hands that sprang from nowhere.

A monstrous thing heaved itself up from a suppurating morass, wallowed forth, and began to trample and gore the very stuff it had issued from. The place grew lesser monstrosities, things all head and jaw tusks, hungry answers to the behemoth. In a protracted pursuit and battle, the lesser things brought the greater to bay and devoured it alive, slowly, starting by eating only those portions that were nonvital so that the monstrosity's great bellows of pain and suffering might go on longer. This was Ojukalazogadit at its most splendid.

As the tusked victors howled over their triumph, a volcano thrust itself up nearby and vomited forth a sticky, acidic fluid that was both burning hot and sentient. The viscous tentacles that were spewed out quickly found and engulfed the now-gibbering things that had devoured the behemothian monstrosity alive. The searing heat and burning acid had their own sport with the things, and then the plain was again relatively undisturbed. Vapors rose from the scarred place where the eruption had occurred, but even that was soon awash in a slimy lake of ichorous secretion.

Here was a place for demon wars. No king of the Abyss, no demon prince or great lord of Evil could work his will upon the stuff of Ojukalazogadit. The plane was itself a demon of sorts. It was uncontrolled, uncontrollable, and uncaring. Content in its madness to torment and devour itself, Ojukalazogadit heaved and pulsed, changed and re-formed, and quietly enjoyed its utter madness without caring, without feeling a need for revenge — for how can something avenge what it does to itself?

Either unaware or cunning in its insanity, the plane allowed vast armies to come upon it and do battle. And, of course, those not *of* it who caused it hurt would certainly pay for their deeds. Whether they were still alive or already dead, many of the interlopers would feed Ojukalazogadit before it permitted the survivors — if any — to depart.

This disgusting layer of chaos was also a gateway to many other strata of the abyssal realm. If counting downward made it three hundred sixty-six steps deep, that by no means meant that the law of orderly progression applied to it. Ojukalazogadit touched a dozen other layers firmly and impinged with varying degrees of tenuosity upon as many others. The eleventh and five hundred second were somehow firmly adjacent to it, as were other key strata seemingly above and below the reeking stretch of it. No other plane touched as many others in the whole realm. Thus, no other layer was so important in controlling the Abyss as Ojukalazogadit.

Into its very heart now marched a vast array from the deeper tiers that were the home place of demon-kind: a great mass of awesome proportion and terrible composition. Only demons could abide such a place, and they but for a short time. Nonetheless, march they did toward Ojukalazogadit. They came to conquer — not the place itself, but the other forces that had taken up temporary residence here, as if daring their foes to meet them on this most loathsome and important of battlegrounds.

A sudden cloud loomed on the sickly pale horizon, a blackness smudging the rotten orange atmosphere above. "Zubassu scouts, King Demogorgon!" a six-legged lizard-thing with human arms and a bat's head chittered as it peered into the distance. Obviously the demon didn't suffer poor vision, as its form might suggest. Its huge, dull red eyes evidently were very keen indeed.

"Attack them, fool — quickly!" said the left head of the towering Demogorgon, even as the right one barked orders to a squabbling flock of vulturelike demons that was clustered nearby.

Multiwinged wasp-demons swarmed upward with a hideous buzzing, heading directly for the approaching cloud of enemy zubassu, while the vultures stretched out snaky necks and beat their huge pinions in order to climb high into the dead-orange sky. From all along the front of the marching horde sprang other sorts of flying demons, some with such gross and bloated bodies, tiny wings, or other oddities that it seemed impossible for them to engage in aerial activity of any sort. Yet not only did they fly out and up, but soon the menagerie of monstrosities was battling fiercely with the thousands of four-winged zubassu demons. As bodies plummeted to the foul plain, whether singly or in tangled clusters still clawing and biting, the ground welcomed them. Wormheads formed to swallow the wounded combatants, or funnel-shaped holes suddenly gaped. Taloned, pawlike growths struggled forth to grab and pull down clusters of the fallen. Ojukalazogadit was already feeding well.

Despite the masses of opposing demons who arose to contend with the man-hawk zubassu, the latter were both fierce and more numerous. They flew over the advancing mass of nonflying foes in squadrons. Gouts of flame, jagged lightnings, thunderous explosions, searing streaks of pure energy, and other releases of magical forces made it seem as though a celebratory display of pyrotechnical virtuosity was in progress throughout the rotten, sickly orange sky. Even as scores of the four-winged scouts tumbled down burning, dismembered, half-vaporized, or simply as ashes, these demons repaid the compliment sent upward to greet them with similar, but less powerful, spectacular compliments. It seemed that even a miss was useful, however. To inflict a lightning stroke or gouting flame upon Ojukalazogadit was to ensure the instant demise of any creature near the wound, as mandible or tentacle, huge head or flopping hand suddenly appeared to seize repayment for the injury. The zubassu were soon in total rout, however, and only a tithe of their original multitude flapped over whence they had come.

"We have crushed them!" The boast was from the

capering Mandrillagon, a monstrous, blue-faced parody of a mandrill. He was a mighty demon indeed, with two strata under his heel. It was Mandrillagon's winged monkey-demons who had finished the pursuit of the fleeing zubassu.

"Fodder!" rumbled both of Demogorgon's heads. "Mere dung for spreading! Worse, many escaped. Now Graz'zt and his lickspittles will know our numbers, the composition of our masses," the heads of the massive demon snarled. Even Mandrillagon, blood kin and long ally of Demogorgon, quailed before the fury evident in the demon king's twin voices.

Mandrillagon's livid blue face wrinkled, baring massive fangs of filthy yellow-gray at the rebuke. This was not defiance on Mandrillagon's part, but simply a reflexive gesture. "We have no need to worry, my brother," he assured Demogorgon in a coughing, barking voice. "No enemy can stand before us. Never has such a horde as this been assembled!" That was true, and Demogorgon lashed his forked tail in acknowledgment of the statement.

A vast force of demons rolled across the disgusting plain that was Ojukalazogadit. On the left of the array were the mighty Var-Az-Hloo and Abraxas, each with an army of lesser demons. Demogorgon's headquarters and personal guard of snake-fish, toad-crabs, and lizard-slugs occupied the right flank. The central mass proper was commanded by Mandrillagon. This body of more than a million of all sorts of demons was the largest and certainly the most varied in the whole host that stretched for miles and miles across the flatness. It marched through pus and ordure, scum and bubbling excretions, heedless of all, even losses to predatious portions of the plain itself. Its tread shook even Ojukalazogadit's self as it squawked, screamed, fluttered, wiggled, hopped, and bounded along in a phantasmagorical symphony of hideousness.

Far away to the right rear was a smaller array. The two divisions that composed it were those of Zuggtmoy and her servitors and Szhublox and his lot of toadstool demons, amoeboid monsters, slimes, fungi, smut, rust, more slimes, blight, molds, and still more oozing slimes. Some hooted or puffed or burbled, but most were silent as they slid and lurched across the plain. Ojukalazogadit recoiled from their touch, so terrible were the demons and demonkin making up this force — not even a quarter-million strong, but so fearsome as to be dreaded. It came slowly, so it was effectively echeloned to the rear.

Lesser princes of the Abyss and a multitude of demon lords were scattered throughout the three great battles of the advancing horde. Telepathically and by various other means as well, they assured that the wild disarray of demons would obey orders to the limit of their ability. Of course, that simply meant that the vast hordes would move in the same direction and not tear each other to pieces. Such was the way of demoniacal warfare. With such a force as he had assembled and not marked against the actual person of the hated Graz'zt, Demogorgon was confident of an easy and total victory. Then he would assume the emperorship of the whole of the Abyss and deal with pretenders too. After Graz'zt came Orcus and Zuggtmoy.

"They retreat before us, brother," Mandrillagon barked. "They hope to wear us down before having to face your awesome might." The latter was a hasty but needed addition to his first statement. The blue-faced master of demons knew that calling Demogorgon "brother" too often was not a healthy thing to do, even if it were a fact. Both were sovereigns, blood relatives, and allies. The towering Demogorgon, though, accepted none as equal. Better to fawn now and save vaunting for the time when his own power enabled him to do away with the two-headed freak permanently. "What shall I do, greater one?"

"Order our horde to halt," Demogorgon commanded, fixing Mandrillagon with his twin stares so that even so mighty a lord as the simian demon king twitched uneasily. "Order the reserves, slaves, and foot beasts to hurry up to the advance."

"I don't understand. . . ."

"Of course not," the right head of Demogorgon said with contempt as the left giggled derogatorily and nodded. "I will communicate with Ojukalazogadit, sacrifice to it and feed it. This plane will then hinder the flight of Graz'zt and his little turds. Then I will bring him to battle and crush him and have the throne and the Theorpart both."

There was no darkness on the near-infinite reaches of the stratum, but some time later the dull orange sky was suddenly shot through with sheets of bilious green. Sacrifice to Ojukalazogadit had indeed been made in copious form, and as the monster that was itself a layer of the chaotic netherworld chomped and crunched and surfeited itself on blood and ichor and flesh not of its own creation, it raised up folds and sunk chasms. The surface of Ojukalazogadit rippled. Pulses boomed, and Demogorgon exulted. "The dirty lump styling himself emperor of the Abyss has been halted in his flight! We now march to render Graz'zt and all his curs their death blow!"

To an ear-splitting cacophony of iron horns and vast kettledrums covered with human skin or dragon hide, to the bonging and whanging of gongs and cy-lindrical bells, to screeching fifes and other instruments of all sorts, while millions of demons raged and roared, the corps and divisions of Demogorgon's horde marched. Soon the stronger began to outpace the weaker as the advance became a race to see who could fall upon the enemy first. Streaming across the vile landscape inexorably, a tidal wave of demonkind rushed upon a huddled array of their fellows not half as numerous.

* * *

"They come, my liege."

This was more a confirmation of some long-expected and delayed event finally occurring than anything said in fear or as a warning. The speaker was Eclavdra the High Priestess, known to some as Leda, a dark-elf counselor of standing and power equal to any of the demon lords who swore fealty to Graz'zt, save possibly the alabaster-skinned Vuron. "All is in readiness."

"Kostchtchie?" asked Graz'zt, turning to the ugliest and perhaps most ruthless of his lieutenants.

"My horde stands ready!"

"Baphomet?"

"To kill!" the bull-headed demon prince bellowed, raising a massive axelike weapon.

"Your demon giants and scum, Kostchtchie, will march very slowly forward. Delay as long as possible the melee with Zuggtmoy's horde. You, dear Baphomet, must fling your ravening demoters and the rest quickly forward so that you strike the enemy on the left under Var-Az-Hloo before the freak and his corps are in range of our own main body. Understood?"

Neither of the great demons understood the strategy involved, but both said they knew exactly what was expected of them. "Go then, and may you savor the death of each enemy slain!" Graz'zt roared.

Dark and dour Nergal remained standing with Graz'zt, both demons bulking huge beside the small and delicate drow, Leda. "I will watch the horn-head Baphomet," she said to Graz'zt softly. "Even though you promised him ascendancy over Yeenoghu should he triumph this day, I trust not his loyalty to you, liege." That brought a dry rasp of a chuckle from the stony depths of the demon-man Nergal, who had been through his own quarrels with the ebony Graz'zt before the latter had acquired the Theorpart he now controlled.

"Yes, little one, and think you not that the weird Demogorgon frets not about the blubber-gutted sheep-face with whom he has made common cause? Time enough to even old scores afterward, say I. . . ."

It was a most unexpected combination, that of Orcus and Demogorgon, but as with Yeenoghu and Baphomet, the foes fought for the same side on different fronts. Perhaps it would suffice. Leda understood full well the principle of biding time to wait for revenge or anything else sought for. "Nevertheless, with your permission, emperor," she said, "I will take my station on the right."

"Take Palvlag and the conflagranti," Graz'zt assented, pointing toward the half-hundred great demons of flame who were his personal guard. "For what is coming I have no need for them. Their presence will be sure to soothe any ill will Baphomet harbors." Again Nergal chuckled. The terrible fire fiends were sufficient to give any, even the greatest of great demons, pause.

Leda made no protest. Turning quickly, with but the slightest of bows, the drow priestess hurried off to inform Palvlag and gather the force to speed off to where the bull-headed Baphomet's corps was already forming for its advance. "Victory, Emperor Graz'zt!" she cried as she departed.

"There is one whose aura is wrong," Nergal said squarely to the six-fingered demon king. "How is it that you allow such a one to exist?"

"She serves faithfully in all ways and counsels wisely . . . for a nondemon," Graz'zt said with a little wave that dismissed any further discussion. He would not admit to any that he simply found it expedient to maintain her because that was what Vuron wished, and the albino was his most trusted henchman. Making a face at the unconscious use of a human term, the would-be master of the Abyss said as an afterthought, "Besides, all of my nobles must soon become used to dealing with such as the dark elf. As our realm expands, more and more such servants will be needed."

Nergal nodded but disagreed in his heart. Any territory under his heel would be depopulated quickly, save for those undead and demons whom he placed there. "Most sagacious, majesty. Ahh . . . Shall I now lead forth the main battle to confront the center of the enemy?"

"No, I shall do that myself when the time is ripe. Go and find Ogrijek and have him bring all of his remaining zubassu and voord too — those should total ten thousand or so. They will be assigned the place of honor before us."

"Honor? Before us? I don't under—"

Graz'zt cut the rest off. "What you understand, Prince Nergal, is of no matter to me. Simply fetch them!" As Nergal started to go off, the ebony demon king added, "And, Prince of Unlife, don't forget to have several of your toughest enforcers with you, for it is quite likely that Ogrijek and his lot are in league with our foes!"

Nergal spun and stared, then bared his fanged mouth in a hideous smile. He whistled and clapped. Shadows gathered around and coalesced into massive demons. Soon Nergal and a growing throng of his own were shoving their way toward the place where the lord of zubassu was resting. Ogrijek would not like serving in the forefront, mused Graz'zt . . . especially when he found that neither he nor any of his kind could take wing any longer.

Not caring now about what was revealed to the enemy by his action, Graz'zt spoke a series of chest-jarring words and shot upward. He mushroomed skyward as a pillar of smoke, growing less and less substantial as his height increased. At three hundred feet he was satisfied. Now he could see all that was needed. Ojukalazogadit had obligingly mounded up a ridge beneath Graz'zt, so that now the demon king was able to view the entire front of his force and the wildly surging line of the charging enemy.

Part of what Graz'zt saw was disconcerting to him. Ojukalazogadit was hungry at all times, and Demogorgon's side wasn't the only one being weakened by the gobbling undulations of the plane. But the enemy force was being weakened to a much greater degree than his own by Ojukalazogadit, almost as though the place itself was showing partiality in the struggle. Graz'zt saw that although his array had been sufficient to prevent the enemy from badly overlapping his flanks, the density of the opposing onrushing mass was about five or six times the depth of his own. He had the most powerful warriors in the conflict, by and large. But Demogorgon and his ass-kissing toadies had a great advantage in numbers. Were they two million? Three? No matter. Whatever the count, Graz'zt could see clearly that less than a million were in the horde confronting their howling onslaught.

There were the zubassu and carrion-eating voord, under the command of Ogrijek, thrust into the very first rank of the center. Demogorgon and Mandrillagon themselves would come here, and Graz'zt saw that their center had fully a million in its mass — ten to one against his force! But Graz'zt's minions, led by the forced labor of the zubassu, were stronger and more powerful than the bulk of their opposition. The zubassu were cowardly and traitorous by nature, but Graz'zt had seen to it that they would not have a chance to flee. . . .

A shout rose forth as Ogrijek perceived what was happening just before the charge of the overpowering enemy force struck. He tried to take flight upward, but it was as if he were tethered. His followers then tried to escape likewise with the same result. Then the rush of the enemy was upon them.

When masses of demonkind fight each other, there is little or no use for magical energies. Light and fear, typical demoniacal weapons, have no effect on others of their kind under such circumstances. Most of their other magical powers are likewise of limited effect, short range, or require too much concentration. Simply put, when demons battle other demons, primitive striking weapons, fangs, claws, talons, pincers, mandibles, and the like are the most effective and immediate means of dispensing with foes.

Some aerial combat would have been taking place in this struggle, but Graz'zt had seen to it that the

153

battle would be held down to the surface of the stratum. This he accomplished through the dark energies he had drawn from the Theorpart, and the effect would last long enough for the battle to be fought to its conclusion. His monstrous sword resting atop one mountainous shoulder, the three-hundred-foot-tall demon king watched the horde of attackers impact raggedly upon his own solid lines. The zubassu fought very well once they realized that they had no chance of escape, no opportunity to turn coat.

Parodies of bears and goats, horses and wolves, apes and gorillas and buffaloes, weasels and boars were jumbled with insect, skeletal, amphibian, bat, reptilian, fish, arachnid, bird, and human parts to form the companies and regiments of demons who fought each other. At least that is how it appeared. Toad-man bit pig-owl as the latter used taloned forearms to rend the former's flesh from its slimy back. Elephantine monstrosities trampled chimerical horrors, as little wolverine-faced demons used iron teeth to sever leg tendons and worm-bodied half-camels spewed acidic secretions over all before them. All that happened in mere seconds, and then the initial wave of the attacking horde was broken, reeling back. Graz'zt laughed, and the sound was like that of a volcano clearing its throat prior to eruption.

"Demogorgon! Come forth and face me alone!"

Naturally, the demon king named failed to come forth as demanded. In fact, although Demogorgon and his allied lords and princes heard the challenge clearly enough, they were busy trying to determine what had gone wrong. Ten thousand of their demon troops had fallen in the first rush. They outnumbered the force of Graz'zt heavily. Yet not a hundred of the ebon-hued demon king's soldiers had fallen, the zubassu had not joined the attackers, and Graz'zt was an enormous figure daring to stand before them all without regard for dweomer or power sent against him. It was true enough that little or no magic played a part in the combat between demon hordes, but their leaders — king, prince, lord, or greatest demon — certainly had recourse to such powers, for they commanded a wide and terrible spectrum of magics and similar energies.

At Demogorgon's enraged command a barrage of lethal bolts, killer forces, and demon-shattering spells were sent to vaporize the insolent figure that rose like a colossus before their burning eyes. The forces struck, visibly and invisibly, and the smoke-black Graz'zt seemed to shake and thin and nearly disappeared under the withering power sent against it. Well it should, for enough force to destroy a small mountain had been expended. "Again!" screeched both of the demon king's baboonlike heads. "Finish him!" Then, suiting words to his own actions, Demogorgon released his most potent and deadly attack, beams of lambent green shooting from the eyes of one head, dull maroon from the orbs of his other. Similar powers discharged from the princes and lords of demonkind there with him, also played upon the foolishly exposed and enlarged form of their hated foe, Graz'zt.

Suddenly the figure shrank abruptly, seeming to collapse upon itself. "Victory, Emperor Demogorgon!" Trobbo-gotath, a greatest demon of earth, rumbled in fawning fashion. "Do I order a new assault to finish them?"

Before Demogorgon could answer, he saw the distant line of the enemy center rolling aside to left and right. Were they about to run? "What . . . ?" said his left head as the right turned to try to peer through the gap.

Then Graz'zt, now but a thirty-foot tall giant, strode into clear view between the parted regiments of his demon horde. In his hand he held a little figure that he tore into two parts even as the demon king watched. The huge ebony arm windmilled. A tiny speck sailed up and out, toward Demogorgon, like a stone shot from a great trebuchet. Lizard-quick, the demon king avoided the missile. Both heads bent to see what had been aimed at him. The thing was Ogrijek's head. "We are undone. . . ." the right head yammered, and the left was too terrified to speak.

Graz'zt was simply walking with impunity toward the horde that had but recently threatened him. With a roar composed of bellows, shouts, squeaks, yammers, and all forms of similar noises, the demon soldiers who served the black one followed with glee. They rushed forth to fall upon a force many times larger than their own. Why not? Before them was Graz'zt, invincible and triumphant! His hands shot forth blasts that blew the opposing horde into nothingness, a hundred at a time. Then the demon king was among the foe, and his massive sword played upon them as a scythe upon a field of ripe grain. Down fell lowly dretch and rutterkin, kerzow and goat-horned clobdroo. Malvachnu demons were as swine in a slaughter, and great lords of ogre size and humanoid form as impotent as lambs before the black blade of Graz'zt.

The left battle seemed unaware of the debacle taking place in the center. Var-Az-Hloo and Abraxas collided with Baphomet's corps and began a terrible melee that slowly ground down the latter force. The bull-headed demon prince and his companies of demonkin were not yielding an inch, only being gradually overcome by the superior numbers of the enemy.

So too on the right. The fungoid and slime contingents of Zuggtmoy and Szhublox were ideally suited to meet the disgusting horde under the even more loathsome Kostchtchie. The foul things commanded by the demon queen and the slime lord felt no revulsion when facing the terrible array of deformed giant-like demons and their ilk. Of course, neither did those minions of the bandy-legged Kostchtchie fear the obscenities that came to do battle with them. Hulking demons spread the plain of Ojukalazogadit with bits and pieces of toadstools and amoeboid monsters while they, in turn, were dissolved, rotted, and made into puddles of putrid ichor by their implacable opponents. It was fortunate for the attackers that there were so many of their own, for a dozen of Zuggtmoy's things, or the smutty warriors of Szhublox, died for every soldier who fell in Kostchtchie's horde. The demon queen hooted and the reserve moved up. The situation was in doubt.

"We must retire, king," Mandrillagon chittered nervously as he hurried up to where Demogorgon had positioned himself. "If we do so immediately, the enemy turds will have to take some time to finish off our cowardly troops, and we can be well away — safe and gathering fresh contingents!"

Demogorgon thought about that with his left brain while the right assessed the field before them. His vaunted mass of demon soldiery scarcely outnumbered the opposition by two to one now, and Graz'zt, accompanied by a half-dozen lords and greatest demons, was beginning to cut a swath through the very middle of the horde to get at him. Then there was a great commotion on his left, and Demogorgon used both heads to see what was happening there. A company of conflagranti, dreaded fire demons, had managed to take Var-Az-Hloo's division in the flank. Trouble there too!

Just as he was about to agree, to slip away with Mandrillagon and leave the others to fend for themselves, Infestix himself appeared to stand beside the demon king. "You! Here?" Demogorgon's heads spoke in chorus.

"You are betrayed by your senses, Demogorgon," the daemon said without bothering with formalities. "The offal heap, Graz'zt, has brought the Eye of Deception. With it, and the Theorpart too—"

"The Eye of Deception!? He dares—"

"Don't ever interrupt me again!" Infestix hissed, cutting off the so-called imperial demon king. Then, considering the circumstances, the daemon added, "Especially when everything you hope for hangs in the balance so precariously." There was no anger evident in the weird, reptilian eyes of the towering Demogorgon as both of his baboon-heads craned down to listen to Infestix speak on.

"You have come alone," Demogorgon said, unable to keep resignation out of his tone. "Then my hordes are defeated!"

"Not so! Not on either count, demon king. I have brought with me Utmodoch and his demodand warbands in their myriads. Not even Graz'zt can see them, for I have covered their presence with our own Theorpart."

"Where—"

"Marching now to take the inky turdheap from behind. Hold fast here for but another quarter of an hour, and you'll feast on Graz'zt's own flesh to celebrate your triumph."

That was what the two-headed creature desired to hear, to accomplish! "And you will stay? Use Initiator to counter the Eye?"

"Aren't we allies?" the daemon asked. He thought, actually, that lord and vassal were more correct terms, but until the brawling lords of the Abyss were eliminated or subjugated by one master, Infestix had to pretend otherwise. No matter if it was Demogorgon, Orcus, or some other who strove against Graz'zt; whichever of the demons eventually floated to the top, Infestix would himself enthrall. "You will have power to counter what you . . . your servants . . . stupidly fed into Graz'zt. Your very attacks were channeled by the relic he is linked to. When I counter that, he will lose that force, return to normal size. Then you yourself can slay him in single combat."

Ignoring that last statement, the dual heads of the demon king began to spit out instructions. Mandrillagon rushed out to bolster the sagging horde, while several demon lords hurried off to stiffen the front. Infestix was very pleased with himself; that Demogorgon could sense, based on that last remark. Infestix knew — as Demogorgon had to reluctantly admit to himself — that despite his terrible powers, poisons, talons, fangs, and the rest, the reptilian demon king had no stomach to confront Graz'zt in single combat — at least not while the black one still wielded his terrible sword.

The daemon was overweening, and Demogorgon would eventually set matters straight. Infestix sought to rule the Abyss, that was clear. Demogorgon knew that the outcome would be quite the reverse: He would rule Hades and the rest of the nether planes too, but only after he possessed the whole of the artifact. Time, only time, was needed. The matters at hand demanded his attention now. In minutes Demogorgon had sent in his last reserve, manlike demons with heads like those of miniature tyrannosaurs. He waded in behind them, going for the monstrous figure that was Graz'zt. Let that one think he would do combat personally. Time too would dispel that idiocy.

Soon enough all occurred just as the daemon had said. The mass of demodands took the enemy by surprise, Graz'zt was shrunk down to normal size, and the tide of battle turned abruptly in favor of the invaders. It was only the lack of cooperation from Ojukalazogadit — or the cooperation of the cursed thing with Graz'zt — that allowed the ebony shitpile to escape, Demogorgon mused as he surveyed the shambles with satisfaction. Even as he watched, Ojukalazogadit began to seriously feed, cleaning up greedily. Good! His troops would not have to view their own dead, which amounted to more than a million. That number was inconsequential; with the millions more available throughout the whole sphere of chaotic evil, Demogorgon would soon be able to field a dozen hordes twice as numerous. The million existences were well spent, a small price to pay for victory. Better still, the puny daemon had hied himself back to his dirty little pit, and Utmodoch and his demodands were left to the demon king's mercy. Those fools would become his shock troops in the next battle . . . which would come soon, soon.

Despite such thoughts, the facts of the matter prevailed. Graz'zt, worn down to his true proportions by the force of Initiator, fought on with demoniacal fury, hardly surprising but noteworthy because the demon king turned and fought to the rear as it were. Thus he extricated himself and the bulk of his surviving troops. And Ojukalazogadit too assisted the retreat.

Put simply, the strata of the Abyss was, when all was said and done, a loyal if imbecilic subject of the mighty, ebony-hued demon. With its assistance, Graz'zt withdrew all three great divisions of his army and arrived safely on his own plane. In time, the enemy would follow, further depleted by Ojukalazoga-dit, but not seriously decimated or long delayed. At least Vuron would no longer have to be concerned about a war on multiple fronts. The enemies of his master had managed to consolidate and compress the action to but a single time and place. Unfortunately, that was now, and the battleground the principal place of Graz'zt himself. The time of the final phase of the war was at hand.

The multiverse was strained by this war, but only because of what was occurring with respect to the power involved. Many were the agents of arcane energy and ancient power employed. The Eye of Deception was one of the most puissant, of course. There were a dozen others, graduating down the scale from it. More importantly, there were three far greater. All portions of the tripartite relic were now in play, and about to so exist on a single layer of a single sphere of reality. Well should the whole of existence tremble. All fabric, the very stuff of existence, strained, groaned and shuddered.

Somewhere, a somewhere that was no-where, no-time, no-place, a massive being stirred and strained and sought to awaken. Tharizdun's time was drawing near.

Chapter 8

HE RAN THROUGH the twisting alleys of Old City, pursued by bullies shouting "Gutless!" after him, and tears of humiliation filled his eyes. . . .

He crept silently and struck the terrible cataboligne demon from behind, feeling cowardly for doing so yet knowing full well that to face it head-on would be useless. . . .

Then Evaleigh was telling him she would wed another, and he wept, for the loss was compounded by the betrayal. So . . .

He turned and was with Leda, and he helped her to enter the portal that would separate them forever, and despite the weight in his heart there was understanding and shared pride. . . .

As Leda disappeared, he found himself slipping sideways along a dark drainage tube toward a cistern wherein an unnaturally animated thing that had been Theobald the Beggarmaster awaited, and as he faced that terror . . .

It disappeared into the lightlessness of the shadow plane's Snuffdark, and before him there was a thing composed of duskdrake and lich-vampire. He was weaponless, but then unseen figures behind him supplied a sword and a charm, and when he was so armed the shadowy threat vanished and all was bright. . . .

Along the checkered squares of an infinite chess-board he wandered, and looming forms bulked to block and threaten. The board became a forest, then a field, a village, open sea, the city of Greyhawk, an endless desert of dust, an expanse of labyrinthine dungeon corridors. . . .

He walked with himself. He was frail, beardless, and just escaped from the prison workhouse, and he was sixteen and reckless, and he was older still and uncertain, and he was *now*. Then he understood and awoke. . . .

"Your doze was a most uneasy one, Gord. Was there some portent you dreamed of?"

The young adventurer shook his head, looking squarely at Timmil as he formed an answer to the cleric's question. "No, not exactly. There was a meaning to what I dreamed, but I think it more likely my mind has simply identified events, meshed them. . . ."

"Then I am happy to not be so enlightened," Chert rumbled. He had observed his friend's troubled dreaming and liked it not.

"There was no rede, then?" Allton the wizard asked, for he sensed something just as Timmil had.

Gord stood up and stretched, trying to work out the stiffness and tension. "Let's be on our way," he said to the group. Then he answered the spell-binder directly. "No omen, but a rede? . . . Perhaps. In my sleep I dreamed of what has gone before — those things which have formed the *me* that speaks to you now, Allton. I moved and was moved by an unseen hand, too. The past was preparation for this future — if the dream was true. Each thing I did was an exercise, preparation for a later test. In the end, time was of no consequence, for I existed in all aspects. Perhaps the whole of it is, then, the schooling for the last event."

The priest made a sign, and Greenleaf spoke hastily. "Don't talk that way, Gord, my old friend! No speaking of a final chapter yet; we all have far too much to accomplish before such a page is turned."

"Of course, of course. I apologize to all of you. I did not mean to imply that we would fail. The words came from the oppression of reliving so many past happenings."

"To be resigned to failure when your moment for revenge is at hand bodes ill," Timmil said slowly. Gord's profession of still being under the influence of his dream when he uttered his words did not satisfy the cleric at all.

It was Gellor who dispelled the tension. "Come, now, good priest!" he said with a smile, but sternly. "If you were recently given the name and identity of the one responsible for the murder of your parents, your life of misery and suffering as a child, and your endless uncertainty and self-doubt — along with a surety that this one likewise plans misery for all — would you be cheerful, positive, and bold? More likely cloistered on your knees somewhere in fearful prayer, say I — begging for divine guidance as to the course to take!"

There was uneasy laughter from the others at that, even Allton and Gord. The priest started to snap off a reply, then clamped his mouth shut.

Chert's booming voice filled the silence. "Yeah! The bastard is in Gord's palm now — all of our palms, in fact. We just have to be sure our fingers are together and strong enough to crush him into the foul puddle of filth he is!"

Gellor was donning the last of his gear, hiding his warlike dress under a great cloak. "Fingers alone can be broken, comrades. Together they make a stabbing wedge or smashing fist. An old martial axiom. . . ."

The others quickly followed suit, and in a few minutes all six of the men stood armed and ready. Outside the window of their quarters, the night sky was slowly paling to a milky color on the eastern horizon, and sounds from the street below indicated that farmers and merchants were already wending their ways toward the nearby market square.

Chert's massive axe, Brool, was slung beneath his voluminous cloak. The magical longsword that Gellor had plied so often and to deadly effect was concealed beneath his own outer garment.

As Gord fastened his new scabbard to his belt, the barbarian wondered again about the ominous blackness of the strangely hilted weapon their leader now possessed. But this time he kept his thoughts to himself. He had tried to speak to his friend about it, but had received only a curt assurance that the blade of his sword would prove itself against foes. Of course, all three of the fighting men likewise sported daggers, Chert having the heaviest.

Strangely, both the half-elf Greenleaf and Allton the wizard favored the curved-bladed knives from the west. The ranger-druid's was of ancient Baklunish craftsmanship, while the mage's was dwarven-forged and thrice enspelled by the legendary dweomercraefter Yartsenag seven centuries past.

Those two, as well as Timmil, also relied on other things for attack and defense. All three were equipped with magical staves and, of course, each had his own repertoire of great spells to call upon as well. Enchanted protections, charmed amulets, rings containing powers and energies arcane; all that and more were secured here, sequestered there.

"Even I can smell the wizardry which rises from us," Chert expostulated, "because it comes like stink from a dungpile!"

That fully dispelled the remaining tension, and after the others had finished laughing at the homely statement Allton said seriously, "The hillman speaks naught but bald facts. Hide as we may under these disguising cloaks, the aura of so much magic as we six bear is sure to alert the most inept of sentries."

Gord was unconcerned. "Trust me, comrades. Much was given to me by the Lords of the Balance. Part of their gift I will use to mask us from any who use magic or even their inborn senses to suss out powers of dweomered or divine sort. Even as we go I will send forth an unseen shielding. It will not cloak the magic, but its force will misdirect and mislead. Strength will become weakness, purpose will be seen as aimlessness, and the aura of opposition appear as indeterminate evil."

"I am humble," Allton said in response, and Timmil nodded agreement.

"We go by twos," Gellor suggested, wishing to have done with this uncertainty. "The sun is almost risen!"

"Yes, we must hurry," Gord agreed. "You and Greenleaf take the lead," he said to the one-eyed troubador. "I'll follow with Allton a score of paces behind. Chert and the cleric will guard the rear at the same interval."

A chill breeze wafted along the street, hurrying folk on their way. The sun would make the day warmer, but autumn dawn was not a time for leisure strolling, whether those about were rich and heavily garbed or poor and dressed in swatches and rags.

The six men issuing from the little inn did so with long strides and a brisk pace. As far as they could tell, no one paid them any heed.

* * *

When would the enemy strike next? The question bothered Gravestone far more than it should, much more than he would even admit to himself. That was because he was empowered to scry the game board but could not discern the nature of the attacking piece. "Black — he is of black," the wizard-priest muttered aloud. "Why fear, then? No demon lord can come near undetected, and anything lesser is of no consequence. . . ."

Yet he mistrusted his tools, those who served as front-line sentries and the ones who were nearer to him as well. The riffraff of swordsmen and petty spell-binders were worth hardly a thought; they were mere stopgaps, placed along the front to give Gravestone advance warning as they died. The minor daemon watchers and mercenaries all were fodder — lesser magic-wielders, stupid warriors, little monsters drawn into bondage from the netherworld. Each was but an impediment to slow the progress of he who was coming. He? Probably male, but it could be a female. . . . That was indicative of how little Gravestone knew for certain, and that thought was disquieting.

As he continued to dwell on what he did not know, was not sure of, Gravestone thought again of the black sword — the blade of evil that he had appropriated so effortlessly from the foolish sailors. He had not desired the sword for his own use, but had reasoned that if he possessed it, then it could not be used against him or his minions. He did not consider it an especially powerful weapon, but keeping it out of play would be one more bit of insurance that his master plan would succeed.

But then, mysteriously, the blade had disappeared from the place in his quarters where he had secreted it. He had cursed his error in not hiding it more carefully, but his anger at the loss was overridden by bewilderment and uncertainty. If the sword was so coveted, then why was it left unguarded aboard an ordinary sailing ship? How could it have been stolen from him without his knowledge that the act was taking place? Why could he not detect its whereabouts now, as he had been able to do prior to claiming it the first time? Doubt and foreboding nagged at him, even as he told himself that the weapon was not worth worrying about. That last observation was almost certainly true, but Gravestone was never comfortable when there was something he was not sure about.

So too was he unsure of some of his henchmen. Sigildark was a potent enough wizard, but a fool is always a fool. The haughty cleric Staphloccus, drawn from Nerull's own precincts here in Greyhawk, was likewise a wretched instrument. In a showdown, Gravestone had no doubt that the priest would sell his master for his own life . . . given the opportunity. That, the lean man thought darkly, would not be an option given to the cleric any more than to Sigildark — because behind them and the others in the front lines he would station Pazuzeus and Shabriri.

Yes . . . those two were more trustworthy, even if they were more powerful than his human assistants. They would serve well as a means of keeping Sigildark and Staphloccus from retreating or turning coat, and would be a dependable second line of defense if needed. Only at the actual moment of confrontation, however, would he bring up his lieutenants to buttress the ranks. And after the battle, the humans would have to be expunged. No trace of them could remain anywhere in the multiverse, for they would otherwise try to avenge themselves against Gravestone for his treachery.

One day soon the Great Evil would know what Gravestone had done, of course, and no doubt would approve. What Gravestone did, how he worked, and those who were eliminated in the process were matters of no real import, merely stepping stones. Let the whole of the surviving worlds bow to dark Tharizdun! Honor also to his right hand, Gravestone, binder of demons, successor to Infestix as Emperor of the Nether Realms, Loyal Servant of the Evernighted. . . .

Those thoughts made him smile, a sly and wicked leer of triumph. It was easy for Gravestone to boost his confidence, assuage his doubts. All he had to do, as he did now, was think of the glorious future in store and how the present situation would lead inexorably to that end. Chaos reigned totally in the Abyss, and the united forces of the Nine Hells and the pits of Hades roamed nearly at will elsewhere. Whatever the green-hued forces of Balance sent to threaten his own position could be nothing compared to those Gravestone had already vanquished, those denizens of the vilest depths he had bound into thralldom. Every space on the tableau was guarded, each opening or escape route covered.

"Master," a voice said hesitantly, breaking the priest-wizard's reverie. "Master, a new group of applicants awaits your pleasure." The announcement came from a tiny daemon in the form of a cockroach, one of dozens of inobtrusive sentinels Gravestone used to patrol the quarters he kept within the city.

Scowling at the interruption, Gravestone sent forth a wave of energy. It washed out and down from Gravestone's magical sanctuary to spread itself imperceptibly over the anteroom in his building in Greyhawk, where those answering his call for mercenary service were kept waiting. This was a group of six, a mixed lot. He read the general mood of the group as hatefulness verging on chaos. They were cowardly and unprincipled, but could be made to serve well. Men of few resources; a vague, diffused aura of magic — perhaps a weak spell-binder among them, plus a few ill-enchanted items. Minds of shallow sort wondering what pay and how little risk. Typical dregs. . . .

"I have no need to interview that lot," Gravestone snapped at the nervous little daemon that had interrupted him. "Go to Sigildark. Have him send Felgosh, Staphloccus, and Wilorne ahead to put our guests at ease. Then Sigildark himself should enter and enspell the group into reliable service."

"Yes, master," the nether-thing murmured, hastily withdrawing from the priest-wizard's sanctuary against material threat. Once beyond the null-place, it giggled and ground its mandibles together. "Oh, yes — yes, indeed, *master*. I will be happy to inform the wise and potent Sigildark of your wishes, *master*." It ceased its capering then and appeared in the heavily guarded chamber of the mage to whom it had been sent.

The daemon was sure that soon it would be free, for it had read in the six newcomers a demoniacal intent, it was sure. It seemed that some dweomer prevented detection of their powers by the usual means, but this did not stop Ilenz the daemon-guard from learning about them. The creature, upon intercepting the group, had skittered up one of the human's legs and used its cockroach's feelers to touch the weapon hanging from the man's belt. Actually, its extremities contacted only the scabbard — but that alone was sufficient to blast the little daemon into senselessness for a short time. It fell, stunned, and only a crack in the flags prevented it from being crushed by a heel.

The human's blade was thick with the greatest demon-force Ilenz had ever encountered. The daemon knew that Gravestone's time had come. If evil displaced evil, Ilenz cared not. He would be free.

*　*　*

The moment that Sigildark stepped into the chamber where the group stood, he knew that there was trouble afoot. Fool or no, the mage sensed the wrongness instantly. As quick as the six were, Sigildark was quicker. He spoke a single syllable and in the space of a rapid heartbeat had stepped from one dimension, through another, and was elsewhere. Unfortunately for the pale-eyed mage, his dweomer-craefting left a faint tracery behind.

"Enemies!" The warning cry came from one of the sell-swords who guarded the thick-walled old building that was Gravestone's headquarters. He had been a couple of steps behind Sigildark when the mage entered the anteroom. He didn't know why the spellbinder suddenly disappeared, but whatever the reason it probably did not bode well — and the strangers must be responsible. As the man shouted to alert his fellow guards, he pulled a small axe out of his belt and hurled it. That was his second mistake. If he had simply slipped back outside the room when Sigildark used his magic to flee, the man would have survived.

Chert darted toward the hatchet as it flew toward Timmil's head and plucked it from the air. In the blink of an eye it was returning whence it had come, and the mercenary warrior who had hurled it took its wide blade full in the chest. Leather parted, chainmail links were severed or forced apart by the terrible strength of the hillman's throwing arm. Even as the wounded man gasped and staggered back, Chert had taken up Brool, and the massive blade quickly finished the work of its little counterpart. Reinforcements arrived in time to see the fellow's headless body topple in their path.

Timmil, busy casting a divination to determine where the mage had gone, hardly noticed that sequence of events. Next to him Allton was likewise engaged in tracing the magic lingering in the room and seeing if he could identify it and where it might lead; thus, the four associates of the wizard and cleric faced Gravestone's household guards and the other three foes already present without the aid of spells for the time being. Discounting the dead man, nineteen other warriors were now quartered in the complex. Only four others were armed and on duty this morning, however, and these were the audience for the death scene of the first casualty of the melee.

Being hard-bitten men, these four went into the antechamber with ready blades. The men were confident of their own ability and the power of the three other agents of the tall, thin priest-wizard who were in the room with the half-dozen intruders. The mercenary soldiers considered the enemy as good as dead.

Considering their three fellow hirelings, it was understandable that the sell-swords felt confident. Bastro Felgosh was a mage of some power, able to wield magics of considerable strength, to summon elementals and conjure forth emanations of death to fell any who dared to oppose him. With Felgosh was the cleric of Nerull who called himself Staphloccus. Not quite as fell a spell-worker as the mage, the cleric was nevertheless able to paralyze with a word, or rot with a touch, those who angered him or threatened his master. Last, although by no measure the least, of the trio was Wilorne the assassin, called "Snapspine" or "Backbreaker" by the few close associates who knew and feared the ruthlessness of that murderer.

Felgosh, furious that he had not detected the nature of the six men before Sigildark had — and certainly fearing the consequences of that one's anger when he returned — had immediately begun calling forth his killing magic when the warning was signaled. Gellor, his eyepatch raised to expose the glittering ocular gem that empowered him with enchanted sight, opposed the dweomercraefter who was bent on bringing magical death to the six.

As if guided by some unseen divinity, Curley Greenleaf had moved so that he stood directly before Staphloccus. The dark priest raised up his vile symbol of death, that disgusting thing sacred to Nerull, and worked to lay low the druid before him. A word to fix the baldheaded fool immobile, Staphloccus thought, and then . . .

Chert, his mighty battleaxe singing as if it was a swarm of angry bees, waded into the four warriors who had rushed to attack. They cleared the headless corpse that was in their path and then came on to sink their swords into the lone man who dared stand in their way. He was a near-giant, but there were four sharp blades to make him fall hard.

When the commotion began, Wilorne immediately dived under a long table that cordoned off the left quarter of the place. Then he rolled and came up on the flank of one of the intruders. Wilorne had meant to get at the spell-caster there, but a small, quick fellow got between him and his intended victim first. Grinning humorlessly, showing a pair of canines he was proud of, the assassin attacked the small one with precise strokes calculated to slay with utmost efficiency. His hook swung out on its thin chain. It would imbed itself in flesh and wound it, or merely entangle in a garment. No matter; then the strength that had earned him his epithets would be used to jerk his adversary down, to him, or off balance at worst. Wilorne's narrow, small sword was darting into play to follow up whichever of the three possibilities eventuated.

The troubador began to shout out a lusty battle song as he waded into confrontation with the bulging-eyed dweomercraefter. Felgosh, accomplished in hand-to-hand combat such as this, was disconcerted not at all. Neither the chanted song nor the long sword that the strange opponent bore seemed threatening. Felgosh wore a magically protected garment, a robe that made him seem to be in one place when he was actually a cubit behind that place. Furthermore, the spell-binder had an enchanted collar stitched to that garment by daemon talons. The cloth seemed supple but was as hard as iron when touched by enemy attack. Last, Felgosh held in his left hand a fiend-gifted blade, a thick-bladed knife with the name "Agonizer" worked in nether-runes on the cleaverlike shank. A mere cut was sufficient to begin sending an adversary into paroxysms of pain as the evil power of the weapon sent fiery agony through the bloodstream of the wounded victim.

"Devil-serving varlet, you'll bleed scarlet!

"Call for netherforce, ride upon demon-horse, soon you'll be wailing!

"Now you feel sharp, clean steel!

"Back you'll reel!

"Down you'll kneel!

"Searching for your head, but it's gone sailing!"

That near-doggerel that Gellor voiced was a simple rhyming chant he had made up long ago to use as a war song as he fought in the thick of melee. At each point of pause in the verse he struck, the tempo giving him a rhythm for his movements and blows. Because he sung it with vigor and loud voice, it likewise lent power to those of his comrades also engaged in combat nearby.

The one-eyed troubador was only just beginning, however, and he knew that he had to be quick with the work before him. The mage with the egglike eyeballs who opposed him was near to completing a black spell that would bring terrible harm to all of them. This dweomer was from the deepest pits of the lower spheres, a magic that would draw out the very life forces of all six of them, even if it was not strong enough to slay anyone outright.

". . . varlet!" Gellor shouted, and his longsword shot out. Felgosh didn't even bother to make a move to avoid the thrust, nor did the mage attempt to parry the attack with his heavy knife. He knew that he would remain beyond the length of the steel brand, thanks to the magic of his garment. Before the foe could make a next stroke, his summoning of energy would be finished, and his enemy would be gasping and howling as the negative power sucked life from his body. . . .

"Eeeyaack!" Felgosh's scream of pain ended the casting short of its completion. Gellor had followed through with his thrust, ending it not in front of the mage but at his actual location.

I see you true, dogturd, Gellor thought even as he spat out the word "scarlet!" and freed the sword's point from the mage's thigh. At "netherforce" he parried a frantic slash from the spell-binder's knife and then slashed the fellow's chest in time to "demon-horse," but that attack only cut cloth, for the enchantment of the robe saved the mage from worse. Felgosh's eyes widened slightly, and he allowed himself a thin smile of satisfaction. The other man's point might be able to penetrate his enchanted robes, but he was still protected against slashing cuts; all he had to do was avoid any more thrusts until he could muster up another killing spell. . . .

But that was much easier said than done. Gellor's next stroke came at the same time that the bulging eyes of the man locked upon his own, and the smug expression was instantly cut short. Gellor's edge left a red line on the wizard's bare forearm, then the point again went home, and once more.

Back reeled Bastro Felgosh, although he sent darts of evil energy burning into his adversary even as he tried to escape the savage pain of the unrelenting longsword. The glittering gem fixed in the sword-wielder's eye socket followed him as the gaze of an adder follows a rabbit. At the chanting of the word "head," Gellor's sword point took the mage in the chest and pierced his black heart.

Meanwhile, Curley Greenleaf was engaged with the other evil spell-caster. The druid had expected just this sort of opponent — so, as Staphloccus went into a ritual calling that was aimed at immobilizing Greenleaf, the half-elf sent forth a spell of his own. So quickly did he finish his casting, so quietly, that the evil cleric had no idea what had occurred. Seeing the druid make the pass that brought forth some power, and discerning no result from it, Staphloccus assumed failure on the part of his foe. With a harsh note of triumph resounding in his last words, the priest of Nerull completed his own spell and paused for a moment, expectantly.

His misapprehension was quickly set straight by the staff that Greenleaf wielded. From its tip shot a long and razor-edged spearhead. Even as the spear came into being, the druid plied the weapon to good effect, cutting a crimson line from Staphloccus's belly to his chest. The cleric howled in pain and rage, now all too aware that his paralysis had failed to affect the druid. Again the priest thrust forth the miniature scythe he held, the dreaded symbol of his deity, thinking to cast his most potent spell upon Greenleaf and end the half-elf's existence then and there. Dancing nimbly to avoid the sharply tipped staff, Staphloccus brought up the unholy thing that was needed to manifest the sending he would use.

Then his eyes bulged, and he froze as if struck by his own power. The symbol of his dark god was now a bent and twisted parody. Staphloccus knew fear then, for he was powerless to bring any spell forth against the druid who had so desecrated his vile adornment.

"The Lord of Death rot you!" the priest screamed in rage as he hurled the useless symbol at Greenleaf and clawed desperately for the macelike weapon he had hidden under his cassock.

The druid didn't waste his breath in replying, only struck and struck again with the enchanted staff with its needle-pointed blade. The first follow-up blow merely served to wound the evil cleric a second time, but the next took Staphloccus in his hand and pinned it to his thigh. The priest screamed in pain then, for not only did the blade pierce flesh, but a terrible rush of vital energy shot from the metal and ran through his body. Staphloccus shuddered and collapsed as the energy burned where it met the negative force that he had drawn into himself to combat these enemies of the netherworld. In such manner Staphloccus went to his reward, screaming and pleading as he realized what his fate was to be.

In the same brief time Gellor required to slay Felgosh the spell-binder and Greenleaf needed to send Staphloccus howling to the pits of Hades, Chert dispatched the four hapless mercenaries who came against him. The first blow from the barbarian's axe shattered his foeman's sword and went on to cleave him from collarbone to stomach. The three remaining swordsmen actually hindered each other in trying to score against their towering enemy, so although one delivered a slash to Chert's forearm and another drew blood from his leg, the hillman was only scratched. With a great shout Chert jerked the battleaxe free of the dead man's body and spun sidewise in a single, blurred motion.

Brool buzzed angrily as it arced to the right, and there its great blade cut through a guardsman's steel and leather chest protector. Then it was cutting back over the same course, and the wounded man was too slow to avoid it. His head rolled to join that of his comrade, while his corpse entangled itself with the mercenary nearest to it.

The other remaining sell-sword was the most skilled of the lot. As his companion struggled to free himself from the gory corpse, the mercenary shot forth his right arm in a thrust that should have pierced the barbarian's exposed right side. Chert wore both mail and a leather jack. Although the latter seemed ordinary, it was fashioned from the hide of a terrible devil-boar that had actually killed Gord and almost done for the massive hillman as well. The stuff was supernaturally tough and resilient. The armor beneath was also enchanted with a protective dweomer. As a result, the sword's point hardly scratched the stuff, although the force of the impact bruised Chert's flesh beneath its protection and made the hillman grunt in pain.

Despite that, Chert maintained his balance and sent the great axe spinning in an upward loop that circled behind and above his head and came down low. It struck the recovering sell-sword on the hip and sent him sprawling. Just as this fellow thought himself safe and able to successfully face the hulking axeman, Chert stepped in close and jammed Brool's spiked tip into the man's solar plexus. It punched through steel and sunk into the soft stuff beyond. The guardsman's wind whooshed out and he too sat down, then sprawled, again entangled with the headless body from which he had just freed himself.

"Relax, friend!" the barbarian said, grunting the last word, for he was swinging his battleaxe out and down with all of his power as he spoke. This time there would be no need for the sell-sword to worry about being encumbered by his dead comrade. Chert's great axe bit deep, and the guard joined that headless corpse in death.

Just as the hillman sent the fellow's black soul down to the pits, the single remaining mercenary struck. "Die!" he screamed, driving his sword point with all of his might where the flesh of the barbarian's neck showed between hauberk and helmet. Instinctively, Chert jerked back, losing his grip on Brool in the process, but avoiding a hideous death from severed jugular and trachea. Cat-quick reflexes notwithstanding, the guardsman's sword lashed out, and blood showed where its edge had sliced the hillman's throat; a quarter of an inch more, and Chert would have no need of his axe ever again.

The grin of triumph on the mercenary's scarred face suddenly changed to a snarl of fear. Instead of falling, fountaining blood, dying, his opponent was suddenly upon him barehanded! Chert grabbed the sell-sword's right wrist as quickly as a falcon takes a dove from the air. With his gore-smeared right hand the hillman seized his foeman's throat and lifted him off his feet.

The fellow was tough, no doubt. Even as he felt his wrist being crushed, his windpipe being shut from the force of the iron-hard fingers there, he used his left hand to draw his dirk and strike at Chert's side. The blade failed to pierce Chert's armor, but the hillman felt the stabbing steel well enough. Even as the mercenary jerked back his weapon to strike again, the barbarian surged ahead, slamming the man's head into the stone lintel with sufficient force to shatter his skull and kill him instantly. Dropping the lifeless body, Chert pulled the dagger from his thigh where the mercenary had driven it in his last, desperate attempt to live.

"You fought well enough," the hillman grunted as he tore off a strip of cloth from the dead man's tunic and used it to staunch the flow of blood from his only serious hurt, the deep puncture just below his right hip; the others were mere scratches to such a one as he. "Then again," the hillman added, giving the corpse a kick, "cornered rats do fight pretty well. But they are still rats." With that he turned and picked up his battleaxe.

While all of this was going on, Wilorne's razor-sharp, barbed hook swished through empty air and entangled its chain around the nearby table leg. Fast as he was, the assassin couldn't let go quickly enough. The small, dark-haired man he had meant to snag with his weapon struck as fast as lightning. Up and across shot the dull-hued blade. Wilorne felt a sudden, sharp pain, and there was bright crimson on the sooty brand, more on his left arm, as he dropped the hook-and-chain's bladed end.

The assassin cursed his opponent under his breath, but he otherwise wasted no time or effort. A wounded arm was simply a reminder to be quicker, more careful. He would take special pleasure in slaying this man now. If he could snap the fellow's spine just right, the small man would be paralyzed but conscious. Then Wilorne would take his time finishing him off.

The gray-eyed young adventurer assessed his adversary carefully, circling to his right, watching for the wolf-toothed attacker to make his next move. Although Gord was armed with a longer sword, he chose not to rush in immediately. The hook-tipped chain was an assassin's weapon. His opponent would have hidden weapons, poison, all the tools of the killer's trade. Besides, there was speed and tremendous power in the slope-shouldered body of the black-garbed foe. Gord stayed back and used his sword's length to threaten and keep the fellow off balance.

There was a scream of pain from behind. Gord barely heard it and kept his attention fixed on the assassin. The fang-toothed killer must have thought that the sound had distracted Gord, however. As the last note of the cry died, his blood-washed left arm darted to his broad girdle, fingers thrust within its inner side and grasping something therein. Out it came grasping a small bladder, and as the killer pulled the thing out his fingers squeezed and a stream of dust-like spores shot forth. The cloud was a deadly one, for where the spores found warmth and moisture they sent forth tiny rhizomes and fed, growing with impossible vigor, sapping the unfortunate host, while the fungi's excreted waste ate away the living tissue, decomposing it for later use.

Because he was watching for such a move, Gord saw the hand and sidestepped to avoid what he imagined would be some poisoned missile flung from the assassin's grasp. At the same time, Gord extended his right leg and arm, thrusting his sword ahead in a lunge that took Wilorne fairly. Although the wound only pierced the fleshy part of his side, that was sufficient to cause the assassin to drop the spore-laden bladder.

Reeling now from two hurts, Wilorne was unable to take full advantage of the situation. The spores had not done their expected work of blinding his opponent, but the hasty move to avoid them followed by the lunge had put Gord into a position from which he could not easily recover. Somehow, Wilorne managed to bring his small sword into play and slash the young thief's forehead. It was only a little cut, but the blood from it would certainly run into Gord's eyes.

"Bloodied you, monkey!" It was a cry of satisfaction far out of proportion to the touch scored.

Gord did not worry about the little slash. In fact, he was glad that the wound was bleeding freely, and it was simple to use his left hand to flick the blood away before the stuff got near his eyes. "Three to one!" he countered as his lightless length of dweomered metal cut another red path along the already scarred visage that snarled menacingly at him. As he danced lightly back, Gord added, "And my blood flows freely, long-tooth. Your poison will have no bane!"

Wilorne was aware of the rest of the fight around them, and the fact that it was not going well for his fellows. Thrice wounded, with the deepest of the cuts sapping strength from him as it bled profusely, with two of his best tricks proven useless, the assassin was growing desperate. Wilorne no longer thought of the pleasure of killing his opponent slowly or using his hands to break the bones. This one was too able a fighter, too wily an adversary for anything other than death of a swift and sure nature.

To accomplish this end, the killer began a crabwise movement, meanwhile drawing forth and displaying a flat, almost rectangular throwing knife. That made the smaller man cautious and brought him into mimicking the dancelike maneuvering that the assassin had plotted. "Eat this!" Wilorne screamed, making the knife throw obvious and clumsy. Then the assassin leaped in with the narrow-tongued sword he still held, aiming its deadly point squarely at Gord's groin. Head and upper body could be ducked, twisted, turned to avoid such a stroke; but the lower abdomen was most vulnerable.

Instead of dancing sideways to avoid the throwing knife, Gord crouched. He had seen the assassin moving to the right as he released the knife. That fact, and his acrobatic ability, saved him from the real peril, Wilorne's true attack. As the assassin lunged, Gord saw the danger of the low-held sword and from his crouch shot upward. The startled killer saw only a flash as the young adventurer sprang four feet into the air, legs pulled up to avoid Wilorne's low lunge.

The assassin's attack carried him forward to a point where he saw nothing of his adversary. Because of that, Wilorne didn't have the terrible knowledge of his impending death as Gord came down on his feet and whirled with his longsword ready. The sooty blade sunk easily through the assassin's armor, sliding between ribs as it penetrated, seeking his heart, driving on to force its tip a full foot beyond his chest.

"Now, dog-tooth, you can tell the devils that greet your whimpering soul that you've met Blackheart-seeker," Gord said loudly as he placed his foot upon the dead man's back and yanked free the lightless blade. "Demon and deity both have made it for me thus. . . ." The chaotic clangor of the melee had diminished as Gord spoke. He glanced around quickly, sword ready.

What he saw was reassuring. Chert was starting to clean Brool, Greenleaf and the one-eyed troubador were watching, Timmil was still holding a particular position as he recited some litany, and Allton was likewise engaged in a magical ritual. Gellor smiled grimly at him. The half-elf shot Gord a quick grin and then went to help Chert treat his wounds.

"What about the cut on your brow, Gord?" said Gellor.

"Nothing, my friend. A scratch." Gord didn't mention the poison that the free-flowing blood had kept from the wound. "A bit of bandage will be enough."

Gellor dipped his finger in a little pot of ointment and drew a greasy line on his comrade's forehead. "This salve will do better, I think," he said. "It'll stop the bleeding and begin speedy mending, too."

"Stop coddling each other and hurry!" That admonition came from Allton. His face was strained, and there was an edge of irritation in his voice. Gord stared blankly at him and the mage added, "I am holding open a gateway for us to use — to follow that gimlet-eyed sorcerer who fled us as he gave the alarm. Come on!"

There were distant sounds of shouting and a faint pounding of feet. It was obvious that other guards were on their way. Chert tossed a pair of bodies out of the doorway and slammed the heavy slab of iron-bound bronzewood that closed it. "Help me barricade the door," he shouted, dropping its bar in the meantime. Gellor, Greenleaf and Gord sprang to comply, using the table, a big wardrobe, and the corpses as well. It took only a couple of minutes.

"I don't see a portal," the young thief said to Allton. The spell-worker nodded in the direction in which his staff was pointed, and then Gord saw a faint shimmering in the air. As he stared, the distortion took on a pale, violet hue. Timmil, the cleric, was still reciting his steady litany. The words seemed to flow into the distortion, making an amethystine current as they went. "You two combine to track our enemies," Gord said as the realization came to him.

"Very observant, champion," the high priest answered dryly. "Now, pray, pass through the gate and along the path of purple. This won't stay open forever, you know."

Because he was the nominal leader of the group, Gord drew a deep breath and went squarely through the center of the rectangle of shimmering force. With his first, long stride the chamber disappeared. Nothing behind, silver-shot walls of ebony close at either hand, an insubstantial floor of shifting lilac fading to deep plum ahead endlessly. Without breaking stride, the champion of the Balance pressed ahead into the strange, dweomered tunnel. There was an eerie oppressiveness that grew stronger as he went on. It was as if he were fighting a current to make progress, a stream that grew in force with every step he took, making progress slower and more difficult as he moved ahead.

Gord felt a hand on his back, then heard Gellor's voice. "The others are behind us in the pathway, Gord. Concentrate on the goal, and we will soon be through; otherwise . . ." The troubador let his sentence trail away.

The result was too obvious to need voicing. If they did not press on relentlessly, they could all be lost in a region somewhere between the ethereal and astral. Perhaps Allton could get them all safely out, but even that might mean losing weeks of normal time. Gord concentrated on the destination of this journey — Gravestone. Surely the mage who had escaped them would go directly to his master, and nothing better could be hoped for. The light of silvery striation and violet path was beginning to grow dim, slowly fading, but a faint speck of magenta glimmered ahead. "Keep your hand on my back, Gellor, and pass the word back to run! I'm going for it now!"

Chapter 9

A DISSONANT CHIMING filled the black-walled room. Despite the monstrous size of the place, the sound was audible everywhere within it, no softer in the farthest corner than in the center, where a number of flying bridges led upward to a platform that was suspended there.

As the nasty sound died away to a tooth-aching whine, a deep violet light suddenly washed over the floating disc in the middle of the vast chamber, its illumination making plain the whole extent of the massive platform that was a bowshot across and covered with dark, jumbled shapes. Into the private realm of the priest-wizard Gravestone suddenly came a wildly gesturing figure.

"Sigildark!"

The wizard of evil had brought himself into the space that was the center of the floating disc, that portion that his lord and master held sacrosanct. "I implore your forgiveness, Great One," he stammered to Gravestone, his arms still flailing in an uncontrolled fashion. "There are enemies in your tow—"

"Be still!" The last word thundered from the tall, gaunt man. It jerked Sigildark into instant immobility. "Open your mind now, and I will see for myself what has sent you into such a state." So saying, the priest-wizard fixed his gaze on Sigildark and shot forth a bolt of tremendous mental energy, a magically enhanced probe that instantly laid bare the compliant mage's mind.

What Gravestone saw inside there made him stand upright with a snarl. In a flash, he had seen everything that the wizard had perceived in his brief exposure to the six combatants. Gravestone could interpret the information only slightly better than his lackey, but that was more than enough to send surges of burning rage and chilly fear through his tall body. Here indeed were foes of unguessable strength. No true auras could be read, but the glow of energy, the traceries of purpose that were evident, told more than enough.

"What . . . ? Who are—"

"Go below instantly," Gravestone commanded, cutting the query off without response. "Immediately, or else I will blast you where you stand!"

That was sufficient to send Sigildark scurrying toward the nearest edge of the suspended space he was upon. Being a dweomercraefter, he had no need of stairs, of course. A leap, a fall that would gradually slow to a gentle float downward, and he would be one hundred feet below on the floor in no time. As he was about to clamber over the low parapet that circumscribed the floating island of stonelike matter, Gravestone's voice hissed in his ear. "Summon Krung. Have him by your side when you confront those who will dare intrude."

The wizard gritted his teeth and stepped into space. He had no qualm about the distance to the hard floor below. It was Gravestone's words that made him fearful. The priest-mage had just told him he must face the enemies he had fled. Somehow, Sigildark knew that they were a test that he could not endure, and the thought of having the netherfiend, Krung, to help fight them was scant encouragement.

"Why not some greater one?" Sigildark thought, hoping that his master would discern the thought and respond. The black mage knew better than to form the names Pazuzeus and Shabriri in his mind, but he did allow the names of several of the more powerful daemons he had met in this place to float near the surface of his brain. There was no reply, though, and his feet touched the blackish purple of the floor before he could bring up more mental suggestions to send to Gravestone. Thinking better of it anyway, Sigildark used his feet to carry him at a near trot toward the summoning place, a tiered pit beneath the center of the platform above.

His hands trembled as he made the preparations and began the passes that would bring Krung from his own disgusting place to this non-plane that was Gravestone's little domain. He drew a deep breath and calmed himself. After all, the netherfiend was a very puissant being; besides, the priest-wizard might be mistaken. Even the most potent of foes would have a difficult time finding this place. Setting even those thoughts aside, Sigildark began his summoning.

High above, Gravestone stopped scanning the man's mind, sneering. The fool didn't even realize that he had laid down a track for the enemy to follow. All the better. It would take some time to bring Pazuzeus and Shabriri, and in the meantime Sigildark and Krung would "entertain" the unwanted visitors. Perhaps the work thereafter would be minimal . . . possible, but doubtful!

Gravestone used a rodlike wand to scribe a glowing form, a thing of impossible lines and curves, chanting equally impossible words as he worked.

As the burning shapes grew and the stream of sound became a nonstop rush of arcane syllables, Gravestone allowed one corner of his evil brain to ponder events. He felt deep, malign satisfaction as he worked, for the priest-wizard understood that he had been presented with the greatest opportunity ever, something he had not dared to hope would occur again. Into his hands was coming the one who could only be the champion that stood between the coming of Tharizdun and the multiverse. The demons he was bringing would be for those who accompanied the one. He, Gravestone, would personally account for the would-be champion. Who then could deny him his rightful place as Tharizdun's viceroy and chief agent when the Greatest of Evil arrived in his dark and malign majesty? None was the answer — not even Tharizdun himself!

* * *

The dark violet spot grew as large as a postern gate, and with a final surge Gord pushed through it. He was suddenly engulfed in darkness, but in a second he began to perceive the weird "light" of visual sense operating in the spectrum above violet and at the same time below red. This special sight had been initially granted to the young adventurer by the strange powers of the green, cat's-eye ring he wore. Now, however, he knew that his own nerves picked up the emanations of infrared and ultraviolet radiation without reliance on the ring's dweomer.

In front of him, revealed starkly in the weird combination of light waves Gord perceived, was the spell-binder who had cried the warning and fled. The fellow's face was a mask of shock and fear at Gord's sudden appearance. That was understandable, for the young champion had his black longsword in hand and death in his eyes as he forced his way free of the interplanar portal.

"Geeyah!" Sigildark voiced the sound involuntarily as his startled nervous system took over. At the same instant he literally jumped backward, thus avoiding the long thrust that the suddenly appearing enemy attempted.

"No use, you fu—" Gord shouted as he sprang to the attack.

"Hee, hee, heeee!" piped the terrible soprano voice of the netherfiend Krung as the creature struck Gord from behind with a ham-sized, horny fist with enough power behind it to fell a bull.

It was the launching of his attack that saved Gord from having his skull caved in or neck broken. The netherfiend's blow caught him as he was moving away from it. Thus, the force of the terrible fist spent much of its power in driving the young thief ahead. He fell sprawling, face abraded by the rough material that floored the place, stunned and unmoving.

"Yumm," Krung said as it saw the smear of blood on the floor. The misshapen form bent, its neck extending obscenely, tongue rasping over the lithic slabs as the thing bent to lap the blood and then devour the still, human body. The tableau was sufficiently amusing to cause Sigildark to devote his attention to it, for the evil mage had an insatiable desire to see just how the netherfiend would consume the fallen man.

"Sluuslupp," went Krung's foot-long tongue as it writhed out and back. It was just being extruded again when the creature jerked back, head withdrawing, mouth agape, muscles bunching. "Eee . . . yeiii!" The high-pitched scream nearly deafened Sigildark.

"I thought that might attract your attention," Gellor said with steely satisfaction as he withdrew his sword from the fiend's backside. Krung was spinning, giving voice to a whining snarl, talons flashing, fangs bared. The bard moved counter to the spin, while Curley Greenleaf, just behind him, brought his magical spear into play. Behind them, Chert had just emerged from the gateway, and Timmil's head was seemingly floating disembodied in the air as he started to come through. Allton was but seconds from also arriving. "Now, Curley!" Gellor shouted as he struck at a flailing arm from his crouch.

The druid uttered the magical word that brought forth the slender spearhead from his staff as he drove the thick pole toward the netherfiend's head. Greenleaf was aiming for the red-rimmed, pain-and-rage-filled eyes of the monster. One of its clawed hands, a member as broad as a plank and tipped with iron-hard talons inches long, interposed. Krung saw the staff-butt and thought to snap it like a twig. Instead, the enchanted steel that shot from it pierced the monster's flesh as if it was leather under a cobbler's knife.

"Yaahg!" This time the netherfiend's cry was softer, for its brain was overloaded with pain. Gellor's sword had sliced deep, hacking its other arm so that it was open to the bone. The fiend was wounded terribly. Both arms and its intestines were injured. These humans were not the soft and easy prey Krung was accustomed to. There was but one answer: flee! In a short time, natural processes would begin to heal his hurts, the awful pains would recede, and then Krung would return, but with certain things of power . . . and with help of other sort as well.

Now, however, the netherfiend knew that it must make the dirty human mage who had summoned it to this torture release it to return to the pits. Krung tore its hand free of the spear point, leaped sideways, and then bounded in a shambling gait to where Sigildark was crouched over the still form of the stunned young adventurer.

"Loose my binding now, man!" the shrill voice of the daemon-thing piped. "Quickly — else I'll tear out your eyes!" To emphasize the threat, Krung reached for Sigildark's face with its ichor-dripping left hand that bore the puncture from Greenleaf's staff-spear. Of course, Krung would not have harmed the mage — at least not until after he had freed the netherfiend from bondage of service there in Gravestone's null-space. Pain and fear made the fiend careless, however, and Krung's talons raked Sigildark's cheek even as the spell-binder shrank back from the threat.

The slaying of the helpless Gord forgotten, Sigildark reacted as anyone of like malice would. "Rot you, dog's turd!" the sorcerer snarled, thinking that surely the netherfiend had gone totally out of control. "Here's how you'll be freed!" And so saying, Sigildark shot forth a series of five glowing darts of burning force from his extended hand. These missiles of fell energy struck Krung squarely upon its broad, deformed chest and caused the creature to jerk upright and dance and howl in awful agony.

Sigildark was both amazed and pleased. He had not expected quite so profound a reaction to his magic, for the attack had been of only moderate power against so powerful a denizen of the netherworld. Often, in fact, such dweomers as he had employed were of no use at all, for the aural shield of nether-things negated many such assaults. Krung gyrated, and in so doing showed Sigildark the true reason for its incredible reaction. Even as the spell-caster had struck the netherfiend with his evoked energy bolts, one of the invaders had simultaneously fallen upon the creature from the rear. Krung's back was laid open to the black-boned spine.

It took only an instant for Sigildark to assess the situation. There were two spell-workers ignoring the melee. Both were seeking a means of ascending to where Gravestone lurked. Good! That one should have to bear his share of the peril, Sigildark thought. Of the remainder, one was knocked senseless, and three others now confronted the black-hearted mage. The one with a glittering, false eye was about to strike Krung again. That one had been responsible for the netherfiend's ghastly back wound. Close to him, a rotund fellow of half-elven sort was jabbing with a narrow-bladed spear; thus, both were likely to be engaged in combating the fiend for a bit of time yet.

That left only one opponent for Sigildark. He was a tall and brawny warrior armed with a massive battle-axe. No doubt a barbarian of some sort — one long on muscle and short on brains, but dangerous as a wild animal!

"Truce, comrade!" the wizard shouted to the advancing axeman. "The daemon is our mutual enemy." The statements were loaded with a heavy dweomer of persuasiveness. Let the fool but join the attack upon the netherfiend, and he, Sigildark, would strike the lot with such a casting as would fry them all and send them to their doom!

Chert was brought up abruptly by the call. He shook his head, hesitated a split-second, then replied, "Aye, I ken your meaning, mage!" Without further ado, the giant hefted his axe and fell upon the embattled Krung, Brool buzzing and then striking home with a meaty thud as punctuation to its drone.

Left unmolested, Sigildark fairly crooned in glee as he began conjuring the spell that would strike his foes dead with an awful blast of fire and force. The bard engaged against the daemon was singing some sort of magical verse, and the pale dweomer was causing Krung to be hacked to bits. Song, spell, combat — none of that disturbed Sigildark in his own casting. A parchment "hand" filled with the material of the spell he was working flew into the air as he gestured. Only a few more syllables now, and the thing would be done.

Many magicians could bring forth fireballs, but Sigildark's evil spell wrought a clinging, purplish flame coupled with a gaseous explosion that was of far greater bane to those within its fell radius. Even opponents as powerful, as mightily protected by enchantments and magical equipage, as the three locked in melee with Krung would have no chance to survive the thunderfire he was about to bring down upon them. Krung would be slain too, of course, but that was of no import.

After the thunderfire had struck, he would take time for one quick slash across the throat of the one the netherfiend had stunned, and then Sigildark would creep up behind the pair of dolts who sought their demise at Gravestone's hand. One corner of the dark wizard's mind wondered about the possibility of those two managing to kill the priest-wizard. Most unlikely. Another corner of Sigildark's mind nagged him about something else, but the spell was too close to completion, so the mage simply shoved the worry-

197

ing voice back. It would have been better for him to have not done so.

"Death!" Gord shouted, a second before he plied both his longsword and his terrible dagger against the spell-caster's unsuspecting back. Normally, the young thief would have struck silently. But in order to disrupt the magic that Sigildark was in the midst of working, in order to do his utmost to prevent the dweomer from striking his three friends, Gord cried aloud just as he attacked.

The great shout did break Sigildark's concentration, but the brief warning it gave him did not enable the evil wizard to avoid being struck by the enchanted blades thrust into him. The sooty length of Blackheartseeker failed to find Sigildark's wicked heart, however. It glanced off a rib and cut a fiery track along the dweomercraefter's side instead. The long dagger did much better, sinking well into his lower back.

"Ahhh! No!" The screech came unbidden from his lips, as the dark wizard felt pain far worse than the wrenching of his mind as the casting was broken uncompleted. He tried to turn, to use his magic against the one who had so sorely harmed him. Then that part of Sigildark's brain that had been trying to warn him burst forth into his consciousness: "Fool, fool, fool!" The prone man had not been where he should have been when the thunderfire calling began! These thoughts were a most unfortunate distraction for the mage. Sigildark should have been fleeing for his life.

Gord released his hold on the imbedded dagger in order to use both hands to grip the longsword. With the double grasp, he brought the blade up and down so quickly that he caught the mage in half-turn. Charm, spell, amulet, enchantment, talisman — none of the protections worn, carried, or placed upon his person were proof against that attack.

The dull ebon of the sword's blade scythed to cut through cloak and robe and girdle. It cut skin and flesh and innards, too. Sigildark grabbed at his stomach, pushing back the sausagelike things that tried to slide forth through the awful wound. Standing thus, partially bent and unaware of all else, Gord struck and delivered the coup de grace to the malign spell-binder, cleaving his head from his body, and Sigildark's rotten soul went from him that instant. Although Gord didn't know it, Infestix did soon enough, and even that one quailed despite his glee at having such a prize.

There was a hooting, a whining behind him, so Gord brought his sword up and spun, ready to defend himself. He was in time to witness the demise of Krung, albeit only the death of the netherfiend's material form used to convey the monster on this plane. As if by whim alone, the young champion who opposed Tharizdun and all his vile servitors came to stand beside the netherfiend as it slowly expired. The thing seemed to recognize Gord. It spat a weak glob of disgusting spittle and stuck out its obscene tongue.

"I tasted your blood, little man," Krung rasped in a high pitch, the voice hardly strong enough to carry now. "It was as good as that of your friends aboard *Silver Seeker* . . . but not their eyeballs!" And with that Krung trailed off with a hideous babbling laugh in the highest register. It was similar to the cry of a hyena, but more hideous, insane. "I'll be back one day for you," the fiend added with a gasp.

"Will you, now?" Gord asked, bringing the tip of Blackheartseeker out to touch the monster's hideous snout.

As if suddenly energized, the dying netherfiend found strength to draw back from the sword, eyes gleaming, fearful. "No, Masterful One, I lied. Forgive me, please! I will be yours to command — I will do anything!"

"Don't you like to be near the weapon of a 'Masterful One'?"

"It is too wonderful to bear," Krung responded. Meanwhile it was slowly bringing its left hand to a place where it could tear out its own throat and finish its quasi-death here.

Gord saw the motion and struck. Krung's arm, severed at the elbow, flopped and writhed with clenching fingers before the fiend's eyes. "And no need to worry, vile thing! Let your fear be sure and certain. I know what you are, what you did, who you serve. Better still, for me, netherfiend, I know what this blade will do to you!"

Krung's eyes bulged and its mouth gaped to make some utterance, but Blackheartseeker struck too quickly. The dull black of its blade glowed with a purplish sheen for an instant as it drew into itself the force that was Krung; then the sword was dead ebon again.

"Gods!" Chert spat, seeing the very form of the monstrous horror from the pits shrink and wither before his gaze. The sword's power had drained the vital forces from the netherfiend, leaving a withered husk that a mere touch turned into dry dust. "Its soul?" he asked shakily, looking at Gord with uncertainty.

"Annihilated," Gord replied emotionlessly. "It is as if it . . . Krung . . . that's what it called itself, you know . . . never existed. That thing has no being anywhere now — here, the pits, or in the endless spheres of probability. It is nothing!" The latter was uttered with vehemence, for the young thief recalled his slain friends Barrel, Dohojar, and the rest as he spoke. Gord had now had satisfaction upon the slave involved in the matter. Now he wanted the master, Gravestone. Turning to look at Gellor, Gord asked, "Where are Timmil and Allton?"

Chert replied, wiping sweat from his brow as he spoke, for he had fought against the netherfiend fiercely and bore a number of bruises and wounds to prove it. "The mage told me they were going above," the hillman rumbled, "to seek out the hand of Nerull who has been the one behind all this."

All four sets of eyes turned to look at the great disc that loomed high above their heads. Gellor's enchanted eye, though, saw more than even the young champion's supernatural vision could discern. "That place fairly dances with evil and throbs with the power of the magical traps and defenses which protect it — and the one whose lair it is!"

"I see neither the priest nor Allton," Greenleaf interjected. "They too must have seen the dangers."

"They should have bided until we had done with those two," Gord said flatly, glancing at what remained of Krung and the decapitated body of Sigildark. "Now our force is divided, and the enemy has a prime opportunity to deal with us piecemeal. Shit! How do we hasten above to join them?"

Chert looked blank, and the druid was silent, pondering. Gellor, however, spoke up again. "My sight of things shows that our companions must have ventured up that spiral there," he told Gord, pointing to a faintly visible staircase about a hundred paces distant. Its darkly luminous steps appeared to twist upward as it hung on thin air. "The aura I see would indicate that the dweomer and malign wardings there have been neutralized to some extent. Can you manage what remains, Curley?"

Greenleaf looked uncertain, but Gord interjected at this point. "I have sufficient imbued energy to resist an accursed spell which might lie in wait for us along the path, my friends. Come on; follow closely. We must find Timmil and Allton before they come to grief!"

The four made a grim picture as they headed for the helix of stone slabs that was their chosen means to ascend to the suspended platform above. Bristling with magical weaponry and enchantments to enhance their innate abilities, few evil opponents, indeed, would readily step forth to confront them. Although already somewhat bloodied by the foes that had tried to stand in their way, these four brave ones seemed quite unaware of their wounds, undaunted by what terrible enemies still lay ahead.

"Were we but in the natural world," Greenleaf said by way of apology to his young friend, "I would be of more service with my castings, Gord — Gellor, too, I think," he added, giving a sideways glance at the troubador.

"True, Curley," Gellor confirmed. "Our muscular giant there would find it more to his taste, too!"

Chert laughed softly and swung Brool to make the great axe sing. "I like the clean air and open land, true; but Brool has no objection to slaying demons or devils wherever they are found." The big hillman laughed again.

Setting foot on the first step, Gord signaled the other three to silence. Without a further word, they ascended the weird stairway.

Chapter 10

IT WAS NIGHT. Worse: dark as a tomb. No, worse than that: the ultimate lightlessness. "I am blinded," Gord announced matter-of-factly, keeping the apprehension he felt from showing in his tone.

Chert jostled him from behind. "I too, comrade," he rumbled.

"Perhaps I can cast a spell to bring us some illumination," Greenleaf ventured.

"Hold!" The command from Gellor stopped everyone in mid-step. "I can see with the aid of my dweomered ocular," he told his companions. "We stand on a little table atop a pinnacle which vanishes in the distance below. Make no move!"

"Pinnacle?" Gord asked uncertainly.

"Aye. Around is a void which seems bottomless. Far, far below I see a dim, black vortex. At the hazard of supposition, that could well be an opening to the anti-plane," the bard told them, referring to the total negative, that place where they would be annihilated in an instant.

"You are right, Gellor. My dark sword tingles in my grasp as it brings such force to itself. That, at least, is a boon to us."

"Turd-snacking wizard's trap!" Chert grated angrily, hating the absolute powerlessness he felt in his blind state. "At least whatever comes hereafter will be a lesser challenge."

Greenleaf spoke agreement to that, but then added, "Are we trapped with no place to go — ahead or back?"

"Behind there is nothing," Gellor informed them all. "But I see another transparent pinnacle ahead. It is about ten feet distant and almost a man's height higher than the place we stand upon now."

"I can shift-shape," Gord volunteered, "and make so small a leap with ease."

"Not so fast, my young friend," Gellor said, grabbing Gord by his sinewy shoulder. "The place where you must land upon is small and smooth . . . probably slippery. It is I who must try—"

"I think not," Gord said with a snap of his fingers. "I have a rope which will solve our dilemma." He slipped a coil of what appeared to be braided horsehair from inside his girdle. "This can be made into a lariat and used to encircle the opposite pinnacle."

"Yes, I think so. Let me try." Gellor quickly fashioned a running noose and after several misses managed to loop it around the crystalline finger. "There, I've got it! What now?"

"Place the line in my hand," Gord told the bard and thrust out his left hand in Gellor's direction. When the rope was in his palm, Gord closed his hand and spoke softly, his words strange and alien. The braided cord seemed to come alive, and as would a python, its loop moved and visibly constricted, almost cutting into the transparent stuff it was encircling.

"Now, Gellor, take this piton and see if it won't hold here." As he said that, Gord sat on the small stone atop their perch and drew out his magical dagger. Straining, he forced the dweomered metal point into the rock, making a hole that was narrow but several inches deep. The troubador took up the steel spike and placed its tip into the opening, pounding with the pommel of his own dagger to drive it down as far as possible.

Gord felt, found the piton's eye, and threaded the rope through the opening, again speaking to the enchanted line as he worked. The rope drew itself into a twisting series of wrappings and knots, and then was stretched taut from one pinnacle to the other.

In a moment the young champion of Balance was again standing, and then he had his feet off the stone table and upon the line. "I'll walk," he said cheerfully. "The rest of you can swing across like apes!" He laughed and walked boldly along the horsehair strand as if it were a broad pathway. The rope barely sagged, and Gord had no difficulty in attaining the far point. There he paused as his toe encountered the crystalline finger, and with his hands he explored the area before stepping onto it. "It is smooth and slick, just as you thought, Gellor. Come ahead, now, and I'll assist arrivals," Gord called, moving carefully onto the rectangular surface that was about the size of a monk's cot.

Gellor assisted first Chert, then the plump druid to a position where each could swing out and move hand-over-hand the ten feet that separated the two places. Despite the dangers of the bottomless void and the slippery landing spot, both adventurers managed the challenge quickly and without mishap. Gellor then crossed, and when Chert felt his hand the barbarian pulled him up as an adult lifts an infant, just as he had assisted Greenleaf. Gord spoke to the rope again, and soon the whole length of it was tightly coiled and hidden within his broad belt once more. The four then turned slowly, guided by the bard, wondering what would be next. . . . And suddenly they could see again!

The instant return of sight made them all dizzy, even Gellor, for the clash of normal vision and enchanted seeing through his gem-eye was disconcerting. The four reeled but managed to maintain their footing. Ahead was nothing more than what appeared to be another ordinary, if magically suspended, stairstep spiraling upward. "No hesitation — onward!" Gord said, and took the next stride quickly with the others just behind.

Within the space of a couple of steps, no longer were they treading on a stone stair slab. The quartet was in the midst of a dense, junglelike thicket. They stood in a tiny clearing amid a tangle of thorns, briars, knife-edged vines, nail-grass, and spike-bushes. Everywhere were needles, hooks, barbs, and razorsharp edges. "Perhaps this is an illusion," Chert said hopefully. The vegetation moved, and as it did so metallic glitterings reflected from thorns and leaves.

"No illusion," Greenleaf said with assurance. "I hate to contradict you, hillman, but this is actual foliage, growth both evil and filled with sorcerous vitality. Now, though, I just might be of some real use!" With that, the druid began his spellworking, calling upon nature and the elements, living things and their departed essences, too, in the process. Grudgingly, and with sinister rustlings and a malign susurration making a constant undertone, creepers crept back, vines untangled and withdrew, grass parted, branches bent.

A narrow, serpentine path formed. "Move along quickly!" Curley said. "I'm not convinced I can hold the way open for long." The strain in his voice was sufficient impetus to cause them to do as he said. Neither the finest enchanted armor nor the most puissant of magical protections could keep anyone safe from the hundreds of sharp and piercing things here. Two twists, ten long strides, and they came to a flat-topped boulder upthrust from the prickling growth that hedged them in.

"Link arms, comrades," Gord said. "Who knows what will befall us next?"

As they climbed atop the boulder, they saw before them a world of old red, a rust-hued plane of metal with no beginning and no end. Hung from the lowering sky of vivid maroon were monstrous iron bells, great cylinders of stained metal suspended no more than a dozen yards above their heads. Almost immediately the bells began to sway in different directions. Although they were hung on nothingness, although there were no ropes to control their movements, the rusted bells swung slowly but in ever-broadening arcs.

"Run like hellbats!" Chert shouted. "Those gods-damned clappers will soon set up such a din as to deafen us — drive us into madness!" The barbarian was right. He had also seen something that none of his friends had noticed. Away in the distance was a bell of more titanic proportions than the rest, and its metal was of greenish color, the verdigris typical of corroded bronze. "There!" was all he said, and he pointed as he shouted it. Then Chert sprang ahead and ran.

Quick as they were to pound along after him, Gord, Gellor, and Curley were immediately a dozen strides behind. The bells began to sound at that instant. Like massive iron maces, their clappers worked, moving in a motion opposite the swaying of the monstrous cylinders that contained them. The world seemed to shake and reverberate as the titanic throats of rusted metal sent forth their bellowing sounds.

"Badongggg, balonggg, kahronggg!" Even these initial noises, ringing not full-toned from a forceful striking of clapper on bell, were sufficient to shake the adventurers deep in their chests and make their heads swim. The resonance was dreadful, the noise growing. There was no hope of speech, no means to communicate unless they stopped to signal to each other. Stopping would mean losing time, and that could prove fatal if they were thereby exposed to the reverberations for too long.

"GAHDONGG! BRRONGG! DOOONGG!!" The bells were now tilting wildly, the strikers hammering the rusted metal with force sufficient to crush anything except metal like themselves as they hit. The noise was so terrific as to nearly drive the four down to their knees. Gord could have sprinted past, leaving his slower comrades behind. Instead, he kept pace with Greenleaf, helping the rotund half-elf along as they ran.

The triple-sized bronze bell was now only a few yards away, and Chert was visible standing under it. Gord was seeing double, his head ached, and his knees were weak. He wanted to stop and scream over and over, keeping time with the iron tolling of the maddening things that sounded overhead. But he fought off the urge, gritted his teeth, and pulled Curley Greenleaf along faster.

Suddenly they were in an island of silence, of bliss. Chert's mouth was moving, but no sounds were coming out. Gord opened his own mouth to tell the big hillman so; then he realized that he could barely hear himself speak, even though the booming clangor of the monstrous bells wasn't penetrating this space under the bronze one.

Directly under the center of the green-hued cylinder was a platform suspended in air — apparently another of the steps that they had to ascend. Gellor moved toward it, but Gord pulled the troubador back. "Wait," he signaled, and did the same twice more to show both Chert and the druid that it applied to them as well. Then the young adventurer pointed to his ears, allowed his tongue to droop out of his mouth in a symbol of fatigue, and visibly relaxed, slump-shouldered. With that, he sat down beneath the bronze bell, took out his skin of wine, and grabbed meat, cheese and biscuits from his pouch. Nodding and looking relieved, the other three seated themselves as well. They ate and then stretched out and rested briefly.

Gord came out of a doze. His eyes fell upon the cloud of bells beyond. They were motionless. "The ringing has stopped," he said absently aloud.

"So it has," Curley said in reply. Then he stretched and tried to make himself a little more comfortable on the iron floor.

"I heard you speak!" The exclamation was from Chert.

"The deafness was only temporary, then, as I thought," the one-eyed bard observed softly. "Time to press on again, Gord?"

"Yes. Who can tell how long we've been here? Not long, I think, but . . ."

The four managed to step in unison onto the next stair. A sea of roaring flame shot up around them. Again it was the druid who solved the dilemma. It took but a brief time for Greenleaf to summon forth a monumentally great fire elemental from the inferno around them. Such a creature as that was quite usual for the druid, although in all of his scores of years Curley had never seen one so large as that which appeared at his conjuration now. The druid and the elemental exchanged pleasantries. Then Curley asked, "Can you transport us through this fiery place?"

"No!" came the crackling basso of the fire elemental's reply. That would have been the end of it, except for the special rapport that existed between the nature priest and the denizens of the elemental spheres. "Yet you can pass by yourselves safely enough, druid."

"How so?" Greenleaf asked, peering at the leaping tongues of fire.

"I will make a cool path," the elemental responded. "Where would you go?"

"There!" said Gord, gesturing toward a spot where pale smoke streamed upward. It was the only place of its kind to be seen in the inferno. "That is the place we must attain!"

Curley nodded and looked at the elemental. The towering creature said and did nothing. "Oh, yes, of course, I was the one who summoned you, wasn't I?" the druid asked rhetorically. He was truly flustered by the immensity of the being of fire. "We would pass from here to the smoke yonder, majestic one," Greenleaf said loudly to the elemental. "Please assist me!"

"It is done!" the fire elemental boomed. Then it turned and swept away toward the column of smoke. Behind it was a path of cinders, for where it went the creature's raging heat and flame consumed the very fires that surrounded it.

"Not too close, now," Curley warned as he stepped

off the safety of the rectangle they had been upon and
followed the elemental. He hunched and hurried, for
searing curtains of flame were on either hand and the
cinders beneath were very hot. The others followed
with alacrity, and although they sweated and felt
flushed, they came to no harm. The elemental ahead
circled the place where the smoke arose, waved a
cherry-red, flame-tongued member, and then sank
into nothingness again amid the flames. Behind them
the fires were creeping onto the pathway, so the four
sprinted to where the column of gray smoke shot
upward. There was no fire generating it, so they took
their chances and plunged into the stuff.

Their coughing became choking and painful rasping almost at once. Passing from the inferno of flame,
the four had entered a place of insubstantial vapors
and rolling fogs. Sickly pastel hues of mist and cloud;
yellow, green, brownish, hideous blue. "Gas!" Gellor
managed to cough the warning. "Poison!"

It was again the druid who saved them. With a few
quick passes and a litany of chanting, Greenleaf
managed to complete a spell despite the lung-wrack-
ing, skin-burning vapors that crawled and swirled
around the four. In the moment of completion, a curtain of flames shot up. Its hot flames encircled them,
burning away the toxic clouds near, creating a growing updraft that cleared the area it inscribed. "Which
direction shall I move it?" Curley asked as the wall of
glowing fire did its work and normal speech was
again possible.

Gord signaled to Chert and, with a spring, landed
atop the great shoulders of the tall hillman. Chert
then held his hands so Gord could place the sole of
each boot in one of his large palms. Without seeming
effort, Chert raised his arms to extend fully above his

head. The young thief and gymnast now balanced with his head no less than thirteen feet above the ground Chert stood on. "I see pure white there," Gord called, pointing to indicate the direction desired. "All other places are naught but colored vapors of ghastly hues. I think the white is our egress!"

Gellor marked the direction, then Gord was down and likewise pointing.

The druid began to move, causing the fiery curtain that surrounded them to progress with him. It was slow traveling, for the four had to carefully maintain the line that would take them to the small place where they could escape the terrible poisons of this trap. By staying in line, one as near the rear, two in the middle, and one as far ahead as the heat of the fire allowed, the distance was covered. The sheet of flames washed over another of the big rectangles that were the manifestations of the steps leading to the suspended platform that was the lair of their enemy, Gravestone.

"There," said Gellor, who was then in the lead. "On to the next welcome!"

"How many more, I wonder?" Greenleaf grumbled as he jumped onto the surface where his companions were standing. The poison gases and the dancing wall of fire vanished at that instant.

The biting wind of this next environment nearly knocked them off their feet. The ground was solid ice. Tiny particles of the frozen stuff filled the air as well. The howling wind whipped them laterally across the frozen, limitless expanse of the place. The ice crystals stung where they touched flesh, imbedded themselves in any fold or crevice where the wind drove them. Soon the four adventurers would be encased in the stuff, icemen frozen into cold death. The temperature was so low that it hurt them to open their eyes. Here was a trap most cunning and deadly. They had to move to stay warm, to locate the step that was their only escape from icy death. Yet the sheet ice made movement slow and perilous, the jagged hunks of upthrust ice turning the place into a maze.

Shivering from cold, their teeth chattering, they searched with their aching eyes, looking in ever-expanding circles for some clue to the portal of escape. "Shall I use more of my power to conjure fire?" Curley Greenleaf chattered. "We could warm ourselves a bit, then spread out to search for the hidden stairstep."

Chert instantly assented to the suggestion, and Gellor was uncertain, but Gord vetoed it. "Only as a last resort should more of your spells be used, Curley. We won't separate in any event! We must stay within sight of one another, and we should be moving now, too." The words were reasonable, Gord's assessment accurate and requiring no further explanation. His comrades nodded, and the four returned to scanning, peering.

"Any clue?" Gord shouted over the shrieking gale.

That question drew only negative responses — and then another shout blared forth: Gellor had slipped and fallen on the iron-hard ice. Curley thought the bard's cry was one of pain and distress, and in a flash the druid was hastening to the fellow's side by making skating movements with his frozen-stiff boots, using the staff's spearhead to balance and pole in the process. "How badly are you hurt?" he called.

"Hurt? Hurt?" The bard was actually laughing, so hard that tears were forming . . . and freezing to his cheeks! "It is ironic!" Gellor bellowed over the wind. "Come here! Look!" He pointed to a silver-white sheathed fang of old, black ice that was nearby.

213

"My fall has saved us, dear friends," the troubador went on — in a lower tone now, for the others were all clustered near. "See that darker ebon in the hummock?" Not one of the three could spot what Gellor was directing their attention to. He laughed again, then said, "No wonder, I suppose. Even though it was within a few feet of our entry point, the combination of ice and dweomercraeft cloaked it from us completely. Only from the edge can I discern the thing, even with my enchanted orb! The stair is imbedded there, hidden in the icy mound before you!"

Chert needed no further encouragement. He swung Brool with vigor unusual even for that hulking barbarian. Shoulder muscles rippling, arms corded as he worked, Chert chopped with the battleaxe. The massive blade sent ice flying in chunks, slivers, and a spray of finer stuff was instantly borne away in the wind. There was no room for the others, for the axe described mighty arcs as the brawny hillman sent it biting into the ice-fang time after time in a furious frenzy.

In a handful of minutes the little mountain of frozen water was a waist-high plateau. Chert ceased his titanic hewing then, and Gord and the bard relieved him, doing the finer work of clearing the metallic rectangle with their swords first, then daggers for the inch or two that remained atop the thing's surface.

"Done," the champion said with a last chiseling of the long dagger he plied against the ice. "Six tests have we passed. This might be the stair which brings us to the enemy!"

"Hey," Chert said unbelievingly, "I saw about a hundred steps when we first started on this stupid exercise. What makes you think that there aren't pretty near that many left for us to go!" The query was accusative in tone. Despite the severe cold, the words sent a chill through the other three.

Seeing the effect on his comrades, Gord shook off his own foreboding and managed a grin. "One more or one hundred — will it matter? We will win through the rest, just as we've managed the traps behind. There's no choice, comrades. Either we succeed, or we die . . . and if we die, so does all hope everywhere." That bolstered them, and even the young adventurer felt heartened by his own words. They reminded Gord that this hunt was for more than personal revenge. Gravestone was the one responsible for the deaths of his father and mother, for the murder of his ship's crew, and the killing of his friends Dohojar and Barrel. Only the archdaemon, Infestix, was more culpable than the vile priest-wizard.

Still, there was far more at stake. Gravestone was a very powerful agent of evil, one of the greatest working for the awakening of Tharizdun. It would be a double blow then, the satisfaction of personal scores settled being secondary to the lessening of the ability of the nethersphere to achieve its malicious ends.

"Come on, Gord! We'll freeze here soon. What's wrong?"

He realized he had been standing, lost in thought. "Sorry, Chert. I was considering strategy, more or less. You're right, though. I can't stop for that sort of thing now. Tarrying is death. Let's climb up and see what's in store for us next." And he again shot his friends his boyish grin.

Although his eyes did not laugh, the three with the young champion understood and smiled as well, each hefting his own weapon as he did so. Come what may, they were four men who together would face and overcome anything that was thrown at them, or else they would lay down their lives in the trying. "On the count of three?" Gellor called out.

"Agreed," Gord replied.

"One!" shouted Curley.

"Two!" the big hillman boomed immediately.

"Three!" Gellor cried as he hopped up to the surface.

They were in a warm, green-lit forest glen. It was, in fact, a druidical grove, and all four of them were standing upon the smooth altarstone in the center of three rings of standing stones. There was a crowd of the faithful there, too, and the circle of faces showed shock and surprise at their sudden materialization atop that holy place.

"Gord, what are you doing here?" The question was from a female voice. Gord recognized it instantly, even before he turned to face its owner. She was Evaleigh, the Baroness of Ratik — the first woman Gord had ever loved. She was here!

Chapter 11

LORD NELBON GELLOR RECOGNIZED the beautiful
woman just as quickly and as happily as Gord did.
The troubador was a nobleman of Nyrond, just as
was Evaleigh's father, Count Dunstan of Blemu. In
his service to the crown, Gellor had traveled often the
lands of the Count, seen the pretty little child grow
into a lovely girl and even a more beautiful woman. It
had been his intervention that had brought Gord,
who was then Evaleigh's lover, from the count's dun-
geons on the pretext that the young thief was actually
a secret agent and captain of Nyrond's king.

How would Gord react now? Gellor wondered, then
dismissed the question. The real issue was, how had
the four of them come to this place? A place somewhere in or near Ratik was a long step indeed from
the quasi-dimensional places where they had been
hunting the malign demonurgist.

"Our apologies for this unseemly intrusion, Lady
Ratik," Gord said with utmost aplomb, giving a court-
ly bow as he spoke. Then he sprang lightly down from
the stone block. "We were brought here by sheer mis-
chance, and no sacrilege is involved."

"Most assuredly, lady, most assuredly!" Greenleaf
said as he too hopped off the altar and signed to

make pardonable the transgression that he and his associates had committed. The nature priest who was evidently officiating at the ceremony that the appearance of the four had interrupted recognized Greenleaf as a fellow druid and saw the little ritual of asked-for forgiveness that the half-elf had silently performed after vacating the hallowed stone block.

"The All-In-All will accept with understanding," the druid said to his fellow. Then something clicked in the tall man's mind; that was evident from the play of emotions across his face as he stared at Curley. "I . . . I . . . beg *your* forgiveness, Great Harmoniousness. To have one of such exalted standing in my humble grove . . ." He let his words trail off as he wrung his hands and looked hopefully down at the bald, rotund little man, for the fellow had recognized Greenleaf as a very, very high druid indeed.

Just at that same moment, Lady Evaleigh called out, "And you too, Lord Gellor?"

That caused the tall nature priest double anxiety, for Gellor's was likewise a well-known name in these parts. Who might the other two be? The baroness had recognized the small, gray-eyed man first. Could he be of greater station than even the Great Harmony named Greenleaf and the renowned nobleman of Nyrond called Gellor? The druid decided to take no chances, so he addressed the rest of the visitors as a group. "And to you also, gentle lords, I extend my sincere pardon, and that of those faithful here gathered in celebration of the coming of Midsummer this night—"

"Midsummer?" The demand came from the one-eyed bard. "Did you say Midsummer?"

"Well, of course, I . . . . Yes, your lordship. Tomorrow is Midsummer's Day, none other; and naturally we . . ." Again the druid lapsed into silence in mid-speech, for Gellor had turned away with shock on his face.

"We have been trapped for the better part of nine months," he said to the three who now faced him. Gellor's face was as pale as ash. "Such time, such time lost. Surely we are undone."

Dire as those words were, Gord could not help but believe that his comrade spoke true. So long a period would certainly have allowed the dark foes to have done their worst, free of serious challenge from the only force capable of opposing them. He, Gord, had tried and ultimately failed. But . . . no! This place was not in despair, overrun by the forces of evil, groaning under the yoke of slavery and degradation. The young adventurer turned directly to Evaleigh, ignoring the rest of the assemblage. "Good Baroness, Lady Evaleigh, we have been absent from this world for a considerable span of time and have just now returned — as you yourself witnessed. Tell me, pray, what of the great battle between Evil and Good? Has the Ultimate Darkness made headway?"

"Darkness?" Evaleigh's pretty face showed incomprehension. Then her lilac-hued eyes widened, and understanding was plainly written in them. "Oh, you mean the evil deity, the one they name Tharizdun."

"That is exactly the one I mean!"

"There is a great temple under construction in his honor in our capital," Evaleigh said. "This last spring there was great rejoicing amongst those who serve the netherspheres — and a great deal of bloodshed between them, too."

All four of the men gathered closer to her, unbelieving. The baronial husband of Evaleigh was not present at the grove, but various knights, officials, attendants, guards, and servitors were thronged nearby. So, too, other groups of petty nobles and their entourages, and many other folk from the surrounding area, had come to honor the druidical festival. The grove was very large, the glen and rings of stones of moderate size. Perhaps three hundred or more people were there.

As the adventurers came near, Evaleigh's knightly retainers and guardsmen moved to interpose themselves, half-drawing swords or aiming crossbows as they did so. "Hold, sirs! Guards!" Evaleigh ordered. "These are noblemen of great standing. They may approach as they will!" There was a little grumbling among the cavaliers, but the matter was settled.

"I fail to understand, lady," Gellor said slowly. "It seems we have been too long out of touch. Although this is not a meet place for such, I beg your indulgence. Will you favor us with an account in detail?"

"Of course, Lord Gellor," Evaleigh said with a smile so sweet it would win any heart. "Those darklings who honored the Abyss and demonkind were taken to task by the rest of those who give service to the netherspheres. With them were strangely garbed clerics, priests of the newly risen deity Tharizdun. After much rioting and fighting amongst themselves, the demon-lovers were either slain or converted. There is now a general amnesty. The old temples dedicated to such as Orcus and his ilk are being torn down or simply abandoned. All the darklings now swear allegiance to Tharizdun."

"I am not hearing right!" The exclamation sprang from Gord's lips before he could prevent it. "Well," he quickly added, "you are in a far better position to know than I. But the great one of All Evil — surely he has brought blood and suffering to our world!"

"Not that I have noticed, Gord — Sir Gord," Evaleigh hastened to add, seeming a little flustered at using such familiarity before the crowd there listening. "We collect and pay out from and to fewer of the nether sects. Tharizdun's priests have demanded and received recognition and a place in our council and those elsewhere, I assume. But blood? Only that of the demon-servers. Suffering? Nay. The ones obedient to Tharizdun seem to have quieted evil doings, stopped much of the activities which those of other persuasions objected to, and brought reason and order — reason which goes beyond those formerly convinced of darkling principles. I have heard that many folk are actually converting to service of the one you call 'All Evil.'"

The four exchanged glances. "This is astounding news, lady," Gord managed finally.

"Perhaps. Why do you all have so much interest in a matter of passing concern only to those who devote themselves to the nether regions?" That seemed a fair question indeed at this juncture.

Greenleaf looked around as Evaleigh spoke. When she mentioned the last, the tall druid who was the priest of the grove gave the half-elf a strange, questioning look. It seemed to ask, Have you become a minion of demons? and Curley was troubled. "I can perhaps explain that—" he began.

"No," Gellor interrupted. "Better I do — or you, Gord."

The young champion of Balance looked at his friend for a long moment, then nodded. Evaleigh watched the exchange from atop her little dais, that platform that set her apart from the rest as the greatest noble there. "My lady," Gord said, turning to face her directly, "it is because of a solemn charge placed

221

upon me directly, and these three stout comrades indirectly, that we express such concern." He took another step, so that he now stood a full pace away from his friends but still two long steps from the Baroness of Ratik.

"Upon my soul and sword I swore an oath," he said earnestly, placing his hand upon the dead black of his longsword's hilt to emphasize his point. The hand closed upon the hilt, and with a motion so fast that the eye had difficulty following it, Blackheartseeker was drawn from its scabbard. Even as the blade shot forth Gord was leaping ahead and striking. The sooty length of the blade entered Evaleigh's chest on an upward angle, pierced her heart, and passed through to show itself above her shoulder blade. The thrust was accompanied by a piercing scream from the beautiful mouth of the woman.

Chert was uncertain what was happening, but he swung his great battleaxe up anyway. He would stand by Gord. Then he heard the troubador singing a song of doom to evil, and at that sound the big hillman was reassured. The knights and guards who accompanied the baroness were rushing in to attack, and Chert happily hewed into their ranks with the angrily buzzing axe. Brool began its bloody execution.

Greenleaf held his staff ready, but called first a great summoning word. This took but an instant. Then the staff swept out in a semicircle. Wherever its butt end pointed, the ground gave forth a furious growth of briars, thistles, and thorns. Three quick passes of this sort, and no attacker could approach the four from the rear without first contending with the tangled barrier that was yards high and thick as a castle wall.

Satisfied, Curley turned to confront the swarm of

angry attackers that Gord, Chert, and Gellor were engaging with their gore-smeared weapons. Still the druid didn't cause the spear tip to shoot forth from the stout length of ancient wood. Instead, he held it almost as one would wield a wand. "Back to me, comrades!" he shouted. As quickly as possible, his three friends disengaged from the enemy and sprang back to where Greenleaf waited.

It seemed as if the heavens were being torn open from where Gord stood. Chert clapped his hands to his ears, letting Brool swing free on its thick thong. Gellor hunched and half closed his eyes. From the druid's staff had come a terrific noise, a clap as loud as the most fearsome of thunderclaps splitting the sky just overhead. At the same time there issued from the thing a sizzling bolt of dual lightning.

The sound bowled over the onrushing opponents and sent others of them away howling. So, too, the eye-searing discharge of electrical energy played havoc upon the foe. It struck, leaped in great arcs, striking again. It burned, charred and killed indiscriminately with an awful snapping and crackling sound as the lightning discharged itself into flesh. Between them Gord, Chert, and the bard had slain a half-dozen of Evaleigh's retinue of warriors. The single magical attack that Greenleaf unleashed from his staff felled that many more and a score of the rest as well. Even so, the four heard the crowd behind howling and raving as they attacked the thorny barrier.

"That is a marvelous sword, Gord," the one-eyed troubador said with grim admiration.

"In a manner of speaking, yes," Gord agreed. The young adventurer unconsciously sent his gaze to where the shriveled husk of the dead hag who had been pretending to be Evaleigh lay decaying into noisome powder. "It finds the heart most often, and from those of evil it draws forth all force."

"I'm prone to favor old Curley's staff there," Chert said reflectively as he rested both of his massive, calloused palms on the steel butt knob of Brool's thick haft. "Still, considering the number of the foes still quick, and their obvious desire to rend us limb from limb, I think we need to save our breath for the coming fight."

Gellor laughed at the sarcasm, and Gord was nodding grim concurrence, when the rotund half-elven druid said, "If you enjoyed the effects on those dirty buggers, wait until you see what's coming!"

"Why?" Gellor asked.

"To teach them a lesson," was all the druid said in reply.

"No need," Gord said. "All we need do is to mount the dais the hag stood on."

"Let's get out of this godsdamned shithole, then," Chert rumbled. "I'll have enough of killing the blasters soon enough anyway!"

Without hesitation all four climbed up the one step that would move them from wherever they actually were, take them from this place of evil and illusory familiarity to some new danger. The powdery husk of the destroyed hag from the pits was crushed underfoot as they mounted the dais step.

The sylvan scene vanished, but the green light did not. They were surrounded by a deep, emerald color, the hue of sunlight filtered through fathoms of seawater. Massive sharks swam nearby, and not one of the four could say a word about it.

In fact, the suddenness of their precipitation into the submarine dilemma gave them only seconds to react. Perhaps they could survive for a minute or two, even though they had been given no chance to draw air to fill their lungs prior to coming into the underwater trap. Before the last of their oxygen was gone, the step that led from this new place of death had to be located.

Visibility was limited to twenty or thirty yards. Within sight there were several possible places where the next stair could be located. Ahead was a thick growth of giant kelp, to the right a gradual drop leading to rocks with a cave opening plain to see. Off to the left were a dozen giant clams, while behind them, just at the limit of sight, was a long coral reef. Tiger sharks swam overhead and around. Big blue sharks circled there, too.

Gord, his hair waving above his head as if it were some fine, black sea growth, tugged at Gellor's clothing, pointed, and began to move as rapidly as he could in the direction of the huge mollusks. The others had no real choice. They followed.

The clams varied in size. The smallest ones were less than three feet across, the larger ranged from three to five feet, while one monster was fully eight feet in diameter and nearly as deep. That one was Gord's target, and the young thief darted straight for its yawning valves. Both failing lungs and closing sharks lent speed to his movement.

Just short of the thing, Gord stopped, picked up a stone from the sandy bottom, and hurled it toward the clam.

The missile traveled in slow motion, but Gord's aim was true. Into the open shell it went, and as it struck the muscle within, the clam closed its shell with such force that there was a current created of sufficient strength to make the young adventurer sway. His three comrades arrived just after that, and the stiff-finned sharks were not far behind, making rushes and coming ever closer.

Chert was in the lead. He saw Gord place his feet upon the closed shell. Then he was gone. The big hill-man immediately imitated his friend's action. Gellor followed next, with Curley bringing up the rear. An attacking blue shark was but a fraction of a second late. Its teeth closed on empty water, and it shot off into the green gloom with dull disappointment registering in its minuscule brain.

They had been transported to a tiny island of sand and rock. Nothing grew there, and around it was nothing save an endless expanse of ocean. The sun was overhead, beating down remorselessly. There was neither shade nor fresh water.

"Marooned with a vengeance," Gord noted. "But at least it should be a simple task to locate the magical portal to escape the place." All but Gellor voiced ready agreement. They set to work immediately, searching the few dozen square yards of the islet for the hidden stairstep. Not even the troubador's enchanted ocular detected the slightest hint of what they sought.

"Now here's a terrible thought," Greenleaf finally said. "What if that filthy scum put a false step into that last trap?"

It was something that none of the four adventurers had considered. Could Gravestone have managed such a dweomer? A second gate to take them into a place with no escape? "It might be done," Gord said, "but the Law of Balance isn't that weak — not yet. We are simply looking in the wrong place, I think."

"Where else can we look?" Chert asked crossly. Gellor pointed outward and swept his arm in a complete circle. The barbarian gulped audibly. "Yeah. I hadn't considered that, comrade," he said, eyeing the rolling waves with obvious distaste.

"No, again I disagree, bard," Gord said firmly. "Each time we have had to actually go *up*. To search under the water would be folly, I think. There has to be a place above. . . ."

Greenleaf shrugged and commenced going over the little bump of dry land again. The other three followed suit. They passed back and forth across the islet a score of times. Still nothing. "There is no step up," Gellor said finally. "You were wrong, Gord."

"Perhaps, but perhaps not. I have another thought on the matter."

"Well, we have time enough to hear it, I think," Curley said, sitting down with a huff of tiredness as he did so. "But let's not be too long about it. The salt water is drying, and my garments are beginning to become itchy and irritating."

"The initial step was nearly transparent, all save Gellor were blind, and it was separated by a gulf of ten feet. Now, why shouldn't the location of the next place we must ascend be likewise hard to locate?"

"No reason at all," the one-eyed bard admitted. "But where do we look?"

"Up!" said Gord with firmness.

"Into thin air?" Curley said with a derisive laugh.

"You can turn into a bird, can't you?" Chert said with sudden inspiration. "Why not do that? Take a little wing around this stinking bump and see what's visible from up there!"

Gord slapped the broad back of the barbarian. "I hadn't thought of that, my hulking friend, but you hit the target fairly there. Curley, do just what Chert has suggested."

In a moment the druid wavered before their eyes,

his outline shifting, his form condensing, until a big pelican stood before the three. Gord made upward gestures with his hands and stamped his foot impatiently. Curley-pelican gave a squawking protest but broke into a lumbering waddle, beat his wings, and flapped heavily into the air. The bird then commenced to flap its slow way up and around until it attained a height of a hundred feet or so, then tilted, spiraled, and glided down in a corkscrew path to land beside them.

"Well?" Gord demanded irritably.

"Braawk!" the pelican said with equal ill temper.

"All right, all right," the young champion said with resignation. "Please, respected druid, return to your true form and relate what you saw."

Greenleaf seemed to sprout out of a pelican. When his feet were no longer webbed, but the properly booted appendages of a half-elf, the druid beamed a smile at the trio of expectant observers. "It is there, plainly visible, not more than twenty feet overhead. The step is directly above the center of the islet."

"How do we get up to it?" the hillman queried.

"The rope again, I think," Gord murmured as he freed the coil and began to work it into a noose. The rest was easy going, comparatively speaking. The line anchored itself around seemingly nothing, Gord swarmed up it, and hung from the top of the cord as if levitated.

"It hasn't taken me to some other place yet," he called down, "so I suppose the rope is hanging on the edge of the portal. Chert, help Curley to climb, and I'll pull him up before I change position. Then you come up and haul Gellor on after you. Be sure one of you brings the line, too!" When the druid arrived and forced Gord to move closer to the center of the opening that was invisible save from above, the others saw Gord vanish. Chert then climbed up and took Greenleaf's place. The druid, too, disappeared as he moved elsewhere.

"I don't know how to free the rope," Chert said loudly to the climbing bard. "Can you manage it?"

"No, blast it!" Gellor was thinking furiously as he replied. He could almost recall Gord's magical words of command that controlled the enchanted horsehair line, but what if he made a mistake? Just then he attained the platform, and the matter was taken out of his hands. As Chert moved to make a place for the bard to clamber onto, he tripped over his own foot and fell. Clutching out desperately, one of his huge hands grabbed onto Gellor's studded leather jack and held fast. Both men were thus precipitated into an unceremonious heap within the next of the intradimensional pockets devised by Gravestone.

There was nothing in the new place. Some grayish illumination seemed to fill the air, but there was no sun, stars, moon, or even sky. All of them were within a bubble — a bubble of stone. "Out of the great worm's hole . . ." Chert said slowly as he looked around.

"And into the maw of the waiting dragon," Gord supplied. "It is worse than before!"

"This time I might have to agree," Gellor said. "I see no step anywhere, and there can be no invisible one in this place."

"Which of you has the rope?" the young thief asked without taking his eyes off the dome of the ceiling overhead.

"Ah, well . . . err . . ." Chert managed.

"It is behind. Lost, Gord, by no fault of ours," the bard told him. How exactly he didn't relate to Gord, naturally. "Did you think it would be useful in this cyst?"

"Perhaps . . ." the young acrobat-thief replied distractedly, seeming to dismiss the magical cord as unimportant. "See there at the apex of the ceiling? That appears to be a hooked stone projecting there."

"I see it. So what?" Chert demanded.

"It seems evident that we escape this trap by going there," Gord related patiently, still studying the dome of granite. "As feet are placed on the ceiling, the counterpart of this floor, it is my guess the individual will be sent on to the next stair."

The dilemma was finally solved by Gord. He rummaged around in another of the magically expansive pockets hidden in the thick girdle banding his waist. There were several enchanted rings therein, and one possessed power over air. "It is sufficiently strong to carry two upward. You, Gellor, will wear it, and bear Curley upward with you. As your boots touch the ceiling, you must drop the ring from your finger. Be swift, for if it is transported through the portal with you, then Chert and I will be stranded here forever."

The troubador managed the trick — barely! Gord then jammed the rune-worked circlet of ancient metal upon a finger and floated up, he and Chert clutching each other like long-lost relatives reunited after a generation of separation. A push against the curving wall, a mid-air somersault, and the two were with their comrades.

The place all four were in now was a totally alien one, its landscape of such distorted shapes, sky of jarring coloration, atmosphere so noxious that all of the adventurers were shaken to the core. Whatever it was that pervaded this far world, its effect was to erode the mind, tear away sanity, insinuate madness.

Somehow Gellor managed to begin a heroic ballad, draw forth his little kanteel of ivory with silver strings and gold inlays, and turn back the insanity that would have overwhelmed them otherwise. The stair was the most revolting feature in view, but they found the mental strength to mount it nonetheless.

Next was a jungle, but not of vegetation. The wild growth around them consisted of various tentacles. Some were one color, some another, with suckers, poison, claws, barbs, and so forth. Each set of the waving members sought to seize and slay and devour. Two, three, four, five, even as many as a dozen tentacles surrounded each of the sphincterlike mouths into which a victim would be thrust. The solution was simply to hack and slash the attacking tentacles, to strike them with magic and weapons. It was the thickest and largest cluster of the things that hid a step in the midst of the viciously hook-fringed and venomous tentacles.

That step took the four into a reeking moor whose fetid, miasmal air was filled with swarms of biting insects and whose mud and water swarmed with leeches and similar forms of hungry parasites. The place where the next step was located was evident; an expanse of high ground far in the distance. It lay but five or six leagues distant as the crow flies. Translated to the real terms of the place, that meant five or six days of hard going on foot through the low-lying, infested swampland.

They tried that mode of travel only for an hour. It was soon evident that they would be infected with a half-dozen diseases, anemic, and worm-ridden at the very best after much more of the same. Then they heard the monstrous bellowings and croakings and splashings of the native fauna of this stinking swamp world, and that decided the matter promptly. Curley Greenleaf, as a last resort, used some of his remaining magical capability to create a fiery vehicle that would carry them to the ridgelike step. It took the four of them quite a while to build a fire of sufficient size to effect the magic, but it was accomplished, and the aerial journey was simplicity itself. The chariot set firmly down upon the monstrous-sized next step.

The next stratum was worse, for the stair-portal shot them into the space between galaxies, and the heatless, airless void would have slain them in an instant except for the presence of the champion of Balance. The power vested in him was such that all of them were sent to the next entrapped step in the instant after the malign dweomer left by Gravestone precipitated them into the freezing, suffocating void where they were meant to die.

"Time to rest," Gord said with tiredness and strain filling his voice.

"This is a far less lethal area than any we have encountered so far," Gellor said as he surveyed the surroundings. "At least on the face of it. . . ." What they saw was simply a strange landscape, a plain of infinite dimensions. It was covered with flights of stairs.

"We all need some strong, prayerful treatment to rid our bodies of the pestilences of that miasmal fen," the druid said firmly. "Some of us bear wounds and other hurts which would do with some treatment and healing. As we take our ease here a time, I'll see to that," Curley told them.

Gord was given preferential care because he alone was the Balance's hope. Then Greenleaf cared for himself, just in case some unperceived disease was affecting him. Chert had fallen asleep immediately, as was his wont whenever the opportunity permitted. The troubador had spent some time scrutinizing the surroundings, but soon he too was dozing. "Seeing those sluggards makes me sleepy, too," Gord yawned in Curley's general direction. "After you've done your best for Gellor and Chert, wake me up."

"I'll wake him myself," Gellor mumbled. "I'm not really asleep. I watch with one eye open."

Gord chuckled at the joke, and Curley laughed, too. "That's fine, dear woods-running minstrel," he commented. "After curing myself, I will need at least a catnap and some time to meditate. Rouse yon hulk, or Gord, if you need fresh eyes to watch, but disturb me not." Gellor nodded affirmation, and Gord was already asleep, so the druid stretched out on the soft, semi-yielding terrain and was soon mimicking Chert's snores.

When the druid regained consciousness, there was no way to tell how long he had slept. He saw that all of the others were still asleep when he awoke, but seemingly nothing untoward had occurred during their unguarded period, so Curley simply shrugged the incident off and began his period of prayer and concentration. It would be no real trick for him to maintain watch with a corner of his mind as he managed the rest of what he had to do, especially when he felt so sure and comfortable.

"How goes it?" The comment startled the druid, for he hadn't noticed the young thief awaken and move to stand beside him. Gord saw the surprise and smiled. "You were deep in your meditations, comrade, so I moved softly. I'm myself surprised to find the only one alert is you, though. Usually, grizzled-beard there would be prodding us all before this."

"Hmmm . . . You have something there, Gord. I am

nearly ready for renewed effort." Greenleaf shook his head, then corrected himself. "I haven't managed to restore my greater powers. Perhaps it hasn't been so long a napping as we supposed."

"No. . . . My instinct tells me we have slept very long," Gord countered. "Hey! Useless sentry and would-be guard! Wake up!" As he spoke, the young adventurer moved over to where Gellor slept and toed him gently and cautiously. There was no telling what reaction he would have upon awakening. Gellor stirred and sat up slowly. He looked tired still, and his movements were sluggish.

"Sorry," he said. "I'm a bit muzzy with sleep yet." With a lot of stretching and eye-blinking, the bard finally stood and joined Gord.

Waking the barbarian hillman was a more difficult task, but finally Gord and Gellor managed it in tandem. "Let me rest just a bit longer," Chert said. He was only half-conscious. "These damned traps have worn me out! Besides, there's no hurry. The stair we need is the smallest we can see from here, and time has no meaning here. We can snooze as long as we wish and then get away easily."

"Rubbish," Gellor shot back. "What makes you say all that?"

"It was my dream — as clear as glass from Hardby, too. I'll wager my life it was a true sending."

"That you will, should you attempt to stay here longer," Gord said with a sarcasm-laden voice. "Nothing which Gravestone prepares is true in any sense save evil and death!" He dragged on the hillman to get him into a sitting position, and with the help of Gellor eventually managed it. Then he shouted, "Come here, druid, and use your hands and words to heal these two deserving heroes. As soon as that is done, we must find out how to escape this slumber-filled nothing. It is a most perilous place which will lull us all into death's bed."

Gord was correct, of course. Lethargy, weakness, and a growing need to sleep, sleep, sleep forever were imbued into the substance of the quasi-real space that the fourteenth stair had brought them to.

As they went toward the flights of steps that sprang like strange growths from the slightly yielding surface of the ground, each found it harder and harder to place one foot in front of the other.

The environment would possibly have proved fatal, except that Gord correctly gambled that one portion of Chert's dream was true. They had to choose one stairway and head for it, wasting no time, so Gord thought and hoped that the stairway Chert referred to was the actual one. He was right, and they barely made it to the new plateau before succumbing to deathly lethargy.

Draughts from an enchanted flask that the bard supplied gave the four sufficient strength and refreshment of vigor to deal with a place that was like a giant plane of fly paper, populated by flying horrors ready to saw off choice bits of any creature stuck down and unable to defend itself. Chillingly, they had to step up on just such an unfortunate creature in order to be magically moved to the next test.

The residual strength from the elixir that Gellor had shared round, plus his own signing too, gave the four the ability to resist the terrible pain that pervaded the next area — agony borne by the sights, sounds, smells, and very touch of the place. Where the torment was worst, there too the stair for escaping it.

"Upon my life, Gord," Chert spat, "never was a

sheer ice cliff before and an angry cave bear behind half so fun as the entertainments you have always managed for us!" He said that as they came floundering down a slime-coated slope toward a precipice.

"If you and Gellor hadn't botched up and lost—" he began to retort, then stopped wasting his breath to do something about their dire situation. Tumbling and somersaulting to the lead of the group, the young adventurer plied his enchanted dagger to dig in and make a firm place to hold to. Greenleaf, immediately behind, slid past, while Chert caught onto Gord's belt and Gellor grabbed Chert's leg. In desperation the druid used one of his least powerful spells and succeeded. The dweomer caused the slime to stiffen and grow, and the stuff caught Curley and held him fast just as he was on the brink of destruction.

Eventually they found the way to free themselves from the slime world, but wound up in a place where gigantic gears with grinding teeth of spiked surfaces threatened to pulp them all. "This is a nightmare of some mad technologist," was all Gord could manage. Chert pointed out the way, and then he set the example by grabbing fast to one of the free-rolling spiked wheels and rode it upward to where a small ledge was visible. It was the wrong one, and getting down was trickier than getting up, but after managing it they found the correct ledgestep and were gone from the clockwork plane.

There followed an acid world, a place of animated metal shapes of geometric form and malign purpose, a desert of alkaline sort, a quasi-plane where they had to hop from tooth to tooth of a giant mouth as it clashed open and shut trying to swallow the four. From there to a globe of prehistoric sort that teemed with dinosaurian monsters they went, and thereafter to a brazen city filled with fiery denizens. Of course, Curley Greenleaf handled the City of Brass and the efreet well enough. In fact, the sultan of those elemental beings actually directed the party to a place where there was a portal that bypassed many of the stair-traps that Gravestone had devised. The four adventurers used it to ascend the helix to a point twice as far along as that of their previous progress.

But on that fiftieth plane the druid suddenly found himself face to face with the avatar of Infestix known as Nerull. Chert saw the devil-duke Amon. The troubador confronted the netherlord, Hafdoligor Kaathbaen, master of the undead realm. And Gord stood before none other than Tharizdun himself!

Here at last, it seemed, was the final challenge for each of them. How would they react? How would they fare? They all reacted the same, but not in their usual way. Instead of leaping to the attack or poising themselves for defense, each of the four simply stood, motionless and uncaring. They were filled not with courage and spirit, but with the heaviest, most oppressive despair that any of them had ever known.

Chapter 12

"LEAVE ME," Infestix uttered in his worm-ridden voice. The various daemons and netherworld things that served the great lord hastened to obey. "Let none enter until I personally command," he added as the last of his servitors was departing. That ghastly daemon, one of the Diseased Ones, bowed low and firmly closed the ancient door behind itself.

Infestix was now alone in the chamber, a minor audience room he favored because its location allowed him to access so many places easily. The master of the netherplanes sprawled back on the wide chair. His form shifted to that of Nerull, the skeletal god of death, and in his hands appeared the terrible scythe wielded by that deity. Then the terrible figure bounded up from the seat as quickly and nimbly as if he were a young man full of vigor and life rather than a bony monster eons old and laden with plagues. Infestix laughed a booming, iron-throated laugh, as in his Nerull avatar he swung the scythe in great arcs around the chamber, the rusted, blood-stained blade singing a death song that was most pleasant to the being as he danced thus and laughed in pleasure.

"The planets come slowly into alignment, and all signs and portents are favorable," Nerull caroled loudly. There were none to hear, of course. He shared the news with nobody, for none save he would soon ascend to be the Chosen of Tharizdun. No master of devils, no chief of any other power in the whole of the netherworlds had come close to accomplishing all that Infestix-Nerull had managed.

Now the culmination of all he had worked for and labored to produce was at hand. With an abrupt cessation of motion, Nerull stopped his cavorting. The terrible being swished his long-edged instrument through the air. There, where it had passed, Oerth and the Flanaess appeared at his feet.

"Let me see the struggle," he ordered. From east to west tiny lines of figures sprang up, fighting and killing in a replay of events of the last few weeks. The soldiery of the Great Kingdom fought on all fronts, slaying and being slain by the knights and footmen of Nyrond, Almor, and the League of the Iron Knot. The forces of Iuz and his allies hammered south, east, west and in turn were hit and driven. Scarlet Brotherhood legions marched, battled, and bled. Baklunish hosts fought nomads and wild kinsmen, as dwarves and elves defended valiantly against the unending hordes of humanoids swarming out from the Pomarj. Everywhere there was destruction, hunger, suffering.

Nerull laughed the rust-throated laugh of death again, and as he passed his scythe over the little depiction, all save the dead vanished. Those, in their thousands, arose and marched in ordered formation at their master's will. In fact, many of those dead would come to Hades and those other netherspheres serving Infestix and become new soldiers still fighting for the dark cause of Tharizdun.

"It is perfect," the daemon hissed as he allowed the phantom figures to vanish. "Neither law nor chaos attains ascendancy now. What war ever brought weal?" he added with a sardonic chuckle. "I am readying all for you, Great Master of Evil," Nerull shouted, and a faint pulsing in the dim atmosphere seemed to indicate that the bound lord of all darkness heard and strained to come forth again.

"See, Lord Tharizdun!" the nether-king shouted as he again cut a path through the thick air of the chamber with his scythe. There appeared scenes of the war being fought in the netherspheres. Demons great and small fought with their own ilk and against the minions of the Nine Hells and Hades, too. Three amethyst lights, tiny and bright as stars, showed where the Theorparts were, each a key, a third of the relic that would free Tharizdun.

Infestix-Nerull noted absently the smaller, black gleam where the Eye of Deception gathered chaotic power for its demoniacal wielder, and even smaller motes of rubine hue, orange fire, deep jet. Those were merely indications of the many great weapons being used, artifacts of evil force employed by the warring factions. Together, perhaps, the rest would surpass the power of the Eye wielded by Graz'zt, and it, with the other weapons of the Abyss, might just surpass a single Theorpart.

"My Lord of All Evil," Infestix-Nerull said more softly, "see how the three parts draw ever closer to each other? Soon, soon!" But there was no further indication that a channel remained to that no-space where the dreaded Tharizdun was imprisoned, so the daemon dissolved the scene with another swish of the groaning blade.

Thinking carefully to himself, Nerull pondered the situation. The keys were so close, yet they remained disjoined, separate, and contentious. "The one-who-stands-between still lives!" The words were loud, iron-toned, rust-dead damnations echoing in the fetid atmosphere as the sound rebounded from the walls of livid purple, skipped off the polished porphyry floor, beat against the dull plum-tinged dome that capped the place as the lid of a sarcophagus. "Where?" Infestix-Nerull demanded, giving the great scythe a twitch that sent it slashing with the sound of a thousand death moans.

There appeared before him his own scrying room. The Diseased Ones were not there, of course. All of them were guarding the door to the chamber he was in. In the vast basin was the situation envisioned as a chess game. The daemon concentrated on the vision of a vision, and the squares ran, shifted, changed. From a vast survey of planar scope it contracted, shifting to a different scale. Yet the field was still multiplaned. Transparent level upon ghostly level it formed. First came the golden brown and pale tan of the material world. Its hue and conformation showed it to be Oerth. There the board shed a fading emerald light, and the violet garments that covered the array of slain pawns and minor pieces there told a tale that brought fury to the daemon's visage. Ghastly lilac light shot from the hollows where violet specks writhed like worms. The beams swept the phantom field, and the depiction of the chess board sank, so that Nerull's gaze was now fixed on a weird and distorted field. "Better," he hissed in his metallic voice. "Much better, little human."

The twisted, distorted helix that was depicted as the playing field of the game was the work of Gravestone. The convoluted layers writhed out and back, and each stratum was filled with the stuff of Nerull — death! For a brief span the daemon lord watched the tableau. The clear emerald of the sole champion, the resister of Evil's coming domination, was pulsing, moving, but struggling from one tier to the next.

"A fly in the webbed tunnel," Infestix-Nerull said gleefully, the sound of his mirth like rusted metal scraping on rough slate. A force of the green-hued pieces moved on the strangely colored spaces of the extradimensional board built by the priest-wizard who so faithfully served the cause, but the way grew ever more perilous, each move more fell; and upward, ever upward, the serpentine helix writhed. Those four men were gone from the main field and entrapped in a mazed board that would isolate them for . . . how long?

"Too long!" The daemon's gaze slid upward to where the misshapen squares terminated in an infundibular form. There another pair of the green pieces stood. "What is this?" Nerull was surprised; concern tinged the iron of his voice as he muttered the exclamation aloud in the empty chamber.

The conformation depicting the enemy men relayed what force they had. Minor pieces, but strong ones. Perhaps one could be likened to the promoted bishoplike piece, a mixture of the conventional moves of bishop and king. The other showed power of a shorter range but good strength in the area immediately around it; a great mage and a high priest.

Infestix-Nerull saw his own chief piece on the field of the material plane, Gravestone. He was larger, stronger, than the two attackers who had attained the funnel's disclike rim. In fact, there in his own place, the no-where he had constructed as fortress and refuge, power base and armory, Gravestone was nearly godlike in strength. "But why?" Again the words sprang unbidden from the lipless mouth of the

243

daemon. "Are those black wings? Shadows? Or something else . . . ?"

He was pondering that, and also thinking how fortunate for his lieutenant that the little force of green antagonists had been split into two parts, when the images of the many-layered board wavered and began to fade. "No!" Infestix-Nerull boomed the command, and as he so shouted he bent his entire will upon the vision, demanding it to solidify, become sharper, grow. Pale fog of pea green color was obscuring the scene. The phantasmal vapors shot upward from the ground that was Oerth and rose through the unnaturally formed planes above.

"Slow, too slow," the daemon-master said with hard satisfaction. "I will see more before you manage to cloud the scrying, Basiliv!" The smoke roiled and darkened. The intensity of its hue tried to shoot upward, but the convoluted parody of creation disallowed such speed. Laughing foully, knowing that his hated antagonist would hear, the daemon again stared upward to the place where Gravestone was about to combat the two minions of the Balance.

The vivid vert of the mage and priest were barely discernible through a growing gloom. "Black? Black?! What demon scum dares to interfere with Me?" Infestix-Nerull bellowed so loudly as to make the whole room shudder and shake. Nothing was heard outside, of course, but the very stuff of the bronze-bound planks closing off the chamber danced from the force of the daemon's wild outcry, and the Diseased Ones beyond huddled within themselves in fear.

No answer was forthcoming, however, and try as he might Nerull was quite unable to discover some intruding mental force indicating the interference of Orcus, Graz'zt, or any other of the mightiest of demonkind. "Plagues smite you!" he thundered, and scythed the old-blood blur of metal through the vision. Black smoke and verdant fog alike vanished. Filled with rage, the ruler of the netherworld stalked out of his chamber, scattering the lesser daemons before him as wind whips dead, dry leaves in autumn. Now it was time to intervene directly. For the second time Nerull would go forth to find and lay low the puny champion of Balance. He would not be foiled twice.

* * *

Of all the powers who adhered to the middle course, among all those who strove for neutrality and balance between the dichotomous forces of the multiverse, Basiliv, Demiurge and dweller on old Oerth, was perhaps the single most powerful. Yet even that might was of limited sort. It extended to the material, reached forth into the elements, and touched those other spheres that in turn touched the material.

Basiliv was an earth giant, as it were. With his feet upon Oerth, he was formidable if not omnipotent when opposing any similar force. When allied to and aligned with the other great ones of like ethos, only the evil strength of the triune relic of Tharizdun could stay Basiliv's hand. Would that hand have been reached forth at this time, the struggling hordes of evil, men and mock men and monsters, too, would have been hurled back into the dark realms whence they had marched. With but another single blow, the Demiurge and his allies would have extinguished all lesser evils, leaving demonkin and devils' own and nether-server alone and trembling in their exposure and vulnerability.

But no such attack had ever come in the past. To cripple and destroy the dark would be to misalign Balance forever. When Tharizdun first arose, the Demiurge had pondered the issue. He concluded that Order, Chaos, and Wealsome deities too would serve to disarm the threat of the totality of malign rule. He and the disparate ones of neutral bent assisted, but they did so sparingly and with a cautious eye toward the time after the Great Evil's binding. Now Basiliv dared not reach forth to strike at the swarms that wrought such havoc in the kingdoms of the world, for all of his attention was needed elsewhere. . . .

"Did I err?"

"Pardon, Lord Basiliv, I didn't hear the question," Mordenkainen said.

The old archwizard was there, serving as a conduit connecting Basiliv to other groups of Balance — Hierophants, the minor lords of planar sort and of specificities, the quasi-godlings. In short, all the might of the alliance save the One of Entropy. Mordenkainen, deep in concentration, had sensed the question Basiliv had asked of himself, but had not heard the words. "I am sorry, old contestant," he murmured to the archwizard. "I was merely mumbling to myself. Excuse me, and return to your work."

"You're growing older than I," Mordenkainen cackled, one bushy eyebrow raised in mock alarm. Then he shrugged and returned to his task. "Dealing with that deranged dabbler Gigantos is hard enough without having to put up with you, too," he snapped, recalling the times he had opposed the Demiurge for one reason or another because of what Basiliv had called him. "Mad Archimage, bah! *You* are as scattered as Gigantos ever was, and *I* have better claim to the crown of—"

"Enough, please, Archwizard, enough. We must strive together now, or else . . ." Basiliv let his sentence trail off. Mordenkainen took the point and said nothing further, expending his full attention on the linkage once again. His attendant mages, led by the portly Bigby, joined again in the circle. All was quiet.

With a final glance at the spell-binder, Basiliv thought, I am as much older as he as the world itself, and yet I wish it otherwise. Then the Demiurge turned away from Mordenkainen and the eight mages with him and focused his power. It was his duty to observe the progress of Gord and his comrades, to communicate what he learned to the others, and to help — if he could.

Information floated into his consciousness and out. Thoughts sent from Shadowking regarding the state of the warfare in the netherspheres, intelligence on the movements of devil-legions, the escalation by inclusion of yet another great malign artifact. Important! The thought stayed and was filed for ready access. The triple keys of our undoing are in close proximity to one another, but still each contests against its counterparts!

The Demiurge saw at the same time the stalemate that locked good and evil in long lines across the whole of the Flanaess, which sent riot, rebellion, and red war spreading in waves over the whole Oerth, but whose waves smashed against each other in a moil of uncertainty. It would culminate in death and destruction without victory to either side.

Another portion of his mind received facts pertaining to the higher spheres. Embroiled in bickering, factious, the beings of Good argued relative worth and precedence, fought for disciples, and were of scant assistance against the looming threat of evil.

That is not by mere chance, Basiliv noted. The great tripartite force which they wrought to bind Tharizdun now rebounds upon its creators. Perhaps a few devas, possibly a planetar. Just enough to check the hells, the undead and maelvis of Acheron. Enough, barely, but enough nonetheless. Dreggals and Hades were now interlocked in the demon-war. There was balance . . . Balance.

Not all of Oerth was festering under conflict. The Cabal hedged its places on and near the material world. The Bladelord evened things in favor of the less rapacious, Rexfelis maintained his own place untainted and reinforced his allies at strategic points. Even with Mordenkainen gone, the others of the Obsidian Citadel were strong enough to hold fast. Soon they would join with the elves of Highfolk and the freefolk of Vesve to drive off the invading scum sent by Iuz. Precarious, teetering on all the manifold fronts, but the scale was steadying at the midpoint again. Good, but . . . something bothered the Demiurge. Another corner of his mind nagged. Let it nag for now. He had to center all of his force on Gord.

Basiliv's view alternated between the actual and the representational. There were the six, champion and attendant heroes, leaving the secluded inn and heading into the district of Greyhawk where Gord's first and most personal foe laired. Determination, cold anger, purpose radiated from Gord in particular. That was so strong, in fact, that it came through the network of supernatural energy with which he was charged.

Then the depiction was of a board. The six moved as a unit, entering the space of the enemy. There was a veil of plum-colored mist surrounding the square, but the Demiurge had no difficulty penetrating the screen. His dweomered sight pierced the obscuring cloud of power and saw the multi-piece contest with lilac-hued opponents. Immediately before was a minor piece, and a pawn suddenly entered the area too. No, wait. There was also a greater figure, but it fled at the coming of the six, abandoned its position before the attack.

With barely a thought, the Demiurge's sight widened and deepened. He discerned a trail of angry purple, a weaving of dark powers left as one of the enemy fled. There! A sick and perverted ladderway in the noplace of extradimensional existence. Only one such as the priest-mage called Gravestone could construct such a place. The purple pathway led to the foundation of the twisted tiers, then deepened.

I will see the reality, Basiliv thought firmly. Again his vision shifted, and he saw the wizard Sigildark and the netherfiend Krung. They fought with malign fury and died before the mental gaze of the Demiurge. The six were well, unharmed. Most of their energy quite untapped. The sword! Basiliv thought hastily. Its aura is black, yet there is a veining of verdigris wound through its fabric.

He was shocked at the terrible power of the weapon Gord possessed. He had formerly received no hint of the sword's potential. None save Vuron the demon lord could have alloyed such malign prowess into the magical metal of the weapon, but even that great demon was quite helpless compared to the force of the blade. Was it our gifting? Basiliv asked himself. Entropy? Gord's own inner forces? None of those possibilities fit. Another unknown, another nagging question. Later. . . . For now, all that mattered was that it served Balance.

His view of things jumped back to the representa-

tional. The six had divided into two groups. Allton
and Timmil were bypassing the mazetrap. This was
occurring even as Krung was expunged and Sigildark
sent gibbering away to his fate in the pits. Why? How
could those two be so foolish?! In their desire to confront their evil foe, both the mage and high priest had
separated from their acknowledged leader, the champion of their very cause, to strike Gravestone immediately. The rashness was unbelievable, especially considering that the priest-wizard undoubtedly had both
reinforcements and a bolt-hole. Perhaps the two
thought they could prevent Gravestone from summoning the dire beings who were undoubtedly at his
beck in the lower planes: cleric to ward off the rising
evil, spell-worker to hold fast the adversary and prevent his flight. With Greenleaf, Chert, Gellor, and
Gord coming immediately behind, such tactics would
be superior.

The projections that were the chessmen of the envisioned board moved. A dual-piece of intermediate
value confronted a towering figure of pulsing violet
hue. The purple was more potent, but to strike would
expose it to the duality of the other. Standoff . . . for a
time. What of the others?

He was part of a weird, four-sided construct. It
was a piece of unguessable force, but it moved only
slowly. One square at a time it wound its way labori-
ously up the hideous squares of the distorted helix,
the ladder of spaces that eventually culminated in the
place where the devoted wizard and priest held off the
evil priest-wizard. There was another, far easier route
for the four-fronted chessman to follow, only its power of movement was inadequate to follow the simple,
untrapped checker of upward-soaring cubes. Instead
it moved and fought along the hundred steps of the

deadly helix. Basiliv watched in horrified fascination as the Gord-Chert-Gellor-Curley Greenleaf figure went on, space after space, slowly, fighting the form or foe at each step, moving haltingly toward the lairboard so far above.

Wrenching himself from the spectacle, the Demiurge concentrated on the ultimate goal that Gord struggled toward. Gravestone's image appeared, seen as from a bird's-eye view of a bowshot above. He stood at the apex of a triangle formed by himself and his antagonists, Timmil on the right with a potent staff held ready, Allton at the other corner, likewise armed. The two who held Gravestone at bay had so many protections and tokens of power that even the great evil one was uneasy, it seemed. He neither struck at one or the other, only stood still and slowly moved a long wand, or a slender rod, first left, then right, and back again.

Was this to ward against the two? No! Some new presence was gathering behind Gravestone, slowly, becoming more palpable with each slow, measured sweep of the priest-wizard's malign wand.

Where were the others? Basiliv thought frantically.

Gord was plodding upward still. The four had just overcome a place of living metal where iron spheres and steel cubes sought to crush nonmetallic life with savage ferocity. Next was a wilderness of alkali, then a primal jungle-swamp filled with monstrous dinosaurs. Somehow the four managed to win past and gain the place of the efreet; and despite the evil nature of those denizens of the City of Brass, the foursome prevailed again.

A monstrous efreeti transported them past the next fell space, a square wherein things of negative force waited to leech life from them, onto a formless void where not even the Demiurge could guess what awaited.

But then . . . "I understand!" Basiliv spoke aloud, not caring if he disturbed the others. They too must know. The revelation was sudden, and the shock was sufficient to make Basiliv curse.

"How could I have been so stupid?" Now the others were staring at him. He'd tell them in a moment. Two things first. Quickly concentrating on Gravestone again, Basiliv saw the shape of what formed behind.

"As I feared!" Shifting instantly to Gord, the Demiurge then viewed the formless expanse where the four were now held. Yes. It was as he thought. There was a . . . Never mind thinking it! He had to communicate directly with the champion.

"Gord!" The name, thought and shouted at the same time, was sent with all the energy the Demiurge could muster. "Gord! You are— "

"That is quite enough of that," a dry voice said, an interruption heard only in the Demiurge's brain just before . . .

Basiliv's mind went blank.

Chapter 13

"WE NEEDN'T BE ENEMIES, YOU KNOW."

The words were addressed to him only, so Allton responded. "That is true, daemon-kisser," he mocked. "You or I will die, and thus we will no longer oppose each other."

"That is the solution toward which we now steer, I grant," Gravestone said without rancor or threat. "There is another answer, though. A better solution for you and your associate." As he said that, Gravestone allowed his eyes to slide easily, head turning slowly, to include Timmil in the offer.

"Another?"

"Cease the bantering now," Timmil barked to the mage. "He is as sly as any archdevil and as vile as Nerull!"

"Yes, another, better way," Gravestone responded to Allton even as his stare stayed fixed on the high priest. "Join me. You are a spell-worker of great puissance. Become my lieutenant. Your priestly friend here says that Nerull is vile; still, I think you know otherwise, for you seek the balance, do you not?"

"The lord of the pits is reviled!" Allton shot it out without having to consider.

"True," Timmil affirmed in support.

"False, quite false," averred the priest-wizard. "Is death wrong? How is there balance against the riotous spawning of life without quiet death? And light — would it not gladly sear your eyes constantly were it not for sweet darkness?"

"Sophistries!" the priest barked.

"The words of Balance," Allton admitted.

"The Weal would suppress Balance were it able. Long and long it has oppressed us of the netherspheres. We strive now against those above — not you, not Nature. How could we know our own if our actual aim was to destroy all save those who served the same master?"

The mage found a grain of something in what Gravestone uttered. Nodding slowly, Allton began, "But all know that Tharizdun—"

"Beware again, Allton!" Timmil interrupted. "He lies with scant truths!"

"Beware yourself, priestling called Timmil," Gravestone fired back unheatedly. "Might not your 'truths' be formed of scant lies? No? You think not? No matter! Think on this, mage Allton, and you too, cleric, if your brain is not too filled with propaganda to remain open to reason." That seemed to have an effect. The priest-wizard shifted his eyes back to the mage, who now stood uncertain.

"Ponder the enmity which exists now," Gravestone continued. "Has any hostile action been taken on the initiative of the netherspheres? Yes, of course! But only, and I repeat, only, against those who fight us. Balance has interfered, made cause with Good, because its leaders betray it!"

Allton took a moment to consider that, but Timmil did not hesitate.

"The fallacies of your statements, blackheart, are

exceeded only by your deceitful actions!" The cleric had picked up the gauntlet, for he was all too aware of the nature of their opponent. Gravestone had evil powers of persuasion that could overwhelm both of their defenses if allowed to insinuate their way into their minds unchecked.

Upon hearing the high priest's denunciation, Allton snapped back to himself. The staff he grasped with knuckles now white sprang up to point at the malign figure before him. "Yes, liar and deceiver, I am aware of your summoning!"

"Too late, you puny fools!" Gravestone shouted the words with malign laughter rolling after them. It was as if a curtain had been raised behind the priest-wizard. As his peals of maniacal laughter died away in the measureless distances that were no distance at all, there appeared behind him two towering forms. The burning eyes of Pazuzeus seared into Allton's brain, while the stunned cleric tried to defend his sanity against the assault of Shabriri's many-orbed stare.

"They are yours, body and soul, my servants!" Gravestone shouted at them at the top of his voice, his tone still laden with unholy joy. "Take them! The sport is yours!" So saying, the priest-wizard made a tiny gesture. Instantly he was gone from the setting, leaving the great elder demons to deal as they could and would with Timmil and the archmage. Gravestone reappeared in the same heartbeat that he vanished, now well removed and comfortably reclining on a divan. Cacodaemon whores from Gehenna fawned around him, and dumaldun slaves from Tarterus fanned and fed him. Now he could relish the coming spectacle in proper comfort!

That the two mighty demons were sufficiently formidable was beyond question. After all, no human mage could stand alone and unprotected against the likes of ancient Pazuzeus, four-winged lord of aerial nethercreatures. Shabriri too was of incalculable power, and even so great a cleric as Timmil would be helpless to defend against the mental, magical, and physical assaults that the elder demon would send and employ. Taking no chances, however, Gravestone was ensconced at a long distance and employed a distorting dweomer to appear closer. The best part about that spell was that it also allowed him to see as if he were only but a few rods distant.

Even removed as he was, Gravestone also took additional precautions. He activated protective magics and then used a personal spell to construct a globe around the area he was in, so that stray energy or spells would not penetrate. Of course, such defense precluded any direct intervention by him, but the priest-wizard was more than confident that his demoniacal servants would need no assistance from him. Gravestone was commensurate at his black art; he was *the* demonurgist. These netherbeings who were enmeshed by his power were studied, known, and controlled as well.

Allton felt the meshes and lines of dark force that flowed and held the pocket of created space together. Without conscious volition, he knew the spaces and distances. Allton was, after all, one of the greatest of dweomercraefters; only a handful of spell-binders anywhere surpassed him. One was here. Mordenkainen worked elsewhere, as did Tenser, the one who had sent Allton. None of the dark ones other than Gravestone came close to his power. Sigildark had approached the mark, but that one was no more. Bigby was perhaps on a par. There was one of awful weal who was likewise, and one of chaos far to the west. There were none other than that.

Allton's many talents included knowledge of energies, and thus he knew now what was surrounding him. Gravestone's sudden disappearance and reappearance stood out plainly to the mage's mind. Allton saw the means used, the currents of power tapped, and the distortions that indicated reshaping and continued usage. This was the same talent that had made it possible for him to trace Sigildark so easily. It was the reason he had been the one chosen to accompany the champion.

He could utilize Gravestone's own forces here, but only if he were allowed time. Somehow the demonurgist had duped Allton, lulled him into a mental stupor while calling forth the demons, but aside from that, the mage's skill was such that the demonurgist would be hard pressed to contend with him even on his own demi-plane. With the aid of Timmil, Allton thought he could best the priest-wizard. But he needed time! Now two terrible demons confronted them, and there was no time to study the energies here, to plan, to seize and reshape the surging forces and reshape them to his will. Nevertheless, Allton had his staff. That would serve as a conduit of sorts. Together with his chosen spells and the many tokens of magical containment he carried, he was armed well enough to withstand the demon who came for him. He could hold out, stand under the siege, until help in the form of the champion arrived.

"I abjure the evil, turn back the nether, set forth a barrier for all time between Right and Oppression, the Natural and Malign!" Timmil's words rang clearly through the strange atmosphere of Gravestone's place. The priest was calling for a protection against all wickedness, and of course that included the many-eyed Shabriri.

"I confound all evil power and strengthen that which resists its purposes," the great high priest continued, and as he spoke the air began to shimmer around him. Somehow the forces of his own calling were coalescing here, even though it was a place of darkest evil. "All who strive against the wrongfulness will prosper and strike true. All wicked ones will falter and grow weak." Timmil recited the chant rapidly, but it came from his heart. The innate powers he possessed were sufficient to keep Shabriri off for just long enough for him to complete the work. It included Allton positively and Pazuzeus negatively. It was then that the demon struck, for Shabriri was now sure of exactly what his human foe was doing.

"A petty nusiance, priest!" Shabriri roared as he sent forth his attack. It was a withering blast of negativity, a death force meant to turn Timmil into a husk.

Coruscating ebony vomited from the ancient demon's mouth. It came toward Timmil in a broad gout, but it failed to harm him. The null-stuff of the demon's assault splattered as if it were indeed vomit, then ran to the ground like electricity, disappearing with a sharp, explosive crack. The high priest's defenses and the protective power of his abjuration defeated Shabriri's force.

It was merely the first exchange of the first round of a duel to the death, and well Timmil knew that. The cleric understood clearly what had happened. How their foe, Gravestone, had distracted their attention, used his power here to mask his true actions, as he delayed Allton and Timmil with seeming willingness to avoid conflict. Because the two had meant to prevent just such a summoning as Gravestone had accomplished, and to fix him to a spot in order to slay the demonurgist, the task the priest-wizard had managed was, in retrospect, not surprising.

Yet now they were in real trouble. He and Allton had seriously underestimated their enemy. Timmil hoped the mage would know the forms of attack that Pazuzeus could employ as well as Timmil himself knew them — and the abilities of Shabriri. It could be said that the high priest was very much the antithesis of Gravestone, for Timmil was an exorcist, abjurer of evil and demonkind, exiler of netherbeings from the realms of mankind. The demonurgist had known his name. The hideous expression apparent on Shabriri's visage as he drew near showed Timmil that the elder demon now knew who and what the high priest was.

"My apologies, demon. I shall not trouble you with petty nuisances again," Timmil said, as the monstrous being strained to break through the barrier that the cleric had created to hedge himself from the demon. "Is this better?" From Timmil's staff came a golden halo, a thing of light no larger than a finger ring. It floated for a split second, then shot toward the demon, growing from bracelet-size to the circumference of a large man's waist as it flew. Shabriri cursed and ducked, swatting at the shining stuff. He touched it, and the gold flickered, dimmed and went out. More were issuing from Timmil's staff, though. Seven such circles came forth, and the demon could not stop them all. One found him untouched and settled over the thing's head as a halo.

"Noooo!" Shabriri bellowed in his multitoned, discordant voice. The radiance of the nimbus was the light of Order and Weal. It was of its very nature diametrically opposed to the demon. Its radiance burned Shabriri's eyes, its warmth blistered the creature's horn-plated hide, and the music it emitted gave such terrible pain that Shabriri could hardly think. Somehow, though, the demon managed to gather his wits and work a counter-spell against the searing force of the halo. "That will cost you much when the end comes!" Shabriri hissed in a voice as loud as a dragon's roar when the force of his counter dissipated the nimbus and the pain left him.

"In all the multiverse, nothing is free, and all must bear some cost," Timmil countered. "Come, then; let us see who shall handle the reckoning!" So challenging, the priest loosed one of his most potent spells against the demon, as Shabriri cast forth his own power to sunder the enchantment that protected Timmil from his fangs and talons.

Allton had not fared quite so well as his comrade. Pazuzeus had leaped into the air, circled at blinding speed, and struck with a blast of air that took the archmage from the rear so unexpectedly as to knock him sprawling on his face. The potent staff Allton held was knocked from his grasp and sent rolling away in the course of the attack. The spell-worker was not so dazed, though, as to be powerless, and as the demon plummeted down for a killing attack, Allton released a barrage of energy at the winged beast. There came a half-dozen or more little bolts, shining streaks of positive energy that struck the arched chest of the demon with snapping cracks as each took its toll.

Pazuzeus swerved and faltered momentarily, giving Allton enough time to roll and scramble erect. He stood in time to face a pair of lightning bolts from the angry demon's outstretched arms.

Pazuzeus grinned evilly as the electricity shot out and took his foe just as the human's little darts of burning energy had struck him. His malign glee was quickly transferred into a hawklike shriek of pain and rage, however, as much of his own lightning arced back from the mage to play around his multiwinged body.

The mage was protected against his powers, Pazuzeus knew, but not well enough. In the blow and return, the human had suffered much, while the innate force of the elder demon had dissipated most of the harmful effects of the encounter. Pazuzeus would be more circumspect in his applications henceforth, but in a battle of attrition, the mighty netherbeing knew that he would prevail. Just as Shabriri sought to use brute force to slay his opponent, so too Pazuzeus now rushed to seize and destroy Allton.

From his distant but magically close vantage point, the demonurgist contentedly watched the initial and subsequent exchanges with relish. Gravestone was content that his demon-thralls were suffering punishment from the two humans. Let both understand just how deadly even such lesser men as those could be in mortal combat. Shabriri and Pazuzeus would both be more obedient after this.

The priest-wizard had little doubt that they would triumph. But if the unlikely happened, and the so-called heroes who had thought to confront him personally began to get the upper hand, Gravestone would intervene directly. He had a carefully stored reserve of dweomer prepared. It could be tapped instantly, and then there would be no contest at all. "Let us see something exciting!" he shouted. That statement was simply meant as general encouragement to all concerned. Gravestone was rewarded with

261

a ferocious melee between the many-eyed Shabriri and the staunch Timmil.

It was painful, even damaging, but Shabriri broke through the screen that hedged the high priest. As the demon sought to grab the man who stood un-flinchingly before him, there was a nasty surprise, for the staff held by the cleric did more than send forth magical forces. Its metal-shod foot caught Shabriri squarely on his massive, horny knee with such force that the demon was toppled backward and sent into convulsions of writhing agony. Despite that, one of his massive hands swiped out, and as Shabriri fell, the razor-keen talons sliced crimson tracks across the face of his opponent. The demon concentrated, expending some of his power to ease the pain and repair the damage caused by the magically enhanced blow he had suffered.

Timmil had nearly lost both eyes. He was wounded seriously, and blood from the wounds caused by the demon's raking nails was making him virtually blind. Thus the high priest was unable to take advantage of the opportunity presented to him when Shabriri broke off the attack. Instead, he too expended some of his forces to cast a healing upon his own flesh. It was an easy enough thing to do, and it required no effort and little time.

When he finished and could see clearly again, Timmil was greeted by the sight of his monstrous adversary erect and grinning a fiendish grin. "Blow and return, it would seem, you dark dungheap of perdition," the cleric said calmly. "But your breaking the protective ward cost you more dearly than you know!" The last was said with triumph, and to punc-tuate the claim, Timmil loosed a combination of word and rune, the one spoken as the other was etched in the air in green-gold with the cleric's talisman-bearing right hand.

A cloud of intense black appeared instantly around Shabriri as the demon understood what was occurring. He knew that in his desire to rend the hated priest into bloody bits, his impetuous action in forcing himself through the guarding magical globe had stripped him of his own protections against dweomers sent by the cleric. "Korb! Haklo! Meemgul!" He shouted, even as the inky darkness surrounded Shabriri.

The power of the syllables spoken by Timmil made the ebony obscurement vanish, to be replaced by a storm of silvery motes. Those nearest Shabriri attacked the demon as if they were wasps. The priest smiled grimly as he saw the demon dance and howl as the thing tried to beat away the fiery tormentors. The glowing glyph he had drawn was likewise still extant. That saved the cleric's life, for in the next moment appeared a trio of ghastly, chimerical demon-things.

These lesser beasts were thralls of Shabriri, just as the elder demon had been forced into servitude to Gravestone. They had been brought to their master's side by the utterance of their actual names. Terrible indeed were these three, and their numbers would have served to finish Timmil then and there; but the symbol that hung in incandescent glory in the air struck them as they appeared. The lesser demons were frozen into agonizing immobility by its force.

"Banished forever, Korb, Haklo, and Meemgul, too! Torment and dark doom upon you eternally in the stinking cesses of your home!" The high priest too had their true names, given to him by the very cry of their master, Shabriri. There was a hideous sound as the exorcising magic seized the three and jerked their life forces back to the lowest portions of the abyss.

"You fecal-headed pig fornicator!" That was a mild thing for Shabriri to shout, but the raging fury that filled him spoke volumes. He belched a cloud of poisonous gas as he came forth, leaping and roaring, to grapple with his hated foe. Long and long had the three chimerical ones been his. Now, stripped of their vassalage, humiliated, weakened in imagined and real power, Shabriri had only one choice. He must kill the demon-baiter, Timmil, and return to his own plane with the corpse of the priest or else be forever consigned to lesser status and ever-shrinking power.

"Much better! Much, much better!" The words sounded as if they were spoken in his ears, but Timmil knew that they came from the distant form of Gravestone as the demonurgist lay back in obscene relaxation, ministered to unspeakably as he watched the spectacle. Ignoring his tormentor's words, Timmil met the elder demon's rush with the full might of his blessed, glory-filled staff. Although the great monster was twice the priest's height and ten times his weight, Timmil wore magical armor of finest make. His determination, weapon, and plate mail made the match an even contest. Demon and cleric sparred, struck, cast spells and circled in a dancelike routine of deadly intent.

Pazuzeus had attempted to change his own opponent's flesh into stone, force the mage into submission by sheer mental strength, rot the man's eyeballs with a sickly green ray, as well as to wound Allton by blows from his taloned feet and iron-nailed hands. In turn, the battered mage had somehow not only managed to resist but actually serve out more punishment to the demoniacal foe than he took.

Both archmage and elder demon knew that certain of their powers would not function on this demi-plane of Gravestone's creation, so rather than take the chance of wasting critical energies and precious time with something that would prove fruitless, both kept to basic assaults. Allton sent forth spells and struck blows with his mage's thick staff. Pazuzeus used his innate powers, both mental and magical, to assail the human, occasionally meleeing with the fellow so as to prevent the employment of some greater dweomer by the spell-binder.

The demon was now aware that Allton could see and know energy sources and uses. This ability put the mage at an advantage here, and the four-winged monster began to feel unease, fear. No mere human should be so puissant in the face of one as mighty as Pazuzeus!

"You two lumps of shit disappoint me!" The rebuke was clear to men and demons as well. Gravestone was again speaking, this time clearly disturbed that the gladiatorial combats were taking so long and still hanging in the balance. "Show me that you have testicles, both of you! Finish the fart-smudges; stop playing with them. Do it now, Shabriri, Pazuzeus, or else . . ." The demonurgist let his angry warning fade into what both of his thralls knew was no empty threat.

The effect was quite the opposite of what Gravestone had desired. The words he had grated out distracted both of the elder demons. A tiny distraction was all that either of their adversaries needed. The archmage was hurt, bloody, near exhaustion, but from somewhere deep within himself, Allton managed to draw up a reserve of energy. Flashing into supernormal speed, he struck Pazuzeus a stunning blow with his magical staff, then dropped it and jerked forth an egg-shaped thing of iron. With an exclamation of desperate hope, Allton hurled it squarely at the proto-demon's feather-crested head. "Die, darkspawn!"

Pazuzeus's reflexes were superb. He ducked his head with a motion too quick for a human eye to see, shrieking his own glee as he did so. The missile would have no chance to strike him, and the dolt had tossed his deadly staff aside, too!

The glee turned to stark terror in the next instant, for the sphere suddenly froze in mid-air. From it shot thick tongues of metal, iron bands that caged and held Pazuzeus. The unyielding metal was proof against the demon's power, and the bonds constricted to crush him into helplessness.

Simultaneously, the high priest employed his most potent weapon against Shabriri. As the red-orbed elder demon had his attention drawn by Gravestone's threatening voice, Timmil spoke a word and his own staff sprang into two. Each portion was a rodlike weapon. The one that was held in the cleric's left hand sent forth a blinding beam of hot, golden radiance brighter than the sun itself. The right-hand portion shed a cone of cool, soothing dimness. Each seemed a living thing unto itself.

With sweeping motions, Timmil plied the solar rod as if it were a broom. The palpable touch of the brightness sent Shabriri cringing and scurrying back. The demon was being moved inexorably into the umbral cone projected by the second rod held in the priest's now-confident grasp. Timmil knew that in a second the confused demon would retreat into the dimness, and once shaded therein, Shabriri would be helpless. He would diminish, grow weak, and come to his end as a tiny, doll-like monster unable to resist being sealed into some specially prepared container and condemned to some perpetual prison evermore.

"You are mine!" Allton gasped as he reeled and panted from fatigue. Pazuzeus, being slowly compressed by the deadly bands of iron, could make no reply to the claim.

"Minimus!" The thundering cry sprang triumphantly from Timmil's throat as he caught Shabriri in the demon-band cone and began the process of disabling and diminishing the fiend. Shabriri ranted and beat against the dimness that surrounded him, but no sound came out of the gray haze of the dweomer, and the ancient one of demon-ilk grew measurably smaller before the satisfied gaze of the high priest.

With a word Timmil ceased the brightness that radiated from the leftmost portion of the staff. The other demanded his full concentration, as the ancient precursor of demonkind struggled to get free. Soon now Shabriri would be no larger than a halfling and as powerless as a chattering monkey to free himself. There were weaknesses in the device, but as long as the wielder of the rod knew how to move the dim cone of diminishment, the demon or other netherbeing entrapped in it had but small chance of escaping. The high priest and demon-exiler had no intention of allowing his mighty foe to win freedom. Here and there he moved the rod, first with a slow motion, then a sharp twist followed by a series of jerky lateral motions. The shrinking, raving demon was foiled, bounced, battered, and confused. Just a little more time and it would be all finished.

"Your cage is a fine one, Pazuzeus?" Allton inquired sweetly. A thick band of magical iron clamped fast the demon's jaws, encompassing Pazuzeus's head and chin in a viselike grip. Other straps of enchanted metal wrapped shoulders, chest, abdomen, legs, and taloned feet. The great wings were flattened and there were cracking sounds initially when the iron clamped fast. The elder demon's wings were surely broken.

"Later, perhaps, I shall have you sing a little song for us . . . then you'll have nice seeds to eat." Allton couldn't restrain a little laugh after that. He glanced around. The cleric was just finishing his work. Shabriri was but a foot and a half tall. Where was Gravestone? Gone? No, the mage detected a cloaking screen of energies that had to indicate the place where the demonurgist sought to hide himself.

"Bring your little demonling here, Timmil," the spell-binder called. "I'll need your help with my caged fowl . . . foul? Heh! Heh! Heh! Ha . . . Then we'll spy out the hidey-hole which the cowardly Gravestone has dug for himself and keep him corked there until the others arrive."

"I hear," Timmil replied, drawing Shabriri's little form with him in the cone as he came over to stand beside Allton. "It was a hard fight, but easily enough accomplished in the end. Need we await Gord and the others?"

"Here is a flask of dweomered glass shot through with webbing, filaments of spun metal from a falling star." As the high priest took the bottle from his hand Allton added, "Lock up your atomie, and then pray shrink yon buzzard-king into a tiny mockery of itself, too. I have yet another of these jars for Pazuzeus."

"Are you gravely hurt?"

"Nay, although that bastardly demon fought stoutly and delivered many blows. Your ministrations would be appreciated."

"As soon as we have dealt with the winged one, then, you shall have them — my own self too needs some healing, mage. What of the bounding bands of iron which constrict Pazuzeus so well? Do they too shrink?"

Allton shook his lionlike mane as he looked at the demon. "No need of concern, my priestly friend," he told Timmil. "Turn that bird into a little wren, and the enchanted bonds will remain unaffected. With a command I can return them to their relaxed state, and thereafter they'll appear as naught but an iron egg of curious sort."

"In you go, Shabriri!" The high priest shooed the protesting little monster into the waiting bottle with a reed-thin beam of brilliance from the lefthand portion of his staff. "And now we have jugged Shabriri," Timmil said with a droll smile as he sealed fast a special stopper and set the container down to admire his handiwork. "Now for you, clip-wings," he added, turning to Pazuzeus and playing the cone of dim radiance upon the encaged demon.

"That's splendid, Timmil, splendid!" the archmage said with enthusiasm as the four-winged monster shrank slowly, giving forth two barely audible squawks of protest under the effect of the power. "Better still, our chiefest foe still cowers away behind his thick walls of magic. Methinks that the loss of these two demon servants has unmanned him!"

"Don't become so cocky, Allton," the cleric cautioned with a stern anxiety. "We managed the demons easily enough, I grant, but they were but slaves serving a greater master."

"Greater?" The mage's face showed a look of incredulity. "You can summon a storm, Timmil, but does that make your power greater than the fury of the winds and flash of lightnings? I think not, not at all, sir! The two of demon-ilk were undoubtedly the greatest of all the many vile servants of the demonurgist. He sent them against us because he himself was unable to face the combined strength we possess. Now he cowers."

"Are you sure? Perhaps the screen hides his next attack. Perhaps he is readying it now, while we preen ourselves here." Timmil was very concerned as he spoke.

"Perhaps," Allton agreed slowly. "Yet dealing finally with the two demons is necessary; and we both must restore ourselves as much as possible if we are to face Gravestone, don't you agree?"

"It will take but a short time, so I concur. Make ready the other flask now, and I'll insert the prisoner therein."

The latter task accomplished, Allton quaffed a draught of an elixir of restorative sort, while the high priest used healing powers first upon his own body, then on the wounds of his comrade. "Thanks, good priest," Allton said sincerely. "The mesh of forces yonder seems to be growing thicker and more active. Perhaps we should investigate."

"Wait a bit. Some hidden bane might still lurk within us from the foul touch of those netherbeings. I'll use some curatives and antitoxin workings to see us whole and sound. Then we can go and deal once and for all with the demonurgist."

Allton hefted his staff. "Yes, I think we must. I don't know where our champion is, but we should be derelict of duty if we tarried awaiting his eventual appearance."

"Where could he be?" Timmil said as he rummaged through his pack.

"Don't be concerned, priest." The voice sounded like Allton's, but as if the mage was speaking from a long distance away. "He is mired in a maze which will entertain him and the three who accompany him for hours — perhaps days or weeks. There is also the distinct possibility of him not getting through it alive!"

"Just how do you know that?" asked the cleric without glancing up.

"He doesn't," said the same voice. Then it changed to a deeper, more threatening tone that was also familiar to Timmil. "It is I, Gravestone, who speaks to you. Rest assured I know where the reputed champion is, and what he must overcome to arrive here at all."

The cleric's faced paled as he turned and stared at his companion, for Allton was frozen with shock at what he was hearing. Before either of them could move or act, the disembodied voice of the demonurgist spoke again:

"You have rested and recouped your strength, questing heroes. Let me now even things out. After all, it is Balance you seek, isn't it?"

Even as Gravestone said the latter words, unseen forces lifted the pair of magical prisons that held the shrunken demons. The crystalline bottles rose, and as they flew upward they expanded. Far above the heads of the two men the containers suddenly burst, raining down a torrent of sharp, jagged shards of glass as deadly as spears hurled by great giants. Both the cleric and the mage were too busy protecting themselves to notice what occurred immediately thereafter.

"Yes, this is much better," Gravestone said with arrogant satisfaction. "Round two commences!"

"May the gods deliver us," Timmil whispered. Allton gripped his staff grimly and remained silent. Before them stood the two demons, normal-sized again and with no sign of any harm ever having befallen either.

"Do we switch opponents?" Shabriri asked in his horrific, grating boom.

"No, brother, no," Pazuzeus replied as he fixed the mage with his dreadful stare. "I have personal business with a little human spell-tinkerer who thinks it amusing to break wings with a nasty little device he has. Perhaps it will expand from inside his intestine after I have shoved it up his ass!"

"Don't hurry with your fun, brother," Shabriri said. "That's the kind of sport I wish to enjoy!"

Chapter 14

THE SHIFTING NOTHINGNESS was oppressive. The nothingness-that-was-something made Gord's spirit sink, his courage shrivel and grow small. He wanted to hide somewhere, anywhere — even within himself, if necessary.

The terrible foe that Gord had faced upon entering this dismal world had vanished in the blink of an eye. It was only an illusion, and a short-lived one at that, but that knowledge did not hearten Gord. In fact, everything about this place had precisely the opposite effect on him. His very soul was shot through and through with despair and hopelessness. Even though he knew it was an artificially induced effect, he could not fight it off with the power of mind or magic. The force seemed to be strong enough to get through all of the defenses and protections that had been placed on his person.

He turned for some encouragement, looking toward Greenleaf. The druid was shivering, and his eyes were shut. "Curley!" Gord shouted with all the volume he could muster. It came out as a croak, but the half-elven priest of nature opened his eyes for a moment.

"Curley, don't allow this place to get to you," the

young adventurer continued as he saw the stark fear in his comrade's eyes. "We can manage it together."

"I can't manage anything," Greenleaf replied. "I can't look at the obscenities here." As he spoke, the druid shut his eyes, screwing up his face to close them tightly. It was evident that the formless place was not conveying the same sights to him as it was to Gord. He saw terrible things, while Gord saw nothing. Still, the effect on each of them was similar. Greenleaf, like Gord, acted as if all the fight had been drained out of him.

"Sit and remain calm," Gord said with a soothing voice that he managed to make strong and confident now. He had to, for otherwise his friend would surely go mad. "Gellor," he called, touching the druid still as he looked over his shoulder for the troubador, "please sing a song for us. And Chert, you sing along in that barbarian basso you so favor when giving voice to war songs!" It made him feel better to speak, to issue instructions. With each word Gord's voice gained in volume and the sound made his spirit rise, his courage expand.

Gellor had covered his enchanted eye, so that he was not forced to view this terrible place as it actually existed. "I'll do so," he replied when Gord spoke. The bard's voice was as harsh and croaking as his champion's had been at first, however, and his shoulders drooped. His fingers played upon the strings of his little kanteel, but only a discordant jangling arose. "Help me find the right note, Chert," Gellor whispered.

"Huh! No, no! I can't sing here," the hillman whispered back, licking his lips and trying to clear a parched throat. "You can do it without me. . . ." And then Chert went back to staring around, jerking his head wildly from place to place every so often as if trying to keep his eyes on some hovering threat.

"Come on now, both of you! I require it — and old Curley, here," Gord said as he squeezed the hunched shoulder of the druid, "wants very much to hear a stirring ballad of heroic sort."

Chert was turning now, wary, staring around his position with wide eyes that didn't see his comrades. No words spoken reached his ears. Gellor spat when he saw the antics, saying, "That oaf was ever too stupid and useless in a press!"

"Then sing alone, Lord Gellor," Gord urged.

"Sing for yourself," the one-eyed man replied in a harsh whisper. "I've no voice in this place. You've been placed above me — above us all. Go ahead and make music on your own, mighty champion." There was scorn and derision in the last word. Gellor made "champion" sound vulgar and dirty.

Anger began to wash over Gord. His brain sent a score of attack modes forth, a means of displaying to his critic just how potent a champion was and how painful his wrath could be, even as blood suffused Gord's vision. Seeing red, he did nothing for a split-second as the various means of punishing this detractor for his scorn flashed across his mind. The troubador was paying him no heed. Gellor was now directing his sarcasm and scorn toward the others.

"A giant too puny to shake away bogeymen he thinks are hiding out there, and a cringing druid who can't even speak. Why am I in such company? Because noble lineage and long accomplishment account for nothing with the addle-pated 'Masters' of balance." Gellor was barking now, his words still harsh and dry, but louder than before as he warmed to his task. "A lowly thief, that's who they give the laurels to. Oh, yes. Clever. A claim of illustrious parentage, substantiated only by the tomcat king, one always seeking to lord it over all the rest. Let this whelp—"

Gord's open palm struck Gellor's face with sufficient force to make the troubador stop talking and reel back. "Now, you half-assed, one-eyed old has-been!" Gord said with ice in his tone. "I'll make you masticate and swallow that talk. The eating will be most unpleasant — but you'll do it, or eat this!" The steely hiss of metal on metal seemed to fill the whole of the place as Gord's long, dead-black sword shot from its scabbard.

The slap seemed to have sobered Gellor, to have cleared his head and galvanized him to action. His own brand of enchanted steel shot out, the longsword giving forth a deadly sheen as he drew it with rapidity that matched that of the young thief who threatened him. "Cease your childish prattle," Gellor grated with a snarl to match his expression. "The time is overdue for such a settling of old accounts!"

The two blades cut through the air, rang against each other, darted, danced, circled. Close and apart and into intermediate ground the opponents leaped and danced, lunging and circling as they exchanged feints and attacks.

Gellor was the better swordsman, but only by a hair's breadth, and his advantage was outbalanced by the sword that Gord held. Each time its lightless metal struck the glowing steel of the bard's weapon, a tiny filament of deepest jet played along Gellor's blade. The tendril shot up and touched the hand that held the sword, and a minute fraction of Gellor's strength, speed, and energy was drawn from him through that leeching filament. Both men were pant-ing with tension and exertion, both bore small red badges attesting to the skill of the other.

"I use only my own force," Gord sneered after a quick exchange that resulted in a pricking of the bard's left forearm. "Come now, let's see your vaunted prowess, windbag!"

"Bah! You lean on a demon-cursed brand, whelp!" the troubador countered. "You'll need more!" His attack came so close on the heels of his shout that Gord was unable to react quite quickly enough, and now he had another little crimson-dripping cut to prove the excellence of Gellor's bladecraft.

"It is time to settle down to a conclusion," Gord said with a voice as hard as the steel of Gellor's sword. "In a trice, now, we'll find out just who is indeed fit to be champion."

"Save your wind," Gellor panted back. "You don't have long to enjoy such anyway."

"Gord! Gord! You are—"

Those four words were spoken inside Gord's head by a different voice, and the sound rocked him. A long lunge by Gellor at the same moment would have done for him, but his reflexes and enchanted mail both served to save him.

The voice had been Basiliv's. Gord knew it with certainty, just as he understood the communication had been mental, not physical. What disturbed him was the suddenness of its cessation. The Demiurge had been interrupted in mid-sentence by some force so powerful that not even Basiliv could resist it.

But despite the break, there was an image, a strong series of impressions, in fact, left in Gord's mind. There had been a message on two levels sent by the Demiurge, and the forced interruption had only partially succeeded.

The long thrust left Gellor off balance standing close to Gord. He was too near for an effective sword-thrust, though, and neither man was about to ply his dagger; this was a sword-to-sword duel. As the bard tried to recover, Gord smashed the hilt of his weapon against Gellor's temple with tremendous force. The one-eyed man dropped as if pole-axed.

"Sorry, my dear old comrade," Gord said aloud as he gently picked up the crumpled form and laid it beside the silent, withdrawn figure of Curley Green-leaf, where the druid huddled in introspective escape from the terrible nothingness around him.

All anger was gone from the young champion. He now had only purposeful resolve. "Now for Chert," he said softly to himself. As the struggle between Gord and Gellor was coming to a conclusion, the barbarian had begun to circle and pant, his eyes as huge and wild as those of a bull sensing lurking wolves nearby.

He attempted to come near, but Chert swung his battleaxe in a circle. The hillman uttered not a word, but Gord knew that Chert somehow believed that anything that came near was a deadly foe to be slain. Here was a problem indeed. In order to save them from this trap, Gord had to get his associates into a single spot, each in proximity to the other. Finally, he rolled Gellor and carried the withdrawn druid to a place as near to Chert as was possible without risk-ing their lives to the humming axe. "This will have to do," he said uncertainly. "I hope it will be sufficient."

As Gord moved to place himself as near as pos-sible to the still forms of Gellor and Curley, position-ing himself as close to the berserk hillman as he dared, the formless void that surrounded them all suddenly began to seethe and shape itself. Chert bel-lowed a challenge then, at last seeing the dreadful foes he had known were lurking just beyond his vision. Whether the visions that appeared to his eyes were the same nightmare forms that Gord saw was immaterial. The sudden activity in the place was due to Gord's resolution, his formed purpose. The nothingness sensed this change and was reacting. "Too late," the young thief said confidently.

Ignoring the threatening things that were now growing to loom on all sides, Gord sheathed Blackheartseeker and calmly began to shut out all distractions, gathering power within himself, yet at the same time remaining acutely aware of his comrades. As he did that, the roil of confusion that had just before seethed and stormed quieted to a mere brooding menace again. Chert settled down at the same time, seemingly exhausted from his recent expenditure of physical and especially mental energy. He sat, then slumped as if he was asleep.

Gord thought nothing of the place, so there was no stimulus for the plane to respond based upon his thoughts. In truth, Greenleaf had been correct in his reaction, at least in part. He was now safe, but he had no personal means of escaping other than withdrawal into a shell and eventual dehydration and death. Gellor had fallen prey to the terrible trap almost as easily as had Chert. "And I not far behind them either," he said wryly to himself as he thought momentarily of what had transpired. "Had not Basiliv's thought managed to reach me, we might all be dead by now." So pondering, Gord closed off even such reflections as that and did what he knew he must do.

Using the great store of force that had been granted to him by the diverse group of beings representing Balance, Gord mentally reached out and "felt" the form of the place. It was small, confined, restricted. It was but a single step amid a whole series that twisted upward to a place above. By the same means through which he was able to determine the nature of the space, the young champion also discovered the location of the next accessible step beyond the obvious, that which came next in order. He no longer needed to use single steps in order to progress upward; the Demiurge had depicted the means of bypassing the line of deadly traps mentally, and Gord had managed to grasp the idea shown. They had come but one-quarter of the route so far.

Reaching and grasping with his mind, Gord created a series of clean, small steps, a stairway within a stairway. He envisioned himself as a parent, his comrades as children. Mentally Gord swept up the three in his huge, fatherly arms, clasped them to his bosom, and bounded up the light, fair flight of steps he held firmly depicted in his brain.

Then he had to stop and rest. Carrying the three limp forms was heavy work. He thought about it, wished for it, and there suddenly appeared before him a landing, a platform with a long, padded bench. He placed the forms down carefully there, Curley first, then Gellor, and lastly the slumbering Chert. Even the latter was no larger than a big lad of six years. Seeing that the three were safe and resting quietly, Gord took a place at the end of the long seat and stretched his legs out. The muscles ached from the strain. It felt good to work the knots from his muscles, to let his arms hang limp so blood could course freely through veins and arteries, taking away lactic acid, bringing oxygen and nutrients. It required but a moment for sleep to overcome him.

Sometime later he was awakened by a tugging on

the hem of his leather jerkin. "Will you wake up?" Gord opened his eyes and saw the barbarian standing there on the alabaster floor of the landing. Chert's voice was a reedy piping, not the familiar rumbling tone that Gord had grown so used to.

"I'm awake, I'm awake," he snapped back rather grumpily. Chert clapped his hands to his ears.

"Not so loud!" he called, looking up.

Gord shook his head; then it came to him. The hillman had not shrunk — Gord had become gigantic. His voice was now that of a monstrous giant. "Sorry, Chert," he said as softly as he could. Gord peered around and spotted the druid and Gellor standing a short distance away, appearing to be torn between laughter and admiration.

"There's no doubt that you've grown," Gellor said. "The question is why?"

"To be able to cart you three useless heroes up the stairs," Gord responded with a bit of irritation affecting his tone.

"Where did those steps come from?" Curley Greenleaf asked with a puzzled frown. "Those aren't natural, if that term can be used to describe anything in the universe created by Gravestone."

"No, of course they aren't from the demonurgist," Gord explained. "I got a message from Basiliv, a warning, but it was interrupted, and — never mind. I'll tell you the whole lengthy tale later. Right now we have to go on. Suffice to say I made myself large to tote you three up the stairway. I thought these steps into existence in order to avoid the pitfalls waiting on the staircase which Gravestone would have us use."

That made the troubador smile. "So you managed to find a means to outfox the demonurgist? You've slipped us around his death maze?"

"I think so, Gellor, but it is difficult, even though the distance seems short and the climb minimal."

"How far?" Chert's question cut to the heart of the matter.

"I think," Gord replied slowly, "that there are about half of the step-dimension-traps left. We came through about two dozen, and I have already carried you past as many more. We should be able to make the rest of the journey quickly — now that you can clamber upward without need of my lugging along sleeping babes."

"Clamber is aptly put," the druid observed, eyeing the stairs. "Those are high!"

"But climb you must, no matter how strenuous it may be. Time is on the side of Gravestone, I fear. And what of Timmil? Allton?" Gord paused to let that sink in; then he arose and put his mind to the task. "I must concentrate on the actuality of these steps. It becomes more and more difficult as I ascend. If you must, ask for assistance, but I'd prefer it if you'd manage yourselves."

"Of course, giant-sized master of all," Chert said crossly. "We'll not disturb you." It was evident that he was quite unaccustomed to having his old companion be so much larger than he. Bad enough that Gord was the champion, but to be twice as tall, too, was almost more than the hillman could bear. That made the others laugh and broke the near-desperate gloom that had been hovering over their heads.

"Think to the time of your childhood," Greenleaf admonished.

"Barbarians have no houses, let alone stairs," the bard chided. "Think of them as hills, instead," he suggested. Gellor and the druid then were treated to the sight of Chert making a rude sign and stumping off to the task of climbing. Thus the four resumed their interrupted journey.

Time had no meaning in this no-place within no-place. Gord had mentally wrenched a portion of the demonurgist's quasi-universe from the control of its maker. Using the infusion of power granted to him, the young champion of the Balance had welded that force to the energy used by Gravestone to make the deadly planes between the real spheres to the multiverse. Using his own force was tiring enough, but to manipulate the evil energies that the priest-wizard marshaled in the making of his personal demesne and the multitude of death traps therein was so strenuous as to bring constant fatigue and near collapse to Gord. Somehow he managed. The four struggled up the tall steps. The change was gradual, but Gellor, Chert, and Greenleaf grew taller with each upward plane. They also grew more tired.

"This is not at all like climbing up normal steps," the barbarian said with consternation. His size relative to Gord was now back to normal. He towered over the dark-haired young man, head and shoulders, and his body was that of a Hercules. He was puffing, though, and Gord was not.

When Gord allowed another rest, Gellor asked, "How are we being drained so? Aren't we slipping past the demonurgist's traps?"

"Slipping? No, not hardly. I am struggling to keep this way open, using my force to bend his, as a bar pries and levers a greater weight. We must move on soon."

"Why are we tiring so?"

"That, good druid, is because I am using your strengths as well as my own to manage this all."

Whether or not there was protest from his comrades about to be voiced at that revelation, Gord would never know. They were all about to speak when the pale stone of the staircase, the bench, and the walls that seemed to support all began to turn dull yellow and crack. "The demonurgist is trying to wrest his energy back!" With that shout of warning, the champion leaped to his feet and sought to re-form the alabaster stair by concentration. His three friends stood close at hand, likewise concentrating on the reality Gord desired. The stone went to dull brown and began to crumble away despite this.

As the stuff fell away beneath their feet, Chert lunged sideways. He had spotted a new plane there, a place of possible refuge from endless plummeting, if not safety from danger of other sort. "Grab Curley!" he roared to Gellor as Chert himself clamped his hand around the bard's left arm and pulled him toward the opening that led off into somewhere.

Gellor managed to snag the druid's short cloak, so Greenleaf too was pulled off toward the refuge. There was a rumbling crash, and the whole of the alabaster stairway fell. Its now blackish walls cracked and slipped down, slowly at first but then quickly dropping off into a nothingness that seemed to terminate on broken rocks a mile below. Gord was plunging downward with the discolored stuff of the stairway.

"Save him!" the hillman shouted desperately.

"I can't!" the druid screamed. He thought desperately, and Gellor was tugging out something from his girdle to likewise attempt some rescue, when the opening snapped shut. Chert, Greenleaf, and the one-eyed troubador were simply standing on a strangely illuminated platform. It was a place of uncertain substance and indeterminable distances.

"What happened?" Chert managed to ask.

"We escaped. Gord didn't," Gellor told him flatly.

The druid broke into the conversation with a bitter tone. "We were already at the top when we rested. Look!"

There, in the distance, they saw Timmil and Allton in combat with a pair of terrible demons, while the hated Gravestone reclined in comfort on a divan, enjoying the battle in ease and comfort.

"Rot that stork-legged bastard's eyes!" Chert had Brool ready and was striding toward the demonurgist as he spoke. "He'll find out how true men avenge their friends!"

"No, Chert, wait! We must help Allton and Timmil first, then deal with that spider."

The barbarian half turned. "Somebody's got to keep the bugger occupied, and I'll vote for me." He glared at the druid as if daring Greenleaf to dispute his words.

"You and Curley hurry to our friends' need," Gellor said firmly. "Hew the demons down! I'll counter Gravestone's dweomers with my music — I *can* work much with it for a little time, even against one as powerful as the demonurgist. But as soon as possible, come to my aid. This will be no easy task!"

For a moment the big hillman hesitated, torn between his desire to hack the priest-wizard to pieces and the logic of what the bard said. "All right," he growled. "You keep the filthy scum in check for a few minutes, then we'll come to help you finish the business. Come on, Curley. We've got a couple of lousy demons to deal with."

Greenleaf would have laughed at those words, only his throat was somehow constricted and no laugh would come. Deal with a pair of demons? Chert made it sound like a hawking after hares! More likely it would be doom for them or Gellor. No, probably doom for them all. Without Gord they didn't have much chance. Still, the plan Gellor had sketched was the only one that had any hope at all.

"I'm coming, Chert," the druid managed to say, hurrying and puffing as he trotted after the barbarian. "Slow up a bit, for we should fall upon the enemy together as a force!"

As the two dashed off to assist in the fight against the demons, Gellor drew forth his slender little harp, placing a ring upon his right forefinger as he gently touched the silver and gold strings of the kanteel. With care he sang a song whose verses had immediate effect. The one-eyed man was suddenly beside the demonurgist, and the latter was just as quickly immersed in black rituals of magic to counter the dweomer of the music Gellor played and sang. The denizens of the netherspheres who had been surrounding Gravestone vanished at the first of the troubador's notes. The two were alone in their contest.

Shabriri happened to be the closer of the two ancient demons to Chert, so Brool sang its song for the multi-eyed demon's discomfiture. Chert came running, swinging the massive battleaxe at waist height as he rushed into the fray. Its edge took Shabriri's scaled calf, laying it open. Ichor flowed, and the demon snarled at the stinging pain. It was far from a telling blow, but the hillman saved Timmil's life by his sudden onslaught. Shabriri had been about to finish the priest. Now the great elder demon had another foe to contend with. As Shabriri turned and battled with the wild giant, Timmil crawled off a little way and tried to gather strength to resume the fight. He was weak, nearly dead, but the old cleric was not ready to surrender to the mercy of a demon!

It was much the same with the druid's reinforcement of Allton. The lion-maned mage had nearly exhausted his spells, and was in sore straits when Greenleaf arrived to do battle with Pazuzeus. The enchanted staff that the druid wielded and his store of dweomers sufficed to save Allton from death, but the archmage was in no position to take advantage of the arrival of help by pressing his own attack. As Greenleaf contested with the huge demon, Allton retreated out of harm's way for a moment and sought remedies for his ebbing strength.

There was a series of terrible exchanges between demon and druid. The latter dealt great harm to Pazuzeus, no question. Allton saw the ancient one of demoniacal evil reel and writhe from spell and staff as Curley Greenleaf fought valiantly against the fiend. Even after all that the mighty demon had undergone before, however, his power was too great for the druid. Inexorably, the might of Pazuzeus was wearing down Greenleaf. Allton had to rejoin the battle and even the odds. Only a short step from the gates of death himself, the wizard set his face in a determined line and came forward again. Just then, the demon struck Greenleaf with some spell or force that caused the druid to scream and fall senseless.

Nearby, Chert was faring but little better in his fight with the huge Shabriri. Seared, battered, bleeding from many wounds, the barbarian still stood firm and struck. Brool's kiss had left the demon a gory reminder from leg to torso, but no blow from the edge of the enchanted axe had been telling. Hurt, weakened, but by no means on the verge of defeat, Shabriri was devising his final stratagem, the attack with which he would slay the barbarian who dared stand and fight against him, when Timmil re-entered the melee.

"Demon!" The priest's voice was an unnatural boom. Shabriri spun toward the challenge, startled and surprised. The cleric's staff was cast aside, its force exhausted, but Timmil grasped his amulet of faith, and the pure metal of the symbol glowed with a radiance that nearly blinded the demon.

"Back to the dark netherworld forever!" Timmil commanded as he advanced. "Never return, spawn of the elderdregs!"

Shabriri took a small step backward, more in uncertainty than fear. The cleric was no longer powerful enough to exorcise him, that the demon knew with certainty. Then his long-nailed foot slipped just a little on the blood his raking talons had drawn from Chert's body. Shabriri directed his multi-eyed gaze down to the floor for a second. The demon had no intention of slipping and falling, of being laid prone and vulnerable.

That was all the opportunity Timmil needed. With a resounding shout of triumph, the priest launched himself through the air, grabbed the huge creature, and spoke a word of condemnation. That potent word carried Timmil and Shabriri both from the place to the depths of the netherplane that was Shabriri's own. Chert saw the flash, heard the rolling thunder of the consignment, and wept.

As if in a ritualized ceremony, a tragedy with a prescribed conclusion, Allton was engaged in a desperate act even as the old antagonist of demonkind sacrificed himself to exile Shabriri. The mage had no great spells left, no power in his castings, no repository of energy with which to continue on against Pazuzeus — except one. His staff still contained some strength, and Allton now used it to smite his demoniacal foe. As he struck, he recited the syllables of release, of unleashing, of direction. Each had its purpose, one to channel dweomer one way, another to send energy another, a third to free power, a fourth to change forces in some fashion.

Four and more Allton cried aloud as he struck. Each took effect. The staff was a tuner, a receiver and transmitter of energies as well as a store for such forces. It resonated, opened channels, sent forth rays, drew power, and it did so all in an instant of time.

"Cease, foo—" was all Pazuzeus managed to bellow before the ancient construction of wood and metal and magical bindings malfunctioned. The event occurred just as its wielder knew it would. Too many energies flew from it, too many currents were drawn into its confines — far, far beyond the capacity of its strength.

A tiny rupture between its forces and the negative flow of the anti-world occurred. The fabric of the multiverse mended itself quickly enough. Only a brief spurt of the dark energy came out to meet the raging blazes of power from other places. But even as the demon tried to shout, to delay, even to beg a truce, the dark and light blended and devoured each other. Only a little of the bright disappeared, enough to balance the negative — but the great force of that brief transfer of energy blew the ancient staff to nothingness. The eruption of power from that explosion devoured demon and mage alike in a pink-white flash that sent Curley Greenleaf farther along the path toward death's looming gates.

The condemnation of Shabriri to the depths of wherever he sprang from, Timmil's sacrifice, and that of Allton at nearly the same time, made Gellor falter in his contest. The demonurgist blinked too, but he recovered more quickly. He sent forth a wave of unmaking, a power stolen from the archmage Morden-kainen. Its force disjoined the song of his enemy, scattered its dweomer, broke the strings of the kanteel the troubador held. The rebounding of the bard's own casting stunned him, and Gellor was laid low instantly.

"Five in the pot," Gravestone said with a sneer. "One more to make the dish better still, and then my feast is done!"

Chapter 15

THE SHARK-TOOTHED ROCKS rushed to meet his body, to impale his helpless flesh upon their waiting points. But Gord simply willed it otherwise, and it was. He fell no longer; rather he strode along a dun road in a wild land of twisted trees and formless evils.

Was this another of the demonurgist's creations? Perhaps . . . but there was a subtle difference here. Wherever he looked Gord could see clearly, as if mighty beams of light sprang from his eyes, and nothing could escape his gaze here.

"I would the road were smooth," he muttered. At his command the surface under the soles of his high boots became as a polished floor of marble.

"Let me ride a mighty destrier," he thought, and suddenly the young champion was astride the broad back of a stallion. Despite different saddle and barding, Gord knew the animal instantly. "Blue Murder! Valiant steed of younger days, how came you here?" The stallion whickered and shook its head at the words as if relating his surprise at finding himself as Gord's mount in this strange realm.

"Gellor! Timmil! Greenleaf!" he then called out. "Chert! Allton! To me, all five!" That demand brought nothing at all save a graying of the horizon toward which Blue Murder now carried him. The place was not totally his — or, at least, things beyond its confines could not be called here by its forces. No matter. Gord would discover the nature of it soon, deal with it, and find his companions. "I will discover the guardian of this plane," he said.

The road was now a shimmering pathway with no end. It ran unsupported through space. Fields of stars were everywhere. Some glowed near, revealing their spheres in pure violet, white, green, deep red. Some twinkled so distantly as to seem but a single mote, but Gord's magical sight revealed them as whole galaxies of suns burning in a remoteness so vast as to make the heart falter in its beating.

The sudden change had affected his steed as well. Blue Murder was even bigger, more magnificent, and wore the twin horns of a dragon-horse, a ki-lin whose hooves sent trailing sparks of silver and gold behind as they struck the surface of the strange pathway.

"Swiftly, swiftly!" Gord urged, and his mount responded. The stars began to fly past, as if they were comets with fiery tails. Now to either hand, below, and above the champion of Balance could discern other places. By hue or scent, and some even by actual vision into their expanses, Gord saw the whole multitude of the many-sphered cosmos whip past. Elements, probabilities, ether, the yawning hells, bright planes of splendor and exaltation, dim places of disorder and chaos. There was the all-present realm of the Shadowking, above it the broad vault of the pure astral plane, and far, far beneath the scintillating trail the ki-lin left were the dreaded sinks of Hades, the nadir of all the manifold netherspheres. "No dark glow emanates therefrom, Blue Murder," the young champion shouted. "Onward!"

Myriad shades of verdant green, hues associated with green, too, from deep olive to citrine to pale aqua, spun now beneath him as the dragon-horse galloped. Tiny wedges and broad archways displayed the various means of entry to the multitude of hidden and arcane places. Whether partial plane, demi-sphere, or quasi-dimension, each such place was visible to the young champion as the ki-lin raced along the multiversal highway. Gord shook his head and turned away. There was an infinity of these places, but not one held what he desired. Blue Murder, if the strange mount was indeed that great stallion in a transformed body, was now bearing him toward an opalescent roadway, a flowing path that intersected with the ribbon upon which they had traveled so strangely.

"What is this you take me to?" Gord demanded.

The ki-lin made no sound whatsoever in reply, only redoubling its efforts so that the suns and stars blurred and disappeared. Abruptly the steed gave a strange, mournful call and leaped into the river of opaline light. Then the young champion who bestrode it knew that he was within the very flow of time itself.

"No," he commanded the steed. "You must battle the current! Go backward!"

The ki-lin shook its horned head and continued on. After only a few heartbeats, they were thundering up a metal-like bank and out of the glowing stuff with its myriads of scenes and standing stock still upon a flat and featureless expanse of what could only be purple chitin. The horizon was a knife-edge in the ultimate distance, the sky made of strata of pale, grayish stuff, each layer tinged with a faintly different hue.

Gord urged his steed on. The beast must know the

place where the guardian of all this was. "I still seek to confront the one who will enable me to pass beyond," the young man said to the dragon-horse. "Whether Blue Murder or some imitation, you have obeyed so far; now fulfill your obligation!" At that the mount simply vanished, and Gord fell with a crash onto the unyielding stuff beneath.

The sudden precipitation dazed him, but in a second or two Gord was recovered and standing erect. He did so in time to see that the horizon was coming closer . . . no, the plane was contracting! All was shrinking, drawing toward the center — the place where he himself stood. This was disconcerting, threatening. Gord sensed a looming presence, a lurking evil that would manifest itself at any moment.

Crouched slightly, sword now drawn and ready, the champion of Balance waited. A faint wind blew, hardly stronger than a zephyr, yet its force was sufficient to tug at Gord's body and nearly drive him along before its path. He looked down at himself and saw that he was transparent. "Oh, shit, no! I can't be dreaming!" Gord pinched himself. His fingers encountered firm flesh and hurt as they closed and nipped. "Yowch! No, this is something other than a dream, I think. . . ."

Now he could no longer see himself at all, not even Blackheartseeker as he held the dull ebon of its long blade before him. "Why?" he whispered the question as he peered nervously around.

Voices. Behind him stood the demon queen Zuggtmoy in her most hideous form. Conversing with that horror was an ancient and equally loathsome crone. It could be none other than Iggwilv, the mother of witches.

Each held a darkly luminous object with her pride

and arrogance plainly displayed. There was a slight disturbance, a darker place in the air between them, and each moved slightly so as to make the distance that separated them greater. In that instant another form appeared suddenly. It was the naked, red-hued form of the cambion demi-god Iuz. Demi-god? No longer, it seemed. Iuz was fully a head taller than the demoness, and his bulk was as great. The cambion had grown larger, more powerful, and more assured. He too held a luminous object in his hands, and his huge mouth opened to show the rows of pointed teeth that filled it as he fully materialized.

"Welcome, my son," the greatest of hags croaked.

"Greetings, Lord of Pain," Zuggtmoy breathed in her dank, fungoid voice.

"Ho! Ho! Ho!" Iuz boomed his mirth, allowing it to roll and play into the distances of the plane. "This is the place you have chosen, is it?"

"Yes, dear boy," the cambion's horrible mother said gleefully. "It is a place where none but ourselves can reach. Not even that corpse-lover Infestix can disturb us here," she simpered, looking to the fungus heap that was Zuggtmoy as if seeking approval.

The fungi demoness didn't disappoint Iggwilv. "A most clever notion, don't you agree, Iuz, my pet?"

She might have said more, but the cambion spoke rudely in interjection.

"Never call me that again, toadstool slut!"

"Be nice," the crone-mother admonished without force. "We three are an inseparable group now. Give me your Theorpart, dear Iuz, and mother will make the two a great tool for your power—"

"Tush! Don't interfere now, 'Wilva. The key must be given to me for the initial joining." Zuggtmoy shifted shape as she spoke, becoming a beautiful and seductive human as she conversed. "So I will accept your offering now, Iuz," the demon queen said in her now-sultry voice.

Iuz shook his head. "If we are conjoined, then we must act so, my lovely consorts!"

"What?" Iggwilv demanded somewhat irritably, even as she too shifted form to appear as a brightly clad and gorgeous young woman.

"How is that?" The beauty that was now Zuggtmoy demanded almost simultaneously.

"Each must hold forth that portion of the tripartite relic which she has, just as I do now," the cambion said smoothly, smilingly, as he extended his right arm and held the oddly shaped portion he possessed in such a manner so that it pointed toward the chitinous surface of the place. "Now you two must do likewise, and so doing we will gently bring the three together so as to form a whole!"

Zuggtmoy hesitated, looking at Iuz, then at Iggwilv. The ancient witch was likewise uncertain. She stared at her offspring, then looked at the fungi queen. The two exchanged glances, each suspicious, doubting the cambion, questioning each other as well. As if by some silent mutual concord, both then turned to stare at Iuz. He stood as before, still amiable, a faint smile upon his huge face.

"Come, come! This act is to make us the unquestioned masters of all, the most powerful beings in the multiverse. Our wills alone have sufficed to keep the relic disjoined, to maintain the bindings upon Tharizdun. . . . See? I freely speak that turd's name without fear! It is we three who will rule, not he!"

Zuggtmoy hesitated, then nodded, and slowly extended her Theorpart. "Come on, Iggwilv, you too!" Her tone was harsh.

"Oh, very well," said the witch. "Here is—"

"Ieeuuzzz!"

The ferocious, rising shout that the cambion let out made both of his tensely extending arms twitch reflexively. Iuz had instantly dropped his portion of the relic when the other two had been held forth, and his long arms shot forth to seize the extended artifacts of the evil one's prisoning. The long fingers of his hands clamped with an iron grip, and the muscular arms jerked back with lightning speed. The horrified eyes of both Iggwilv and Zuggtmoy saw events as if in slow motion as the cambion brought his twin prizes to him, then lifted both overhead in exultation.

All of this time Gord had watched without attempting anything. He was uncertain if he was invisible, undetectable, to the trio. When Iuz tore the two keys from the grasp of his supposed co-masters of all, a shout of horror rose unbidden from the young champion's chest and was out of his mouth in a rush. His cry went unheard, however, for even as it vented forth, the three were themselves screaming at the top of their lungs.

"Nooo!" Zuggtmoy bellowed, trying to shift shape again.

"Wait!" Iggwilv screamed, hoping to gain time.

"Mine! You are mine!" Iuz shouted in triumph as he placed a massive, clawed foot upon the last portion of the relic. As he did so, the cambion used the other two together, bringing left and right parallel, portions touching.

"Dry dust!" he thundered, aiming the weird pair directly at his mother. Iggwilv blew away in the breeze, a little whirl of powder.

"Empty air!" he shouted, as he turned and leveled the twin Theorparts at the half-female, half-fungoid

297

thing that was Zuggtmoy. The demoness vaporized, and the little haze of smoke she had been was instantly gone, too.

Iuz pranced and capered at that. "I am King! I am All! None can stand before Me! All, all, all is Mine!"

Gord was rooted to the spot. He watched as Iuz bent, scooped up the final portion of the dreaded artifact, and without hesitation fitted it into the other parts to form a whole. "This cannot be. . . ." Gord managed to whisper. As if in answer to that, thunder rolled in the distance somewhere. Thunder?

"Thunder?" The question in Gord's mind was echoed by the mouth of Iuz. The cambion left off his cavorting and stared at the horizon. It retained its pale, varicolored strata, yet the rumbling came from there. It was like thunder, but it was continuous. Iuz stared, immobile.

"It draws closer," the huge demon said at last. "Who dares to disturb the Master of the Multiverse?" Iuz finally demanded in a voice almost equal to the thunder itself.

There was no answer. The plane itself contracted, though, and the rolling boom of thunder grew louder still. There was no doubt in Gord's mind. The source of the noise was closer still. He could move now, but there was nowhere to go. Even as those thoughts raced through the young champion's mind, the place shrank still more. Now it had definite boundaries, perceivable dimensions. It was a rectangle of miles in depth, leagues in breadth. Still huge, but contracting, diminishing. Iuz raged and thundered in reply to the booming of the plane itself, and when they so contested, Gord saw the dimensions of the chitinous layer grow smaller and smaller until he and the cambion occupied a space no larger than a few hundred paces deep and thrice that across. Then the noise stopped, as did the shrinking, when a thin plume of dark smoke appeared against the pearlescent horizon.

Iuz noted the column of smoke and strode toward it. "Who dares to intrude upon Me?" he demanded. "What entity is so bold as to defy the wishes of Iuz?"

There was no reply. The smoke thickened, grew taller, and from its uppermost portion gleamed motes of bright amethyst hue, a purple fire within the dense, dark cloud, perhaps. The cambion was non-plussed but determined. "I sense your presence," he shouted, standing not fifty paces from the stuff. "I grow tired of this game," the half-demon added. Casually he lifted the awful form of the ancient relic he held and pointed it at the smoke. "Now, thing of folly, you see the might of Iuz!"

A blazing beam of violet light sprang from the arti-fact, stabbing into the cloud. The dark smoke seemed unaffected by it. In fact, the smoke fractured the ray, splitting it in twain, and the twin beams thus created seemed to stoke the purple glow within the cloud of smoke. Now there were two gaps in the blackness, and from them burned the amethyst light. Holes like eyes, light as of lambent orbs within those sockets.

"I . . . Nooo!" It was the cambion's turn to shriek denial, to try to flinch back to escape what he saw.

"Oh, yes!" laughed a gigantic voice of pure evil.

The top of the dark column had formed itself into a head. The bright amethyst fires were Tharizdun's own eyes, of course. The being's vast maw was a purple-black deeper than endless night, a lipless mouth with teeth and tusks and fangs in size and profusion beyond belief. Hide as black as Graz'zt's own midnight skin, as hairless as a newborn babe's skin, as hideous as the leathery coverings of the

299

gates of doom. Every unspeakable evil, each blemish of the world's ugliness covered Tharizdun — at least all of the terrible being that was now visible to Gord's horrified gaze . . . and to the eyes of the shrinking cambion.

"Greatest of Great Evils," Iuz whimpered, "forgive your worthless spawn, Iuz. I beg you to accept my homage, this . . . this artifact which is truly yours." As he spoke that, Iuz held forth the tripartite instrument. This time, however, he made no attempt to wield its power against the half-formed lord of the netherspheres.

Tharizdun chuckled and drew a deep breath. The relic of his binding, the hoped-for eternity of unending slumber, crumbled into bits, the pieces themselves into flakes. Those in turn became motes, and all vanished into the flaring nostrils of the most vile one.

"Better, little demon, much better," Tharizdun said in a whispery voice. "Now come! Kiss the hand which will rule you!"

The cambion almost flew out of his own blood-hued skin at the command. Then Iuz managed a shaking, trembling bow, and literally leaped to obey. He flew toward the ever more complete being of evil incarnate, saying, "I am your slave, Most Wicked. I am yours to do with as you will."

"Very commendable, Iuz," Tharizdun boomed. The cambion now stood close to him, very close. Tharizdun reached out. Iuz was a rabbit before the paw of a tiger; nonetheless he stood steady and actually kissed the massive hand of the ruler of the depths. "I accept your homage," Tharizdun whispered.

He then spoke further in a voice that rose to a thundering volume again. "I likewise accept your slavery, and now grace your unworthy existence with an act of my own — the first in eons."

"Unto me, Utmost Darkness?"

"Unto you, Iuz-that-was." With a deep laughter that was totally an expression of malign hatred and ineffable wickedness, Tharizdun took the cambion into his monstrous right hand and lifted him high. "Observe the view as your Master sees it," Tharizdun bellowed, still with a voice brimming with evil mirth. Then the terrible god tossed the cambion up, caught him again, and squeezed. A piercing shriek came from Iuz as his bones were splintered, organs ruptured. Pinkish ichor started to flow from his orifices — eyes, ears, nostrils, mouth, everywhere.

Tharizdun's talonlike nails sank deeper into his victim's flesh as he looked down with satisfaction at his handiwork. "Yes, slave, I choose your death now, rather than wait for betrayal and rebellion at a later time." Then the glowing eyes of pure purple looked up from the corpse of Iuz clutched in his hand and out across the chitinous plane. "Now for you, little champion. . . . Muoohhahahahaha!"

Gord had soiled himself in far less threatening circumstances — years before, at a time when he was little and helpless. Yet he thought of that time now, and he felt as powerless as "Gutless Gord" had felt in the grasp of the bully-boy called Snaggle. His knees sagged, his spirit quailed. Gord had found revenge against the ones who had made his childhood a nightmare of fear, hunger, and self-disgust. His reason told him that no such evening of the score would ever occur hereafter. "If that be the case," Gord managed to say to himself aloud, "then why not go as a wolf rather than a rabbit?"

"Go? You will go nowhere!" Tharizdun had heard.

The amethyst eyes bathed Gord with a wash of brightness. "You think to fight against Me. You will attempt to, even though I can break you in one hand as I did the bloated spawn of Iggwilv and Graz'zt! That is stupid. I will kill you easily, if you try."

Gord lowered the tip of his sword, uncertain. It had taken all of his strength, his resolve, to point it at the terrible creature of darkness. Tharizdun was taking time to speak to him, and that made the young man pause.

"Good! Well you might ponder, wonder, consider. I will crush you in an instant if you think to fight against Me. I will accommodate your talents if you serve. Think you that I love or trust the vile dregs of the netherworld who fawn upon Me? Never! They are a race of liars and backbiters, each seeking to usurp My headship. If you swear oath to Me, Gord, accept Me as your King, then I will make you the Lord of Arms of My Kingdom, and that is All . . . Everything. You will repress all the others, be a Viceroy, have everything I do not desire personally."

*　*　*

"He is a deceiver, Gord."

"What? Oh. . . . Tharizdun is false?"

"That, too."

"Of course, but I—"

"You what? Listen? Consider?"

"No. I seek to not fulfill my obligation."

"That one slew me, Gord."

"I think otherwise. Tharizdun has been chained and helpless till this moment."

"Remains thus; and you do not heed. The one you see is the murderer."

302

"Now . . . I understand."

"Blessed culmination of my being, all fortune to you."

"Will we speak again thus?" Gord's mental voice was strained, then almost pleading.

"That cannot be, as you know in your heart . . . not yet for ages of your time will we meet otherwise. It is naught. We shall. You are. Let that suffice."

"Thank you, my father."

There was no reply, no form visible to his mind's eye. Gord was again alone, his brain unoccupied by anything save his own thoughts. The voice of the dark, nearly formed Tharizdun penetrated his consciousness.

* * *

"Well? What is your answer, man? I grow impatient. Those who think to be Mine must instantly obey!"

"Obey you? That is a jest!" Gord spat in the general direction of the monstrous being, raising Blackheartseeker as he did so. "I'm loath to spoil this fine weapon by thrusting it into such corruption as you, Tharizdun — but I shall!"

Iuz was still clutched in Tharizdun's huge left hand, the long, misshapen fingers of the malign monster smeared with the cambion's blood. The great right hand stretched forth toward Gord, purple talons as long as scimitars, clicking and rattling eerily as the digits writhed in anticipation. "Come then, Gord-the-dead. It is your doom!"

As the hand suddenly shot toward him, Gord leaped to meet it.

Chapter 16

THE LONG, SALLOW FACE of Gravestone was beaded with sweat, but otherwise there was no sign that he was alive.

He sat, in a trance, upon a flat pad on a steplike dais. It was circular, dark, and graven with sigils and writings of power and warding. Near to him three candles burned, each with a flame the color of its wax — black, plum, deep crimson. From a brass bowl resting on his crossed legs arose smoke, tiny columns of vapors. Each was of a different hue, each betokening one of the netherspheres.

The faint haze reeked of noxious drugs, an odious stench. These drugs aided the priest-mage in his work. When he needed the stuff of flame and incense, the candles flared and smoke streamed upward. A sudden inhalation, more sweat, then absolute stillness again. The flickering tongues of the candles' flames receded to mere glimmers then, and the tiny streams of noisome stuff resumed their slow rising.

Nearby, watching for what seemed hours, Gellor gazed upon the scene. But the bard was by no means idle. He was struggling to free himself from the bonds that held him as Gravestone sat in his trance. The bonds were of both physical and magical sort, however, and the attempt to win free of them was proving to be long, if not fruitless. Curley Greenleaf was nearby, his condition very serious. Gellor thought the druid was sinking toward death. Chert was there too, battered and bloody but awake and silently straining to free himself just as the troubador fought against his bonds.

A figurative "third eye" watched the three. Despite the trance, Gravestone was not so foolish as to allow enemies to be in proximity without being under observation, bonds or no bonds. This mental watch would trigger an alarm instantly. The priest-wizard had a special surprise awaiting, and his attention would be needed for only a moment if the spell was required to deal with one or more of the captives.

The demonurgist was not thinking about all that, however. At the moment he was deep into the dweomers he had spun. A final trap was in action, and he personally must oversee the occurrences, utilize his powers to operate the whole of it.

It was a masterful and deadly piece of work. The trap had three levels of complexity, three ways of snaring the enemy therein. First and least likely was despair and withdrawal. Both the spectacle and information imparted by the magic were set to promote the proper mood for dejection and hopelessness. Those emotions, that mental state, was enhanced as fully as Gravestone could manage by powerful spells. The adversary within the trap was very potent, charged with magical energy himself, so Gravestone dismissed the likelihood of the initial snare actually functioning as was hoped for.

The second level, that of persuasion and subversion, was insidious in that it played off of the first grouping of power. Even though the enemy might ultimately reject the dweomer of forced surrender and inaction, it would surely affect him nonetheless. Thus primed, there was a greater potential for the acceptance of offers meant to appeal to the base and low desires contained in even the best of persons. Together, then, the demonurgist gave the first and second ploys about four chances in ten of success.

Five in ten was the probability he placed upon the final tier of the trap. That was physical combat based upon mental conviction. Accepting what was seen and experienced, the victim mired in the snare would accept and fight back against the threat. More insidious than the second snare, this portion played off both foregoing magics. Best of all, Gravestone was there mentally to channel energy and force. The attacks of the illusory opponent would be far from imagined. The vision of Tharizdun he had enspelled and now operated would utilize very real attacks of terrible power against the would-be champion.

Even if that fool discovered the figure he opposed was naught but a false image, it would be too late. Blasts of magic from the demonurg ʼs own store of dweomer would cut him down before he could escape. Gravestone recalled for an instant his pleasure in slaying this young upstart's father and mother. He had enjoyed the woman's terror as—

The extrasensory alarm in his head blared its warning. This was terrible! The final confrontation and fight between the champion and the illusory Tharizdun was commencing. The demonurgist mentally set a fixed program of actions for the phantom deity of all evil, sufficient in force and deadliness to keep the man occupied for a minute or two. That was ample time, for he needed only a few moments to deal with the three prisoners. Gravestone had thought to

307

keep them alive for questioning and amusement. Under the circumstances, though, he would now simply kill them, then return to the direct handling of what would be the demise of the last hope of all who opposed evil.

It was at the instant that Gord leaped toward the illusory Tharizdun that the mental warning was triggered in the demonurgist's mind. Even as he shut off the telepathic link with the trap, leaving it on a program that included triggering of actual magical energies, and turned his attention toward the bound captives, Gord did what the demonurgist had not anticipated. The phantasmal form of the dark god was nothing, but the hand that reached forth to seize the young champion was enspelled with dweomer and meant to crush Gord. Instead, Gord used his acrobatic ability to bound up and actually stand upon the bundle of force that was the enspelled member. *That* was the last step. . . .

* * *

"What's this?!" Gravestone blinked and stared, using magic as well to examine the three bound enemies. None of them were actually loose. "But why did the warning sound . . . ?" Thinking about that, the demonurgist decided to slay them instantly anyway and return full attention to his chief antagonist. He raised his arms to set in motion the power that would kill the helpless prisoners.

"Whump!"

The soft sound of something falling behind him distracted Gravestone. He spun and readied the dweomer's force for some possible new opponent. Somehow, one of the trio of captives must have managed to summon another to assist. As the demonurgist turned, arms half raised, mystic syllables ready to trip from his tongue, something struck him a blow that drove the air from his lungs, the spell from his mind. "Sorry to drop in on you like that, old sorcerer," a mocking voice said as Gravestone scrabbled to gain his feet and face the opponent.

He saw Gord. This was impossible! The alarm . . . the trap. It all came together suddenly. It had been this one's action in leaping that had triggered his mental warning bell. There could be only one result of Gord's action, coming here to this plane to threaten Gravestone personally. His own mind had tricked him, worked too quickly, betrayed him! The demonurgist knew of his opponent's prowess as a thief, gymnast, acrobat, swordsman, adventurer. This was no mean opponent, as the blow to his back indicated — probably a kick delivered at the end of a leap. Gravestone felt confident still, despite all that. He was supernormal, far greater than any foe the so-called champion had ever faced. Even stripped of the great elder ones of demonkind, the priest-wizard was filled with self-assurance regarding any contest with this one before him, remarkable or not. "I'll have your balls for that, shitpile!"

"Then you'd have two, eh?" Gord laughed as he spoke, but the young man's clear gray eyes were as cold and humorless as the winter sky.

Gravestone moved back, hastily weaving wards and protections. The dull black of his adversary's sword disconcerted the demonurgist. "Let us fence a bit then, braggart," he chided, drawing forth a wavy-bladed dagger. It was a ruse, of course. He had no intention of physically contesting with the young champion. The next spell he planned to use would require just a little more time, and Gravestone hoped to buy that interval with his offer. "Do you fear to cross weapons with an old man?"

Instead of moving toward the priest-wizard, Gord suddenly did a backward vault, rolled sideways, and struck at the chains that held his comrade Gellor. Although he had a dagger at his waist whose dweomer made steel as weak as tin under its edge, Gord didn't employ that weapon. The ebon-bladed sword he wielded was of far greater enchantment here, for the bonds that imprisoned his friends were of the sort utilizing dark power and netherforce. Sunder the evil dweomers that fortified them, and the chains and cords would be as nothing. The sword rang dully against the thick links of metal, and the chain rattled and clanged upon the stonelike floor.

"Free yourself quickly!" Gord managed to call as he sprang away, putting as much distance between himself and the bard as possible.

"Nyeeyah!" Furious at being outfoxed thus, Gravestone gave vent to a cry of rage even as he loosed a shackling spell meant to slow his enemy for but a little bit. The demonurgist needed more time to work his greater spells, to bring forth things to deal with the now-freed troubador and possibly the barbarian axeman, too. His conjuration manifested itself in whirling chains of magical sort that headed straight for Gord's legs.

As the shackles spun toward Gord, he countered with a downward thrust of his sword, which interposed the blade between the chains and his legs. Gord saw the demonurgist begin immediately upon another casting. Although the conjured metal of the shackle was already visibly corroding where it touched Blackheartseeker, the impatient adventurer didn't wait for the chains to fall away from this erosion. With a flick he had his long dagger out and drawn across the stuff. The magic broke and the shackles fell into bits of rust.

"Now, my tall and gangly fellow," he called to Gravestone to distract the priest-wizard from his ritual, "we have some business to finish between us."

Just then Gellor called out. "Gord, help me free Chert!" The bard's sword and the hillman's battleaxe were on the dais near the storklike demonurgist, but Gord had no time to assist the troubador by grabbing the weapons.

"Here," he shouted, sending his dagger spinning toward the one-eyed hero. "This will do the work!" Then he leaped ahead and cut viciously at Gravestone's neck. Suddenly a forest of mottled tentacles sprang up between Gord and his foe. Their purple and maroon blotches were poisonous-looking, and the fanged sucker-mouths that adorned these wildly waving appendages threatened to fasten to him and tear the young champion apart.

His sword cut down upon these tentacles instead of upon Gravestone. The lightless black blade sliced the things away easily, though. In a few strokes all were severed, and Gord had only slight damage from the things, although the one place he had been well struck burned and ached from the toxic secretions of the tentacle.

It was working. Even though the cursed little thief had managed to win free of each spell, virtually unscathed from any damage in a dweomer's content, Gravestone was gaining time. Now I'll deal with the reinforcements he hopes to gain, the demonurgist thought as he wove a powerful vortex that spun from his own little universe into another place nearby along the flow of evil. Out from that place came a stream of hideous things — dumalduns, members of the disgusting race native to the plane of Tarterus.

A dozen at most had come gibbering and howling into the place when the vortex vanished. In the time it had taken for the disgusting monsters to arrive upon Gravestone's quasi-sphere, Gord managed to seize and hurl Chert's great axe and Gellor's sword belt, with longsword and dagger thereon, in the general direction of where his friends were.

Then, almost in the same motion, the young champion had used a precious item he possessed — another of the benisons he had received before setting forth on this mission. It was a Talisman of Balance, a dweomered sign that took years to fashion and fill with the proper enchantments. Gord stood upright, grasped the little token in the shape of a scales, and sent it high into the air. As the talisman came to the apex of its flight, Gord said the word of activation. Another vortex shot forth, and as it manifested itself the one created by the demonurgist's spell was negated. Down through the new vortex came a single being. The dumaldun were unaware or uncaring, but Gravestone grew pale at the approach of the single one summoned by the talisman.

The one-eyed troubador managed to snare his belt from the air, and in a trice Gellor held sword and dagger ready to face the rush of the nightmare creatures who were gleefully bounding and capering toward him and his two chained comrades. Chert was almost free, his battleaxe within reach as the brawny hillman plied Gord's dagger to cut through the last of the bonds that held him.

Gellor began a heroic chant, a ballad reciting the deeds of great warriors who had faced and fought the most evil of foes, even at the cost of their lives. As he sang the brave words, Gellor was not otherwise idle. He met the rush of the first dumaldun with dagger point and sword edge, and the monster recoiled with a yowling cry of pain from the wounds inflicted by the enchanted steel of those blades.

As the second of the apelike dumalduns appeared from the vortex and bounded forth to do battle, Chert finished his work and stood free. One muscular arm scooped up a long length of chain while the barbarian grabbed Brool's leather-wrapped haft. Thus armed, Chert straddled the still-comatose form of Greenleaf and waited for the monster's assault. The dumaldun was there almost instantly.

The monster that charged toward the hillman was gorillalike, while the one Gellor had repulsed was a baboonlike thing. Others now appearing resembled orangutans, grizzled old chimpanzees, gibbons, mandrills, and other sorts of hideous monkeys. Each dumaldun was huge and strong, with long fangs and poisonous nails.

Stupid, lusting for blood, and maniacal by any standards, these denizens of the sphere of vile purple were indeed the perfect tool to accomplish the demonurgist's aim. Although his might had summoned far more than a dozen, that number would have been quite sufficient to dispose of Gellor, Chert, and the unconscious druid. With Gord's help they might have a chance of defeating the creatures, but that meant Gravestone would be left unmolested, free to work still more evil with his spells and magic.

The distorted visage of the gorilla dumaldun came open in a howling challenge, splitting wide to reveal a mouth big enough to encompass a man's entire skull, teeth long and sharp enough to crush bone, tusks of length so great as to meet where the teeth splintered a fang-pierced cranium.

The monster was indeed planning just that, but the hillman's battleaxe struck first. Brool sent its angry buzz all around as its deadly curve came upward at an angle. Barely grazing the dumaldun's paunch, it nevertheless left a foot-long cut that was only a nail's breadth short of disemboweling. Then it clipped the lower quarter of the yawning mandible and sheared it off. The dumaldun rushed on still, grabbed Chert, and sank its remaining lower tusk and upper fangs into the hillman's shoulder. Despite his dweomered leather and magical mail, those terrible teeth penetrated flesh.

The baboon-thing fighting the bard was likewise at close quarters. Recovering from the pain of its initial wounds, the dumaldun crouched and ran into the fray again, coming on all fours as would a dog. Then the bestial thing leapt. Dagger and sword met that attack, but the dumaldun came on heedless of the steel thrust into its throat, the long blade of Gellor's sword shining with gory wetness where it protruded from beneath its shoulder blade. The baboon-thing bowled the waiting man over and tore with nails and fangs at the frail human body. Gellor's helmet was knocked off, and his head struck the floor. A thousand stars sprang into the troubador's vision, then all was dark.

At that same moment, Chert loosed his hold on his axe and used his big hands to seize the jaws of the dumaldun. With a titanic effort that made the barbarian's muscles bunch and his veins to seem like snakes writhing across those rugged mounds of power, Chert pried the massive jaws open. Teeth were forced from flesh, then apart farther still. There was a loud crack, and the monster's jaw dangled limply, held in place by rags of its filthy hide.

"Son of a diseased dungheap!" Chert bawled as he grabbed the monstrous dumaldun, lifted it over his head, and hurled it into the faces of the next two demoniacal things as they came at him. The corpse sent the pair back and down, but the effort was too much for the barbarian. Head spinning, muscles uncontrolled, Chert toppled backward at the mercy of whatever beast came upon him next.

Gravestone had seen Gord's action, noted the sudden cessation of his evil gateway to Tarterus, and for the tenth time cursed mentally the young champion who opposed him. There was no time for the luxury of a true and proper curse, though. Besides, the priest-wizard thought, the efficacy of such against one so filled with supernatural powers would be questionable at best. What was needed to best the little thief were strong spells and malign forces. Gravestone still had a considerable arsenal of both. Another weapon must be brought into play now, instantly.

"Hellsblades!" the demonurgist shouted triumphantly. That dark calling would not only keep his foe at bay, it would pursue him and at best embroil Gord in combat with the howling, capering dumalduns.

The champion of the Balance heard the exclamation as it sprang from the priest-wizard's lips, saw the red-hot metal of the hells-spawned glaives as they came into being and began to twist and spin. Nine long knives, glowing tongues of terrible metal forged on the floor of the furnaces of the hells. They rotated with blades in varying planes so as to describe a moving sphere, a ball of grisly death for any creature caught by them. Nine feet across, nine feet high, nine deep. A devilshine called up to slash and chop a globe

of red destruction from razor-edged, searing-hot fal-
chions of diabolic making.

"You grant them to me?" Gord called to the vaunting Gravestone.

"Oh, yes, yes! Dear 'champion,' they are yours — a
freely bestowed gift," the demonurgist called back,
wondering why he had spoken so even as he articu-
lated his response. There was a feeling of unease in
his heart, but he shrugged it off instantly. He had not
erred; he could not.

But he had. Gord knew this the moment he saw
the nature of the dweomer Gravestone had brought
into being before him. He knew right away what to
say and do. "It is a generous present, and I freely
accept!" Gord shouted the response as if responding
in a ritual. "Blackheartseeker and I now take your
gift!" With that the young champion thrust forth his
dead-black sword, sending its length toward the center, the heart of the Hellsblades' form. The demonurgist had only a heartbeat to wonder what madness
had overcome his adversary. He was throwing himself
into the centrifuge of his doom, and the blur-quick
blades would devour sword and champion alike in
the blink of an eye, spewing both out as steely slivers
and minced flesh as instantly.

"Die, dirty little . . ." The shout of final triumph
died to a murmuring standstill as the demonurgist
saw what happened next. As Gord's sword pierced
the sphere, the whirling slowed. Lightless sword
touched red-hot glaive, and the hell-forged metal
darkened, flowed, and then became a part of the ebon
blade. One after another were affected this way, until
all nine had melded with the black brand.

Although the horrified gaze of the priest-wizard
saw no change in the sword itself, Gravestone under-

stood. "Aid me, Infestix," he wailed as Gord brought the dark blade down and a hell-red trail glowed in the air where the long edge passed.

"Demon-hand and devilshine, Gravestone," Gord called as the demonurgist shrank back. "Let the greatest filth from Hades' cesspool come bubbling up to heed your bleating and whimpering for help. He'll come too late! My sword needs yet one more component to complete its energy — the heart of the nether-pits' force. You!"

Gravestone turned and ran. The ravening dumal-duns would screen him from the terrible blade, from the champion who bore it. Not long, but long enough for him to effect his escape.

Then the demonurgist saw the full effect of the use of the Talisman of Balance. Four of the ape-beasts were tearing at their dead mate where it lay atop the stunned troubador. Two were engaged in a cannibal feast upon the carcass of the dumaldun slain by Chert, as the remaining quartet of the horrible deni-zens of Tarterus alternately tore into the motionless druid and the felled barbarian, trying to decide which was better feasting. All of them were unaware of what was about to transpire, but Gravestone saw and knew too well.

"No help, no help," he wailed, clawing desperately in his dark robes for an instrument therein, a thing of power to rescue him.

A shape of pure light, a form of deep blue in which meteors of gold shot and played, stood near the scene. It was the ultimate guardian of the upper spheres, a solar. Gravestone needed but a single glance to know what it was and flee shrieking from it. Gord, however, was uncertain. Despite the rout of his foe and his desire to catch and slay the demonurgist, the young champion felt compelled to observe what the being was doing. Its work was fell indeed.

The glowing form of lapis hue sent forth jagged bolts from its hands. These crackling, ragged-edged arcs did not flash forth, then disappear into nothing but a burning after-image as would lightning. Each played forth with angry snapping to a distance of five paces — just about the height of the solar itself. Then, as if extensions of that bright being's arms, the arcing bands of energy stretched forth, their tips forking pincerlike, and each seized a dumaldun.

The sound of the beasts as they died was a terrible music to Gord's ears. The translucent being from the upper spheres, however, seemed totally unaffected by the hideous yammerings and bellows of the dumalduns as they melted into stinking jelly under the crackling force. Again the pincered bolts reached out, and again another pair of the evil monsters were slowly vaporized into fetid gas and jellylike slag that puddled and bubbled on the floor. These sounds also attracted the notice of the other beasts from the netherspheres.

Leaving their quarreling and feasting, the half-dozen remaining dumalduns sent up ear-splitting howls of anger and hatred as they espied the towering solar. Though small by comparison, the beasts of Tarterus were undaunted. Eight-foot mandrill and nine-foot gibbon snarled and sprang. A monstrous orangutan parody, as wide as its seven-foot height, bounded and gibbered as it charged. The others were no less fearsome in aspect; yet the being from the higher planes stood unperplexed.

Twin rays of molten gold sprang from where the solar's eyes would be, had the tall quasi-god had such. The scintillating beams struck the massive orangutanlike dumaldun, and the beast was transfixed. It took but an instant. The light died, the dumaldun stumbled and crashed down. Where the rays had touched the thing, there was no longer any substance; the orangutan had no chest or heart left. Still the survivors came on. Giant-sized tusks from a demoniac chimpanzee slashed and ripped at the lapis form of the solar. A dumaldun with the long and spindly appendages of a parody spiker monkey used its teeth and venomous claws to inflict its worst upon the being of glowing blue as the monkey-thing perched atop the gigantic head and shoulders of its foe. The five monstrous beasts swarmed upon the solar, and for a split-second Gord couldn't see it or speculate on the damage being done to the godling by the ferocious beasts from the foul sphere of Tarterus.

The solar spoke a bell-loud word, and the spidery dumaldun fell from its place atop the being, its iron bristles aflame, its bodily fluids boiling into steam. It exploded into stinking fragments when it struck the floor of Gravestone's space in no-place. The bolts of energy had vanished, but the solar used its own broad hands to seize another pair of the four remaining dumalduns. Each was held by the scruff of the neck.

The herculean arms came together then, and the beasts were smashed as if they were cymbals. The sound was by no means melodic or even ringing. Instead there was a disgusting thud, a wet squishing accompanied by snapping and breaking sounds and a spray of crimson and gray. Two limp forms flew up and over the massive being's shoulders. They didn't move after bouncing from their impact on the hard flags behind. Darker places of midnight hue showed plainly on the solar's form, mute testimony to the terrible weapons that the dumaldun employed. No mere fang and claw would so wound a being of this sort. The denizens of vile Tarterus used other malign energies as well, to inflict such hurts.

Without regard for such, and with singleness of purpose, the glowing solar drew a silvery rod from where a man's girdle would be. It was small-looking in the being's vast grip, but the instrument was potent nonetheless. Down it came, crystalline light flashed from it as it impacted upon a gibbonlike fiend, and the dumaldun thus struck howled and retreated, with weird, mercurial incandescence lighting its whole form. The sole remaining attacker left off its ferocious assault at that and tried to flee. The right arm of the solar struck again, and the result duplicated his first smiting. Both dumalduns glowed and yowled and capered. This time it was in agony and fear, not as wild lusting for blood and death. Because it was a creature of the higher spheres, the solar dealt quickly with the two. A quick snap of the wrist, a repetition, and the rod took each beast again, giving them a cleaner death than such fiends ever deserved.

"Thank you, One of Weal!" Gord spoke out of true gratitude.

"Stay back!" The solar bellowed to the man who had taken a step toward it. "I read no malice in your heart, but you have no pure aura, either. Keep your distance, whatever you may be, and keep that weapon you hold away, too!"

"My friends and I serve Balance, fight the evil of Tharizdun. This brand is made potent by the very strength of Evil. Fear me or it not!"

"Fear? No solar ever fears, creature of convictionless spawning. It is the stench of the blade, your lack of righteousness, which repels me. Common foe or not, I will have no association with you!" The being of lapis light then moved as if readying to depart.

Gord was taken aback by the attitude the minion of Weal displayed. It felt no fellow-feeling, showed no common cause, disdained any proximity to him. No wonder that the vile ones who labored for Tharizdun's ascendancy were virtually unchecked by the might of the higher planes. Such beings as this would never accept others who were not of identical ethos and action.

"Have pity, Bright One," he called to the solar despite his welling indignation. "There lie three heroes, brave men and true, felled in the fight against those who oppose you and all Weal, too. Show mercy and aid them!"

The solar paused. "Your heart is filled with repulsiveness, your head with sin, your hand with netherforce. Yet you dare to speak to me of benisons?" Yet even as the being spoke, it hesitated. "Very well, I see the need for some justice in the matter. You serve those both hot and cold, good and evil, the fencestriders and self-lovers. Choose one of the three, and I shall restore him to vitality. That, and the whereabouts of your demon-consorting adversary, will fully even the score between us."

"Even? Score? I speak of combating the very essence of all that is wicked, of driving that one's servants to their demise, of locking evil away forever!"

"Cold untruths, neutral creature. You seek not the end of all evil, the glory of Weal forever. What you work and strive to do is play the wicked against the righteous eternally, thus allowing your gray-tinged existences forever. You will have no such service from me! Name now the one you will have quickened, then follow the reek of corruption left as the slug you call Gravestone crawled away to seek safety."

There was no choice. "Gellor," he said, speaking the name slowly, carefully. The one-eyed troubador was the greatest and most powerful of the three. Gord's heart was leaden in his breast as he said the name.

"It is as you would have it," the solar said in its deep and beautifully resonant voice. Then the lucid blue vanished.

"What happened?" It was the bard, coming to consciousness, struggling erect.

Gord had no time to explain. "You're fine, I think, old comrade, but Chert and Greenleaf are not! See if you can do something for them. I must continue the hunt for the demonurgist. Here, catch!" the young adventurer said, tossing a rune-worked pyramid to Gellor. The troubador took it from the air but looked uncertain. "It is enspelled and will take you from here. Use it if I do not return in a thousand heartbeats. Speak the name of the Demiurge as you open the thing."

"I'll not be in so great a hurry to flee, Gord. Right protect you and make your aim true," Gellor said. Then he went as quickly as he could to where the torn and bloody forms of his other friends were. "Hurry after the rotten bastard, Gord. Get him, and even if we three here die, it is a good exchange."

"I . . . I'm sorry, but I must leave you. Care for them, do what is possible." Without saying anything more for fear that his voice would break, Gord turned in the general direction in which the priest-wizard had gone and began to peer at the floor, sniffing as he did so. True to his utterance, the solar had used his power to reveal the path that Gravestone had taken.

Curiously, although the place appeared flat and featureless to his normal vision, the dweomer of the being from the higher spheres enabled Gord to see the place as its evil maker did.

Better still, the energy imparted by the solar allowed the young champion of the Balance to follow the demonurgist as he entered the devious mazes of the sub-rosa portion of his creation. What was a disc of a few hundred feet diameter to others became far different now. There was a level below the apparent one on a different vibratory frequency. Its dark resonance expanded the confines of the nullity greatly. Below the featureless oval that held Gellor, Chert, and Curley Greenleaf was a warren of passages and chambers that was three times larger than the space above, even though it existed in the same seeming place. Gord was confused but could comprehend the principle behind it.

He followed the visible smudges of stinking stuff. It was a trail of the very essence of Gravestone; his aura of evil was such that it actually left behind a reek as he passed. Wondering if the solar's reaction to himself and the lightless sword had been based on a similar perception of aura, Gord went down a now plainly visible flight of steps fully twenty feet broad. His body was resonating on the same frequency as the vibrations of Gravestone and his hidden underlevel, only Gravestone wouldn't be aware of it. Not yet!

Despite the possible fate of his comrades, Gord felt a grim satisfaction, an impending doom hanging over the demonurgist's head. Gravestone had been the instrument of all that was truly bad in the young man's existence. It was the priest-wizard who had hunted down and killed both Gord's father and mother. All

323

evil that had followed therefrom, even Leena's degenerative condition, the terrible existence he had suffered in Old City and beyond, all the rest, too. The demonurgist had caused it all and desired worse. There was one beyond Gravestone, of course. Perhaps two, if Infestix were placed in the equation.

But Gord didn't consider the master of the pits as a part of his mission. That one would be taken care of by some other. First came the demonurgist. Then Gord had but one remaining foe to face. The sole master of Gravestone was Tharizdun. That was in the priest-wizard's heart. "No problem," Gord said aloud as he stepped off the last stair and followed the slime of evil. "I'll remove his black heart and quench the burning desire all in one cleansing thrust!"

The foe Gord sought now had no idea he was being hounded by the young champion. Gravestone had activated a great spell, a dweomer contained in a scarab that had been carefully prepared and held ready for júst such need as now. As the dumalduns stupidly sacrificed themselves in combat with the solar, the demonurgist had begun the task of evoking the malign forces locked in the scarab. Layer upon layer of magic flowed from it.

First, the wards against Weal. The quasi-sphere that was Gravestone's own creation in nullity began to glow darkly. Lasting globes of malign force sprang into being. These were fashioned to repel goodness, to drive away anything from the upper planes. Three bands of such malign power manifested themselves from the scarab: the dull, bloody hue of the hells, the ebon of the Abyss, the putrid purple of the pits. True, a great solar might be able to endure such force as those three globes emitted, but even so the evil would begin eroding the strength of any being of Weal.

Next issued the most potent and malign of the sigils of the netherplanes. Each evil sign was disguised, near-invisible even to a being as mighty as the solar. These sigils were themselves repositories of dweomer. Some held black destruction from the depths of demonium, others fiery force garnered in the hells, while the remainder contained the death-powers bestowed from Hades itself. To confront one was to be blasted by the full potency of the evil rune's magic. Should a solar even pass near to one, the sigil would trigger its guarding force to the detriment of the intruding foe. Wards to force away the strength of good, guarding sigils to lay the enemies of Tharizdun and his servant low. Great was the power of the scarab. Yet a third came beyond.

The complexities of the dark castings that the device contained had taken years of time and great effort to form. As the wardings and guards sprang into existence, so too the final portion of the dweomer. The dark power of the netherspheres formed a labyrinth of corridors and rooms, halls and passages, galleries and rooms in which the priest-wizard would be hidden. No bright creature could discover the secret of that maze, for the aura of evil was nowhere and everywhere at once. That particular pattern that was Gravestone's was replicated, mirrored, and spread throughout the complex whose confines were broad and confusing. The being of Weal who entered would be so affected as to find the whole ever greater. Each step added two to the evil complex, each turn created a branching, a fresh twist, so that the very operation of such an enemy in the black maze caused the labyrinth to expand and become more confusing.

A portion of it had existed from the time Gravestone had fashioned his web using the netherforces at his command. There, safe in the center, hedged round with every protection years of effort could build, the demonurgist hid. Pentagrams and circles graven into the stony stuff of the floor kept him free from magical intrusions, as did the mystic triangles and horned seals of evil. The entrance was of stone and iron, set with silver and gold runes. All were hidden by secret fashioning and cloaked further with spells of invisibility, illusion, and blindness, which made physical location of the lair he had constructed nearly impossible. Dense metal and dampening magics precluded other forms of intrusion. It was a place of total safety.

In this sanctum Gravestone had stored the treasured things of his craft, the repositories of black knowledge, arcane art, and magical lore. The material of alchemy, the rituals of necromancy, the conjurations of sorcery alone filled the whole of one long wall. Components for spells, the paraphernalia of retorts and flasks for the concocting of magical fluids and powders littered a long bench. A century of malign deeds and accumulation of the fruits thereof were contained in the place. There Gravestone sat, breathed deeply, shook off the awful dread that the appearance of the solar had wrapped around his dark heart.

"I read the enemy wrong," he said aloud. "After all of these decades I made a mistake!" Muttering obscene things under his breath then, the demonurgist began hastily to correct his error. His entire force had been spent on preparing for the coming of the man who was called Gord. The champion, though, had nearly triumphed despite all that Gravestone had done. This would be rectified.

Drinking from various of the multitude of vials

and flasks that littered the secret chamber, Gravestone restored his confidence, energy and strength. Elixirs and black potions of human blood were consumed, along with a half-dozen less savory draughts. The demonurgist then began selecting an array of potent devices and evil objects with which he armed himself as a precaution. There was no telling when such would be needed, even though his chief armament would be the dweomers he would soon prepare.

"Yes, bastard of balance," he spat aloud. "Soon, indeed, I'll have restored my power, prepared the castings which will blast your guts into food for the worms, and myself eat your heart and liver while your soul goes into Hades for the amusement of the daemons!"

Gravestone pictured Gord as he spoke. The human had brought a solar to aid him. Despite the aura he possessed, the demonurgist now knew the true nature of the warrior of Balance. That one could be no neutral median, not when the greatest minions of Weal came to his bidding. The emanations were naught but a cloak, a hoax. The one called Gord was actually of the spheres of light, and now Gravestone would know exactly how to dispose of him. "The Cursed Codex, I think. . . . Yes! That and the Everlasting Damnations of Dilwomz should serve."

He found the vile tomes where they stood on the shelves amid the ranks of wicked lore in his library. Seated at his high desk, black candles burning, the priest-wizard began his preparations. The process would take a while, but time was the ally of Tharizdun, of Gravestone. If his adversary managed to win free of Gravestone's web before the demonurgist came forth again to confront him for the last time, no matter. He would be the hunter, Gord the prey. There

327

was no place in which the champion could hide, for if he tried then the nether realms would automatically succeed. Gord would have to come again to seek him out, and the demonurgist would deal with the puny little human then, once and for all.

"Human?" Gravestone asked the question aloud in the dark chamber. The flames of stinking candle and burning brazier leaped and flared at that. "No, another false assumption. The little turd is of Rexfelis's spawning, too. He is of mixed heritage — the weakness of man, the vacillating dearth of neutrality. Each is riddled with flaws and lacks conviction. This mixture assures the victory of Evil's dark purpose!" He leaped off his chair, gathered up another grimoire, then returned to his reading once again.

Hours passed in this fashion. The priest-wizard sought the words he needed, burned the malign syllables into his brain, tapped the energies of every hellish and demoniacal place, too, for good measure. Now and again he sought further works, gathered strange and evil things for the casting of a spell, or actually worked some minor casting in the process of equipping himself. The philters he had drunk earlier gave Gravestone unnatural energy, unsleeping vigor. After hours and hours of time spent thus, the demonurgist wrote furiously in his own collections of dark spells and then began his final preparations. He felt the life force of Gord ebb as he worked. There was no chance of failure this time.

Chapter 17

COULD A SOLAR LIE? Gord asked himself that as he realized there was no longer a trail for him to follow.

No, that wasn't exactly true. Actually, there were endless trails leading everywhere and nowhere. The slime-path left by the fleeing demonurgist covered each and every route in the whole of the maze. "Let me think," he said slowly, and pondered what the being from the higher spheres had said. " '. . . Follow the reek of corruption . . .' " But there were dark trails of the slime visible everywhere!

" '. . . Follow the *reek* . . .' " That was it! He was relying on his eyes, not on the literal words of the instruction. The slime was a secondary trail. The solar had actually told Gord to use the odor of the demonurgist's evil to track him down. Let me see what I can do to correct my stupidity, the young champion thought as he sniffed the air.

"I am a fool!" he muttered. For what seemed an eternity he had been wandering up and down the dark byways and broad halls of the labyrinth trying vainly to discover which of the plain paths was actually the essence of Gravestone's passage. Now, his nose revealed what the truth was. A sharp, acrid stench was obvious. Its reek was stronger in some places than in others. Eventually, by carefully sniffing out his way, Gord would be able to trace the priest-wizard to his lair here. "Doubly a fool, and I have not much time left!" he chided himself.

Instead of using his human nose, Gord shifted from two-legged to four-legged form, and where a short, slender man had stood a moment before there now crouched a huge black leopard. It crouched in order to get the scent from the hard floor.

The olfactory power of Gord as a panther was more than ten times greater than that of Gord as a human. Gord-panther now swung his head this way and that, sniffing the flagstonelike floor, testing the still air. Then the great cat rose and padded up a passage, back down, and across a place where three other corridors met. Although he was unaware of it, the chamber was dweomered to expand to massive proportions, to have four, six, or a score or more adits, but there was no force to spring the evil magic. The champion in leopard form had a far easier task than ever the one who devised the labyrinth imagined. Soon enough Gord-panther's nose had the strongest scent, and he leaped ahead, following the noisomeness that was the sign of the demonurgist's passing, with increasing speed.

There was a turn here, a doubling back there. No matter. The duplications of Gravestone's trail were each weaker. The immediate mirrorings were very close, of course. That made the tracking more difficult, but the replications from replications grew progressively weaker, stale in their evil stench, as it were. The task was hard but by no means impossible. As if following footprints plainly set in smooth sand, the black leopard that was Gord traced the frantic passage of the demonurgist, and eventually came to the place where it ended in stone, plain blocks no different from the thousands of others that formed the walls of the place.

With a low panther-sound still rumbling from his chest and along his throat, Gord became human once again. "A cat to suss you out, demon-clasper; a thief to find your hidey-hole," he said softly as his hands felt and eyes observed the place. There was more to it, of course. Gord thought the rest to himself: A swordsman to fight you; a sword to take your heart. Dwell upon that later. Now he had to discover the way to enter Gravestone's lair.

There was a portal here, surely. It was hidden by natural craft and dweomercraeft both. It would be similarly closed fast by bolts of steel, bands of wizard-work. Gord felt for his dagger, then recalled he had left it with Gellor in his haste to pursue Gravestone. Knowing that no skill of his own could ever open the secret door, the gray-eyed thief put aside that strategy and drew Blackheartseeker from its scabbard.

"Come, sword, show me the power you have in your metal!" he growled softly. Blackheartseeker trembled slightly in his grasp, and a red-black glow seemed to come from the heart of the long blade whose tip was centered on the portal. "Your completion lies beyond, but I cannot get you to what you must have without help!" As Gord urged the weapon to release its might, however, the glowing waned; yet the vibration of it seemed to increase. Uncertain, the young champion held his arm steady, sword tip still and unswerving from in front of the barred door that must surely lead to his quarry.

Heartbeat after heartbeat he stood thus until a full minute passed. Gord was almost ready to abandon this tack and try some desperate device when the whole length of the sword leaped convulsively and the portal it pointed at sprang into sharp relief as violet energy played over the entire place it was. The violet darkened, intensified, turned to a sullen plum hue. As the length of Blackheartseeker recoiled, the purple energy covering the secret entrance flowed together, coalescing into a burning amethyst ball of force that jumped as if a bolt of lightning to kiss the sword's tip and vanish. The flow of evil force made him reel, his head spinning, his stomach twisting, but somehow Gord managed to retain his grip on the hilt of the weapon.

"Now open the way," he said softly, still shaken and uncertain. The stone before him ran down and flowed out as would dry sand. Weird and twisted forms of metal fell from the air, no longer supported by the stuff that had been granitelike only a second before. Vile rune of brass, evil sigil of frozen quicksilver fell soundlessly into the soft, powdery stuff that mounded out to near where he stood. So too dropped steel bars and iron bindings, bronze and gold workings of all sorts. In that raid came some faint clangings and dull clinks, so thick were the pieces upon the little hill of powdered stone.

Blackheartseeker no longer trembled. It was stable again, and all along its length was the lightlessness seen as black to mortal eyes. "You have done it!" Gord exclaimed in fierce joy. "Now I'll do my best to fulfill my part of this bargain!"

A short, narrow passage was revealed beyond the destroyed gate. There was a dim illumination coming from its end, and Gord could hear a murmuring sound. It could be none other than Gravestone's voice chanting some evil litany of dark magic, as the demonurgist sought to gather strength for renewed combat. Not hesitating further, the young champion stole along the little hallway leading to the inner sanctum of the priest-wizard. The time of vengeance was come finally and at last.

Gravestone stepped into the open end of the narrow passageway just as his foe was slipping along it toward him. When the demonurgist beheld a form moving into his supposedly inviolate lair, the fellow started and cried aloud in shock. "Out!" At the same instant he pointed a wand and moved it so as to cause the instrument to shoot forth a stream of searing fire.

"In!" Gord countered to the priest-wizard's denial, and charged ahead, Blackheartseeker lancelike before his rush. The fiery wash of magical power shot forth then, crackling and leaping as its tongues sought to consume all in their path. Gord was seared, his flesh blistering under the intense heat of the burning discharge. Still he came on. In fact, the dull ebon of the longsword held in his hand seemed to cool and lessen the flames of the demonurgist's wand, and the power of the blade washed back to cool and soothe its wielder as well. There were scorches and red burns to be sure, but the effect of the burning gout of energy was far less than it seemed.

The steely shaft aimed at him forced Gravestone to leap back and get away before he could send another withering spray of flames from his wand. He was readying it for another attempt nonetheless even as he retreated in haste. His adversary followed too closely. The ebon blade darted out as if a serpent's tongue, and the wand was broken, one piece still held in the priest-wizard's hand, the other portion spinning away. "Devils take you!" Gravestone shouted, throwing the useless stump of it at Gord and then using his greater powers to evade the next blow that the young swordsman aimed at him.

The terrible dread was filling him again. The sword that seemed to fill the whole room was a weapon against which Gravestone had few defenses. He utilized all of them, though, in order to escape death. Between the demonurgist and his foe sprang up a huge and bestial form. It was almost as high as the vaulted ceiling of the chamber and as broad as a span of oxen. It was formed of darkly shining colors, transparent layers of color describing the creation's dimensions. Evil orange was its outermost hue, and beneath that thick sheen was another of vile gray light. Then there followed a diabolical red, a clear black fire, an ugly maroon, and a ghastly purple. Innermost, and of a disgusting incandescence that hurt the eyes to look upon it, was the violet sheen of the deepest nether-pits of evil. It was as if the priest-wizard had formed seven nether-beasts, each slightly smaller than the foregoing, each inside the other, and then himself gotten inside the whole to animate and empower the hideous agglomeration into assuming unnatural life.

"Hide, rat, but you can no longer escape into some rathole!" Gord shouted angrily.

"Hide?" the multilayered, evilly hued monster surrounding Gravestone bellowed. "This for hiding!" and it struck a terrible blow.

Gord cut at the creation at the same moment. Sparks of brilliant orange shot from where the dark blade touched it, but the thing hit its target nonetheless. Gord was knocked back, sprawling, blood streaming from his nose. "*Your* hide!" Gord managed to say, rolling aside from a massive foot that was trying to stomp on him. "I mean to have it!" And as he said that, the young thief was upright again and his lightless brand hacked a second time at the strange glowing agglomeration of nether-hues.

Now a torrent of fiery orange flowed from the thing, and it gave vent to a scream as the stuff of its outermost shell poured out upon the floor. "A mere trifle," a sinister voice mocked as the scream died away into nothingness with the last flicker of orange light. The sound was putrescent, as hideous as the deep gray outline that was now the outermost part of the varicolored creation of evil.

Again the monstrous form struck, this time a pair of swift blows. Gord dodged the first and met the second with the keen edge of Blackheartseeker. Dead gray flickered, globs of luminosity were sent flying. "A mere trifle," Gord mocked, stepping in as the thing tried to move back to get a better swing at him. Staying close, darting and weaving, the champion of Balance stabbed and stabbed again at the corpselike color of the form; and each blow he struck made the gray lessen in intensity, thin, dim as its stuff was sent oozing forth and away. "Yet it seems effective," he added as the gray went out and the hell-red was clearly visible.

Inside the construction of evil power, Gravestone was still safe, but he was weakening with each loss suffered. There were yet five layers of protective force shielding him, and serving as weapons too. But the loss of the two was severe, not to be discounted. He would have to redouble his efforts to slay his opponent immediately.

Because he was who he was, the task was far from an impossible one for Gravestone. Many spell-binders had the means to produce multilayered spheres to protect themselves with. A few of the most evilly adept could form beasts of energy to encase themselves in and serve as extensions of themselves.

The demonurgist, however, went far beyond either of these accomplishments. This many-colored beast of force was drawn from all of the netherspheres, fought as well as any great devil or demon, and protected its creator behind seven barriers of malign energy. It had a life of its own, too, and Gravestone could lend the quasi-thing his own powers to employ.

"Touch of rotting death," the priest-wizard said softly. The disgusting crimson of the right hand of the beast that encased Gravestone glittered with a darker sheen from the power thus bestowed. Mage's spell and cleric's power both were known to the black-souled demonurgist. By transferring either to his construct, Gravestone could utilize his fell energies beyond the confines of the many-hued beast. Then he feinted with the thing's left, and as his foeman moved to avoid the blow, the deadly right hand came flashing forth to deliver its killing charge of dweomer.

It almost worked. The huge fingers brushed Gord, and the death contained in each digit hurt him to the center of his being. Yet by instinct and long training the champion managed to leap back just far enough to prevent Gravestone's tactic from having its full intended effect.

Using the sword to shield him from another such trick, Gord circled and drew several deep breaths, trying to regain lost energy. He knew that the demonurgist desired a melee at this long range, where he could watch Gord and strike more efficiently at him, but there was no choice. If he went closer, the touch of the beast would be fatal, for the energy that generated the scarlet color was a force that would burn flesh and destroy bone if it came in solid contact.

The groping, pawlike extremities of Gravestone's agglomeration swiped wildly at Gord. He danced, ducked, and slashed with Blackheartseeker as he avoided the attacks and regained strength. The pain subsided to a dull aching. That he could put aside with effort of will. Now it was time to take the offensive again. Gravestone made a clumsy rush with his beastlike thing, and the longsword slashed into the glowing maroon with cut after cut upon the defenseless flank and back of the nether-fiend.

"Howoou!" The hell-red layer seemed to give vent to the sound from every portion of itself, not just the near-featureless head and hint of a mouth it possessed. Then the light was gone, replaced by the glitter of abyssal ebon.

His sword seemed to leap for joy as the black sheen sprang clearly forth. With volition that seemed to come from itself, Blackheartseeker plunged its tip into the darkness and drank. The jet instantly lost its lustrousness; then it was gone, vanishing without sound of protest. There were now but three layers of the construct left to protect the demonurgist, but Gord had to retreat without striking a further blow as the thing of maroon light spun and attempted to sweep him into an embrace. It was but ten or so feet tall now, and narrower too, but it moved with greater speed.

"Come, champion. Stand and fight your enemy." Gravestone used "champion" as a dirty word, and scorn dripped from his voice as he taunted Gord.

It was easy to ignore such a ploy. Instead of paying the slightest heed to those words, or the many that followed, Gord played cat-and-mouse with the priest-wizard. Sometimes the multihued beast was the cat, and then Gord darted and fled. But then he

would see an opening, seize an opportunity presented, and ply his brand against the maroon light of the
thing's fifth layer. All too soon for the demonurgist
the maroon-hued force was bled off, the purple spent,
and still his adversary stood ready, dreaded sword in
hand.

No human, no quasi-deity or heir to the mastery of
one of the planes of creation, could do this. Gravestone knew then that he had made still another error.
Gnashing his teeth in fury, the demonurgist allowed
the thing he had created to lumber as it would in
search of its elusive foe. Gravestone was busy with a
dweomer of his special creation, one as fell as that
used to make the thing that shielded him now . . .
but not for much longer. By rapid voicing of unnatural sounds, and with little movement save for a
strange twisting of fingers and slight shuffling steps
that seemed to be nothing save the footwork of attack, the priest-wizard created a replica of himself
within the hideous violet beast. At the same instant
his actual form was transported to an alcove, a place
screened by an arras, so that his opponent would
suspect no such trick.

Safe for the moment, Gravestone placed a dweomer upon himself. It was a powerful working of
priestly sort that would enable him to see unerringly
the play of forces that made up Gord the champion
and were employed by him in fighting the demonurgist. Now I have you! he thought to himself.

"Now I have you!" the violet-colored thing of trans-
luscent energy echoed in a booming voice. Ready in
the upper levels of Gravestone's consciousness were
spells of thundering fire, blazing lightnings, extradimensional pits, spiked walls of pure evil power, and
utterances to jolt time into temporary cessation, twist

distances into confusion, and alter the course of actuality. Before he dared to employ any of the dweomers, Gravestone knew one fact. He had to determine exactly what strengths the champion possessed, see where his weaknesses were. Silently chanting the ritual of revealing, and with vision able to discern aura and energy, the priest-wizard moved to a place where he could peep out from behind the hanging and view the battle.

The blundering moves of the evilly glowing energy-thing alerted Gord to a change the instant that Gravestone left it, leaving behind an illusory figure of himself. Although he wasn't positive of what had transpired, Gord understood that the demonurgist was no longer housed within the shell of the beast he had formed. When he slipped to a position that enabled him to strike it unimpeded, and the monstrous thing bellowed "I have you!" the champion of the fight against Tharizdun and his evil minions understood what had occurred. Ignoring the creature, he rushed to the only place where Gravestone could be concealed, flattening himself against the wall beside the arras. The semi-intelligent energy beast blundered here and there, seeking its adversary, and Gord waited. The monster's noises were sufficient to make it seem as if it was still in combat with him.

Magical sight and supernatural sense gave Gravestone just sufficient warning. He was leaping back from his intended spying even as the keen-edged sword shot out to pierce his chest. Gravestone's recoil was as fast as an adder's, Gord's stabbing lunge as quick as the strike of a leopard's paw. The demonurgist was wounded, but only an inch of Blackheart-seeker penetrated his flesh; then the evil spell-binder was back and free of the metal, gasping and cursing.

It was still the opportune moment for Gord. One more thrust and the storklike worker of mischief and murder would be dead. The moment was taken from Gord by the violet energy-beast.

"Whump!" The sound of it striking him seemed soft enough, but the evil power that flowed from the thing into Gord knocked him away. He was driven into the arras and tangled up in its folds. The monstrous thing stepped ponderously forward and struck again. Gord kicked up, and the fallen fabric of the arras bellied upward. The thing struck that, and the force of its blow went on to impact upon the stone where his adversary had been but a heartbeat earlier. Half-dazed, weakened, but still able to fight, Gord was tumbling and rolling to get beyond range of another immediate attack by the monster. It hurt, but he continued the gymnastic display by springing upright and crouching en garde. The sickly lavender of the thing's form moved to close the distance between them. It was what Gord wanted, for that movement placed Gravestone's construct between Gord and the priest-wizard.

"I should have known better than to leave an enemy behind me," the young man said with feigned sadness as he readied for the assault. It came quickly. The beast struck a sweeping blow, almost as if it sought to sweep Gord's feet out from under him with its long, evilly shimmering arm. Blackheartseeker's edge was there, but Gord was not. As the thing's thick arm swept forth, the sword's cutting edge struck a backhand blow that passed cleanly through the dark violet force. The featureless head of the beast went back and its voice howled from the opening that might have been a mouth. It now had but a single arm, and where the right one had been there came drops of dirty violet color, little drippings of energy that dissipated into nothingness as they struck the floor.

"Sing loudly for me, pitspawn," Gord cried as he leaped in and cut again at the beast. The longsword sliced through the violet force as if it wasn't even there, and the creature crashed down, its substance bleeding away in dark flashes of impotent evil. The beast was no more, but Gravestone was ready.

The demonurgist saw plainly what he faced. There was an aura surrounding his adversary that caused the priest-wizard to shudder. So deep its colors, so brilliant their glowings, so varied their spectrum as to show no weakness. Here indeed were the hands of all the most potent foes of Tharizdun who formed the Balance. Gifted power of supernatural splendor encased Gord in a halo that brought fear into Gravestone. That dread was nothing compared to what he felt when he looked at the lightless sword. Its power was of evil, but an evil distorted and made over to serve the opposite force. It was an instrument made of malign energy to destroy evil!

Mistake after mistake. . . . The majority of Gravestone's spells had been selected to have effect upon an opponent aligned to the ethical outlook of the upper spheres, thus in harmony with certain patterns and subject to set counter-frequencies. The appearance of the solar had caused the priest-wizard to make false assumptions and base his strategy of attack thereon.

It was also an error not to have considered the possibility, however remote, of having to deal with an enemy loose within his sanctum sanctorum. Gravestone could not now utilize the powerful spells based on fire, lightning and the like because to bring up such dweomers here would destroy centuries of work, an age of collected arcana, and who knows how many valuable magical repositories such as wands, scrolls, and apparati for demonurgy. As his foe fought with the construct, Gravestone wracked his brain for the single most effective attack he could now employ against the Champion of the Balance. In seconds, minutes at best, the last force of the spell-beast would be drained, and then the priest-wizard had to be ready with some sending that would stop the man who wielded that terrible, dull-black sword. The weapon he could not destroy, but the one who wielded it was an altogether different matter.

"Entrance to the Pits of Hades," Gravestone began to chant, making the formal, ritual gestures as he did so. His hands were filled with the correct materials to activate the gateway. All that was necessary for the priest-wizard to do was send them forth at the proper intervals as the incantation progressed. He was evoking his Doompit, a dweomer that would plunge Gord bodily into the depths of the nether spheres' lowest plane.

"Now conjoined with Gravestone's playground," he sang, fitting words to suit the circumstances. Meter was important, as was rhyme and constancy of the chant. "Force of Nerull death and disease, keep it fast and make it stay bound," the demonurgist continued, trying not to rush the spell but unable to keep his eyes from the melee. There were four stanzas needed to effect the junction and open the tunnel-like portal under the victim's feet, a one-way chute straight to the nether-pits. Just as Gravestone finished his first quatrain, the dark-bladed sword struck the beast's arm and destroyed it. But he still had time!

"Spinning vortex now created, Barrier magics all

abated," Gravestone chanted as he spread black powder before him and moved his hands just so. A tiny whirlwind suddenly sprang up, and the sooty stuff was turned into a miniature tornado, a vortex that moved toward the unsuspecting man who was now in the act of delivering the final blow to the figure of ghastly, violet-hued force. "Here to Hades now instated, Doompit passage generated!"

The second stanza was completed. Only two to go, but the champion was staring directly at him. The demonurgist felt cold beads of sweat spring from his brow. He knew it was not from the effort of casting the dark dweomer of the spell, but from the stark terror that came directly from the blade that would soon threaten him again. The single touch of it, the slight wound Gravestone had suffered in the fleshy part of his upper arm, had sent an agonizing wrench through him. The metal of the longsword seemed to tug at his heart as it was pulled from Gravestone's flesh when the demonurgist leaped back from its touch. To die by that weapon was to die forever!

Gord saw his foe clearly as the thing of netherforce collapsed and sputtered into nothingness, dispelling the illusory Gravestone within it as it did so. The priest-wizard was intoning a spell. Although the young adventurer had no idea as to the nature of the dweomer that was being called for by the ritual, Gord understood all too well that nothing cast by Gravestone would be weak or not calculated to cause total calamity to his person or goal. Gord had to remain quick and capable so the demonurgist could be slain. Perhaps the magic was one of escape for Gravestone. Either way, it made no difference. The binding had to be interrupted, the spell's completion unattained. The tall man's mouth began to move faster, his arms and hands making passes that seemed to occur in light-ninglike sequences. Gord leaped into motion himself then, dashing across the chamber.

The words the demonurgist now shouted in a rapid stream were indecipherable to Gord. He was intent only upon one thing. Blackheartseeker must strike the chanting spell-binder before that vile mouth of Gravestone's managed to utter the final syllable of his evil evocation. Only a half-dozen more steps, and the blade of his sword would be buried in the demonurgist's foul chest.

Then Gord stumbled over a small object. A crystal flask, knocked from a table in his struggle with the varihued beast of nether-force, had rolled into the young champion's path. It was a thing of enchanted substance, so it hadn't broken from the fall, nor would it break beneath anything so puny as the foot of a man. It rolled under the pressure, and Gord's foot went with its roll.

Gravestone had but one more quatrain to recite and his antagonist would be consigned alive to Hades! How he would delight in seeing it, in actually traversing the planes himself in order to enjoy the sight of the one called Gord trapped and tortured for an eternity in the nether-pits! The last words were on Gravestone's lips even now, but it looked as though the lightless metal of the dreaded longsword would strike before they could speak their fulfilling sounds.

He rushed along as quickly as he dared — faster, perhaps, than any other mage could have managed. Yet the first couplet was just completed when Gord was but a handful of paces distant and coming for him like a rushing wind. At that moment Gord fell, and it was all the demonurgist could do to contain his joy, repress his wild laughter. That would have spoiled his work as surely as the thrust of the sword would have. Instead, Gravestone paused and drew a deep breath. It was a very minor interruption, one that would in no way disturb the casting. There were but two lines to recite, sixteen beats to toll in measured form. When that little was accomplished, the Doompit would seize the Champion of Balance and consume him.

The first of the dire sounds issued from Gravestone's mouth, one of sixteen needed. A deep voice sang back, two beats for his one, and at a disturbing pitch. The demonurgist turned his eyes sideways at this disturbance.

One of the small fellow's companions was at the chamber's exit. It was a man Gravestone recognized, a singer of magics, the troubador called Gellor. That too was laughable. The priest-wizard would have enjoyed a contest one on one with the stupid minstrel, but not now. He fixed his thoughts and chanted forth another pair of the sounds needed to complete his casting. Gellor countered with more lyrics of his own, louder still, and coming closer as he sang. Gravestone was uneasy, but not worried. His chief antagonist was still on hands and knees, trying to recover the sword that he needed to harm Gravestone. The demonurgist knew that he could complete the thirteen beats still remaining before Gord was up and again at his throat.

With evil delight spread upon his features, the tall demonurgist raised his arms high, booming triumphantly the completion of the line, and the five syllables flowed as a mountain freshet down its steep course. Then Gravestone commenced the completion of the binding. The sounds poured forth, but he had to slow them, to articulate each with greatest care.

The bard was now bellowing a counter-ballad to the demonurgist's rhyme, and the dweomer of that singing made it exacting work to accomplish. Now the last sounds were forming, but the priest-wizard was forced to enunciate each with excruciating slowness. To mispronounce might merely negate the power of the spell, but it could as easily open the vortex for Gravestone himself. An entrance thus before Infestix would be far from pleasant. Failure was never tolerated, of course. . . .

It was a nightmare in a world where Gord's every motion was taken as if he were underwater. The fall was not serious, except that Blackheartseeker slipped from his hand as it occurred. Then, as if he and the weapon were opposite poles of a magnet, his hand couldn't seem to properly grip it as he tried to regain his feet and strike the demonurgist. It was a matter of trying to accomplish too many actions at once. Gord's hands were sweating, his nerves frayed, his body battered and wounded, his brain filled with desperation.

The sudden sound of Gellor's voice as it sang forth in counter to the dark spell of the priest-wizard brought Gord to his senses. Even as the troubador's singing hindered Gravestone in his incantation, the ballad forced the Champion of Balance to pause a split-second, get a firm grip on his sword hilt, then come erect and attack.

Had Gord possessed his dagger then, he would have hurled it at the demonurgist, trusting that the blade would suffice to break the binding that the demonurgist was surely about to finish. That would have been a fatal mistake, for the dweomer of that weapon was by no means potent enough for the task. Not being thus armed, though, and seeing that the distance was too great to close with a single step and long lunge, Gord decided that his only hope was the sword.

He shifted his grip on the hilt and threw the weapon as if it were a javelin. The long blade made that very difficult — the balance was all wrong — but there was little space between Gord and the chanting demonurgist. Of the incantation, but a single word remained to be uttered to create the Doompit when the edge of the lightless blade struck Gravestone.

The sword's point didn't sink into his throat, where Gord had aimed when he hurled the weapon. In fact, the sword was already turning and no longer flew true when it touched the priest-wizard. Gravestone, in completion of his spell, was just in the act of bringing both of his arms down, fingers to point at the exact place where the opening of the spell's vortex was to appear, when Blackheartseeker's edge contacted his flesh. Only a little of the flesh was touched; three fingers, to be exact. The descending fingers of Gravestone's right hand met the flying blade of the sword almost gently. The weapon fled past them, hardly checked, rang against the wall, and fell to the floor with a clang. Nearby lay the three blood-spilling fingers that had been severed very cleanly by the sword.

Gravestone's scream ended the casting with a single syllable wanting.

Gellor shouted in exultation when he saw what occurred, his ballad also interrupted by the sight of Gord's thrown sword.

Still feeling as if he were immersed in a great depth of water, Gord sprang toward the demonurgist. He reached his foe in three bounds and grabbed the tall man by the throat, bearing the fellow down with the savagery of his bare-handed assault.

"At last, you devil!" Gord was beating the bushy-haired head upon the hard stone floor as he tried his best to force his thumbs into Gravestone's flesh. "I"—thump — "know"— thud — "what"— bash — "you"— bump — "did"— thunk — "to . . ."

He got no farther. Despite the choke-hold, Gravestone managed to mutter a word, and suddenly Gord was trying to strangle a huge, amoeboid thing. His hands sank deep into its soft surface, and the acid of the monster's stuff burned them with searing pain.

Gord extracted his injured members and rolled and somersaulted away. The amoehoid thing that was Gravestone came after him. It was too slow to catch him, but it prevented Gord from getting to his sword.

It was a stand-off that the demonurgist would eventually have won, except that Gellor was there to intervene. Even as his comrade sought to flank the monster and get to the sword that the shapeless blob of acidic stuff guarded, the bard struck.

"You like swords, do you? Then try this one!" Gellor cried as he stabbed his blade into the formless blob. The amoeboid writhed and retreated from the attack. Gellor had no such weapon as Gord's, but the troubador's sword was of potent enchantment nonetheless. Had the priest-wizard been in his true form, it would have failed to do the slightest injury to him, so puissant were the evil protections that Gravestone had woven around his body. In this shape, however, it had effect. No mere slicing or stabbing would have harmed the amoeba either, but Gellor's blade exuded a chilling cold. The thing drew back instantly from that freezing brand, but the troubador kept up his assault. "Or this? Or this? Or this one?"

It was almost impossible for the demonurgist to think clearly or quickly in the form of the amoeba he had taken. The pain from the sword sent him back and back with involuntary motions. Then somehow he recalled there was more than one reason for his choice of becoming this amoeboid monstrosity. There was an escape route that this form could take and no man follow! Gravestone-amoeba flowed toward the place where there was relief from the pain of the gelid metal — only when he-it tried to do that, the icy spear of metal was in the way. The hurt and anger became too much. Gravestone would take no more.

"Gord! Your weapon, quick!"

When the bard yelled that, Gord leaped over the jellylike mass of the amoeba. It had stopped its flow and was gathering itself for some renewed attack perhaps, but there was space and opportunity. His leap carried the young man onto the little space that existed between the monster and the wall. Blackheart-seeker lay there, and the amoeba's sudden inactivity and contraction gave him the opportunity to reach the sword. "Look out, Gellor!" Gord called as he picked up his sword and turned to look at the thing he was about to strike with its deadly blade.

The change took only seconds — a split-second from the compaction as amoeba to his human shape again. Gravestone uttered a minor spell even as he had tongue and mouth to do so once again. The one-eyed scum who had been tormenting him with his icy-bladed sword was moving to strike, even as the smaller man was hefting his black-hued weapon and readying to do the same.

Neither succeeded in their aim, for suddenly there were six of the demonurgist where one had been, and the half-dozen forms immediately began to disappear and blink back into existence in a random fashion all over the place. Gravestone was now replicated and alternately moving off and onto the vibratory plane he had created. Before the two foemen could discover which of the six was the real priest-wizard, Gravestone would be far enough distant to do what he had to. Better to be alive without all than die with possessions intact. The demonurgist was desperate now. He would bring into existence a Hellsfire, an inferno of flames and raining lava in the center of this chamber. Of course, when that occurred Gravestone would be beyond the furnace-heat of his dweomer.

"The egress! Guard the passage out!" Gord shouted that to his comrade, for he saw that the blinking in and out by the half-dozen Gravestones was not as random as it might seem. Two of the figures seemed to appear constantly behind Gellor, moving a little closer to the lone exit each time they became visible again. Taking no chances, the champion of the struggle against Tharizdun dashed toward that place himself, striking a could-be-Gravestone with his ebon sword as he went. The figure popped as the metal edge cut through it.

Gellor, too, was quickly moving. He didn't stop at the mouth of the corridor, though; he continued on until he was a few paces along the passage. Then the troubador turned and faced the way he had come. A Gravestone figure suddenly appeared just a yard away. Out darted the steel tongue of his blade. The image vanished without blood. Now only four of the replications of the demonurgist remained.

As he winked back and forth from another nondimensional space to this quasi-plane, the priest-wizard was busily concocting other surprises for his foes. He was in control of his movements, while the duplicate, insubstantial forms were moving randomly. The figure that was Gravestone, along with a special mirror image that behaved as he did, moved steadily closer to the place of safety, the passageway out.

The demonurgist was already speaking the words to trigger a new dweomer when Gellor blocked the passage. That made no difference to Gravestone at all. He was summoning his most prized staff to himself. That he would now use to combat the bard when the time came. He willed a duplicate into the corridor then and spoke the last syllable. The replica vanished into nothingness just as the staff appeared in the priest-wizard's hands.

It was as Gord had assumed — the figure of Gravestone just beside the mouth of the passage was indeed the true one. The sudden appearance of the twisted and ancient piece of wood in that one's hand, while the three others jumped in and out of sight with no such accoutrement, confirmed the young champion's assumption. When the staff came into the demonurgist's possession, Gord was halfway across the chamber and closing as rapidly as he could travel in the cluttered place. It was clear that Gravestone planned something to deal with both of his adversaries. Logically, that meant some calamitous spell being cast into the chamber that housed Gord while the demonurgist dealt more personally with Gellor. There was no question in the young man's mind as to his foe's stark terror when facing Blackheartseeker's blade. "He comes!" Gord yelled at full cry, trusting that his companion would act.

He had no need for concern. When the false Gravestone vanished at the touch of his sword, Gellor knew that the true one would come quickly. Because he was also a veteran, the troubador also understood that the priest-wizard would attempt to arrive unex-

pectedly. Thinking thus, the one-eyed bard spun and
prepared for Gravestone's manifestation. Gellor said a
silent prayer as he did so. Gord had better be close,
for the troubador was leaving his back totally exposed
to the enemy should Gravestone try to transport himself beyond Gellor's position in the narrow hallway.

It was almost correct. He had considered doing
just that, but the bard would have been in the way of
the Hellsfire that Gravestone meant to send into his
sanctum. Because he could control his movements
between the two places his spell enabled him to exist
in, the demonurgist simply remained on his own
plane and physically stepped around the corner into
the corridor. There was Gellor in the act of turning
his back. It was all that the priest-wizard wished for.
Almost casually, Gravestone tossed the twisted staff
onto the man's unsuspecting back.

The thing had many, many powers bound into its
ancient form. One dweomer it possessed was that of
becoming a snake. This it did, thickening and growing longer even as it struck the bard. The crushing
coils of the reptile-staff circled Gellor's head and
neck, even as a skeletal head tried to sink venom-
dripping fangs into its prey. That was sufficient for
the demonurgist. He faced the chamber, uttered three
terrible words, and released the pent-up power of his
anger into the place in a thunderous explosion and
inferno of flame.

As the Hellsfire erupted in the vaulted room, Gord
was leaping for the exit. The explosion of magical
energy blew him squarely into the startled Gravestone. Gord's hair was aflame, the leather of his jack
charred, but the awful blast had not slain him as
Gravestone had supposed. The young champion was
blown straight into Gravestone's arms. He knocked

the storklike man down with a tangle of arms and legs.

Gord was injured, stunned, but the demonurgist was merely shaken. Gravestone untangled himself and stood erect. One step, a leap, and he'd be clear of the bard where he struggled with the constricting coils of the snake. Let the staff go, too. He would escape and cause the whole of his created plane to annihilate itself. Such an act would drain his power to nothingness, but life was foremost now. In a few years he could recover his force, and in that space Tharizdun would come. Gravestone's sacrifice would be amply rewarded!

There were whumps and bangs rising above the sound of the inferno of molten lava and burning gases that had been evoked by the Hellsfire spell. The many strange things filling the laboratory and store for magical experimentation and implementation were reacting violently to the heat and fire. The gangling demonurgist was in the act of turning, crouched to spring over Gellor where the latter lay wrestling with the python-adder that the staff had become. Gord heard the sounds of the lesser explosions, the crackle of burning tomes, and even had time to wonder what terrible thing would arise from such a strange conflagration, as he observed Gravestone's action. Then the bent man straightened his legs, leaping, his tattered cloak soaring out and up as if the priest-wizard were truly a winged storkman.

"Too late," Gord whispered to himself as he too sprang, coming up and leaping after the demonurgist in a single, smooth motion. As fluid as a coiled snake striking at a fluttering sparrow he attacked, and the lightless length of the sword's blade ran up and in, traveling through Gravestone's kidney, lung and heart in a thrust that the demonurgist had no chance of avoiding. "Too late by half!" he added as the fellow's limp body crashed down upon the unyielding stones of the maze's floor. Gord jerked the blade free, and Blackheartseeker seemed to dance in his hand as he held it upward in victory.

"Ahhh, no. . . . Please, no!" It was a gasp from Gravestone. Such a thrust as he had suffered would have slain an ancient dragon instantly, but the demonurgist was imbued with unnatural life. "Make your . . . your sword . . . give me back my . . . life," Gravestone coughed as dark blood trickled from the corner of his cruel mouth.

The sword seemed to tremble in Gord's hand again, but this time not in exultation. In that instant Gord understood that perhaps he had the power to make Blackheartseeker return whatever force it had drained from the dying man, to give Gravestone back his evil vitality. "I . . . I beg you!" the demonurgist wheezed. Gord moved the gory tip of the sword to a place before the man's eyes as Gravestone lay his face slightly turned to one side, allowing his lips to move, voice to speak. "Oh, yes. . . ." he murmured as he saw the blade.

Gord laughed, spat loudly, and jerked the longsword away. "Die now, you unnatural abomination, and may you rot forever in Hades!"

Blackheartseeker shone with deep ebon splendor as Gord turned and gave succor to his comrade. One slash and the skeletal adder's head was parted from the thick python body. Another cut and the coils were in two lengths.

"Gellor!" he cried as he yanked the man free from the writhing segments. "Are you bitten?"

Chapter 18

BASILIV AND THE MANY LORDS who formed the
Great Council of the Balance were gathered together
in a special place. It was a hushed conclave.

The Demiurge was silent. Basiliv had not spoken
or given any sign that he was aware of what was
happening around him since . . . something . . . had
struck him down while he had been scrying on the
champion's activity and trying to warn Gord of something. Now all the other powers were met and watching as well as they could. What they observed was
abstract, cloudy, the events of uncertain occurrence
in a temporal sense but positive in their finality.

The two contending pieces, the livid lilac of the
demonurgist and the emerald light of Gord, had shifted shape repeatedly as they maneuvered across the
checkered field of battle. Parts sloughed off and de-
cayed before the watching eyes of the assemblage.
The fall of the two elder demons brought a somber
cheer to their throats; then the death images of the
heroes reasserted the muffled silence over all once
again. Allton, Chert, Greenleaf, Timmil. . . . The
names were as the sound of a bell tolling a dirge.

All were shocked to see the glaring lapis of a solar
appear to contend with the enlarged foe. Had Basiliv

been able, the Demiurge would have explained that he had worked the dweomer that summoned the mighty being to Gord's assistance. The loss of the dumaldun addition to Gravestone's figure, and the fiery black ring suddenly added to the champion piece, made the group sit up and wonder. Yet they were powerless to intercede, to take part in any form at all. It was a duel to the death between the mortal manifestation of those who supported Tharizdun and that body of heroes who sought to thwart the arising of the great one of evil. Board and men in place, neither side could now make moves for its benefit. This game was strictly played out under the volition of the pieces themselves.

When the final duel began the figures of the antagonists blurred. The power each possessed, the result of their combat, could not be discerned. Then the board itself began to melt and crumble. The Lords of Balance broke the scrying immediately.

*   *   *

In his depths, Infestix, too, watched the struggle. Because of the critical nature of this confrontation, the daemon monarch was again alone. None of the other mighty ones of the netherworld were privy to what Infestix watched. Neither devils nor demons had any piece in this portion of the game. They had no direct channel to the event, and the great magics surrounding it easily screened out any attempt to penetrate and observe. It made the daemon's dark spirit exult to know that even Gravestone was unaware of being so observed. The priest-wizard was too powerful, too ambitious. Infestix would always watch his every move henceforward.

When Shabriri and Pazuzeus appeared at Gravestone's beck and call, the master of the pits grew
paler still with his fury. He was almost gleeful when
those fell beings were blasted, but then the horrible
form of the solar sprang onto the board. *Almost* gleeful; the emotion was repressed by the growing doubt
Infestix felt. If the adversary, a mere once-thief, could
bring such things as solar beings into the battle,
what outcome could be expected otherwise?

Still, the daemon allowed with grudging admiration for his human lieutenant, Gravestone had managed to bind the two elder demons to himself without
alerting Infestix to the fact. The priest-wizard might
just have other secret powers to spring on the enemy.
Gravestone could be annihilated for all the daemon
monarch cared. The demonurgist meant nothing —
less than nothing — to Infestix. He must not fall to
the one of the Balance, though. Never! That would
create a new force for the enemy, place them one step
closer to success in their desire to prevent the rising
of Evil, the return of Tharizdun. Let Gravestone deal
with Gord; then he, Infestix, would squash the overweening little priest-wizard as his final act before
freeing the great dark soul.

Parts of each force fell away. The daemon was
happy to observe the losses to Balance, uneasy when
he saw the damage being inflicted on the compound
figure that was his own right hand, his chosen force
there. Although he was unaware that his foes too
watched, Infestix observed and saw in finer detail
than they did. First came the utter destruction of
much of his lieutenant's power. Then the innermost
citadel was blasted and the whole field of play, the
terrible place Gravestone had created, began to disin-
tegrate. With a vile oath, the master of the nether-pits

forced the scrying into closer, sharper image. He would see the outcome down to the last!

Just then a dark veil seemed to drop, and the daemon was left unseeing. Infestix was powerless to prevent that from happening — as helpless as Basiliv had been just a short time before.

* * *

In the place of no-time and no-space where Tharizdun stirred, there was a ripple. The nothingness wavered. The dark form of the greatest of evil convulsed. Then it sat upright with a sound that was like the rattling of ethereal chains of adamantite.

* * *

Observe the observers. . . . The thought made the entity laugh. Ordered steps bringing chaos. Good and evil now locked in melee, now ignoring one another. Balance, those tiresome little neutrals seeking vainly to triumph. Well, perhaps . . .

Then the entity laughed silently again to itself. It had succeeded with interference so subtle as to be undetectable until now. And what matter if it had been revealed? The steps taken were so clever and potent that none could ever discover that the players of the game were themselves made pawns of itself . . . until it was too late. The contest would play itself out to the conclusion, but that end was predestined now, a forced game above a game, and the entity was the sole master of both struggles. Soon, there would be no need for subterfuges such as this. Soon all would be as was inevitable.

Chapter 19

"NO, I AM SOUND."

That reply from Gellor was all Gord needed to hear. "Then get up, and let's get out of here," he urged, grabbing the bard by one hand and pulling to help him stand.

The entire place was shaking. It wasn't much more than a gentle swaying now, but a few moments earlier it had been only a barely imperceptible trembling. "Thanks," Gellor said as the two men ran along the dark passage that led up and out of the labyrinth. "But how in the blazing brass buckets of the hells are we going to get free of this place? I think it's beginning to crumble!"

"The same stairs we came up," Gord panted in reply, "must be the link that son of a bitch maintained between this place and his headquarters in Greyhawk."

"You're not certain."

"Uh-uh," Gord grunted the admission. "What's the difference? You were right. The whole plane is falling apart now that the dirty demonkisser has gone down."

"Okay," the bard said and let it go. He was in no shape to waste further breath, not after the pounding he had taken. Gellor looked at Gord, seeing his comrade was in rough shape, too. Then the one-eyed troubador grinned. "We just booted that bastard's ass into the pits!"

"You got it," Gord said tersely. Then he grinned back. His face was lined, older-looking than it had been before all of this started. But at that moment he looked almost boyish again.

Gellor had tracked Gord to the demonurgist's lair. That hadn't been hard, for the champion of Balance had scratched marks all along his route — the instinctive procedures of a master thief. The two followed these same signs now, and they reversed their route as quickly as they could. The deep purples and violent lavenders of the dead priest-wizard's domain were paling. The stuff of the quasi-plane was cracking, flaking, crumbling around the edges. "How much longer?" Gellor shouted as they pounded toward the dais area.

It was getting difficult to run. The whole little universe was now shaking violently with an increasing swing. It took concentration to maintain balance and force one running foot to come down ahead of the other so as not to tumble and sprawl. "Not long enough to worry about. There's the staircase — can you manage Chert?"

"I'll manage," Gellor shot back. "You just take care of Curley."

Just then the whole of the floating disc tilted. The troubador was thrown against Gord, and both men tumbled uncontrollably toward the canted edge. With a wild surge of effort, the small champion forced his body to roll in the direction of the spiral steps. Gellor was already heading that direction after caroming off his comrade. The one-eyed man grabbed the metal of the staircase, Gord snagged Gellor's belt, and the platform they had been upon a heartbeat before fell into nothingness, crumbling away as it plunged into an ever-widening chasm of nullity. Gellor pulled his friend up beside him on the uppermost step. "What now?"

"Down those stairs like the wind, Gellor, and keep your mind set upon the wonders of Greyhawk!"

Scenes of various sort flashed past as the two bounded downward. The spiral was now beginning to twist and rock just as the disc had done before. That it still stood at all was mute evidence of its existence on more than the one plane that the demonurgist had made for his lair. Thirteen stairs down, and then they were standing in a tower room.

"We made it," Gellor panted.

"Chert and Greenleaf didn't," Gord growled. His face was drawn and tight.

The bard placed a fatherly arm around Gord's shoulders. "We all knew there was a chance of that when we took this mission, Gord. Look," he said, turning his comrade toward one of the diamond-paned windows. "There's the city. You're alive to fight on. . . . I'm here to help however I can. The man who killed your parents, the chief agent of the enemy on all Oerth, is dead, slain by your own hand, Gord. And you're alive to take the fight to Tharizdun himself, perhaps!"

"But four of us are gone. . . ."

"They died to enable the battle to continue. It was a worthwhile sacrifice, my friend. Without you, all of us are doomed! Don't belittle their deaths by maudlin words — they died as heroes."

That made him realize the futility of his feelings and expressions. "Of course, Gellor. Your level head and firm advice make you a friend, indeed. Let's get out of this filthy place — it belonged to that rotten shitpile Gravestone. I find it a cesspool."

"Agreed," his comrade replied, opening the door to the plain, unmagical stone steps that would take them down from the tower and out into the streets of Greyhawk. "Best of all, that one will have no memorial of his own," Gellor said with rising heartiness. When Gord looked at him with a cocked eyebrow, the troubador explained, "No gravestone for Gravestone!"

It was mid-morning, that time when the laborers and other working class folk of the city took a brief rest to drink tea or beer, eat a bite and prepare themselves for the remaining eight hours before employment ceased with the evening.

Both men had taken time to clean up from the grueling ordeal they had undergone and used cloaks found in the complex that had belonged to the demonurgist to hide the condition of their garments. Nonetheless, there were a number of odd looks and hard stares as Gord and Gellor passed along the streets. It was too obvious that these men had been engaged in strenuous activity of a very questionable sort. City watch and citizens alike presumed the pair to be bandits or hardbitten thieves.

"Down this alley," Gord said in a hushed tone, steering his comrade into a narrow, dirty passage that curved off toward the northeast.

"This makes us look even more suspicious," Gellor hissed.

The champion made no reply but increased the pace. The alley widened into a little plaza where another similar way met it. There were steps there, both leading to cellars and going upward to a balconylike walkway above. Gord chose the upward direction, and after they had attained the upper tier he led the troubador into a little place that served a half-score of different teas and had a fragrant array of breads and rolls to go with the infusions.

"We can be compromised still," he told Gellor after the proprietor had set tall glasses of smoky-flavored tea and a basket of rolls made of heavy rye flour whose tops were sprinkled with tasty seeds and crystals of rock salt. The food was consumed quickly, neither man speaking for a time, for both were absolutely famished from their exertions.

"I know that all too well," Gellor remarked, harking back to what his friend had said minutes before. "It's your city, though, Gord. I don't know it anywhere near the way you do. How do we avoid being embroiled in more trouble?"

Gord signaled, and a boy hastened over to the table to bring more tea and a different sort of food, this time a loaf of bread on a long board. Patrons supplied their own knives, naturally. The lad left as quickly, grinning at the extra bronze coin Gord had slipped him. "The fall of Gravestone is an event," he said softly to Gellor after making certain that there were none nearby to overhear. "His lord and master will be filled with fury and desire for revenge, and by now agents of the pits will be sending word to all who serve them."

"How does that respond to my query?" Gellor asked in irritation. "I am as aware of all that as you. How do we get from here to the safety of our rendezvous?"

"We don't. That's exactly what they'll expect. Every known meeting place for . . . our side, each dwelling place of the ones who belong, will be watched."

Gellor was indifferent to that. "Who cares if their

spying dogs yap of our passing? By then we'll be far away."

"If they would only watch, old comrade, I'd agree with your assessment, and we could hie from here now. Many in Greyhawk openly serve the nether-spheres, though — not just the priests of evil, either. The dead enemy served the assassins, for instance."

"And the rulers of the city too, I am told," the one-eyed bard supplied. "You think that such as those will intervene directly?"

"The great ones of evil will send word to the power-ful here in Greyhawk. Of that I'm sure! If we are seen, you can bet a squad of watch will be there to make an arrest. Clerics of evil and assassins will league to see we never live to protest the injustice."

"So we come back to my original question."

"If we can get to one of my own places of hiding—"

"Then we could use the pyramid to move . . . else-where," Gellor finished.

Gord seemed uneasy, uncertain. "I wonder about that, Gellor. If we were observed closely, then the aura of that object could be known, our route plotted, and a detour prepared."

"Why have it at all, then?"

"When I held the device it was safe from scrutiny, because I have a warding against prying magics. It passed to your hands in time of jeopardy. You could have used it without fear. Now I think it most unwise to try the pathway it would open for us."

"Then we have only one hope," Gellor said softly. "We must try to go to the main headquarters in this city, fighting our way if need be, or . . ."

"Or?"

"Or we can slip quietly out of Greyhawk and speed to the stronghold of the lord-mage Tenser."

"That is an option I wasn't considering," Gord admitted. "His castle is the nearest place of true safety, but the passage there is difficult and dangerous."

"True, true," Gellor nodded in agreement. "Perhaps the very reason why the enemy won't place the likelihood of our doing that high on its list."

"The water route?"

Gellor shook his head. "I know you have a fondness for the Rhennee, Gord, but too many of those folk are unscrupulous. What think you the reward for your head at this very moment? Ten times its weight in gold orbs, I'll wager."

"I hate to mention this, Gellor, but traveling by land is dangerous, because it is no problem to note a one-eyed man."

"But a blind man being led to the Shrine of St. Cuthbert By The Lake for healing would raise no notice, I think. Two pilgrims amongst a whole troop of the faithful trudging through the fringes of the Cairn Hills would be quite unremarkable."

"And the holy ones and relics borne with the train, the blaze of the aura of such a body; there would no chance of discovering us two in such a crowd!" Gord was enthused now. "It will be no problem to slip from the city between afternoon and evening — but we must be disguised ere then. Here's my plan. . . ." And the Champion of Balance eagerly set forth his ideas on what they should do in the seven or eight hours time that remained before then.

In half an hour the pair departed. Using the less traveled routes, and with hood and cowl raised, they managed to get to a small set of rooms that Gord kept as a second hideaway. They were in the River Quarter, at a place where a fishmonger had his shop in the front of a ramshackle building. The man and his family lived above the store. A small, cluttered storage room was left vacant, though, by terms of the agreement. This place had a concealed entrance that led into a narrow room beyond and from there to the larger basement room below. It was damp and musty, as were the various garments cached there. Such garb suited both men. It would draw no notice.

"Not much in the way of coin," Gord noted sadly, parceling out the few coppers and silver nobles between himself and his comrade.

"A blind pilgrim and his devoted nephew will have few riches, Gord," the troubador noted with a smile as he returned the money to his friend. "You are the master of the purse, for a blind old codger such as I could mistake a zee for a common . . . or vice versa."

Just after the fourth hour, at the time of early evening when the streams of visitors to the city began their long treks homeward, Gord and Gellor slipped out of the place and found a ferry to take them across Hook Harbor to the place along River Street outside Greyhawk where pilgrims gathered to make their journey northward to the fabled shrine. Dressed as they were, and haggling over the price of smoked fish and wheat loaves, nobody paid them attention, not even the sharp-eyed men who moved here and there along the quay and wharves searching for wanted men. At sunset the two were camped with a half-hundred folk preparing to begin the march into the hills next day. They did so without molestation when the warm red of the sun's great disc pushed above the horizon a few hours later.

It was a slow and arduous passage. The pilgrims wished it thus. How else could one benefit? The trials and perils were tokens of faith and offerings, as it were. Days later, just short of the shrine that was the object of the pilgrimage, Gord and Gellor disappeared, leaving in the dark when all the good folk, and even the tough and not particularly prayerful soldiers guarding the flock of pilgrims, were sound asleep or nodding by fireside or sentry post.

The slow pace of the train had been beneficial to both men. Bruises and cuts had time to heal, damaged internal portions of the two began to mend. To veterans such as these, twenty miles of walking each day, plain fare, and seven or eight hours sleeping on the ground were both restful and restorative.

Gord worried about the sword. He had wrapped it carefully, but its length made the bundle rather noticeable, he feared. Because the group was large and the champion kept the weapon near his person at all times, nobody took interest in it, and no good priest or faithful paladin sensed its dark dweomer. Many of the members of the long stream of pilgrims undertaking the trek were taciturn, somber, and remote. Those more sociable and garrulous simply steered clear of the few who wished to be left alone. Although Gord and Gellor did not announce such a desire for privacy, their attitudes and introspective silences quickly placed them into the category of those not active in the pilgrim train's social community. Neither outcast nor shunned, for that was unthinkable to such persons as these, their attitude was simply accepted as part of what these men held dear. In fact, a score of others were similarly not a part of the activities. Most of the introspective ones had afflictions that were similar to or worse than that which the bard supposedly suffered from.

"I feel rather shoddy," Gellor whispered one night. "How many of these honest men and women are truly in need of help?" It was a rhetorical question. "It bothers me to pose as another blind one seeking the blessed cure."

"We are helping them all to live, old comrade," Gord noted as softly. "Not one of the truly decent folk here would say aught of it if they were aware of our feigning and the cause thereof."

"Yes, I know that's true, Gord. Yet it disturbs me nonetheless. I also am forced to wonder why more of such disabilities cannot be cared for by the great clerics."

"Too few are the priests with the power to heal such needs as these, too many are those with serious deficiencies to be rectified. I would not be a priest for any reason, Gellor. The need and my shortcomings would soon bring dementia to my brain."

There was more bothering them than either could articulate. Curley Greenleaf had been the bard's oldest and closest friend. The druid had been Gord's mentor for a time and dear comrade since. It was not possible for either man to speak of the loss they felt, not yet. It was too deep, too strong.

So, too, the death of Chert. He and Gord had shared a youthful time together in such fashion as bound man to man in bonds of brotherhood. Gellor had patted the big hillman's curly head when Chert could barely toddle, hunted with him when the lad received his first bow, advised him as a man. The four had undergone desperate adventures together, fought the enemy side by side. Two comrades in arms as well as old friends had gone outward and would be with them no more. The aching void that left within each breast was indescribable. The two kept their own counsel about that feeling and made each day as busy and mundane as possible. It was in all ways a beneficial journey.

When they slipped off into the darkness, each felt a particular tug. It was the poignancy of leaving behind a painful yet needed time of healing. Soon now they would have to deal fully with all that had transpired, undertake new missions without their old comrades there beside them.

It was as if the two were facing manhood again, having to leave the things of a childhood behind. Each sense was in part correct. Yet Gord and Gellor went forth without hesitation, and the mourning for their dead comrades was now something that would be retained in a special, deep place inside each of them, a badge in a place of honor where none but them could ever view it. That sharing was known to both men, but it too was unsaid.

"Mounts," Gellor said. "We need them now, and there's not enough coin between us to buy a single old plug!"

"No problem," Gord rejoined as he dug around in his gear. "This little pearl necklace should take care of the need nicely."

"I know that you didn't have any such thing when we began this trip," the bard said with rising suspicion in his tone.

Gord laughed. "Too long a thief, perhaps," he admitted as he admired the string of oddly shaped freshwater pearls. "The lantern-jawed merchant who purported to be a pilgrim — he was a dealer in stolen goods, too. I recognized him, Gellor, and relieved him of just a little of his ill-gotten gains."

Sound horses were soon found in a village, and with saddlebags well-provisioned and bedrolls tied behind saddles, the two heroes set off along the narrow trail that wound upward into the high hills and steep bluffs of the northeast. There, lost amid the wild terrain, was the keep of the mage they sought. In but a short while the two were safe within the walls of Tenser's castle.

The great archmage was absent. That surprised neither of them. He would be with the others, of course, working in concert to bring dismay to the hydra-headed gang who sought to free Tharizdun. The venerable Poztif greeted them warmly, however, and after formalities were concluded, Gord and Gellor related all that had transpired.

The high priest was shocked. "Timmil . . . the laughing barbarian lad, too . . . and the others, even Greenleaf," he said slowly, shaking his head. "It is a dark victory, but what else can be expected when one contends with the vilest of evils?" He led them to a place where they could rest and refresh themselves, saying, "I'll prepare immediately for your departure, of course. As soon as you have taken what sustenance you need and rested sufficiently to feel capable, I will have all in readiness for the next step."

Gord slept only a little, Gellor scarcely more. It was only hours after their arrival at the lonesome stronghold of the lord-mage that both of them were sent elsewhere. Neither of them knew their destination, not exactly. It would be someplace where Balance held sway, but Poztif kept his lips sealed on the subject. That was proof enough of how desperate the time was and how strong the foe.

Chapter 20

THE CHIAROSCURO PALACE. Shadowrealm. It was so unlikely a setting in so improbable a plane that Gord wondered aloud, "Have the Lords of Balance lost theirs?"

Before Gellor could say anything to that, however, another voice spoke. "Quite the contrary, Gord! We selected this place because Basiliv is unfit to participate, and we are under strenuous assault by the nether spheres!" Those words were from the bushy-browed archwizard Mordenkainen, come to fetch the arrivals.

"Almost misheard you, sir. I though you said that the Demiurge was ill," Gord said, rising to follow the crusty old spell-binder.

"You have remarkably dull wits for one supposedly serving as champion, young fellow," Mordenkainen snapped. "I said that Basiliv is unfit. In truth, the man is a vegetable. Left all the responsibility to me, he did! Imagine! And Tenser and the Hierophants are blessed little help either. . . ." He allowed his words to fade, for the three were already at the Vault of Veils. When Gellor and Gord both started to speak, the archwizard hushed them with a sharp gesture, saying, "No time for chatter now. You must intelligence the Council, and then we will give instructions. Come along now."

The assemblage was as expected. Basiliv the Demiurge was there too, seated next to Shadowking, but his face was blank, eyes empty, mouth slack. "He has been struck by a most potent foe," the ruler of shadows told the newcomers curtly. Then he launched into a session of questions and answers. The questions were put to Gord and Gellor, and they supplied the answers. Finally Gord and the troubador were asked to relate the whole of events from their own perspectives. The whole business took several hours. When it was finished, they had the strange, shadowy wine and cakes of the plane set before them and were surprised to discover that these offerings satisfied their thirst and hunger.

"Had one of the urgists mumble over the lot," Mordenkainen said under his breath as he leaned near to Gellor. Gord overheard the words and thought that the aged wizard was perhaps a trifle less cantankerous and absentmindedly thoughtless than he had supposed. Then the Hierophants took over, enunciating in their fluted, speaking-as-one voice.

They explained that despite the severity of the blow struck to the enemy, rather than being weakened, Nerull and the forces who fought to free Tharizdun were suddenly strengthened. "That infusion of dark force flows from deep, deep below," the Hierophants noted rather off-handedly. "It is the one of all evil who sends it forth. The nether spheres are mere beneficiaries of it."

"Who is so potent? What power strives against us and succeeds with such ease?" Gord demanded. "I have brought victory, made the sword a weapon of might against any malign being — any! Gravestone is lost to the evil ones forever. Gellor and I have done as you have requested — yet we hear only of defeat?"

"Peace, Gord." It was Rexfelis.

"He has a right to be irate," Shadowking said in admonition to the Lord of Cats. "It is neither your fault nor ours, champion — and friend! Some new ally of the nether spheres has joined to discomfit us. Here in shadow is the only safe place for us all now. The evil has managed to penetrate into all the other places of Balance — or watches and guards them so carefully as to make our gathering there perilous in the extreme. We are as isolated fortresses besieged."

"Then all is lost?" the bard said unbelievingly.

"By no means!" Mordenkainen interjected. "You proved that when the two of you journeyed safely to the castle of young Tenser, there," the archwizard noted, pointing at the lord-mage who had been of such status for a mere handful of decades or so. "And being here demonstrates much, obviously."

"Much?"

"Much, Gord," Shadowking agreed. "You are our mobile army."

"Some army! The two of us—"

"Managed to beat the living shit out of Gravestone and his whole lot!" That from the rather earthy lord-wizard, who was being restrained in his comments.

There was a brief furor at that, and comments flew around the many-pointed table for several minutes before order was restored. Finally, the ruler of the shadowy sphere managed to silence the score of other Lords of the Balance and say so all could hear, "I understand your feelings, champion. You have evened things, brought the murderer of your own parents to justice even as you struck a blow of utmost severity to the enemy." He paused, and when there came a nod from Gord, Shadowking continued. "There is but one true enemy, though. All the rest are but minor extensions of Tharizdun — even Infestix-Nerull. He would have no legions of devils at his side were it not for the one of ultimate darkness."

There were murmurs of agreement. Cries of "Hear, hear!" and "Speak on!" came from various members of the assemblage.

The dark lord of Shadowrealm smiled. "I only say that which we all know at heart. The loss of Basiliv is a terrible blow to us. It is by no means the loss of all, for we still have you, champion. The new, unknown enemy is a shocking setback to us, but even so great a setback as this one is not fatal . . . nor of great import."

"No import?!"

"What balderdash!!"

"Horseshit!!" Tenser chimed in.

Gord rose and spoke to the clamor. "Truth," he said without heat. "If the ultimate enemy is beaten, the allies of Hades are of no great interest at all."

"We concur, champion," the multitoned voices of the Hierophants chorused. "Yet Tharizdun stirs and sends forth his strength to Evil. The end is near."

"Why does that surprise any of you?" The one-eyed bard suddenly was on his feet beside his friend, his face set in hard lines. "We all know that there is but one purpose for the champion, one reason why the power we have is his — our power and that of . . . elsewhere, too, as you know. It is to face and fight the greatest evil when — *when*, not if, he arises!"

Silence.

"We do not agree." That from the Hierophants after a full minute had passed without any sound save breathing.

"They have always been fools," Mordenkainen quipped dryly. Tenser nodded and made a rude gesture in their direction.

That brought a flurry of name-calling, charges, counter-charges, and insults flying across the table. After quite some time, Shadowking managed to restore enough order to the conclave to make a call for adjournment.

The members of the council readily agreed to that. Immediately thereafter, over half of the lordly masters of Neutrality departed for their own places.

* * *

"What terrible disaster is now wrought?" Gord was sitting in dejection when he said that. With him were Rexfelis, Shadowking, Murlon, Heward, Lord Thomas, and Gellor, of course.

"Why, none!" the master of the shadowy sphere said happily. "It went just as we'd planned. You were superb, both of you!"

"Superb? Planned? All I am doing is asking questions, and I am getting very tired of that." Real anger was in his voice and his face.

"With evil so powerful, menacing us everywhere, we dared not keep so strong a force together, united. Now we appear weak, factious, disjoined, and plainly ineffective to contend against anything. Had you known, then there might have been a warning, and the foe might have discovered the ruse."

"We are not traitors," Gellor said with heat. "You could have explained!"

"You are not, but some agency seems to be able to spy out our great meetings, learn what is decided in conclave. You would not have been so convincing, the quarrel would not have seemed so real, had you been forewarned."

"We are safe enough now from intrusion," Rexfelis said. "Now you will learn all that we know."

"Who has joined with the vile foes, we know not," the Catlord said. "Perhaps Basiliv could tell us, but he is as a shell. His body lives, but his life force is elsewhere. We must assume that there will be no return before the final confrontation occurs."

"That will come soon," Shadowking inserted. "Your success, Gord and Gellor, was great. It dealt a massive blow to evil and made our force greater. The coming of the unknown ally to the cause of Tharizdun has not necessarily strengthened the nether spheres. It has certainly brought the matter of Tharizdun's awakening into imminence."

"That one is now aware of his imprisonment," Murlon said with certainty.

"There is but a single duty for me, then," Gord responded.

"I would it were merely a matter of sending you forth to the lists to meet the black-armored foe," Shadowking rejoined. "We had hoped to have six heroes for what lies ahead. Only you Gord, and the brave bard here, are left. The darkest one must be loosed, and it must be quickly. As things stand, Tharizdun will eventually be freed in any event, and in the interim all of the multiverse will be scourged by the warfare surrounding the tripartite relic."

"In short, you two must venture into the nether planes," Rexfelis told them. "It is in the realms of demonkind that the three parts of that artifact now rest. You must journey into the Abyss itself, seize the three keys, and yourself loose the greatest evil!"

That was absolutely unbelievable at first thought.

Then Gord considered. If none could resist the might of evil, and it was evident none could, then Infestix and his henchmen would soon enough release their master in any event. The struggle that was becoming more intense and spreading disaster and death everywhere would never end until the crux of it all was decided. Was Tharizdun destined to come forth and dominate all into an eternity of darkness? Or would the multiverse deny him and retain its equilibrium?

"The ally who has brought so much to the netherpit's plans for evil is in no great hurry to culminate Infestix's desire," Gord finally offered.

"That seems true. I have observed no evidence to indicate otherwise." That, from Rexfelis, was seconded by the rest.

"There is no benefit to all, to Balance and the multiverse, in destroying the ally of Infestix. To eliminate the archdaemon is simply to clear the place so another might ascend the throne," Gellor reflected. "Only the elimination of Tharizdun has meaning."

"Greater ones than we are could not accomplish that," Shadowking noted.

Gord sat unmoving, saying nothing. His mind raced, and a certain speculation grew in his brain. The others looked at him, and finally he nodded, saying, "Even the wise ones of the malign spheres realize the truth of what has just passed here. It is as if those of the Abyss contemplated this very time long before we realized it was here. Now it is upon us. I am ready."

"Both of you will have much to learn yet, receive instructions that you will need to move freely in the underworlds. Augury indicates that you must leave in nine days," Shadowking told the two. "And that is all any of us can do."

"Not quite," Gord contradicted. "I have a growing suspicion and a dawning understanding, too. Have you still that ancient blade of crystal I left here for you long ago?"

The sovereign of the shadow plane nodded darkly. "I keep it in my own chamber, there displayed as a royal gift."

"Will you give it to me?" Gord asked.

"Of course."

He knew that the monarch would respond thus, but Gord breathed a sigh of relief anyway. "Please have it fetched here, now. I would have all now present observe what I will attempt."

Despite urgings, the champion would say no more until the long, crystal weapon, the sword with which he had slain the lich-gloam Imprimus, was laid on the many-pointed table and the servant bringing it was gone. Then Gord acted.

"This blade was seemingly made by accident," he told the audience, holding up his black sword. "Its lightlessness was made by a foul magic from an even more foul dwarf. Then the demon lord Vuron placed some dark powers into it. The blade is potent. It grew more so by the absorption of other evil dweomers, and all without my willing it. From deep beneath the dusty wastes of the destroyed empire of the Suloise, through demons' spells and devilshine, and to here." Gord paused, drew a deep breath, and then went on.

"The sword of diamond brilliance that lies here before you and me is interesting. . . ."

"It is a duplicate of your own blade, Gord!" The exclamation came from Gellor as he gazed closely at the crystal brand.

"I think it is a weapon of Weal, a sword filled with all that is of good and light. Let me place my own sword beside it." He did so. The result was to view a mirror image, one yang, the other yin.

"I am the champion to face Tharizdun," Gord said with measured words. "I am of Balance. I seek neither the light of the upper planes nor the lightless night of the netherspheres. I require day and dark, happiness and sorrow, the measure which lies between." And as he spoke thus he picked up first the crystalline blade, then the ebon, and brought them together.

The audience gasped as one. "They have merged!" purred the Catlord.

"Aye," said Gord with ringing agreement. "It seems that Balance has been given its weapon to fight the oppressors!"

Other fantasy adventure novels from

NEW INFINITIES™

PRODUCTIONS, INC.

THE LAST KNIGHT OF ALBION   by Peter Hanratty $3.50

Twenty years ago, King Arthur took his last breath in the company of a young knight named Percevale. Ever since then, Percevale has been on a self-imposed mission to find and wreak revenge on Mordred — the man he believes responsible not only for the death of the king but for the collapse of Arthur's once-majestic empire.

The fate of *The Last Knight of Albion* becomes intertwined with a group of complacent townspeople, an ambitious barbarian king, and a mysterious hermit. By the time his story runs its course, Percevale has finally discovered what is really important in life — and the reader has lived with him through a tale that is much more than just another Arthurian fantasy.

THE BOOK OF MORDRED   by Peter Hanratty $3.50

The story of King Arthur and Mordred has been told many times and in many ways, but never before from this perspective. *The Book of Mordred* traces the early life of the man who would be king, and paints a picture of Arthurian society and culture that is remarkably different from historical myth and legend, yet still believable and captivating.

The Book of Mordred is a tale of one young man's disillusionment and awakening, a story of his coming to terms with himself and the world in which he plays such a significant role. The story combines the magic of sorcery and strange creatures, the mystery of the coveted Grail, and the mayhem of men fighting for their lives, and weaves the elements together in a tapestry of words that will adorn the reader's memory long after the book is finished.

SKRAELINGS   by Carl Sherrell $2.95

Raum, a denizen of the netherworld, is brought to Earth in the time of the Vikings. Influenced by the world he now lives in, Raum forfeits some of his magical abilities and his great physical strength in return for humanlike qualities — including the ability, and the desire, to love.

Skraelings is the story of Raum's search for his beloved Vivienne, who has been kidnapped by a Viking warrior. The quest takes him and his companions across the sea to the mysterious wilderness known as Vinland — a land populated by fierce and proud savages, known to the visitors as "skraelings," who both hinder and help Raum in his efforts.

Even if Raum succeeds in finding Vivienne, he must still face the challenge of escaping from the land of the skraelings with his life — and even his unearthly powers may not be enough to save him!

THE PATH TO FUN
FOLLOWS THE

LINE!

Nothing but the best — that's what the FANTASY MASTER™ game accessory line is all about!

For too long, players of fantasy role-playing games have been frustrated by the abundance of adventures, scenarios, and accessories that can only be enjoyed by the people who play a particular game. **New Infinities Productions, Inc.**, in cooperation with **Gary Gygax**, is out to change all that.

Every FANTASY MASTER adventure or accessory is designed and written by one of the top creative talents in the field, and each product in the line carries Gary's personal seal of approval. Best of all, each of them can be played or used with any fantasy role-playing game — even those yet to be published! Other companies have tried to produce so-called "generic" accessories before, but no one has done it the way New Infinities is doing it. Try one, and you'll be back for more!

Town of Baldemar, a medieval setting description created by Bob Blake, is the first release in the FANTASY MASTER line. The second one is **Aesheba: Greek Africa**, written by Bob Blake, Jeff O'Hare, and the New Infinities staff. This is a fantasy setting based on an alternate history in which Greek explorers and settlers colonized and dominated north and central Africa. When you see the craftsmanship and creativity that went into these accessories, you won't want to wait for the others in the series. And fortunately, you won't have to wait long; New Infinities plans frequent and regular releases in the FANTASY MASTER series. Ask for them at your favorite game store or hobby store, or wherever role-playing game products are sold.

FANTASY MASTER is a trademark owned by New Infinities Productions, Inc.

MANKIND'S LAST HOPE . . .

. . . AND OUR FIRST GAME!

CYBORG COMMANDO

It is the near future, and Earth is on the verge of an unprecedented era of peace and prosperity. Then, one day, unusual . . . things . . . begin appearing in the sky, and everything is changed: Our world is under attack by despicable aliens who don't even have the guts to fight their battles themselves! Instead, they attack with Xenoborgs, strange constructs of metal and flesh, grown in their vile starship laboratories.

The Xenoborgs spread destruction and terror, and man's conventional weapons are all but useless against them. However, scientists and technicians have been laboring in underground complexes since the invasion, and just when things look bleakest, they unleash the fruits of their labors: the CYBORG COMMANDO fighting men/machines.

Every CYBORG COMMANDO character is a combination of man's best feature — his intellect — and the latest advances in technology. Sophisticated weapons systems, defense mechanisms, and sensory devices are contained in a manufactured body that looks like a human being, and all of the technology is controlled by the finest computer known to man — the human brain!

Each player character in the CYBORG COMMANDO game is part of an elite group whose goal is as simple as it is challenging: Turn back the alien invasion force and save the Earth! Using their individual special talents and abilities, player characters perform singly or in groups — with the fate of the world in their hands every time they set out.

The CYBORG COMMANDO game set, published by New Infinities Productions, Inc., is supported by scenarios and other accessories, the first of which are **San Francisco Knights** by Penny Petticord and **Film at Eleven** by FantaSimulations Associates.

Designed by Gary Gygax, Frank Mentzer, and Kim Mohan, the CYBORG COMMANDO game will revolutionize the role-playing game hobby. Look for the game and accessories in a game or hobby store near you, and get in on the excitement — save the world and have fun at the same time!